The
Galway
Girls

Also by Susan Colleen Browne

The Village of Ballydara Series

It Only Takes Once
Book 1

Mother Love
Book 2

The Hopeful Romantic
Book 3

The Secret Well
short story ebook

The Christmas Visitor
short story ebook and the sequel to *The Secret Well*

**The Morgan Carey Series for Tweens,
set in the Pacific Northwest**

Morgan Carey and The Curse of the Corpse Bride
Book 1, a lighthearted Halloween and Day of the Dead story

Morgan Carey and The Mystery of the Christmas Fairies
Book 2, a gentle paranormal fantasy

The Secret Astoria Scavenger Hunt
Book 3, a haunted house adventure

Memoirs of Country Life

*Little Farm in the Foothills: A Boomer Couple's Search
for the Slow Life*

*Little Farm Homegrown: A Memoir of Food-Growing, Midlife
and Self-Reliance on a Small Homestead*

The Galway Girls

A Village of Ballydara Novel, Book 4

SUSAN COLLEEN BROWNE

WHITETHORN PRESS

The Galway Girls

Print ISBN: 978-0-9967408-6-9
Ebook ISBN: 978-0-9967408-5-2

Library of Congress Control Number: 2017917501
Published by Whitethorn Press

www.susancolleenbrowne.com
www.littlefarminthefoothills.blogspot.com

Cover Design by Courtney Lopes
Interior Design by Author E.M.S.

Published in the United States of America.

A little help with the Irish...

Ailish—pronounced "Ay-lish"

Craic—sounds like "crack," which generally means fun, a good time. *Craic* and crack often used interchangeably.

"Do"—party or event

Bodhran—a hand-held drum, pronounced "bo-run"

Slainté—an Irish toast, pronounced "slawn-cha"

Grainne—pronounced "Grawn-ya"

Slean—a peat cutting tool, pronounced "shlawn"

Aislin—pronounced "Ash-lin"

"Put two fingers up"—giving someone the finger, Irish-style: making a "V" with one's index and middle finger, hand facing outward.

"The wee man"—the devil

Muirnín—"darling," pronounced "moornyeen"

A Word from Susan

Hello!

Welcome to the Village of Ballydara, my fictional little town in County Galway, Ireland. If you've already read some of my Irish novels and stories, thank you so much! If not, I'm delighted you're taking a look at my Ballydara series, set in a rural area that was inspired by a few other places, real and imaginary. As someone who lives in a somewhat remote area, several miles from a tiny town nestled in fir-covered foothills, I brought a few of my favorite elements of home to the Galway setting: not only my village's beautiful scenery, but a small shop, post office, church, and of course, a pub, where, as they say, "everybody knows your name." In creating Ballydara, I also drew a bit of inspiration from two beloved BBC series: *Ballykissangel*, set in a little Irish community, and *Doc Martin,* which takes place in another picturesque locale in the British Isles, on the coast of Cornwall. Hopefully, the residents of Ballydara are as entertaining as the television characters, but not quite so daffy!

Kerry McCormack, the heroine of *The Hopeful Romantic* and this sequel, *The Galway Girls*, has long dreamed of having a farm. Her country place grew out of my own little foothills homestead as well as my visit to a real-life Irish farm: Glen Keen Farm in County Mayo, just north of County Galway. The rolling, sheep-covered hills I describe in my Irish books are very similar to the Irish landscapes I loved seeing for real. Speaking of true-life, some of Kerry's farming challenges were created from my own experiences on our homestead!

It's funny, how a story world evolves and grows…I originally intended to make *The Galway Girls* a novella, with plans to release it a few months after *The Hopeful Romantic*. But as

Kerry and Stephen's love story went in some unexpected directions, I had to toss that plan out of the window. Then, when Fiona walked onto the pages with her storyline and romantic dilemmas, I knew I had to let my second heroine shine, take the time to intertwine her journey with Kerry's, and allow my book to grow into a full-length novel.

Speaking of story evolving, this novel, and I, also owe a great debt to reader Gayle Brosnan-Watters, descendant of "The Fighting Brosnans of Ballycasheen" from County Kerry—Gayle shared an absolutely terrific idea for Kerry and Stephen's story arc. Their journey in *The Galway Girls* wouldn't have been the same without her input.

I'm always grateful for insights and comments from readers about my characters, storylines and books! Many thanks for your support, and I'd love to hear from you via my website or blog.

www.susancolleenbrowne.com
www.littlefarminthefoothills.blogspot.com.

Warm wishes,
Susan Colleen Browne

Kerry

1

$\mathcal{S}$aying goodbye at the airport had been a mistake.

There's a guilty conscience for you. I *could* have embraced my family in the privacy of Mam's kitchen, then had a good cry over a steaming cup of tea as soon as they left. Yet here I waited in the chilly departures hall at Dublin Airport, gripping Stephen's hand. As if that could keep him from leaving.

We stood together near a wall, inches from the river of people moving through the terminal. Stiff with dread, I kept my eyes on the flights' display where the digital clock ticked down inexorably. It was easier than watching my husband's set face, pale in the wintry morning light. Or looking at Jamie's, his spots standing out on his pinched features.

Stephen's hand tightened around mine before he let go. "Right, then—we've got to get into the security queue."

"I know." My voice shaking, I turned toward Jamie. "One more hug for your mam?"

I'd begun to embrace our teenage son gingerly, always bracing for a rebuff. When Jamie didn't move, I wanted to burst into tears. But seeing his woebegone expression, I put aside my own hurt. "It won't be for long, we'll be together in March—"

He suddenly threw his arms around me with such force I nearly lost my balance. "Mam, why won't you come to Vancouver?"

"Son, we've been over this," said Stephen.

"Don't you want to be with us? What's the big deal, leaving

Ireland? You've no job, we don't have a house, so there's nothing to stay for."

"A little respect," Stephen warned.

"Jamie." I loosened my hold on him to meet his brown eyes, so like my own. "You know I've things to sort in Galway."

Stephen put in, "You've been telling your mam you're going to love Vancouver, that you'll be grand without her."

"But Mam...Dad—" Jamie colored. "You said you're not... um, separating after all. Married people are meant to be together, everyone knows that."

Every fourteen-year-old certainly did. "Please understand," I said, my heart aching. "The farm needs looking after. And your dad is supporting me in this." I patted our son's narrow shoulders—one more excuse to touch him. "If you think you'll miss me so much you can always spend the winter with me in Ballydara."

He backed away instantly. "Aw, Mam, you know that's not on."

"I didn't think so." My voice trembled again. But this task I'd set for myself—it was now or never. "We've made our family plan, and we'll stick to it."

"We're really cutting it close." Stephen pulled me into his arms for one last, hungry kiss. For an instant, the passion and familiarity of his mouth made me forget we were saying goodbye. Then I remembered we were in a busy airport, and that I was hurting the two people I loved most.

I broke the kiss, bracing for Jamie's recent refrain, *Mam, Dad, enough PDA's!* But he stayed silent. After the months of estrangement between myself and his father, I sensed my son would rather we kissed in public than not at all.

Stephen murmured, "You'll not change your mind about... you know."

I shook my head, the yearning in his voice almost making me lose control.

"I could..." He swallowed hard. "I'll ring the office, change the ticket—the team can manage a few more days without me."

"It's better this way," I somehow got out, and kissed my husband one last time. "You'll ring me?"

2

He held me an instant longer, then turned away and picked up his briefcase. "As soon as I can. Off we go," he said to Jamie, and the pair of them stepped into the flow of people. They didn't look back.

A knot in my chest, I watched Jamie's curly brown head until he and his father were out of sight. Exiting the terminal, I walked slowly toward the car park. I'm doing the right thing, I told myself, scuffing my shoe against some blackberry vines growing over the footpath. It was a mystery, how that bit of green could thrive in the city when I simply couldn't.

As I neared the airport chapel, a small oasis in the middle of all the concrete and cars and roars of aircraft, I remembered it was Sunday, and that we'd had to skip Mass. I was tempted to go inside. Light a candle for my aunt Rose, make a vow for the life I was choosing for the next few weeks.

You really don't *really* have to be in Galway, a small voice said inside me. Yet another part of me knew how desperately I needed closure on the farm—and the way it had come into my hands.

Squashing my doubts, I walked determinedly past the little church. Still, my conscience nudged me. *A proper wife and mother would have gotten on that plane to Vancouver…*

"You *do* know what you're about?" said Mam an hour later, standing in the doorway of my old bedroom. Arms crossed, she held a damp wooden spoon in one hand.

"Would I be here if I didn't?" Sitting on the bed, I forced a smile. The scents of home cooking drifted into the room, redolent of roasting meat and the sweet tartness of rhubarb crumble.

"If she hasn't a clue what she's doing," said my sister Suz from the floor, where she was playing with her daughter Ailish, "you're going to give her a whack with your spoon?"

Mam glanced down at the spoon resting against her shoulder, as if she didn't know how it had gotten there. "Letting Stephen and Jamie go off to Canada seems completely mad to me." She bent and handed the spoon to nine-month-old Ailish, who waved it vigorously. "So you can spend the winter in some drafty old farmhouse in the back of beyond."

I shifted uneasily on the lumpy mattress. "It's true, Ballydara's way out in the country, but perfectly civilized."

"The farm's got no phone service," said Mam.

"Not at the moment, but—"

"Jamie told us you haven't any mobile signals up there either!"

"No mobile service!" Suz looked aghast. "How do people *exist*?"

"This is no time for smart cracks," Mam scolded. "I'm surprised this farm has electricity!"

"C'mon, Mam, living off the grid is cool these days," Suz said. "And you know how Kerry *luurves* stories about pioneers." She waved toward my vintage set of *Little House* books, in a place of honor on top of my girlhood bureau. "Maybe she'll want to shut off the power for more authenticity."

Mam rolled her eyes. "Kerry, I suppose you'll tell me next that if Aunt Rose were here, she'd take your side."

A lifelong country woman, Rose would have probably been all for my plan. I didn't want to agitate Mam any more than she already was, though. "I've rung to have the phone line reconnected," I reassured her. "I already know some people in the village—a lovely neighbor called Fiona, and the pub owner, who's quite nice. The woman who owns the shop is very kind too, and…" I searched for more glowy things to say. "She likes to buy her produce from local farmers."

"You could've had a wonderful garden in Rathfarnum," said Mam craftily. "If you'd kept your house."

I ignored that. I'd stopped missing growing vegetables, now that I owned a farm—well, I'd own it only temporarily, but still. A farm! "There's even a golf course in Ballydara," I went on, "if Dad wants to try out the links."

"Your dad's not going to go all the way to Galway to take up golf," said Mam. "And don't try to change the subject."

"Mam, don't nag," Suz began. "Don't you have potatoes to mash?"

"Nag!" Mam stuck her hands on her hips. "What's a mother meant to say when her girl's marriage goes on the rocks?"

"On the rocks?" Suz snorted with laughter. "Didn't you catch Stephen and Kerry snogging when they thought no one was looking?"

I blushed. "I *told* you, Mam, Stephen and I have reconciled." *Even if we don't agree on everything.*

"Most people reconcile by being together," Mam said tartly.

I ignored that too. Mam giving out at me was such a rare thing I felt I should let her have at it until she ran out of steam. "Stephen is perfectly supportive about our living apart for now."

"So you say," Mam all but *harrumphed*. "Your husband told *me* he and Jamie were very keen on you being in Vancouver for Jamie's winter term."

He did, did he?

"Your mother-in-law said the same when she and Brian came to visit last week." Mam shook her head dolefully. "Poor woman. You saw the way she was hovering over Stephen. Her only son."

I felt bad for Mary, but leaving Ireland *had* been Stephen's doing.

"I've heard Vancouver is fantastic," said Suz, ever the devil's advocate. "Jamie had gone on about the Aquarium, Stanley Park, all the places he'll visit with his dad."

I sent my sister a scathing glance. *Whose side are you on anyway?* She only grinned. Turning back to Mam, I said, "It's true, they wanted me to come, but Stephen understands why I'm staying on the farm."

"How so?" Mam's tone was militant.

"Wah, wah," said Ailish, thwacking the spoon against the bed.

I smoothed the faded pink duvet. After the snowbound days Stephen and I had spent alone on the farm over Christmas, making up for lost time, we'd dug out of the blizzard. Once we'd left Ballydara, I couldn't face our big house in Rathfarnam—or the unhappy memories lurking in every corner. So the three of us had bunked here at Mam and Dad's house—Jamie in my brother

Liam's bedroom, Stephen and I sleeping in here. Not that we actually *slept* all that much...

I couldn't think of that now. "Stephen knew I'd be miserable cooling my heels in their flat all winter, while he and Jamie would be busy with work and school."

"You could have gone to Canada for a short holiday," said Mam.

No, I couldn't—I'd be too tempted to stay. "Naturally, I'd have loved some time with Stephen and Jamie, seeing the sights—"

"I've watched how Jamie's been sticking to you and Stephen like glue," Mam interrupted, "the fortnight you've been here. And wasn't he going with you every afternoon to Rathfarnam instead of seeing his friends?"

"He was helping us pack up," I said, although Jamie had made my in-laws' hovering look amateur.

"He's likely been afraid you'll break up again," Mam said. "A lot of stress for a young lad."

"Mam, Kerry feels guilty enough," said Suz.

My heart wrung a bit, picturing Jamie's face at the airport, all broken out with spots. "All right, Jamie *was* a bit clingy," I admitted, "but my farm—I mean, this farm I've got to sell needs so much work."

"Didn't you tell me you'd plenty of money saved? You'll be paying someone to fix the place up for you," observed Mam.

"Kerry, Mam's got a point. Isn't Stephen making piles of euro with this Canada promotion?"

I pulled another face at my sister. "After taking a leave from my job, I don't feel as free about money. If I'm at the farm to supervise the fix-ups, I'll save on labor costs." I couldn't tell them the real reason I was keeping our family finances out of it.

"All right." Mam threw up her hands. "There's no changing your mind." Heaving a big sigh, she finally smiled, and reached to touch my cheek. "I'll have to trust that my girl knows what she's doing." She bent down to lift Ailish, settling the baby into the crook of her arm. "Now, give Granny her spoon so she can stir the potatoes."

Ailish gave Mam one of her serious baby looks, clutching the spoon more tightly.

Suz clambered off the floor to pry the spoon from her daughter's clutches and handed it to Mam. "You wouldn't want to spoil Granny's big farewell do for your Auntie Kerry."

As Ailish's little lip quivered, Mam gave her a kiss and passed her back to Suz. "Don't cry lovey, here's your mammy."

As soon as she left, Suz toed the bedroom door shut. "Mam's become rather outspoken since she got over the cancer—I rather like it."

"Me too," I said, smiling. "Except when all that in-your-face talk is directed at me."

"I hear you," said Suz, settling next to me with Ailish. "You're not the only one, though. Liam said Mam gave him an earful when she and Dad visited him Christmas, about how he needs to get over his breakup with that horrible whatsername."

"Alexa," I said. "Although we don't know this girl was horrible."

"If you ask me, breaking up with our brother makes her a complete tosser." Suz lounged back on one elbow.

"Not that we're judging, right?"

"No judgement whatsoever," Suz replied.

"Waaaahh!" Ailish suddenly let out a howl, and stuffed her fist into her mouth.

I gazed at my little niece, the pang I always felt in her presence stronger than ever. "Looks like she's getting hungry."

"I'm famished myself," said Suz. "Isn't it great that Mam's back to cooking us Sunday lunch? Even if her cross-examination is the price we pay." The merriment left my sister's face. "Still, if we're talking about speaking out…"

My own smiled faded. On the outspoken scale, Suz could outdo Mam every day of the week. Avoiding her eyes, I reached out to stroke Ailish's fuzzy head. "Let's not—"

"Oh, but *let's*," Suz said. "You never did tell Mam about what happened to you and Stephen, did you?"

My sister had cornered me four days after Christmas, when Stephen and I had arrived from County Galway—the same day

Mam and Dad returned from visiting Liam in America. In the midst of our informal family reunion, I asked Mam, "Can we stay here?"

"Your house is already let?" Dad asked.

"Not…quite," I said. "But could we?"

Looking puzzled, Mam said, "We'd love to have you."

Suz looked at my husband, then me. "What for?" she said baldly.

"We…" I faltered, looking uncertainly at Stephen.

"We'll be wanting to spend time with you all before Jamie and I go abroad," said Stephen, drawing me to his side.

"*Riiight,*" Suz said, looking pointedly at Stephen's hand on my hip.

I couldn't blame my sister for being confused, what with the estranged vibe Stephen and I had given off last time she'd seen us together. Still, I wasn't prepared when minutes later, she took me aside. "Why aren't you and Stephen staying at your own place?" she muttered. "Having loads of reconciliation sex in your gorgeous master suite? You *know* all you'll get here is stealth quickies in your cramped old bed."

I faked a saucy grin. "As if we'd go in for stealth anything, with Mam and Dad down the hall."

"Jaysus, who are you kidding?" said Suz. "You know you will."

"Well, okay." I glanced at Stephen across the front room. "But it's so lovely here, being with you all after we missed a family Christmas."

Suz looked incredulous. "Stephen's going abroad in a few days, and you want time with *family*?"

"We'll be dealing with the movers at the Rathfarnum house," I said lamely. "The place won't be fit to live in while we're getting it ready for subletting."

Suz only raised her brows.

"Brian and Mary want to visit, and it'll be impossible to have company in such a mess. Mam's never so happy as when she can entertain."

"Your in-laws will be all for hanging over Stephen wherever they are, and you know it," said Suz. "Come on, then. The truth."

My eyes filled with tears. I'd taken her upstairs and told her why our house held too many ghosts. I could still see her stricken face. *Oh, Kerry, after all the times I teased you about having a baby of your own...*

Now, I felt my chest tighten with grief all over again. "How could I share this with Mam?" Ailish wailed again. "She'd feel terrible that it happened when she was recovering from surgery. Like it was her fault or something."

Suz stood up, scooping the baby into her arms. "And we both know what she'd ask next."

"Suz, I'm just not ready to talk about—"

"She'd ask when you and Stephen are going to try again," Suz said gently, stepping toward the door. "So is it a when...or an if?"

After Suz left with the baby, I crawled off the bed to fetch old Beatrice from the chair in the corner. Settling back against the headboard, I cradled the lace-dressed doll Aunt Rose had given me in my lap.

Last night, Stephen and I had spent our last hours together here, spooning beneath the covers. "You're still set on taking us to the airport?" he murmured. "We can say our goodbyes now."

"Not the kind of goodbyes I'd like," I said.

"It'll be better than nothing." He kissed the back of my neck. "Everyone's asleep, we've been able to be quiet all the other times..." Stephen moved his hand lower.

I was still getting accustomed to this newly expressive husband of mine—especially after the months of coolness between us. "You've become quite the impetuous sort." I forced a lightness I didn't feel.

"I've a lot to get impetuous about." He pressed another tiny kiss against my nape. "And since it'll be all work and no play for the next few weeks..."

Being reminded of Stephen's all-consuming career turned my desire off like a spigot. "I'm sorry." I moved his hand to my waist.

"You've..." Stephen loosened his embrace. "You *have* forgiven me, for taking the Vancouver job without telling you?"

I rolled over to face him. "Oh, love, of course." Although the mere thought of that ghastly November day in Ballydara, when he told me he'd accepted a promotion abroad, made my insides clench. "At least our goodbyes won't be as bad as the last time we said them."

"That was rather awful," said Stephen, with his usual understatement.

Parting at a nondescript car hire agency in Galway—following the Ballydara holiday I thought would be idyllic but turned out to be a disaster—*had* been depressing. Yet Stephen leaving right after the implosion with Will Power at the farm, and the second worst moment of my life, seemed especially grim. Because the entire situation had been my fault.

I suddenly burrowed against Stephen, breathing in his familiar scent. "You don't know how hard this is, to let you go."

"You don't have to." His voice was husky. "You know that."

I stiffened. "You *promised* me you wouldn't pressure me to go with you."

"That's not what I meant..."

I heard a soft rap, and the echo of Stephen's soft whisper vanished.

"Kerry?" My dad stood in the doorway. "Your mam's been calling for you—she's got the lunch on."

"Thanks, Dad," I managed. "I won't be a moment."

Instead of heading back downstairs, he said, "She wondered if you'd buried your nose in one of your farm books again. Myself, I wanted to make sure you weren't..." He looked pained. "Well, crying your eyes out, after the lads left."

"I'm not exactly grand," I said, "but I'm coping."

He came into the room and briefly laid his hand on my hair. "We'll miss you," Dad said gruffly. "I understand you'll be off after lunch."

I tried on a smile. "I'll be back to visit, I promise."

"We'd like that. Now, come along. Or it'll be on your head that the roast got dry."

I nodded. "I'll just say goodbye to old Beatrice here."

As he disappeared, I glanced at the doll in my lap. "Shall I bring you to Ballydara with me? You'll be the only baby I'll have to cuddle until Stephen and I are together again."

I closed my eyes, my thoughts returning to last night, when Stephen had drawn me close again. "I'm not asking you to come to Vancouver," he said, low. "Instead, I want to…to leave a part of myself—of us—with you. Let's try again—" His voice cracked. "Let's be mad, and make a baby. Tonight."

"Oh, Stephen." Tears spilled onto my cheeks. "I wish we could."

"It would be our celebration baby. You know, for getting back together."

A sob escaped me. "I don't know if I'm over the one we lost."

He pressed his mouth to my hair. "I'm not—sometimes I think I never will be. But we can't mourn forever."

At the quaver in his voice, I touched his cheek in mute apology. "If I was newly pregnant I wouldn't have the energy for sorting the farm, with morning sickness and all that."

"Kerry—"

"I'm for waiting to try until…" I felt a twinge of melancholy, "until we sell it."

"To hell with the place!" Stephen tensed. "I don't give a *shite* what happens to it!"

That *hurt*—especially since Stephen swore so rarely. I tried to soften my refusal. "If I wore myself out or got stressed, it wouldn't be good for the baby."

"You're not wanting to put off a baby because you still have feelings for—"

"No." I kissed his tight jaw. "You know I don't. Chances are, we wouldn't conceive, trying this one time."

"We could go for it anyway."

I settled my head on his shoulder, regret heavy in my chest. "You know I'm right."

He only sighed. "We'd better get some sleep, with that early flight." He pulled the covers up. "Wouldn't it be great to have just one more day alone? Before life's all about meetings and sales goals and pushing for a bigger bonus."

I knew he felt the pressure of being the sole family breadwinner. Before I could respond, he said, "I sometimes wonder, what's the point?"

I closed my eyes, knowing I'd failed him…

Now, I climbed off the bed and set the doll back in her chair, my heart heavy. *Oh, Aunt Rose, if only I could be sure this is the right decision.*

Stephen had signed a contract for his Vancouver post—and the last thing he'd do is ruin the career he'd built the last dozen years. Going downstairs, I wondered what my aunt would say if she were still alive. Would she tell me, *Go on, have your adventure?* Or would she ask, *Even if you've dreamt of having a farm all your life, what good is a country place if the people you love aren't part of it?*

By evening, stiff after the long hours in Stephen's Land Cruiser, I reached Ballydara. Pleasure filled me at being back in the quiet Galway village, although it was too dark to enjoy the view.

I slowed down, recalling my first glimpse—my delight at the green hills above the little town, covered by a patchwork of stone walls, with cows, sheep and more piles of stones dotting the open spaces. The late afternoon sun had been low in the sky, bathing the pastures with a golden-pink glow, gilt-edged clouds drifting about the hilltops. Next to me, Stephen had gone silent. When I looked at him, I found him gazing at the hills too, a reverent expression on his face.

Now, two months later, I passed Hurley's pub, wishing with all my heart I could have my husband and son back in Ballydara with me. I could see Stephen in my mind's eye, driving the neighbor's ancient tractor, and imagined the three of us hillwalking together. Not to visit but to stay, to create a real farm, a brand-new life in the country…

I rubbed my eyes wearily. Stop fantasizing, I told myself as I headed up the Ballydara road. Not long ago, hadn't Stephen made his feelings obvious? *If I never see another cow again it'll be too soon.* And last night, he'd been even clearer—he cared nothing for this place I already loved.

I had to face reality: Stephen, on a farm—it would never happen.

Fiona

2

*F*iona Whelan paused as she approached the old Power farmhouse. Wouldn't she need an excuse for calling round? Neighbors didn't visit each other like they used to, and she could hardly say I've been desperate for someone to talk to since I moved in with Dad, and you seemed like a kindred spirit...

The house hardly looked welcoming. Its golden stone exterior was dimmed by the low gray clouds drifting along the hills to the west, and no lights shone behind the lace-curtained windows. Still, the big Toyota parked in the drive had to be the McCormack's.

Stepping onto the footpath, Fiona passed the weed-choked garden and a crooked wooden swing dangling from a massive oak tree. She glanced across a stretch of rumpled grass at the barn, built of golden stone as well, the rusty metal roof rattling in the breeze. Near it, a chicken coop listed to one side like it was too tired to stand upright.

The air of neglect around the farm added to her forlorn feeling. Climbing the steps, Fiona considered, *Kerry, I thought you could use some company, stuck out here away from the village.*

Shaking the rain off her mother's old umbrella, Fiona gave the door a brisk knock. As she waited, the bare canes of the rosebush next to the stoop scratched against the stone walls. What if the car wasn't Kerry's? Fiona had never heard of any squatters in Ballydara, but if strangers had gotten into the house she'd have to leg it back home and call the Guards. Dad would get terribly worked up, and he was already in a state—

The door suddenly opened, the hinges squeaking. "Fiona! How grand!" said Kerry. Her curly brown hair was disheveled, her jumper and jeans rumpled, but her dark eyes were bright.

"I wanted to welcome you back to the district," said Fiona. "And if the car in the drive wasn't yours, I'd want to know the reason why." *That sounds all right. Not desperate at all.*

"It's mine, all right." Kerry grinned. "Although as you know, farm equipment is my preferred mode of travel."

Fiona laughed, her tension easing. "Weren't you a modern Guinevere that day, you and your Lancelot driving through the snow." She could still picture the McCormacks bouncing down the Ballydara road on her dad's old tractor.

"Me riding pillion behind Stephen," said Kerry. "Didn't we look a right pair of madzers?" She opened the door wide. "Please, come in."

Fiona snapped the flowered umbrella closed. She liked the ease about Kerry, the kind she herself had once had. "I didn't interrupt anything, did I?" She distinctly remembered that Kerry's husband was meant to be working abroad. But what if he *was* here? And he and Kerry had been in the middle of…oh, *Jaysus.*

"Not a thing," Kerry said. "I had a lie-in this morning. The gray day didn't exactly inspire me to rise and shine."

She hadn't said *we.* Relieved, Fiona said, "I'll take my wet shoes off, shall I?"

"A bit of mud won't hurt this old floor. See?" Kerry pressed her foot against a warped spot. It squeaked like a startled piglet.

"Oh, the state of the place!" said Fiona. When she'd been inside in November, before young Mr. Power arrived with his family, the house had been a right kip. The old fellow who'd rented the property after the grandfather died hadn't kept it up. Fiona had hoped to do a proper cleaning, but with her dad sick with the flu, all she'd had time for was putting fresh linens on the beds.

Fiona looked into front room. "I stand corrected! You and Stephen certainly tidied up the house over Christmas."

"Actually, I did a bit of mucking out...before. While we were visiting the Powers." A flash of discomfort showed in Kerry's eyes.

Brushing off her jacket, Fiona pretended not to notice. "Everyone I know is thrilled you've taken over the farm." When Kerry and her husband had called round last month and told her and Dad about the change of ownership, Fiona noticed they'd been careful not to say, "bought." Something to do with those narky Powers?

"The problem is, the property is bigger than I remember," Kerry said ruefully. "And more run down too. I'm going to fix it up, though—make it really beautiful."

"Fair play to you," said Fiona. "People were saying the village would die on the vine, with this farm going under, and my dad...retiring. So your coming back has sent the lot of them over the moon."

Kerry laughed. "Go on."

"No, really," Fiona said. "Judith Murphy especially. 'A lovely little family like the McCormacks will really perk up Ballydara,' she said about a million times."

Kerry's smile faded. "It's only right to tell you—it'll be just myself. Temporarily."

Fiona's light heart plummeted back into her chest. "You'll be selling the place?"

"I'm...afraid so."

Fiona couldn't speak for a moment. *Just when I thought I'd have a new friend.* "I'm sorry to hear it. Dad was terribly keen to have you and your husband for neighbors." Seeing Kerry's face fall, she added quickly, "Sorry, I didn't mean to lay a guilt trip on you."

"My selling is on the down-low at the moment, but I don't mind if you let your dad in on it." Kerry twisted her fingers together. "For now, have you a minute? I'd love to show you some of my ideas for the redo."

It'll be worth being late to work. "Give me the grand tour," said Fiona.

Kerry stepped onto the frayed rug in the front room. "This area will be easy, since I'm keeping the old-fashioned look— new wallpaper and curtains should do it."

Fiona took in the faded pink-flowered wallpaper, the threadbare lace curtains, and the careworn furniture. "If you had our old blue wallpaper, our front rooms would be twins."

"You like the country vibe yourself?" Kerry asked. Before Fiona could answer, she said, "Wait—I think you mentioned living in Galway City for years. A city girl."

I'd better get used to the country again, thought Fiona. *God knows how long I'll be here.* "City girl or not, I don't see my dad changing anything in our house," she told Kerry. "He still talks about Mam putting up that wallpaper when I was a teenager."

"How is your dad?" Kerry briefly touched Fiona's arm.

She felt a start. It seemed like a long time since anyone had touched her. "Oh, ticking along," said Fiona. *You don't want to get into Dad's situation now.* "Anyway, your easy chairs seem all right, and the couch is, well..."

"Rubbish?" said Kerry.

"*Serviceable*," Fiona said firmly.

"It's *going*," Kerry said, a glint in her eye. "I don't want any reminders of Will Pow—" she broke off, looking uneasy.

So. There *was* something about those Powers. Fiona said diplomatically, "What of that vintage radio?"

"Um...right." Kerry ran her finger along its top, collecting a coating of dust. "I'll keep it for old-timey atmosphere." Brushing her hands, she ushered Fiona into the kitchen. "Speaking of, it's totally the seventies in here, isn't it?" She waved at the cracked brown lino and the beige chipped worktop. "If it was up to me, I wouldn't change a thing—this room reminds me of my aunt Rose's farmhouse in Wicklow. Growing up, she was my idol."

"Not your mam?" Fiona asked impulsively. Her own mother had been her one real ally, who understood that Fiona wanted a bigger life than what she'd have on a small Galway farm. And when she died not long after hanging the new wallpaper, Fiona had floundered. Like a boat without an anchor.

A shadow crossed Kerry's face. "My mam's always been like a best friend. Until recently."

Fiona raised her brows. "Not a serious row, I hope."

"She thinks I'm dossing as a wife and mother, not going to

Vancouver with Stephen and Jamie." Kerry shrugged. "Maybe with this farm I'm going through…I don't know. An early midlife crisis? Or my second big rebellion."

"You don't quite seem the rebellious sort," said Fiona.

"What else do you call it, when you fall pregnant at nineteen years of age?"

"Never." Fiona could hardly take it in: *Kerry, Teen Mammy.*

"And not married." With a blithe shrug, Kerry leaned against the worktop.

"Stephen doesn't seem the type to—" Fiona broke off, reddening. *Jaysus, what's got into me, getting so personal with someone I hardly know?*

"To get a girl up the pole without a wedding ring on her finger? You're right." Kerry's face turned tender. "Stephen was my real-life hero. And Jamie's."

So Jamie wasn't Stephen's biological child. Who knew? "Not that there's anything wrong with unwed motherhood," Fiona said hastily.

"For me, having a baby and marrying young was no picnic. I'd do it all over again, though," said Kerry.

For years, Fiona had done exactly what she wanted—until that idyllic life came to a screeching halt. "I'm happy everything worked out for you."

"Not always. Stephen and I have had our share of…bumps on the road." Kerry's brown eyes clouded. "There've been times I haven't deserved him."

"Surely not," Fiona said involuntarily.

"I've made mistakes—and they've been *whoppers*."

Fiona couldn't imagine Kerry getting up to anything too radical. But then, who would've guessed how far *she* had gone off the rails. "Here's a thought," she said. "If you never drive your parents—or any of the people you love—round the bend, you're living too safe a life."

Kerry rubbed a mark on the worktop. "Even if you disappoint them terribly?"

Being secure was one thing, thought Fiona. Yet letting down everyone you knew was no way to live either. "We're getting ridiculously philosophical," she finally said. "Now, about your kitchen upgrades?"

"Right, back to the tour," said Kerry, sounding relieved. "I can't count on any prospective buyers seeing the charm in here that I do, so I'll be replacing the floors, worktops, and all the appliances."

"That's quite ambitious," Fiona said. "You might be in Ballydara longer than you think." She tried to keep the hope out of her voice.

"I'd be all for that," Kerry said wistfully. "Whatever I do, I'm giving myself a free hand."

A free hand, Fiona thought, following Kerry upstairs. She could hardly remember what freedom felt like. Hardly imagine how it would be to start over, follow her dreams, even if falling in love again wasn't on—

"I just remembered." Kerry paused on the landing. "You were up here when you made up the beds for the Powers' visit. That was incredibly kind."

Fiona corralled her unruly thoughts. "It was no bother. Although I couldn't help noticing all the mattresses were sprung."

"Oh, I'll get myself a new bed," said Kerry. "I shouldn't want a dodgy back once I start whipping the garden into shape."

She paused in the doorway of a room with two narrow beds, one still unmade. "Look at that—if I'm to show the house I can't go for the lived-in look." Stepping into the room, Kerry drew the covers up, revealing a man's undershirt slung across the foot of the bed. "Stephen obviously forgot to pack this." She looked flustered.

"You must like the view from this room," Fiona observed wryly. *Or you and Stephen would've slept down the hall in the bigger bed, or the one downstairs.*

"You've found me out." Kerry's cheeks were pink. "Can I tell you something?" She didn't wait for Fiona to answer. "I told Stephen that sleeping in such a small bed will either A, strengthen your marriage, or B, tempt you to murder your spouse."

The cozy bedsit in Galway City flashed in Fiona's mind. She swiftly forced it away. "I hope you went for Option A."

Kerry turned even rosier and left the doorway, muttering something about new fixtures for both bathrooms. Taking Fiona back downstairs, she moved toward the closed door on the far wall of the front room. "One last dilemma—I haven't a clue what to do with this room." She hesitated, then turned the knob.

The room smelled musty, like the door had been closed for weeks. Fiona had put the nicest linens she could find on this bed. Now the sheets were awry, the patchwork quilt trailing half off the mattress, and one pillow lay on the floor.

"Would you look at this mess?" Kerry poked the pillow with her stocking foot. "There's no excuse, even if they left in a hurry—" she stopped.

Mr. Power and his wife must've stayed in here, Fiona thought. "The Powers weren't the tidiest people?"

"The kids were lovely, but their parents—I think they create chaos wherever they go," Kerry said, her voice acerbic. Gathering up the quilt, she dropped it onto the middle of the bed. "Anyway, I was thinking most buyers might be interested in more living space, instead of extra bedrooms. This room has a nice southern exposure too."

"You might make this area into an office," said Fiona. "Or a telly room?"

Kerry shook her head. "A satellite dish will spoil the country vibe I'm aiming for."

"Ugly yokes, aren't they?" said Fiona. "I know what I'd do with an extra room." And if Dad wasn't completely resistant to the tiniest change in the house. "I'd put in a sunroom, with garden windows to fill the place with light. It would be perfect for—"

"That's it!" Kerry gazed around the room. "Can you see two walls of windows?" She pointed toward the south and west walls. "It would brighten the entire downstairs! An easy chair and a tea table would make things cozy. It's brilliant!"

"I didn't mean to suggest…" Fiona wished she'd kept her gob shut. "Really, it would cost the earth."

"Who cares? It's just money!" Kerry's face was alight. "I could put in French doors for more fresh air—to clear the cobwebs. Exactly what the house needs." She met Fiona's eyes, a trace of defiance in her expression. "And what *I* need, after I nearly ruined my life with Will—" She bent to pick up the pillow, yanking the white cotton case off. "Pretend you didn't hear that, would you?" she muttered.

Fiona got an odd sensation. It took her a moment to work out what it was: a tiny sense of daring. "I'd say 'okay, I will,'" and she took a deep breath. "But now that you've mentioned him, I don't think I can."

Rubbing her wedding ring with her thumb, Kerry straightened. "I didn't have an affair with him, if that's what you're thinking." Her eyes went wide. "Holy Jaysus, I can't *believe* I actually said that."

"I wasn't," Fiona said quickly. *Liar.* Still, she couldn't let Kerry spill her guts while she held herself at a distance, pretending to be superior. "Look, I've done some really stupid things myself," she said frankly. Like get engaged to Enda, the biggest mistake of her life. Then she had to compound the error by making a right fool of herself.

"You? Really?" Holding the white case by her thumb and forefinger, Kerry dropped it on the bed, then flung the pillow after it. "Let's just say Will Power turned out to be a completely useless article."

I *knew* it, thought Fiona. That big, handsome Mr. Power hadn't been the fair-haired boy he seemed. And clearly, he and his wife were still haunting this room. "Sounds like a long story."

"It is," said Kerry, brushing her hands against her jeans. "Maybe I'll tell you about it sometime."

Really intrigued now, Fiona glanced at her watch. "Bugger— I'd better run. Please, do call round to our house soon."

"Maybe this afternoon, after you're done at the shop?"

"Um...how about later this week," Fiona made herself say. "My dad's not quite at himself today—" *I've said too much.*

"Is he all right?" Kerry asked, concern in her eyes. "Tell me how I can help—I'll put the kettle on."

"I…I'd love to stay, really. But I'm late for work." Fiona headed for the front door.

"Can I give you a lift? I was intending to go to the village this morning anyway."

"No need," Fiona said. After what she'd let drop about her dad, she didn't want Kerry to feel sorry for her. "The walk clears my mind before I'm cooped up all day."

"I've got to shower first anyway, get my act together." Kerry's face seemed to go tight. "I've some phone calls to make."

Fiona didn't make the offer she would have liked to—*no reason to go down to the village, you can ring from Dad's phone.* But he was in no state for company, and lately she'd let the house go. "Great," said Fiona. "While you're in Ballydara, you'll want to contact Bernard Hurley—he's your man for remodels."

Smiling again, Kerry opened the door. "That's my plan. He did offer me his services, when you and I first met."

So Kerry had remembered that. It made Fiona feel less…invisible. Her defenses lowered, she said, "It'll be grand, to have you around. Even if it's only for the winter."

"D'you know what you're in for? I may come whinging to you every time I wonder what I've gotten myself into."

"That's what neighbors are for," said Fiona. "Cheers."

Her steps were light as she strode down the drive. Kerry seemed like a friend already. Still, Fiona would have to guard herself from confiding too much in turn. Because if Kerry knew the truth about her, she might not be a friend for long…

When Fiona arrived at the shop, the phone was ringing. "Can you get that in the back, love?" asked Judith, busy at the cash desk with old Nora O'Donnell.

Fiona hurried to pick up. "Murphy's Shop."

"Fiona."

Her breath *stopped*.

"I've been waiting for you. But I've waited long enough."

Kerry

3

Hi Mr. Smythe, hope you had a happy Christmas, I rehearsed silently, imagining the scowling face of my nemesis. Was that a bit strong? Driving down the Ballydara road, I considered Mr. Smythe's cranky power trips and micromanagement, everything I'd put up with for years. So yeah—*nemesis* was bang on the money. *I'm ringing you with an update of my plans…*

I parked the Toyota near Mrs. Murphy's shop, rain blurring the windscreen. Hopefully Fiona hadn't gotten too wet on her way to work. When we'd met at the shop two months ago, I'd guessed her to be around forty. She seemed a bit plain, her manner prosaic. Yet when Fiona was animated, as she'd been at my house, she had a spare, striking beauty in her face. She seemed far younger too—closer to my age. In a way, she reminded me of Stephen, with her lovely calmness and kind grey eyes.

The reason, I suppose, that I'd gotten way too personal. Had I overshared about Will Power? When Fiona seemed dismayed I wasn't keeping the farm, I'd *so* wanted to tell her, *Selling isn't my choice.* If I had, though, I would've had to tell her the lot. Including my marriage meltdown during our stay with Will and his family, and how letting go of the place would be the only way to redeem myself…

Ballydara's rainbow-hued storefronts came back into focus. Murphy's shop was a cheerful sight, its door and window casements a muted pink. Across the road was Hurley's pub, with its bright green sign and door. The shops on either side of Murphy's looked like they'd been empty a long time, the windows dusty, paint peeling on both doors. A shame no one's opened a new business in either, I thought. The fairy lights I'd seen here at Christmas were still strung around the village, but unlit this time.

Okay, back on task, I told myself, swallowing nervously. Stephen always said when you're facing an important meeting, the more you prepare, the more effective you'll be. Okay. The only talking points I had for Mr. Smythe were these: *I've done a runner and left Dublin entirely, and I can't stand the thought of working for you anymore. So sack me, will you?*

Obviously, that wouldn't work. I released my seat belt and bounded from the car. I'll simply have to wing it, I decided, and headed for the shop. A bell tinkled as I entered.

Mrs. Murphy, behind the counter, broke into a smile. "If it isn't Mrs. McCormack, Ballydara's newest resident!"

"Please, call me Kerry," I forced a smile. *How to tell her I wouldn't be living here?*

"Kerry it is. I'm called Judith. Now that you've taken over the Power place, Fiona mentioned you'd be nipping in to lay in some groceries, so."

"That's it," I said, although my freezer was still full of the staples Jen Power had bought for their visit.

"I've gotten in some fresh-picked kale, and Fiona's just now unpacking a new shipment of apples too," said Judith. "Didn't you do a pie in the autumn, while you were here with the Powers? I think I sold you Granny Smith's—all very well, I'm sure, but if you're thinking of making another pudding you'll want something special. I've some Christmas Pippins, straight from a farmer in Clare."

"Lovely," I said. "Now that I'm back in the country I'll be doing more baking." Apparently country folk knew all about your business—often before you did. "Before I shop, though, can you direct me to the nearest public phone?"

"No need to go back in the rain." Judith reached under the cash desk and brought out a clunky black dial phone. "Here you are then."

"Oh—thanks, but I've got to phone up a Dublin number," I said.

"It's no bother," said Judith. "You can square things up later."

"Really, I shouldn't want to impose—"

"Impose! Nothing of the sort. It's the least I can do, to welcome you to Ballydara."

I felt guilty again. "That's very generous—I do have my mobile on me but I understand it's no use around here."

"I'm not a great one for mobiles," said Judith, "but there's a place in Hurley's pub, where one of those thingummies…what do they call them?" She frowned and said over her shoulder, "Fiona? What's there at Hurley's?"

No answer.

"Fiona!" Judith said louder. "That yoke at Hurley's?"

"Um…you mean, a mobile signal?" Fiona's voice sounded… different.

"Signal, yes," Judith said to me. "You'll catch it if you sit in the back booth furthest to the left." The mobile signal sounded like an elusive wild animal. "It's a busy table, as you can imagine. Bernard Hurley parks himself there by the hour to make his business calls, like he owns the place instead of his brother Pat, who by the way, indulges the man something terrible. But doesn't Bernard have a way with him!"

Judith's longish speech was a novelty—I liked that she gave the full explanation of things, not omitting a detail. Before I could take my leave to use my mobile, she reached under the counter again and brought out a binder with a worn leather cover. "You'll want an account, I'm sure." She turned to a fresh page, writing my name in block letters at the top. "So much simpler to pay only once a month."

I was charmed. "I'd like that." My conscience prompted, *You should own up to Judith now, that you'll only be here a few weeks. Especially since Fiona knows.* But I couldn't quite bring myself. "Right, I'd better pop into the pub and get my Dublin business over with."

The shop phone rang. Before Judith could pick up, Fiona called, "I'll get it!" A pause. Then, "What's happened?"

Judith wore a troubled look. "That'll be her dad," she said in a low voice. "He rings nearly every day, and it's never good news."

Fiona was saying, "Oh, Dad…It's okay, we can fix everything up for…right, it's your decision—"

Since Judith was listening unashamedly, I did the same, even more concerned about Fiona's situation. After a moment she said, "See you shortly." The phone clunked in its cradle.

"Poor Desmond," Judith murmured. "A shame, how things have turned…well, that's not for me to pass judgement."

I got a sudden brainwave, and peeked into the back room. "Fiona, can I treat you to lunch?"

Brushing her hands against her white shop apron, she seemed to look right through me. "Sounds lovely, but I've too much to do here."

"It wouldn't take long to grab a bite at the pub," I coaxed.

"Sorry, no," she said abruptly, avoiding my eyes. "I go home for lunch."

Apparently I *had* gone over the top with my TMI about Will. As Fiona turned her attention to some papers at her elbow, I felt snubbed, especially after her warmth earlier.

Judith must have seen my face. She whispered, "Fiona runs up the hill every day to get a meal for her dad—he won't eat unless she's there to make sure he does."

I only nodded. *You can't be so sensitive, when Fiona's worried about her father.*

"The old fella has been losing ground—you know, here." Judith tapped her temple. "There was some dust-up with—" She pressed her lips together. "Well, it's not for me to say. So you'll be back for your groceries? I shouldn't want you up at the Power farm alone without food, in case we get another terrible snowstorm." She closed the big leather book. "Although it's unlikely County Galway will see another snowfall like we had last month, don't you think?"

"Right. See you soon." I headed out, Judith's concern lessening the sting of Fiona's coolness. Clutching my jacket snugly around me, I ran through the raindrops to Hurley's.

As I approached the door, dread pooled in my stomach. *You've been wanting to do this forever. The sooner you make the call, the better you'll feel.*

"Hallo, Missus!" said Pat Hurley. "You *are* back in Ballydara! I thought I recognized that big car of yours."

"I'm happy to be here." Brushing the moisture off my coat, I made myself smile at the pub owner. "Say, might I have a quick go at your…" *You should observe the niceties before you push in.* "Um…I missed breakfast. Have you a lunch menu?"

"I haven't one, no. I can do you a ham sandwich, though. Since you're our new addition to the village, chips on the house."

"Sounds delicious." *You'll have to tell Pat too, that you won't be staying—better start a list.* "And a fizzy lemonade, if you have it?"

"You like a lemonade too, then." Pat reached for a glass.

"Sorry?"

"Every time your husband came in, back in the autumn, a pint wouldn't do for him, he had to have a lemonade, and he had me brother following his lead."

Stephen had hung out with Bernard Hurley?

Pat passed me the filled glass. "So then, you've taken over the Power place. With your man over in Canada, you'll be all right up there, on your own?"

"I'll be grand." Pat Hurley's friendliness helped me forget Fiona's lack of it. "I can pretend the place is a winter getaway."

Grinning, Pat looked past me at the front window, sheeting with rain. "That'd be some class of holiday, holed up in a drafty farmhouse in the West of Ireland."

"But it's my drafty farmhouse," I said without thinking. *That's it, dig a deeper hole.* I looked around furtively, to see if there were any more local people I'd have to deceive. But the place was empty save for a pair of old fellas watching the news at the bar. "Say, any chance I could use my mobile?"

"Ah, here for my special booth, are you? Right this way." Pat led me to the back of the pub. "I'll have that sandwich for you in a jif."

As he ambled away I set my glass on the table. Once he was out of earshot, I took a deep breath, trying to summon the devil-take-the-hindmost cheek I'd had the last time I'd rung work. My nerves on edge again, I pressed the number.

"Smythe's Engineering, may I help you?" said a familiar voice.

"Sharon?"

"Kerry!" My workmate sounded stressed. "Where are you?"

"I'm ringing from Galway," I said. "I've more family affairs to take care of here." I'd told her about the farm last month, when I'd first taken my leave of absence. "I thought I should put Mr. Smythe in the loop."

"Will you be back soon? Ever since Gwen left, the office has been mad, but with you away it's really falling to pieces."

"I am sorry about that," I said. "It was rotten for me to leave without warning, but another day at Smythe's and I'd have done something desperate."

"I know the feeling." Sharon lowered her voice. "I wish I could chuck the place myself. Especially since Mr. S. has been breathing fire since the holidays."

"He's always grumpy on Mondays," I said. "He'll be in better form tomorrow."

"I doubt it." Sharon sighed. "You really want to talk to him? He's on a proper rampage today."

"He is, is he?" I felt a surge of strength. Only weeks ago, I'd thought my marriage was over. After all that, I realized my boss' tantrums hadn't the same power over me. "Better me than you."

Sharon laughed shakily. "That's decent of you, but you're in for a bollacking. I can put you through to his voice mail."

"No thanks, I'll speak to him." I took another fortifying breath.

"Okay then," said Sharon. "When you're next in Dub, let's take Gwen to lunch and catch up. So…brace yourself."

Minutes ticked by. Mr. Smythe was doing his typical power play. At last he came on the line. "Kerry."

He didn't say anything else—another one of his tricks to get people on the defensive. *Two could play that game.* I didn't speak either. Finally he said, "I trust you're ringing because you've come to your senses." Irritation dripped from every word.

"I'm actually going to be away from Dublin for several more weeks," I said.

"Weeks, did you say? You're not serious?"

Again, I didn't answer—playing Mr. Smythe was actually rather good crack. Besides, I didn't quite know what to tell him. Stephen and I hadn't gotten around to discussing when I'd go back to Smythe's.

"Kerry! *Are* you serious? What d'you think you're doing anyway, leaving us high and dry? Haven't I given you a good situation, good pay for…for…"

You don't remember? "Fourteen years," I prompted.

"Fourteen years! And where are you when you're needed? The billing paperwork has been a shambles since you left, a bloody shambles!"

I'd always cowered inwardly when Mr. Smythe was cross with me. But as my sense of freedom grew, suddenly I didn't give a rip how angry he was. "If I'm so valuable, Mr. Smythe, why did you move my workstation to the file room, like I was some kind of junior assistant?"

"Well, I…I—"

"And I was meant to wait for proper office for months!"

"I…er, counted on you to be flexible, for the good of the firm."

"I'm entirely flexible," I said. "I'm so flexible I haven't quite decided on a return date. I'm exploring some new options for my life."

"Options!" Mr. Smythe growled. "What are you on about *now*?"

"Oh, you're busy so I won't get into it," I said blithely. "I'll give you a date when I've a better sense of my timetable— maybe around late March."

"*March*?"

"That's what I said." With the prospect of devoting myself to the farm for over two months, I could sense the future opening before me, like sunlight peeking behind dark clouds. Far from the sickly fluorescent light and cramped desk in a Dublin office block. "When I come back," I went on, *if I come back*, "I'll expect an organized workstation and my own cubicle."

"Kerry, this absolutely won't do," he blustered, "not for one minute—"

"That's a shame, because I've got to run."

"You realize you're giving me no choice but to give you the sack!"

"If you do, you'll have freed up some payroll funds," I said cheerfully. "You could share it amongst the rest of the staff."

"You're giving *me* advice?" He sounded ready to explode. "You've a nerve—"

"If you're shorthanded, you might see if Gwen's willing to help you with the accounts before the baby comes. She could work from home."

"From home!" Flex time and telecommuting had always been dirty words round Smythe's.

"At double her former pay, of course. Oh, and the best to yourself for the New Year."

I pressed off without waiting for his response. Growing a backbone was so wonderfully liberating. Even if I was jeopardizing my job in a way I would have never dared if Stephen and I were living together.

My gaze dropped to the phone in my hand. Only now I'd have to tell him what I'd done. After facing down my boss, talking to Stephen should be a breeze. But it was way past midnight on the West Coast. On the other hand, with all the closeness we'd shared since reconciling, he'd be happy to hear from me, whatever the time…

I resolutely pressed his number. The international connection seemed to take forever. Finally, "Yes?" a man barked.

"Stephen?" I said, hurt.

"Sorry, sorry," Stephen said quickly. "I didn't look at the ID."

"Is something wrong?"

"I…didn't expect to hear from you. I was going to ring as soon as we'd settled in."

He sounded distracted. Where was my ardent husband from…when? Only yesterday? "If you're so pressed we can talk later." I tried to match his businesslike tone.

"I *am* sorry." His voice softened. "I've been emailing my team, and things aren't quite what I—" He broke off.

Quite what I expected? Searching for a safe topic, I asked, "Jamie's all right? Could you put him on?"

"Actually, he crawled into bed as soon as we got to our lodging," Stephen said. "But now that you're on the line, I should tell you—he's gotten himself into a proper muddle."

Kerry

4

*H*ope rose in me. "He's changed his mind about staying in Vancouver?"

"Ah…no, he's as keen as ever." Stephen's tone was apologetic. I knew he felt guilty for taking Jamie away from me. "It's those bloody McElligotts." His voice turned edgy. "They've been hassling our boy."

Mike Senior and Shirley McElligott—Jamie's biological grandparents. "Surely not *hassling*."

"He never told you—they were ringing the Rathfarnum house over the Christmas holiday, leaving messages nearly every day. Shirley even sent him a couple of letters."

Oh, no. The woman was granny-stalking again. "I can't imagine why they'd keep trying to contact Jamie, after he'd written to them about being away for the winter."

"There's the rub," said Stephen. "On the plane, he confessed he never wrote the letter."

"Never wrote—" I nearly dropped my mobile. "I can't believe it—he promised!"

"He'd deleted all their voice messages," Stephen went on, "and tore up Shirley's letters before we could see them."

These past weeks, I'd been in a fog of wishing—that Stephen and I could be alone, that he and Jamie weren't going abroad—and clearly, not seeing that our son was anxious about something. Guilt-stricken, I spoke sharply. "Have him ring me as soon as he's up."

"I will, but he's too young for this sort of harassment," said

Stephen. "Not at fourteen years of age!"

"Last autumn, he was certainly old enough to look up the McElligotts and write to them behind my back," I said tartly. "So he can just get on with the letter."

"I say he should ignore them," Stephen said heatedly. "Jamie has four grandparents already!"

"Stephen!" It was almost comical, my usually mild husband getting so worked up. "What kind of a lesson is this for Jamie, to be allowed to blow off the people he'd invited into his life?"

"Kids his age should be allowed to drop the ball now and then."

"He's got to be respectful to his grandparents." Then I remembered how sensitive Stephen could be about not being Jamie's biological father. "Please, don't make me be the bad guy, when I won't see him until his school holiday."

"He shouldn't have to deal with these people long-distance."

"Wherever Jamie is," I said, "he's got to do the right thing."

"Kerry…" Stephen said, "Jamie didn't say it straight out, but I get the feeling he's afraid if he writes to the McElligotts, they'll keep at it."

"Yes, I see your point." Bernard Hurley entered the pub, brushing raindrops off his jacket.

"You'll recall they had the utter *cheek* to come to our house uninvited," said Stephen.

I sighed. "I'll phone them up myself, make it clear Jamie will be out of touch until the spring."

"Great!" His testiness seemed to vanish. "It'll be a load off Jamie's mind—help him settle into life here."

I felt a pinch, that Jamie could be happier in Vancouver than home in Ireland. Even worse, though, was the possibility that Stephen might come to like Canada a little *too* much… Just then, Bernard caught my eye and waved at me, mobile in hand. "Looks like there's a queue forming," I said, my throat tight. "I'd better get on with the day." If we'd had more privacy, I'd have liked to linger with Stephen for a few sweet nothings, but here was Bernard, approaching the table.

"Bernard, I'll bet." I heard a smile in Stephen's voice.

If I didn't know better, I'd have thought the pair of them were mates. "You sound quite chipper for someone who ought to be passed out from jet lag," I said. "We could have sorted this McElligott issue after you'd had a decent sleep."

"But…" Stephen's voice lowered. "I wouldn't have been able to hear you say goodnight to me."

I smiled mistily. This was the Stephen I knew. "Sweet dreams, then."

"And I wouldn't have been able to imagine nearly as well you lying next to me, or even better, on—"

"Stephen…" Blushing, I glanced at Bernard. He twinkled at me. "I…um, miss you too, but we'd better ring off."

"I can't *wait* for the Easter holidays."

"Me too," I said, filled with longing. "We'll have to make our short visit count."

"Oh, we *will*," said Stephen significantly. I felt myself color even more. "I'm living for the day this assignment is over, and we're all three of us settled in Dublin again."

Living in Dublin. *But you'll be with your husband and son again…* I stretched out the fingers of my left hand and stared at the ring Stephen had given me only weeks ago. As the diamonds glinted the pub's dim light, I felt another jolt of guilt. As lovely as the ring was, it would forever remind me of how close I'd come to losing Stephen… "Fantastic, yes," I said firmly, as if to convince myself. "Now, go have your sleep."

I managed to ring off without tearing up. Only to realize I hadn't mentioned telling off Mr. Smythe. As I set down my phone, Bernard said, "Welcome back, Missus McC!" He gestured at the empty seat. "You wouldn't mind?"

"Not at all." I made to rise. "I'll sit up front."

"Ah, none of that—we'll share, shall we?"

I settled back into the booth, pleased with this serendipity. "Have you a moment? After you've made your calls, I mean."

"Here's your sandwich." Pat Hurley materialized at the side of the table, setting a plate in front of me. Piled high with ham, the sandwich oozed with melted cheese, the chips still sizzling.

"Thank you—it looks great." I glanced across the table at Bernard. "Have you had lunch? This is too much for me."

Bernard gazed longingly at my plate, but he said, "I'll pass." He patted his stomach. "Got to watch my waistline."

"Watching it is all he's doing," said Pat.

As Bernard grinned and drew a chocolate bar from his pocket, Pat eyed his brother sternly. "You're to mind yourself and not pressure Mrs. McCormack to leave the booth before she's concluded her business."

"I wouldn't dream of it," Bernard assured him.

"Bernie, you can't pull the wool over my eyes, and I won't have you trying it with the Missus here either."

"Ah, me own brother doesn't trust me?"

Pat looked heavenward, then left the table.

Bernard leaned in confidentially. "Bridie McDonnell, that's my cross to bear."

"She lives in the village?" I leaned against the banquette and picked up my sandwich.

"She does, with her old mammy Nora—and doesn't Bridie put my business in a desperate state," Bernard said dolefully. "I can hardly make my calls when she parks herself here by the hour, jabbering into the fancy new mobile her niece Deirdre gave her for Christmas."

"Some people get terribly attached to their phones, I think." I took a small bite of sandwich, then pushed my plate closer to Bernard. "Have some chips at least?"

"Don't mind if I do," said Bernard, taking one. "But the nerve of the woman! I nearly lost a job when a client got crossways with meself because I didn't get right back to him."

Talk about a perfect opening... "Speaking of jobs," I said, "I'm going to fix up the Power pl—I mean, my new place. If you're available, I'd like to hire you for the project."

He helped himself to two more chips. "Now there's something that's long overdue. What have you in mind?"

As the image of the farm rose in my mind, my longing for Jamie and Stephen receded a little. "I've lots of ideas—might you come up for a look?"

"Fiona suggested a sunroom, you say?" said Bernard, rubbing his whiskery chin.

Bernard and I stood in the downstairs bedroom, finishing up his tour of the farmhouse. "Do you think it'll work?" I asked anxiously.

"Hmmm." He gave the room another once-over, then leisurely pulled a stub of pencil from behind his ear. Scrawling another note on his small pad of paper, he *hmmmed* again. Before I could say anything he turned to me, beaming. "Genius, that's what it is."

Relieved, I said, "We thought it would brighten up the whole house."

Ever since Fiona had mentioned redoing the space Will and Jen Power had stayed in, I was determined to go for it. Knocking down a few walls would purge the Powers' bad vibes—*and* help me forget what a complete eejit I'd been. Even if the cost banjaxed my finances.

"There's that," said Bernard, "but there *is* one problem you've not considered."

My stomach sank. "Will knocking down the walls spoil the…um, integrity of the structure?"

"Not at all," Bernard said solemnly. "It's that you'll need sun for it."

I chuckled, already picturing an airy new downstairs. Still, after taking Bernard through the house and getting his recommendations for the remodel, I hadn't much else to laugh about.

I'd been focusing on the farmhouse's appearance, when I should have been thinking about infrastructure. It wasn't a big surprise that the boiler required a tune-up, or that the fuel lines for the Aga I'd set my heart on needed redoing, or that the mains were ancient and would have to be rewired. As Bernard's list of measurements, computations and supplies grew, however, I thought uneasily of the papers I'd put in my handbag yesterday, before leaving Dublin.

Don't think about it. I waited as Bernard made more scribbles in the notebook, then led him back to the kitchen. "I've one more thing in mind."

Since the rain had eased to a sprinkle, I went through the mudroom to open the back door. Admiring the grey clouds billowing above, I gestured toward the garden. "When we're done with the inside of the house, I've tons of plans for the rest of the farm."

"Outdoors?"

The wind blew of strand of my hair into my face. "I'd like to shore up the coop—make it look a bit picturesque, maybe? And the barn—when it's windy the roof rattles something terrible, so obviously it needs a new—"

"Missus," Bernard broke in.

I turned and closed the door. "It's a proper wreck, isn't it?"

"What you've in mind, indoors and out, is a *big* job." He pocketed the pencil and notebook. "I'll need to hire a lad or two to give me a hand."

"Hire all you need," I said, though I winced inwardly, thinking of the bank statement in my bag. "Whatever it takes."

"And I've a couple of wee jobs in my queue, before I can work on yours."

"Any chance you'll postpone them?" Wheedling wasn't my style, but I was desperate to have Bernard get going so we could finish the redo over the winter. Without shame—or at least very little, I added, "I'm hoping to have the house done before Stephen's back at Eastertime."

"Easter, eh?" He paused, shuffling his feet. "Missus Kerry, I'll want to be straight with you. I can't work up a proper bid until I run the numbers, but the remodeling you're set on will set you back a *packet*. Is…em…Himself on board for all of this?"

Stephen and I hadn't exactly intended for me to clean out my nest egg. Yet, glancing at my apple trees through the kitchen window, I felt a surge of love for my place. "Stephen's keen to have everything look absolutely fantastic," I said confidently.

Bernard still looked doubtful.

"Well, great anyway," I added. A suspicion crept up on me. "You're not the sort who thinks a wife needs permission from her husband to spend money?" I was still feeling a bit confrontational after facing down my boss.

Bernard looked appalled. "Nothing of the sort. But builders...well, we can get caught up in all sorts of family rows, and before you know it, you're getting shouty phone calls and solicitors' letters, and..." He spread out his hands helplessly.

Okay. I couldn't keep my plans secret any longer. "There's something I haven't mentioned." I gulped. "Stephen and I are doing this remodel so we can sell the property."

"Ah..." he said slowly.

"I've only told Fiona." I gave him a pleading look. "Could you...?"

"Keep it under my hat?" Bernard wore a conspiratorial glance.

I nodded unhappily.

"I'll be as silent as the grave." He made a zip-your-lip gesture. "A builder who wants to stay in business," he said loftily, "doesn't tell tales about his clients." He twinkled again. "Other folk are fair game, yes."

I had to smile. "Good to know." I was growing fonder of Bernard by the minute.

"But before you commit all this money, you'll want to know that..." He looked pained. "When you sell the place it's unlikely you'll get back all the euro you put into it."

"I understand." Overcome by gratitude, I said, "If you can start right away I'll pay you—" I nearly said *double*. "A big bonus."

"Well..."

"In advance!" I said recklessly.

His bushy brows nearly hit his hairline. I thought, *I've gone completely round the bend.* Still, I couldn't turn back now. "I'll make you hot lunch every day too! Do we have a deal?"

For a moment, Bernard wore the same yearning look he'd had gazing at my ham sandwich. "No bonus necessary," he said, "but I might be persuaded to accept a wee down payment. For the helper chaps I've in mind."

After we finalized details so Bernard could prepare his bid, I walked him to his little van. Opening the door, Bernard paused to gaze down the hill toward the Whelan farm. "Fiona and Desmond'll be right good neighbors. That is, while you're here."

"I hope so," I said. *Or I did, before Fiona blew me off today.* Still, if the Whelans were having problems… "A shame about Fiona's dad," I said experimentally. "I understand he's not well." I wasn't a great one for gossip, but your social currency in Ballydara seemed to rest upon expressing either your concern or your opinion—even better, both—about everyone you came across.

"Desmond? Poor man," said Bernard, shaking his head. "The old fella's been in very poor form since he let go of his herd."

Earlier today, I'd noticed that the pen next to the barn was empty of the cows I'd seen there in November. The day Stephen and I had taken a walk, and he told me the secret he'd been keeping all the years we'd been married. That conflict seemed like part of someone else's life, now that our marriage was better than ever. Except for the living apart bit.

"Arthritis, you know," Bernard went on. "Sure, it's put more than one farmer out to pasture."

"How awful." Mam's cancer scare last summer had been terrifying. But at least she'd gotten better. Fiona's dad, at his age, wouldn't.

"That it is," said Bernard, "with man's hands being his livelihood."

"Judith says…" Unsure how much a newcomer should comment, I hesitated. "Mr. Whelan has other worries too? Besides his health?"

"A sad business," said Bernard, shaking his head. Instead of elaborating, he climbed into his van and rolled down the window. "We'll review my bid after you pick out your worktops and windows."

As I raised a hand in farewell, he shoved on the gearstick. With a crash of what sounded like extraordinarily rusty gears, he headed out of the drive. I watched him go, warmed by his friendly presence. And wondering: what had I done to make Fiona go off me?

The next day, I drove home from Galway City in a thick mist. I was tired from the long day of shopping and decision-making—wearier still from being away from the green hills and quiet around Ballydara. I had one more chore, though, that I couldn't ignore.

Since I was meant to have phone service today, I tossed my handbag on the couch and headed to the kitchen to pick up the phone. And there it was, a dial tone. So I'd no excuses. Replacing the handset, I retrieved my bag and ferreted inside for the slip of paper I'd saved weeks ago. But no luck.

Don't think you can get out of making this call! I pulled out my bank statement and shoved it aside. Turning my handbag upside down, I ruthlessly shook the contents onto the dusty couch. After sifting through the day's receipts, I finally spied what I was looking for.

With the number in front of me, I dialed the rotary phone, which seemed to take forever. So how to approach Jamie's grandparents? *Mr. and Mrs. McElligott, it seems there's been a misunderstanding...*

"Hallo." A man's voice tinged with a London accent.

"Mr. McElligott?" Odd. I didn't remember Mike Senior sounding English. "It's Kerry McCormack, ringing about Jamie—"

"*Kerry?*" He sounded horrified.

Not Mike Senior. Shaking, I dropped the phone. It hit the floor with a crack. I hadn't spoken to Mike McElligott Junior, Jamie's biological father, in over fourteen years.

Where's your dignity, for God's sake? Although I hadn't a shred of it when that tosser split up with me, I was a different person now. I retrieved the handset. "Mike," I said in a businesslike tone, "I'd like to speak to your mother..." I was talking into dead air.

"Mum!" Mike was calling. "Mum, come'ere and pick up, quick!"

I heard a jumble of voices, then a woman who had to be Shirley. "...For shame, Mikey, and her the mother of your child..."

"Not now, Mum," I heard Mike say frantically. The *coward.* "Just get the phone!"

"Kerry!" Shirley McElligott said down the line. She was obviously hoping I hadn't overheard her son. "So lovely to hear from you!"

"Mrs. McElligott," I said formally. I went into my spiel about why Jamie hadn't contacted her—he was with his father in Canada now, and wouldn't be back for some months.

"All that way..." A long silence. "Mike Senior and I had planned on seeing Jamie over Christmas." She sniffed. "We never heard a word, though."

Kind but firm, I told myself. "I realize that, but Jamie was getting organized for relocating."

"If you'd give me his address, we'll send him another letter."

"I'm afraid that's not on," I said. "We'd prefer that you not write to Jamie at this time."

"I suppose this is Mikey's fault," Shirley said tearfully. "His not speaking to you just now, no wonder you've decided Jamie should keep his distance."

"That's not it—my husband, myself, *and* Jamie feel it's best to wait until they return."

"Really, I apologize for Mikey," Shirley kept on. "He's in Dublin this week on business, and wouldn't he have to come round for a home-cooked tea today of all days, and then actually pick up the phone! Please say you'll reconsider..."

I didn't expect Shirley to be so persistent. "I'm afraid not. Please, no letters or phone calls until the spring."

There was a knock on my front door. "Sorry—I've a visitor. In the meantime, we're quite serious. Please don't contact our son right now."

"Oh, but—"

"Jamie will be writing you," I told her. "And you'll hear from me in a couple of months." I rang off before she could plead any more. Feeling guilty and a bit callous, I hurried to the door.

Fiona

5

*S*till having a bit of a freaker after hearing his voice earlier, Fiona waited on the McCormack's front stoop, the mist dampening her jacket. She definitely needed a friendly face—although how welcoming would Kerry be?

As the door opened, Fiona's heart sank. Kerry looked distracted, her dark brows drawn together. "Um...come out of the rain."

"It's only a drizzle." Feeling awkward, she stepped inside. Papers littered the couch, the contents of a handbag strewn around. "I see you're in the middle of...I don't mean to be a pest, calling round uninvited two days in a row."

"Come on, you're anything but," said Kerry and closed the door. She stepped to the couch and snatched the biggest sheaf of papers. Stuffing them into her handbag, she swept the other items off to one side. "I'll put the kettle on, shall I? Go ahead, put your coat on the knob."

"I can't stay," Fiona said. "I'm here to apologize for being curt yesterday, when you invited me to lunch."

Kerry's hand stilled. "Really, it's nothing."

"It was *something*," Fiona insisted. "I was upset, and..." Suddenly, she couldn't take it anymore, trying to hold everything in. "The thing is, I didn't want to lay my troubles on you. But it seems to be common knowledge around the village."

"Your dad?" Kerry straightened, her gaze direct. "Bernard mentioned his arthritis."

Fiona nodded, slinging off her jacket after all. "Unfortunately, it's the tip of the iceberg." She rubbed her temple. "I don't mean to sound helpless, but I don't know what to do for him."

Settling onto the couch, Kerry patted the cushion, a pouf of dust rising from it. "Have you siblings to help out?"

Fiona dropped onto the seat. "Two brothers and two sisters, who are no help whatsoever. All they'll say is, 'Have Dad take more pain tablets.' They pretend not to see that giving up farming is breaking his heart."

"I'm so sorry." Kerry clasped her hands together.

"Yesterday, in the shop, you probably heard me on the line with him." Fiona couldn't help it, she had to tell *someone*. "He'd rung to tell me he dropped his glasses, then he stepped on them and broken them to bits, and he sounded so...so *lost*, like a child. Not like my dad at all."

"Oh, Fiona."

The sympathy in Kerry's voice nearly brought tears to her eyes. "I told Dad, let's ring up the eye doctor, get you a new pair, but he said there's no point—he doesn't read much anymore, and the telly is blurry, even with glasses. I'm afraid pain and boredom are making him feel like he has nothing to live for."

Kerry was staring into the middle distance. "I've an idea." She met Fiona's eyes. "Would Desmond mind if I looked in on him every so often, while you're at the shop?"

"You'd do that?"

"With the house in chaos over the next weeks," said Kerry, "it might be nice to nip out for some peace and quiet."

Fiona's heart lifted. "Dad would be *thrilled*. I have to say, when you and Stephen called round after the snowstorm, he glowed as if the Prime Minister himself was visiting." Still, she had to ask. "Are you entirely sure about this? Dad might start depending on you too much."

"I see what you're saying," Kerry said slowly, "but it'll give me a purpose, while I'm here."

"Oh. Right." For a moment, Fiona had forgotten Kerry would be leaving Ballydara in a few months.

Kerry must have seen something in her face. "My visiting him is only a temporary solution, I get that. It wouldn't be a bad thing, though, to help him get used to retirement? I could bring him lunch now and then too."

"Kerry!" Fiona reached out and hugged her, then drew away, laughing shakily. "Oh, sorry! How could I? You hardly know me!"

"Don't be an eejit." Kerry grinned at her. "With Stephen gone, yours might be the only hug I'll have for a while."

Fiona got off the couch, keeping her smile pasted on. She could hardly remember what it felt like to be in a man's arms. "Dad'll be needing his supper, so I'd better go away home." She released a big sigh without meaning to.

Kerry rose too, her gaze keen. "This situation with your dad—it must be wearing you out."

"I'm all right," Fiona said automatically, but with the concern in Kerry's face, she decided, *Oh, what the hell*. "It's not only Dad—yesterday, before he rang about his glasses, I got a bit of a shock."

"Bad news?"

That depends. "I heard from an old fr—well, not precisely a *friend*, but someone I hadn't seen for ages," Fiona said lamely. The memory of his voice tied her stomach in knots. "When you mentioned lunch, I was still feeling..." *torn in pieces*, "you know, off." She reluctantly headed for the door.

"No need to explain," Kerry said, though Fiona sensed her curiosity. "We'll do it another time."

"Count on it," said Fiona. As Kerry opened the door, she left hastily, before she weakened even more and confided the lot. *I think I can be strong as long as you're around. But how will I be able to put him off once you've left?*

Kerry

6

Crack!

I winced as a massive crash shook the farmhouse. Bernard's builder chappies were knocking out walls for the sunroom.

The Killeen lads, the rangy, black-haired twins Bernard had hired from Galway City, weren't much for chat. Each as solid as the oak tree in my front garden, Davie and Gil worked steadily, like machines. If there was such a thing as a builders' ballet, that's what they did, like a muscular *pas de deux*: one twin ripping out a chunk of wall while the other heaved it out of the way, or one lifting a piece of lumber and the other, without skipping a beat, fitting it into place. Despite their speed, though, the house was a complete disaster.

Sheets of plastic hung all over the downstairs. Bits of plaster littered the floor, and the furniture Bernard and I had shifted squatted helter-skelter like abandoned cars on the side of the motorway. Electric drills buzzed along with the snap of nail guns. I thought I heard a sound outside, but couldn't be sure, the way my ears constantly rang from all the racket.

Shivering, I glanced at Bernard, taking measurements and occasionally whacking at wall remnants with a massive spanner that would be a perfect fit for the Norse god Thor. Shrugging on my anorak, I shouted, "Bernard! I'm off to Desmond's."

He shoved the spanner into his heavy-duty tool belt. "You'll want to stay another minute—a little Yardis just pulled into the drive."

Mam's car? Joy surging through me, I scurried through the detritus on the floor and flung open the front door. "Mam!" I met her on the footpath. "What a lovely surprise!"

"Kerry!" She hugged me tightly. "It feels like months, not weeks since you left Dublin."

I squeezed her back, peering over her shoulder. "Where's Dad?"

"I came alone—a spur of the moment trip." She stepped back, giving me a long look. "I thought I'd see what's what, before your dad has a look at what you've gotten yourself into."

"Mam," I said reproachfully, "I'm perfectly capable of supervising a simple house makeover." Taking her arm, I led her inside.

She took in the mess, a dubious look on her face. "*Simple makeover*?" She headed straight for the kitchen, frowning at the gaping holes where the fixtures had been removed, then strode to my sunroom-in-the-making. Sweeping aside a plastic sheet, her eyes widened. "God give me strength…"

One twin didn't pause, but the other said, "It's not as bad as it looks, Missus." He tore out a massive hunk of exterior wall.

Mam turned back to me. "It's a good job Stephen isn't here to see this—you're lucky to have a roof over your head!"

"Stephen once worked in the building trades, Mam," I reminded her. "Knocking out a wall so you can put in a window wouldn't faze him."

"All the stress he's got now, I think this wreck would put him over the—"

"What stress?"

"Ladies!" Bernard waddled over, his smile broad. Despite his stained gray coveralls, he gave Mam a courtly bow. "Bernard Hurley, General Contractor. You must be Kerry's mammy."

"Anne Ahern." Her eyes narrowed on Bernard. "So. You're in charge of this disaster." She kicked at a piece of rubble. "Exactly what have you talked my girl into?"

"Mam! Bernard didn't talk me into anything, he's carrying out *my* plans! And—"

"Missus." Showing no sign of offense, Bernard turned his full twinkle on Mam. "Yes, doesn't the house look desperate? We're just finishing the tear-down, before we put everything back together. It'll be right as rain before long, I assure you."

Mam appeared to weaken. "But it looks like there's been an earthquake, and it's as cold as a barn…"

"So it is." He waved expansively. "We'll have space heaters set up by the end of the day. And if you come back in another fortnight, you'll hardly recognize the place."

"Well." Mam's frown disappeared. Apparently she was no more immune to that twinkle than anyone else. "I'd say you lot are ready for your tea break, and I've a sweet for us in the car."

Mam got the kettle boiling then fetched her apple cake, while Bernard and I pulled the kitchen table and chairs into the middle of the front room. As I poured the tea and Mam sliced her cake, Bernard filled her in on the various phases of the remodel. I called in the lads, then drank my tea, looking at them covertly.

Davie and Gil ate as steadily as they worked. Given the size of them, they reminded me of Will Power (and with any thought of Will there was no getting around our silly flirtationship), but there was no flirty chat or jokes out of the pair of them. Within moments, they set down their empty mugs, mumbled "Thank-you, Missus," and practically dived back into the sunroom.

"They're certainly hard workers," Mam remarked.

"Yes, yes," said Bernard. "Got them on recommendation from Eileen Larkin."

"I've met her daughter Grainne," I volunteered, to give Mam the impression I'd scads of friends here. No need to mention I'd had a total of thirty seconds' conversation with Grainne, a brash, black-haired girl whose Amazonian build struck me with awe.

Bernard leaned back in his chair. With a sidelong wink at me, he began extolling the virtues of Ballydara and environs. As much as I wanted Mam to think being separated from my husband and son so I could get the farm sold was the greatest decision I'd ever made, I broke in. "Mam, I've promised to look in on a neighbor. You'll come with me?"

Since we were between rain showers, Mam was game to leg it to the Whelan's. I carried the remaining chunk of cake, along with a sandwich I'd wrapped up. "Desmond's the father of my friend Fiona." We strode down the hill, the pastures on either side of us the dull green of late winter. "He's had a few setbacks lately, so I'm helping out with his lunch."

"You're not all on your own here, then." Mam actually sounded chagrined.

"Or else you'd be dragging me back to Dublin with you?" I teased.

"Something like that," she muttered. Mam followed me past the Whelan's cow pen, the skinny little cow I'd seen before chewing her cud in one corner, and we treaded the weedy footpath to the Whelan's kelly-green door. The cottage exterior was overdue for a whitewash, and a few of the roof tiles were crumbling, but someone had kept the door painted.

Desmond had it open before I could knock. "If it isn't yourself, Kerry, as busy as you must be." He always acted surprised when I showed up, as if I hadn't called round at least eight times in the last fortnight. "And you with a visitor too. Come in!"

"Desmond, this is Anne Ahern, my mother," I told him.

"I see the resemblance, yes." He bustled around, plumping up the faded couch cushions, putting the kettle on and setting out teacups. Handing him the cake, I didn't have the heart to tell him we'd just had tea at my house. As we sat in the front room, Desmond poured the tea, and looked at us expectantly.

I could see Mam casting about for something to say. "There's a fine old tractor outside," she remarked. "I understand it saved the day when Kerry's Stephen came up to Ballydara in that terrible storm, at Christmastime."

"Ah, that rusty old relic," he scoffed, but there was pride in his face. "You wouldn't think it, but she's as reliable as the sun rising in the east." He rubbed his knees absently. "I'm not sure what she'll be good for, now that I'm...retired." His expression drooped. "None of the children will be taking over the farm."

To avoid the sadness in his eyes, I glanced at the framed

paintings on the walls. The watercolors were all Irish country landscapes, beautifully rendered—my favorite was of an ordinary pasture. Yet if you looked more closely, you could see tiny creatures perched among the tufts of grass. Fairies?

"Retiring is a big adjustment," said Mam matter-of-factly. "Still, it's lovely you've a daughter to keep you company."

"Fiona looks after the house nicely," I put in.

"Nicely, yes," said Desmond. He sighed heavily.

"Oh, I nearly forgot," said Mam, reaching for her handbag. "I nipped into the shop before I drove up the hill." She pulled out a Brona chocolate bar, opened it, and broke it into three pieces. "I didn't have a chance to meet your Fiona," and she took a bite, "because she was out. But I saw her wonderful adverts."

"She has a talent, right enough." Desmond didn't appear to notice the chocolate Mam had put in front of him. "She's been a trooper for her old dad. Her brothers and sisters are rather…taken up with their own lives."

Narky and selfish of them, if you ask me, I wanted to say, and nibbled on my chocolate.

"I can never get over the way the young people will decide to do their own thing, and there you are, and not a thing to say about it," said Mam.

"The kids do ring up," said Desmond. "They'll say, 'Sorry, Dad, coming out to the farm is just not on now, I've too much on my plate.'" He shook his head. "Too much on my plate," he repeated. "That's what they call it, like it's a bad thing. In my day you'd be right happy to have a full plate. My eldest girl has a new job with lots of traveling, the younger one's busy with her three young ones. Not a moment to spare, they tell me."

It was the longest stretch of words I'd ever heard Desmond utter. "Modern lives and families have gotten so complicated," Mam commented. She was far better at drawing out Desmond than I was.

"That's it, yes," Desmond went on. "My eldest, Gene, had a perfectly decent job in Ireland, but when some opportunity came up in Brussels, off he went without a backward look."

"The kids don't know how good they have it here," said

Mam. "Even with the economy bouncing back, our Liam wanted the big adventure in America. Austin, Texas! Can you believe it? Tom and I went to visit him but I couldn't wait to be home. Even in December, the sun hardly stops shining there till it hurts your eyes."

"Ah, yes," said Desmond. "My youngest, Niall, lives on the West coast, on a little island somewhere. He's gone all that way to work an organic farm."

What Desmond didn't say hung in the air, like a thought bubble. *If he's keen on farming he could've stayed home.*

"He'd made plans to return to Ireland and take over here," Desmond went on, "but just before Christmas, he..." Staring down at his knotted hands, the old man flexed his fingers and winced. "Changed his mind."

That must've been the family trouble Bernard had referred to. Should Mam and I try to get him to talk about it, I wondered, or change the subject? Catching my eye, she said briskly, "Mr. Whelan, it's a lot to ask, but could you spare a moment? I've some boxes to shift at Kerry's."

What boxes? Mam had never been one to play the weak female card, but she'd obviously sussed out that Desmond needed something useful to do.

Walking up the hill to my place, Desmond's pace was halting, yet within a few minutes his stride grew more confident. Mam was saying, "I shouldn't want to interrupt Mr. Hurley at his work—he's on a strict timetable, he says."

"Now that's a one-off." Desmond's mouth twitched. "The man's known for stretching out a job till it begs for mercy."

Mam chuckled appreciatively. When we reached her little car, she opened the boot, which held two mid-sized cardboard boxes. "For you, Kerry," she said, partially opening one of them. I glimpsed a faded aqua, cloth-bound cover. *Little Town on the Prairie* by Laura Ingalls Wilder.

"Oh, Mam!" I pressed a quick kiss on her cheek. "Aunt Rose's books—how thoughtful!"

"With no Internet or telly, and being all by yourself, what's better than a good book?" She pulled on a box without really moving it, then turned a smile on Desmond, and all but fluttered her lashes. "Tom helped me load the car, but unloading…?"

"No bother a'tall." Desmond painstakingly lifted the top box.

Mam opened the front door and I followed them in, keeping a close eye on Desmond for any sign of strain. "Under there?" I pointed to the table in the front room. "It's the one clear spot I have."

After depositing the box, Desmond seemed breathless. "I'll get that second box, shall I?"

"Before you head home," I said, hoping to distract him, "might you take a quick look around? Knowing the neighborhood as well as you do, maybe you'll have some thoughts on anything we missed."

He looked pleased. "Be glad to."

"Outside, first?" suggested Mam. She and I exchanged a conspiratorial smile.

As I led the two into my garden, Desmond pointed out what was presumably a vegetable bed. "Mr. Power had asparagus there."

"Never say I've asparagus!" I was *thrilled*. "I'll get that spot cleared straightaway."

"It's worth a try, though the crowns may have given up the ghost," Desmond said kindly. "But there's a whole row of rhubarb, along the side of the house there."

"Count on some rhubarb cake this spring," I told him, before I remembered. *You won't be here.*

Mam was looking at me. "Won't you be go—"

"The apple trees," I said quickly. "They look positively wild."

Going from tree to tree, Desmond examined each one carefully. "They'll want a hard pruning, to be productive for the long term." He showed me the various cuts I could make.

"It looks…complicated," I said.

"I can give you a hand," Desmond offered, an eager look in his eyes.

"Would you?" Before Mam could point out I'd be long gone

by apple harvest time, I quickly said, "How about the indoors now?" After we trooped inside, Mam waited until Desmond was preoccupied with checking over the house, then she retrieved the second box and took it upstairs.

"I believe there's one more thing you'll want to consider," Desmond said as we wound up his inspection. He stared at the front room wall behind the old radio, took a few steps to the right and narrowed his eyes. "Bernard," he said, "I'll have a chisel in here, please."

"Davie, will you get the man what he needs?" said Bernard.

A twin strode in, holding a tool in each of his big hands. So this one was Davie. Strange, that he could look exactly like his brother, and yet, not. His expression seemed more open, maybe. He'd a more attractive nose, for sure.

"Thank you, son. You'll want to check behind the plaster." Desmond pointed at the wall. "I believe we've a mystery here."

I frowned as Davie placed the chisel where Desmond had indicated. "What are you doing?"

Without answering, Davie whacked the head of the chisel with his spanner. A handful of plaster chips scattered onto the floor.

"Wait just one minute, Davie," I protested. "We didn't have banging out the front room on our project plan!"

"No, Missus." He stepped back. "Mr. Whelan, have a look."

"Just as I thought," Desmond said with satisfaction, brushing his fingers against the battered spot. A reddish-brown layer showed though.

Davie called, "Bernard! Come see this."

Bernard strolled in and squinted at the wall. "Genius! Sure, it runs in the family," he told Desmond. "Who'd have guessed what we had back here?"

"What *do* we have?" I asked. *And how much will it cost to repair the hole Davie just made?*

Davie took the chisel again and started shaving more plaster from the wall, exposing a larger patch of dark red.

"Better lay in a supply of turf," Bernard said. "For your hearth."

"Hearth…"

"What do you think these bricks are?" said Bernard, as Davie chiseled off another bigger section of plaster.

It took a moment to sink in. "I've a hearth?" I immediately had visions of curling up with Stephen on the couch, warmed by a cozy fire. "I've a hearth!" I clapped my hands. "That's fantastic!"

"We'll tear out the rest of that plaster next week," said Bernard.

"Can you believe it?" Desmond snorted. "I couldn't quite remember how your front room was laid out, but I knew I'd seen smoke from this house for thirty years! In his dotage, that old eejit Power plastered over his fireplace. Likely paid a fortune for fuel oil too."

"You *are* a genius," I said admiringly.

Bernard seemed to be giving my neighbor a close look. "Say, Desmond, if it's all right with Kerry, we'd like it fine if you'd nip in here every so often, give us a hand."

"Of *course* it is," I said, giving Bernard a grateful smile.

"We could sure use your help," Davie put in.

Desmond looked as pleased as I'd ever seen him. "Sure, sure, I could do that."

As Bernard and Davie returned to the sunroom, I went to the bottom of the stairs. "Mam, come down, we've a surprise!"

She came straight downstairs and exclaimed over the new find. Desmond rocked back on his heels, wearing a look of genteel triumph. "Kerry, late this spring we'll take you out to the bog and show you how to cut turf, now that Mr. Power's plot is yours. Next winter you'll be warm as toast."

"Oh, Kerry won't need to do that," said Mam, smiling at him.

"Mam—"

"Since she won't be here," Mam went on blithely. "The new owners, though, will likely be grateful for the turf."

"New owners?" Desmond's bushy brows drew together.

"I'll be selling the place," I confessed, my heart sinking to see the hurt in his face.

"Selling," he repeated.

"As soon as Bernard finishes the remodel," I said miserably. "I told Fiona. I thought maybe she would've mentioned it to you."

"Ah, no," Desmond said slowly. "She doesn't talk much to her old dad."

Mam sent me an apologetic look. I felt rotten to have inadvertently deceived Desmond—even so, I couldn't blame her for telling the truth.

Still, the gaiety of our visit had disappeared. "I'd better get myself back to Dublin," Mam said. She popped into the sunroom to say her goodbyes to Bernard, then, "Kerry, you'll walk me out?"

Desmond came down the footpath with us, his gait less steady than before. When we reached Mam's car, he said to her, "I don't suppose we'll see you again, Mrs. Ahern, with Kerry selling."

"Likely not," said Mam, regret in her voice. "Might I give you a lift home, Mr. Whelan?"

"Thank you, no," Desmond said. "With a wave and a distracted "cheers," he headed slowly down the hill. I wondered if he was already distancing himself from me.

As soon as he was out of earshot, Mam said, "I'm so sorry, love—I thought all your local friends knew your plans."

I shook my head, feeling bereft. "They'll soon be ex-friends, once they know I'm doing a runner."

"Darling," Mam said, "why not let go of all of this?" She gestured toward the house. "Come back with me."

"Now?" I asked, incredulous. "You were meant to stop pushing me about it."

"I can't help it—your man Bernard can finish up. There's no reason to stay here all by yourself."

"Mam, you've seen that I'm *not* by myself," I said. "I've good neighbors."

"But they're not family. Come on, we'll shift the books back in the car," Mam said more urgently. "You can pack your kit and we'll—"

"No." I squared my chin. "I'm seeing this through."

Mam crossed her arms. "Tell me, what has this to do with Stephen? Your staying here, alone?"

"What do you mean?"

She gave me a skeptical look. "Have the pair of you not reconciled after all? Why else would you live separately?"

I felt a streak of irritation. "I've not deceived you, or Dad either—we've sorted ourselves."

"Have you," said Mam. "When I was upstairs I saw your beautiful new ring on the bathroom countertop—it's right bad luck, for you not to wear it."

"Mam, that's superstitious rubbish." I certainly couldn't share that the ring only reminded me of my miscarriage, and the months of estrangement with Stephen. "I told Stephen I wouldn't be wearing it—I didn't want it to get banged up." I put on a saucy grin. "Besides, we'll want my ring in prime condition in case we need to pawn it."

"If that's a joke it's not funny." Mam looked grim.

My fake smile disappeared. "All right, we're not keen about being apart this winter, but we're coping."

"Is that so? I'd believe you if Stephen didn't seem so pressurized."

"Wait a minute." Mam had mentioned that before. "You're imagining things—he always sounds so relaxed on the line. Jamie likes his new school, and things at the office couldn't be better."

"He's obviously putting on a good face for you," said Mam. "Because every time he rings, I can tell that—"

"Every time he rings? Exactly how often is *that*?"

Fiona

7

$\mathcal{F}$iona turned up Kerry's drive, checking her step to see her friend in a heated exchange with her mother. "Stephen's not allowed to ring me, to give directions to the farm?" the older woman was saying. Ready to dive into the farm's fir grove and hide out until the pair of them were done arguing, she saw Kerry wave at her vigorously. "Fiona—come meet my mam!"

More accustomed to family silences than rows, Fiona approached them cautiously. "Hello, Mrs. Ahern. I just wanted to thank you for looking after my dad, but I wouldn't want to interrupt anything."

"Oh, you're not," Kerry said blithely. "We're only having our ongoing difference of opinion about my staying here."

Mrs. Ahern wasn't discomfited either. "That's enough cheek from you," she said to her daughter, and smiled warmly at Fiona. "Call me Anne. You'll be the artist whose work I was admiring earlier today? Your fruit and veggie drawings are absolutely true to life—the way you captured the feathery carrot tops, and a shine on the apples."

For a moment, Fiona was overcome by an eejit pride—then she remembered why she'd been out of the shop when Anne had come in. Wouldn't Kerry ask where she'd gone off to? But all Kerry said was, "Isn't it great, hand-drawn adverts in our little local shop."

Relieved, Fiona said, "It's been grand, to practice a bit of my former career."

Kerry's eyes widened. "Former…you're a *professional* artist?"

She hadn't meant to let that out. "I was," Fiona said, super-casual. *Please don't ask me why I gave it up.* "Not anymore."

"I thought once an artist, always an artist," said Kerry.

Fiona's eyes suddenly smarted. "Not necessarily. Drawing a few posters doesn't make you one."

"It *is* art," Anne insisted, "when you have a true gift. But I'll leave you girls to it—time to start on home."

As Kerry hugged her mother, Anne's eyes reddened. She touched her daughter's cheek. "Keep well, darling."

"Dad and I will look after her." Fiona held out her hand.

Anne gave her a kiss instead. "That'll be a weight off my mind." She climbed in her little car and backed down the drive.

Kerry watched her go. "You've good timing," she said. "If you hadn't been here, my mother would've really laid it on thick about my staying here."

And what would my own mam think of what I've been getting up to? Fiona asked herself. Before she could reply, Kerry said, "Enough about that. So tell us! Were you one of those kids who was always drawing, and got lots of art prizes at school?"

For a moment, Fiona let herself pretend she was only on a career break. "Oh, I always had a pencil in my hand." The prizes, she didn't mention. It hurt to remember her parents bursting with pride when she'd get an award at the end of every term. Dad would always whisper, *Well done. But don't get too full of yourself.* Mam would say, *Daddy, be quiet. Fiona should be proud!*

"You went on to study art?" When Fiona nodded, Kerry asked eagerly, "What sort?"

"I dabbled in watercolors," Fiona said, offhand. "What I really loved, though, was graphic design and illustration."

Kerry's eyes sparkled. "So the paintings in your house are *yours*!"

Fiona shrugged. "Schoolgirl pieces." She wished she'd put them in storage. But her dad said, *Your mam would want them to stay, if she were here.*

"All I did was a secretarial course," Kerry said enviously. "And ended up spinning my wheels in an office. I always wished I'd gone for something else."

Fiona thought longingly of her days at art school, living and breathing art 24/7. "You can't regret supporting your family, I hope." A sensible person would say that. "Whilst I was quite a dilettante, doing student shows and odd jobs for the art instructors." As a dark cloud passed overhead, she crossed her arms over her brown cardigan for warmth. "In my off hours I rambled round Galway City, sketching. It was…" *Glorious.* "Rather aimless, really."

"Sounds like great craic." Kerry's voice was wistful. "Living the life other people only dream of."

"Most people prefer security," Fiona said dryly. "I'd often trade my art for food and a place to live. 'Course, I had to look the part." She grabbed her loose gray trousers and waggled the fabric, her smile rueful. "Instead of outfits like this, I wore flowy skirts and fringed shawls, hair fixed in kooky plaits and ribbons, bangles up to my elbows, playing the bohemian to the hilt—"

Fiona broke off, seeing someone in the new gap in Kerry's sunroom wall. Davie Killeen. He was watching her.

"I'm trying to picture it," Kerry was saying. "You, the artist wild child."

Her cheeks warming, Fiona tucked a strand of hair behind her ear. *What's that Davie looking at anyway?* "You'd never guess, would you?"

Kerry glanced at the house. "What about blokes?" Had she seen Davie too? "I'll bet you attracted men by the lorry load."

"Lovely of you to think so, but there weren't many." *Davie's probably looking at my awful clothes. Even if he doesn't seem to notice them when he talks to me in the shop.* "I hadn't time to fuss over guys. After I finally left school, I worked freelance gigs, until…" Fiona's voice dwindled. "Until I got into another line of work."

"But what happened to you?" asked Kerry. "The free-spirited non-conformist?"

Fiona smiled wanly. "The economy imploded."

"Oh…right," said Kerry. "Freelancers are the first to go."

"Exactly," Fiona said. Half her clients had gone belly-up, and the other half had cut their business to the bone. She'd been forced to take a job—a proper one. Which was when everything *really* started to go wrong…"Okay, I've burbled on about myself enough," she said. "Dad will be waiting for me."

After their goodbyes, Fiona saw that Davie had disappeared from the window. He felt sorry for her, that was it. As she jogged down the drive, her throat swelled with unshed tears.

There was no other reason a handsome young bloke would chat up a lonely shop clerk, whose big claim to fame was making signs that only a few people would ever see.

Kerry

8

Robin Keane, Estate Agent
Specializing in Country Properties
Call <u>Anytime</u> –
*"I'm **keen** to find a qualified buyer for your home!"*

I stared at the business card Bernard handed to me.

"You'll want to line up an agent, I think," said Bernard, tucking a tape measure into his tool belt. "Robin's local, based in Galway. A friend of my niece's."

"Um…thank you." I resisted the urge to crumple up the card.

"All right if I take off a bit early?" He was already walking toward the new front door. A beam of early spring sunshine glimmered through the beveled glass. "I've a potential new client who wants to meet with me."

"Of course." I tried to ignore my sinking feeling. "You've done a fantastic job here. And in record time." After my replacement couch had been delivered yesterday, the house was all but finished.

"Let's give credit to our lads too." Bernard thumbed toward the sunroom. "Right then, Robin's expecting your call."

As soon as he left, I stuffed the cardstock into my jeans' pocket. I peeked into the sunroom, where Davie and Gil were doing paint touch-ups. "I'm cycling down to the village," I told them, shrugging on my anorak.

Davie paused, mid-paintbrush stroke. "To the shop?"

Gil made a muffled snicker.

"That's right." With the longer afternoons, I often popped

60

into Murphy's at the end of Fiona's shift and walked her home. And today, I wanted a sounding board in the worst way. "Can I pick up anything for you?"

Another snort from Gil. "Besides Fi—" Davie elbowed him.

"Uh, we're grand,' said Davie, a flush crawling up his neck. "We're here only another morning, after all."

"Right—your last day." I'd caught Davie watching Fiona in the window last month—did he fancy her then? Not that it mattered, since he and Gil would soon be gone. Although I'd intended the remodel to be a rush job, having Bernard and the twins around all day had enlivened what would have felt like a *really* empty house. I opened the door. "You'll let yourselves out?"

"Sure thing, Missus," said Gil. The pair of them persisted in calling me "Missus," despite the forty times I'd said, *Please, call me Kerry*. Clearly, they considered me over the hill. At least Stephen's ardent phone calls proved *he* still thought I was a pretty hot article.

Not that Stephen thinking I was a hottie made me feel better at this particular moment. Wheeling my rusty but serviceable bike out of the barn, I passed the vegetable patch and gazed at it forlornly. Only yesterday morning, I'd joyfully weeded nearly half the asparagus bed, before bringing a sandwich down to Desmond. "I know you said it was unlikely any spears would break ground," I nattered on to him. "But you never know, there might be a bit of life down there."

"You're a right optimist," said Desmond, chuckling. "What of your apple trees—are they pushing out buds yet? They'll likely not produce much this year, with the hard pruning we gave them."

"I'd be thrilled to get even a few apples." Sitting across from the old man, I'd pictured springtime on my farm, and for a moment, pretended I'd never have to leave. In a few weeks, fat green spears of asparagus might be pressing through the cold earth. Already, rose-white knobs were showing in bare soil along the side of the house, hinting at the crinkled, bright green rhubarb leaves that would follow. Once I cleared more weeds,

I could sow peas, then the apple trees would be in bloom...

Now, I tore my eyes from the garden and climbed on my bike. The card in my pocket was my wake-up call: I'd never see any seeds sprout, nor pick any apples from my trees. Beyond the fir grove, my pasture was showing hints of growth. I felt a stab of regret. I'd never have any animals grazing there either.

Flying down the hill, the balmy March wind at my back, I passed a field here, a house there, already missing each one. As I arrived in the village, windblown and warm, my gaze lingered on the late afternoon light casting the buildings in a mellow glow. I had only a few more days here.

My throat tight, I dismounted near the shop window, taking in Fiona's latest advert. *End of Season Special—Parsnips.* She had captured their creamy white roots and abundant foliage perfectly. I could hardly face that my lovely bike rides and my walks with her would soon be over too. As I leaned the bike against the shop wall, she emerged from Judith's cheerful pink door looking more pale than usual. "Things were a bit slow so Judith shooed me out early."

Again? Was Judith hurting for custom? I made myself smile. "Your parsnips have inspired me. If you don't mind waiting I'll grab a few."

"Judith's still got the register open," Fiona said. "I'll keep an eye on your bike."

"Right—the village is swarming with thieves coveting this ancient article," I tried on.

"And no Garda station for miles." Fiona's smile seemed as forced as mine.

Inside, I selected half a dozen parsnips. Judith was counting receipts behind the cash desk. "Just these veggies, then? On your account?"

"I've a few euro on me," I said, and handed them over. I didn't want to add to Judith's potential cash-flow problems. "Desmond's very keen on mashed parsnips for lunch."

"The old fella's been much better since you came along, Fiona tells me," Judith remarked. "He's enjoyed spending time with Bernard and the twins."

Fiona had said the same, many times. "And having an hour free a few times a week has been *huge*," she'd said—though she never mentioned how she spent her lunch break.

"Desmond's a lovely gent," I said to Judith. "Besides having lunch with us, he does seem to like fetching tools and helping out."

"Little things can make all the difference," said Judith. "If only you could..." she lowered her voice, "persuade Fiona to take care of herself. She's seemed a bit low lately." So Judith had noticed Fiona being in a funk too. "She's been buying those frozen meals for her lunch." She made a mock shudder. "Terrible stuff. She must think so too—she'll eat about half, and tosses the rest into the bin."

"Spring fever?" I tried to make light of it.

"To each her own," Judith said. "Or *his* own—those strapping Galway lads of yours fill their trolley with junk food after they've finished work up at your place. You wouldn't believe all the bags of crisps and candy and Cokes they buy! It's a wonder they've any teeth left in their heads."

Both twins had gorgeous white teeth, Davie especially. Had Fiona noticed that too? "They're young."

"Well, their shopping sprees are good luck for me," said Judith. "In fact, they'll be here any minute for their nightly shopping." She glanced down at her pile of receipts. "Although now that your remodel is nearly done, we'll be seeing the last of them."

And once I sold the farm and left the village, Judith would have lost not only the twins as customers, but me as well. Once again, I couldn't quite bring myself to tell her my plans, and made my escape before I could feel any guiltier.

Walking toward Fiona, all I could think of was how fast the clock was ticking. Ticking down to reality.

Fiona
9

What What exactly in God's name am I about? Fiona wondered. *I'm way past the age for this sort of sneaking around.* As Kerry emerged from the shop, it was almost too much effort to smile at her friend, slinging her veggies into the bike basket.

Grasping the handlebars to walk alongside her, Kerry said, "Everything okay?"

"What do you mean?" Fiona tensed, thinking of her stolen lunch hours away from the village.

"In the shop," said Kerry. They strolled past Hurley's. "Do you think there's enough custom in Ballydara for Judith to stay in business?"

"I hope so," said Fiona. *Although the way my head's been in the clouds, I don't know how the shop's doing.* "Working for Judith might not be my dream job, but making the signs keeps me…" *from going round the bend,* "keeps my hand in."

Last year, with the economy getting back on track, she'd actually been tapped to illustrate a book. *This is my big chance,* she'd thought, *I'll be a working artist again!* But that project had fallen apart along with everything else… "What did you say?"

Kerry was looking at her expectantly. "Judith's a decent boss, though?"

"She's lovely." Fiona forced an easiness she didn't feel into her voice. "You know how she's sort of a surrogate auntie for the whole village." She and Kerry turned to go up the Ballydara road. "Speaking of bosses, what'll you be doing with yourself, work-wise, when you're back in Dublin?"

"Who knows—I'd rather fling myself on hot coals than go back to my job," Kerry said. "I finally told Stephen a fortnight ago how I all but told the boss to shove it."

"What did he say?"

"Absolutely nothing." Kerry tightened her grip on her handlebars. "I thought the line had gone dead. Finally, I hear this big sigh. I asked him, 'Do you wish I hadn't quite burned my bridges at Smythe's?' And in his patient way, he points out that my job would've been a good incentive to get back to Dublin."

"The charms of city life don't attract you?" Fiona said lightly.

"They never really did." Kerry scuffed her feet on some loose gravel. "The thought of living in Dublin puts me in the horrors, only I don't know how to come clean with him, being so far away."

"It couldn't hurt to try," Fiona told her. *You're a fine one, to talk about truth and honesty.* "Um, hopefully you'll sort it when Stephen comes home. Next week, is it?"

Kerry nodded. "Still, admitting what a wrench it will be to leave Galway will hurt *him*. So I'm between a rock and a hard place."

Fiona looked up the hill to see the mist drifting along the crest. For once, the sight seemed more welcoming than lonesome. "I wish I could help," she said impulsively. "But I haven't a clue about long-term relationships."

"You must know something." Kerry sounded less stressed. "Even if you told me you hadn't had much time for blokes."

Nonplussed, Fiona couldn't answer right away. She'd never fallen head-over-heels anyway, until… "I got more serious about a guy after I dropped out of design," she admitted. "But he di—I mean, it didn't work out."

"*It?*" Kerry asked. "What—a fling? Or a proper relationship?"

Fiona's steps slowed. Kerry had been open about *her* life… "Some years back, I took a night class in Galway City, to learn a bit more about working with printing companies. The instructor was the co-owner of a small local firm—Enda."

"I knew it!" Kerry's hold on the bike slipped and her parsnips nearly fell into the hedgerow. "See," she said, righting her bike, "I'm a hopeless romantic, and I can sense these things—I just *knew* you'd had a passionate love affair."

"Hardly that." Not the way she'd drifted into being with Enda. "I got a job working with his family's business, and I was a good fit. So good in fact, that I...well, we got engaged. I was meant to help him run the company, but before we'd set a wedding date, he started getting these dreadful headaches. Then his hearing went dodgy."

"How awful—it sounds quite serious."

"It was." Fiona waited for a stab of guilt, and there it was. "A brain tumor."

"Oh, Fiona." Kerry stopped, bracing her bike with one hand. "He didn't...make it?"

Fiona could only shake her head. As Kerry put an arm round her, Fiona's defenses crumbled. "I may as well tell you...Enda died a year ago this week."

"I'm so sorry," Kerry said, an ache in her voice. "No wonder you've seemed low."

"If I am, it's more...well, regret than grief." Fiona took a deep breath. "The truth is, I didn't love Enda properly—we didn't have a lot in common." She smiled faintly. "Actually, I was a bit too airy-fairy for the man."

She glanced at her friend. Why not be totally honest about Enda, since Kerry was leaving Ballydara anyway? "There's something else about Enda I've never admitted to anyone." Except *him*. "About the time Enda's headaches started, I...I told him I didn't think it was working out. Of course, when we found out how sick he was, I couldn't leave him."

Tears shone in Kerry's eyes. "What you've been through..."

Fiona had to look away. Had Kerry worked it out? That your fiancé dying, knowing you didn't love him, would hang over your head the rest of your life. But she'd keep to herself the worst part, how she'd risked everything... "I'm all right. Really."

"I hope so." Kerry gave her a comforting pat. As they resumed walking, she said, "Your heart wasn't completely broken, then."

"No." *Not by Enda.* "That sounds horrible, doesn't it?"

"Not at all," said Kerry. "The pair of you clearly weren't destined for each other."

"Destiny or not," said Fiona, "I think I'm the sort who's not meant to be in a relationship."

"Rubbish," Kerry said stoutly. "You haven't met the right guy yet."

"God love you, you *are* an optimist, like Dad says," said Fiona. "Everyone knows that by the time you're in your mid-thirties, all the good ones are taken."

"More rubbish," said Kerry. "Someone else is going to come along who'll be absolutely mad for you, and you'll live happily ever after."

"In Ballydara?" As a small Isuzu pickup rounded the curve, Fiona stepped to the verge, Kerry quickly following. When the vehicle stopped, Fiona looked at it quizzically. *Not again.*

The passenger window came down, and Davie poked his head out. "You've left the shop early, Fiona?" His white teeth flashed in the dim light.

What is *this bloke about?* "Looks that way, doesn't it?" Fiona said carelessly. She couldn't help it, though—she was *flattered.* She started walking again.

"Well, color me gobsmacked," Kerry muttered, falling into step beside her. "Davie never has two words to say all day at my house."

Davie said, "Here then, Fiona, we can give you a lift to your place."

Fiona quickened her stride. Davie's brother Gil crashed the gears into reverse, and backed up slowly to keep up. "You can squeeze in between us," Davie said roguishly.

"I'm grand with walking," said Fiona. "And I'd hardly leave my friend Kerry here at the side of the road."

Gil's shoulders were shaking. "Oh, right!" Davie flicked his eyes at Kerry, surprised. "Sorry, Missus, didn't mean to, uh…"

"That's all right," Kerry said. "You've no room for four, unless Fiona sits in your lap."

"Kerry!" hissed Fiona.

Davie's gaze intensified. "Fiona, I can give you a ride tomorr—"

"Oh, go on, Davie!" Was he actually serious? "You'll want get down to the shop before Judith closes."

"See you...next time." Davie sounded perplexed. He rolled up his window and the pickup proceeded down the hill.

Kerry giggled. "Did you say there was no chance of meeting anyone round here?"

"Come on! He's a child—I've at least ten years on him."

"Nobody cares about that anymore. I think he really fancies you."

"If I don't encourage him—and you don't either—a guy like Davie will move on to the next girl soon enough," Fiona said.

"Though he's good for the ego?" Kerry teased.

Fiona couldn't deny feeling a tiny thrill at the look in Davie's eyes. "Okay, but not much else."

Kerry gave her a playful poke. "You don't know that until you give him a go..." The smile in her voice faded. "Fiona, I understand if you feel bad about your fiancé, but please, don't give up on yourself."

Reality settled like a low cloud over Fiona's head. "I've my dad to take care of, and that's what's in front of me for now—although things could be worse."

"How?" asked Kerry.

Fiona wondered if she was thinking, *Your fiancé's dead, your dad's getting frail, and ridey Davie is leaving town...* "If I wasn't working at the shop, I'd have felt obligated to take on the farm."

"Oh, surely not," said Kerry. "Everyone has choices."

"Do they?" Fiona couldn't help feeling bitter. "With my brother Niall living on his island paradise, if I wasn't out of the house all day I'd have been stuck for sure." Approaching her dad's gate, she thought of the lonely evening ahead, and the gleam in Davie Killeen's eyes... "I'll walk you up to your place, all right?"

Kerry nodded. "I still say your prospects aren't as bleak as you think."

Fiona was silent as the dusk deepened. Finally, she said, "Most women my age have a family, a thriving career. Instead, I see nothing but dead ends. I really try not to resent my brothers and sisters, or God help me, resent Dad, but sometimes—" she broke off, swamped by remorse. "Jaysus, listen to me go on."

"If you don't let off a little steam," and Kerry's grasp on her bike seemed to sag, "all you'll do is get depressed about things you can't help." Righting the wheels with a shove, she pulled a business card from her pocket. "Like this."

Fiona looked at her friend carefully. "You *really* don't want to sell."

"Bernard was kind enough to give me a referral, only all I want to do is bin the card. How can I possibly tell Stephen *that*? And I can't bring myself to even think about where Jamie and I are meant to live in Dublin."

"Now I *know* I shouldn't have bleated on about my life," Fiona said.

"Although I can't wait to be with my family, at the same time I dread having them back in Ireland," Kerry said bleakly. "I've turned into a right gobshitey wife and mother."

At the foot of the drive, Fiona had no reply for that. She caught sight of a careworn, unfamiliar vehicle parked beside Kerry's Toyota. A light went on in the front room. "Wait—someone's in your house!"

Kerry seemed frozen. Ready to push her friend's bike down, grab her to flee back to Dad's, Fiona saw the door open. A man's silhouette appeared.

"Surprise!" he said.

Kerry
10

I let go of my bike. As it crashed to the ground, I hardly noticed Fiona's relieved, "Well! Dad definitely won't be calling round tomorrow." Before I could gather my wits, she was gone.

Stephen was already striding across the garden to pull me into his arms, his mouth hungry on mine.

"Oh, Stephen." I broke the kiss to catch my breath, pressing my face into his neck. "I can't believe you're here—wait." I stepped back, searching his eyes. "I saw your parents' car—is Jamie okay? You weren't meant to be here until—"

"He's grand." Stephen kissed me again, laughing against my mouth. "I couldn't wait ten more days to see you."

"Mam!"

I released Stephen and ran to the stoop to embrace my son. "Jamie!" I had to go up on tiptoe to kiss him. "What did you do the last two and a half months? Grow an inch or three?"

"Aw, Mam." He tried to move away.

"No," I said, holding him fast, "even though you're home to stay I'm getting in my hugs." I smoothed the brown curls he was wearing longer.

"Come on, don't fuss."

Resigned, I let him go. As Stephen retrieved my parsnips I saw two people behind Jamie, hovering near the front door.

"Kerry-girl!" said Brian McCormack.

"We wanted to be part of the surprise," his wife Mary said at the same time.

Stephen's parents. "Oh, hi," I said weakly. *I'd so hoped Stephen had only borrowed your car.*

"I tried to talk Mary out of coming," said Brian, wearing an apologetic look, "but she said she couldn't wait until your visit to Wicklow."

"I said no such thing," Mary said gruffly, but her eyes nearly glowed as she gazed at Stephen.

I plastered a smile on my face, reaching out to hug Brian, and kiss the cheek Mary offered.

"You'll want to shut the door," said Mary. "Think of the heating bill."

"I've got it," Stephen said, hugging me to his side. "Mam and Dad picked us up from Dublin Airport and brought us all the way to Galway!"

"Why didn't I see you on the road?" I asked.

"We drove the roundabout way—over to Oughterard first, then east to Ballydara." Stephen slung the veggies he was holding to Jamie. "Mam and Dad got a nice look at Lough Corrib."

"Had a lovely tea there in Oughterard," said Brian. "At the Harmony Hotel."

Mary sniffed.

"The hotel had sort of a Zen vibe, super plain," said Jamie, "but the tea was yummo." Setting the parsnips in the kitchen, he returned to the front room and collapsed onto the plump new couch, crossing his arms behind his head. His face had cleared up. "Scones with butter and jam, and cream cakes you can't get in Canada."

"Ireland's good for a few things, is it?" I teased him.

Mary's mouth turned downward. "The tea was very dear, for such an odd place. I wanted to wait and have supper here but Stephen insisted on giving us a treat."

"Mam, it's all right," said Stephen.

"And the room expense too!"

"I wasn't sure what the state of the house would be for guests, so I booked my parents a room," Stephen said. He moved his hand from my waist to the curve of my hip.

Mary looked more distressed. "I told Stephen we'd sleep on the floor if the bedrooms here weren't ready, but he wouldn't have it."

"We'd want you to be comfortable, Mary," I said. Obviously, Stephen had decided we were done trying to make love with parents down the hall.

"I've a thought," said Brian. "What if the pair of you go off to the hotel, take the room yourselves, and leave Jamie with us?" The tips of his ears were red. "We'll see you back here in the morning."

"That'd be fantastic, Dad," Stephen said immediately. "I'll fetch your cases from the car."

I certainly was all for making a quick getaway before Mary got a proper look at the remodel. "But Jamie—" It felt too soon, to be separated from my son.

He was pulling a shiny new smartphone from his pocket. "Seriously?" He frowned at the screen, then looked back at me. "Mam, didn't you get cell service? I need to text Con."

Righto. My son couldn't *wait* to spend time with me. "It's not available," I told him. "You'll have to get used to less technology, now that you're back home."

"This," and Jamie gestured round the house, "isn't *home*—"

"Let's not go there," Stephen said mildly. "Your mother's got a phone." He nodded toward the kitchen.

Jamie looked incredulous. "You mean *ring* Con? No one does that anymore! And only total *dweebs* use landlines."

"Now, Jamie," Mary began.

"*Dweebs*," I repeated. "Who *are* you?" I didn't know whether to laugh or cry. "An alien?"

"No." Stephen kissed my temple. "A teenager."

Stephen drove with one hand, and held mine with the other. We headed uphill, toward the setting sun peeping through violet, gilt-edged clouds. "I wasn't very hospitable," I said. "Letting your mam and dad make up the beds, and not laying out any breakfast things."

"I'm not a proper son either," Stephen said ruefully, driving well over the limit. "I was pretty annoyed when they rang me about visiting us in Galway. Until I got the idea about booking them a room."

I thought of the thousands of euro I'd put into the farmhouse. "I can only imagine the cost of this hotel."

"Please don't," said Stephen. "This is our break from parents and teenagers and expenses and everything else. I even texted Bernard so he wouldn't come until lunchtime tomorrow."

I gave Stephen a curious look. "You know Bernard's number?"

"I got it...online," Stephen said vaguely. He let go of my hand at the Oughterard turning. "Starting now, let's not talk about the outside world. Just us."

Happy not to discuss money, I stroked the hair at his nape. "I see Jamie's not the only one with a new look."

Stephen's hands tightened on the steering wheel. "No one in the office has time for haircuts," he said quickly.

Arriving at the hotel, I hardly noticed the two-story brick building set in a grove of beech trees. Once in the lobby, I had only the most cursory impression of stark white walls, futon-like chairs and bamboo flooring before Stephen led me up a wide, curved staircase. I tugged on his hand. "Don't you want some dinner? The dining room's still open—"

"Not hungry," said Stephen. "For food, that is."

Smiling, I hurried next to him down the hall. "I'm not full of tea and scones like some I know."

"We'll do room service," Stephen said grandly, carding the lock. "After."

Closing the door behind us, he enfolded me in his arms.

We slept late. Or to be more accurate, we stayed in bed all morning.

When I finally, reluctantly, rolled out of Stephen's arms, I stretched languorously. A night of making love really had made the outside world fade away. On the way back to the farm, Stephen held my hand again, this time driving even slower than the two farm tractors we followed on the lakeside road. "I could get used to that," I said a few miles from home.

"You mean the hotel?"

I gave him a sidelong grin. "The massive shower with the two showerheads, and the tropical rainforest spray…"

"That was pretty nice," said Stephen. "I'm afraid we used an awful lot of water." His eyes crinkled with a reminiscent smile. After a minute, his expression turned serious. "But there's something we didn't use—how are you feeling about that?"

"You mean…" *Birth control.* After our miscarriage in August, I was scared to even consider we might have started a baby. Not that I'd any clue how fertile I was, since I'd stopped paying attention to my cycle since Stephen had left in January.

I put on an insouciant smile. "Let's not worry about that now." Leaning toward him, I quickly kissed his jaw. "So, we'll go back to the hotel tonight? I'd like another go at that posh shower."

"Kerry." Stephen's voice held a different urgency. "This visit—it's going to go fast as a blink so I've got to get this straight out. Come back with us."

I jerked away from him. "Stephen—"

"The Vancouver flat is great, but I could get us something bigger, really special, if you'd only—"

"Stephen, you know I've the farm to take care of." Suddenly feeling cornered, I resented him for breaking the spell of our reunion. "I'm just now lining up an estate agent," *well, almost,* "and before anyone comes round I've got to tidy up the garden and outbuildings."

"You can let go of all that, can't you?" Stephen pressed. "We can hire a property manager for the sale, Bernard can find someone for the garden—you can have the whole lot off your hands."

But I don't want it off my hands. As we came down the hill, I caught a glimpse of the farm, *my* farm, and in the distance, the gray slate rooftops of Ballydara. Although my heart ached at the thought of Stephen going back to Canada, it hurt nearly as much

to think of leaving here. As for living in a huge, foreign city…
"We'll discuss it later," I said.

Stephen turned into the drive, parking behind his parents' car.
Bernard's van was next to it. "But I'd like to have everything
sorted before Jamie asks you—" He broke off.

I frowned. "Asks me what?"

Without answering, Stephen pulled the key from the ignition.
"Everyone's waiting for us."

I opened the door. The soft, cozy world of Stephen's arms
was gone. And now that he'd forced the issue, like the coward I
was, I would put off talking about selling—and leaving—the
farm as long as I could.

"This sunroom is sure to add value to the place, wouldn't you
say?" Brian said to his wife.

"Looks really super, Bernard," said Stephen in his fakey-
hearty voice. Trying to make up for his mother's narky vibes, no
doubt. "Any buyer would go for this."

Bernard had volunteered to give a tour of the remodel while I
prepared lunch. Actually, I was hiding out in the kitchen,
pretending to make a meal.

I'd seen Mary's grim face a few minutes earlier when
Bernard showed off the Aga, the new worktops and the flagstone
floor. Of course, after the spending the night here, she'd already
seen them, but with Bernard waxing eloquent about every feature
and advantage, she had to be imagining what I'd spent. And
she'd not said a word since they'd walked into the sunroom,
despite Brian's and Stephen's complimentary remarks. I reached
into one of my new units for teacups, two in each hand, still
eavesdropping.

"Kerry's got a real up-and-comer for an estate agent,"
Bernard said. "Our woman'll have the place sold in no time."

I nearly dropped all four cups. The business card was still in
my jeans pocket. With Mary's disapproval permeating the house
like a bad smell, I hadn't a moment to lose. I could handle
Stephen thinking I was procrastinating, but if he caught me in a

lie... With my in-laws still occupied with Bernard's tour, I quickly set down the cups, pulled out the card and reached for the handset before I could talk myself out of it.

Robin Keane's voice mail came up. A reprieve. I left my number, thinking, *I'm not committed—yet.* As I finished, Jamie trooped into the kitchen and dropped a book on the table. "What's for lunch?"

"Soup." Pulling a tub of vegetable soup from the fridge, I dumped it into a pot to heat up. "And bread."

"Is that all?" He flopped into a kitchen chair with his new outsized teenage energy and opened his book.

I tapped his chair leg with my foot on my way to fetch a spoon. "I'm all for reading, but we won't be doing it at mealtime. Especially not with company here."

"Dad and I read when we eat," he said.

"How you do things in Vancouver is between the pair of you," I said, feeling like I had to reassert myself as his parent. "Here, I'm still your mam."

He closed the book, and I saw the title. *A Game of Thrones.* Were his previous reads, like *The Mists of Avalon*, too tame for him now? He really *was* growing up. "What are you expecting for lunch anyway? A ten-course gourmet meal?"

"Aw, come on, Mam." He stretched out his long legs. "Dad and I have been economizing—we hardly get takeaway anymore."

I stopped stirring the soup. "Is that so?"

"Dad even stopped getting haircuts—they're really dear in our neighborhood."

"But he told me—" *That he hadn't time.*

"Anyway, soup's kind of lame," Jamie was saying. "Can't we go down to the pub for a burger?"

I knew what Mary would say. *You're spending hard-earned money going out, when you've a fridge full of perfectly good food?* "We'll have the soup," I said firmly. "And get burgers another time."

I suddenly noticed a public library label on Jamie's book. Stephen's thriftiness didn't jive with his offer to get a bigger flat. "So, Vancouver is expensive?"

"Yeah." Jamie turned a page. "Dad says prices are mad, compared to Ireland."

"He mentioned housing costs?" I asked carefully, taking a loaf of wholemeal soda bread from the cupboard. "Flats and so forth?"

Jamie looked up sharply. "I dunno," he said, vaulting from the chair. "I'll go get everyone."

Before he reached the doorway, Brian entered the kitchen, Stephen, Mary and Bernard right behind him. "Ah, nice and warm in here, with that big cooker of yours."

"We can turn up the heating, Dad," Stephen said.

Brian glanced at his wife. "No need. Kerry, now that Bernard here has fixed you up with a proper hearth, you can burn turf, once you get some."

Poor Brian. Always walking on eggshells around his frugal wife. "If I'd been here last summer, I would have laid in a supply," I told him, and opened my knife drawer. "My neighbor tells me I've a plot on the commonage."

"It's just up the hill," added Bernard.

"You mean, the new owners of the farm will have the plot," Mary put in.

My hand tightened round the knife handle. "That's right."

"Dad knows how to cut turf," Jamie said unexpectedly.

I glanced at Stephen. "You never told me that."

"He learnt it on his granddad's farm," Brian said proudly. "Helped my da out every June."

Stephen shrugged, with sheepish smile. "No one's cutting it this time of year, son."

"Was that a vegetable patch I saw in the garden?" Brian asked.

"You've sharp eyes," I said, grateful for his interest. "Although it's in a desperate state—two years of weeds at least."

"Once it's tidied up," Mary said, "that'll be another selling point, what with more people cultivating their own vegetables these days."

Selling point. Mary was researching real estate? Alarmed, I began, "But my asparagus—"

"Jeez, Mam," Jamie broke in. "No mobile phones, burning turf, growing your food—this place is like one of those survival shows Griffin and I watch on telly at home."

Home? I flicked my eyes at Stephen, but he was fiddling with the controls on the Aga.

Once I'd served lunch, I let the conversation wash over me—mostly Bernard talking my father-in-law's ear off about his next project. *Home*, I thought, picturing Stephen with me on the peat bog. It would be summer, and he'd be digging with the *slean*, the breeze ruffling his hair, while I'd help him stack the turf for drying. I found myself staring at fixedly at him. After, we'd need a shower…how many hours until bedtime?

The phone rang.

I blinked as Stephen jumped up. "I'll get it." I went back to my little daydream, hardly hearing him say, "The timing's great. See you soon."

"See who soon?" Jamie reached for more bread.

"Your mam's estate agent." Stephen didn't look at me. "Robin. She's outside Knockferry, and wants to come round, get a look at the place."

My daydream vanished. "I'm—we're not ready for visitors!" I was still trying to deal with the *possibility* of selling—not the reality.

"Seems like a stroke of luck she's close by and available," Stephen said reasonably.

Before I could answer, Bernard said, "Robin's got a big client list. I'd not recommend some slacker. And country properties are her specialty."

"That *is* lucky." Mary looked almost cheerful. "Maybe you'll get the place sold more quickly than you thought."

I couldn't eat. Not with Stephen and his mother ready to sell the farm out from under me. "Sorry." I rose from the table. "I'll do the washing up before she gets here."

As the rest of them finished lunch, I tidied the kitchen automatically. It looked too good in here, I realized. I suddenly regretted the Aga, the lovely new units. There had to be some way to put off the agent. Show her the old-fashioned bathrooms first? Bring up the lack of an Internet connection or mobile phone signal, and the improbability of getting either in the near future?

When Robin Keane arrived twenty minutes later, I still hadn't come up with anything.

"Thanks for ringing me?" she said in a girlish voice. She must've learned that inflection from American telly. Robin was attractive, with her flat-ironed blond hair and stylish eyelash extensions. She wore high heels and a Burberry coat over her business suit—and couldn't be more than twenty-five. "I can't wait to show your house?"

I immediately felt better. *An expert in country properties, you say? Not in that get-up.* I couldn't imagine such a young woman being any sort of tough negotiator either. Although my confidence wavered a bit when I saw her Range Rover in the drive.

Bernard offered to do another tour of the house. Jamie stayed at the table to read, while Stephen and his parents sat with him for another cup of tea. I trailed Bernard and Robin around the downstairs, mentally preparing a list of the house's defects. *There's a terrible draft in the sunroom. The water pressure upstairs is dodgy.* As the three of us entered the kitchen, I saw Robin's expertly made-up eyes sharpen. *With the big cooker,* I was ready to point out, *it's terribly cramped in here…*

"Mam?" Jamie set down his book. "I need to ask you something."

"In a minute," I said. *I can take Robin to the barn, poke at the rubbish I haven't binned yet and hope a rat jumps out…*

Stephen set his teacup down with a snap, then stood. "Jamie, hang on. Your mam won't be much longer."

"Now for the upstairs," said Bernard. "There's a grand view from two of the bedrooms."

"Actually, I've seen all I need to." Robin was all smiles. "Everything is simply lovely."

"Great!" said Stephen. "What can we do to make this happen?"

I tensed. "But the bath…" *Really, the pressure is crap, hardly a trickle!*

"I'll just nip out to my car," said Robin, "and fill out the paperwork."

"Paperwork?" I hadn't expected her to get down to business quite so fast. She'd lost that girlish uncertainty too.

"Listing agreement, that sort of thing," she said. "Bernard, have you a moment? Let's review your renovations for any change in square footage."

I stared at the back of her as she and Bernard left the house. She could actually sell this house. And fast...

Brian shifted his chair. "Kerry," he said, "I'm thinking Mary and I should head back to Wicklow. I understand you three will be leaving for Dublin tomorrow?"

"You've no time to lose finding a place for yourself and Jamie," Mary said.

As I felt the walls of inevitability closing in, Jamie closed his book with a thump and got to his feet. "Dad, I really need to talk to Mam now."

Kerry
11

Stephen made a choking sound. "Let's wait until we say goodbye to your granny and granddad—"

"You're always telling me that when you've got something on your mind, you should speak up, not put it off."

Oh, Jamie. Forgetting my in-laws' presence, and that I still had Robin and Bernard to deal with, I looked at my son for what seemed like the first time since he'd returned. Right before my eyes, his face, so beloved, was turning into a young man's. Love and a kind of resignation settled around my heart.

When it came to putting things off, I'd become brilliant at it. I had to get real here—if not for my sake, then for my son's. Let Robin do her job. Life back in Dublin was waiting for us. And if I didn't go back to work at Smythe's, I'd need to start hunting for a new situation. Probably another office job, I thought dismally, surrounded by the city noise and rush...

"Dad," said Jamie, insistent, "You've said it's not right to spring things on people at the last minute either."

Stephen seemed to sigh. He nodded almost imperceptibly.

"Mam, I need to sort something—make my intentions clear." Jamie met my eyes, two spots of color blooming on his cheekbones.

"Intentions?" I got a sinking feeling.

"Grandad and Granny ought to hear it too. But Dad said it was up to you."

I could tell Brian and Mary were as puzzled as I was.

"All…right," I said slowly, and glanced at Jamie's book on the table. "I get it—you want to *watch* 'Game of Thrones.'"

He grimaced. "That's not it at all." Then silence.

"Then…what are you trying to tell me?"

His Adam's apple shifted. "I…I want to go back with Dad. Stay with him for the rest of term."

Ice entered my veins. "All term?"

"Till summer. Can I? Please? I'm having such great crack."

I grasped the edge of the worktop for support. "In Vancouver."

"I've a new mate, Griffin—he's taken me skiing, we go to a skateboard park near his house, and his little brother is *hilarious*."

I stared at him. My son, the boy who was swiftly growing into his own person, had no problem being separated from me for another three months. What could I tell him?

If I said no, Jamie would resent me. He'd have to return to the smaller life we'd had in Dublin, just when his horizons were expanding. "Of course…" I forced the words through my stiff lips. "Of course you may."

"But Jamie," Mary said. Her mouth was trembling. "You've been away, aren't you happy to be home?"

"Dad!" Jamie wasn't listening to his granny. He raised his palm high into the air, and after a tiny pause, Stephen lifted his own to high-five him. "She said yes!" The joy in his voice wrung my heart. Then he threw his arms round his dad.

Stephen's eyes met mine. *I'm sorry.*

As Jamie let go of him, I sent Stephen a cutting glance. "So. It's decided."

"Jamie," Mary said suddenly, "might you show me your book? In the front room."

Jamie looked uneasy. "I don't think you'll like it, Granny."

"Show her anyway," said Brian.

Frowning, Jamie left the kitchen with Mary. Unable to wait until Stephen and I were alone, I said to him, "How long have you known about this?" I kept my voice even with an effort.

He waited a beat. "A few weeks."

"Weeks," I repeated. "And you kept it to yourself." Feeling betrayed, I rushed past Stephen to the back door.

"Kerry…" he said behind me. "Please—"

"No, son," Brian said quietly. "Let her be."

I ignored them both. Desperate to escape, I flung the door open and ran into the garden, not caring about the mud on my shoes. I made it as far as the asparagus patch, and sank to my knees.

And let the tears come.

I wept there in the dirt, my head bowed. A moment later, I remembered Robin and Bernard were sitting in her Rover on the other side of the house. I wiped my sleeve against my runny nose, tears still dripping down my face, and began yanking out weeds with my bare hands. The earthy smell of soil rose to my nostrils, black earth accumulating under my fingernails. I'd a pile of buttercup when I realized the situation wasn't entirely hopeless.

Jamie's decision meant I could stay here through the spring.

It wasn't much of a consolation. What if Stephen made his Vancouver assignment permanent? And Jamie decided to finish secondary school in Canada? Maybe attend university there? More tears leaked from my eyes. Within days, my son could essentially be gone from my life.

I stilled my hands as the wet and cold penetrated my jeans. A proper mother would drop everything and go with him. Let go of her dreams. I tried to see myself in Vancouver, back in a sprawling urban setting. What would I do with myself? Pace Stephen's high-rise flat while he and Jamie were gone all day? I'd have to sell this farm long-distance. And any trips back to County Galway to finalize the process would be torture—

Stop. You're catastrophizing. I knew one thing, though—I would resent being in Canada. And maybe take my unhappiness out on both my husband and son… Heartsore at the thought, I tore again at the stubborn greenery until my hands ached.

"Kerry," Brian said behind me. I felt a gentle hand on my shoulder. "Sure, it's not the end of the world, Jamie leaving?"

I shook my head without looking up.

"It'll be good for the boy too, won't it? All those adventures he's having in Canada. It's only three months."

"Yes." I took a convulsive breath. "If Jamie stayed with me, he would miss his dad too much."

"They've a special bond, those two." Brian gave my shoulder a pat. "If you like," he said awkwardly, "Mary and I can stay another night, so you and Stephen can have some time alone. To sort things," he added quickly.

I didn't answer. Staring at my hands, I squeezed the rich black dirt between my fingers and pictured asparagus spears below the surface, waiting to poke through. I glanced over my shoulder, taking in my greening pasture down the slope, hearing the soft *whissht* of the breeze through the fir grove and Desmond's lone cow bellowing in the distance. I felt a strange pressure in my chest, love and resolve pressing in on me until only words could release it. Suddenly, I knew what I would do. "I'm not selling," I murmured.

"What's that?"

I struggled to my feet, looking straight at Brian. "I'm not selling my farm. Robin Keane can hoof it back to Galway."

"Kerry." Brian hesitated. "What'll you do with the place?"

I brushed my dirty hands against my jeans. "I don't know— keep it for a holiday home? Rent it to visitors?" Brian wouldn't know Ballydara had very little tourism. "I don't have to decide anything until Jamie's back in Ireland."

"You're not thinking of farming it?"

I opened my mouth, ready to say *no*. A lie.

"Farming's not like gardening, Kerry-girl." He reached out and brushed my cheek. He'd never done that before. "Once your livelihood depends on Mother Nature...well, she can be contrary. She can even break your heart."

My heart's already been broken. When I lost our baby. And nearly destroyed my marriage. Yet this little plot of land, tucked in the hollow of the Galway hills, was mending it. "Are you saying just because I love my farm doesn't mean it'll love me back?" I smiled shakily. "But nothing's going to change my mind. I'm keeping it, and I'm staying here until the summer."

Brian didn't say anything for a long time. Finally, he patted my shoulder again. "I'll let your woman know things aren't quite a go. Bernard too."

I nodded. He was far too tactful to say, *You're in no state to face them.* I wiped my eyes with my sleeve and brushed the worst of the dirt off my jeans as Brian sent our visitors on their way. Filled with a new purpose, I strode back to the house, toed off my shoes and went straight to Jamie, clasping his arms.

He stiffened, looking wary. "Dad said you're not…happy about my going."

"I'm all right." He was old enough to make what he liked of my swollen eyes. "You'll go to Vancouver for the spring, with my blessing."

"Mam—you're great!" He gave me a quick kiss and shrugged out of my grasp.

I finally looked at Stephen. "Your dad says he and your mam can stay another night. So as soon as I pack a few things, we'll go back to the hotel."

He took in my tear-stained face. "And the estate agent?"

"She's leaving. Bernard too." As Brian came inside I added defiantly, "Without finishing the paperwork."

Stephen looked somber. "I'll book a room."

On my way upstairs, I heard Jamie say, "Could you take me to the village, Gramps? Dad says there's a hot spot at the pub where I can text Griffin, and my best mate in Dublin."

Clearly, Jamie had sorted his way for smooth sailing right back to Canada. I changed into clean trousers and tossed a fresh shirt and pair of knickers into a tote, my middle churning at the prospect of the almost-certain row with Stephen. Rushing downstairs, I hugged Brian and kissed Mary's cheek. "Thanks for looking after Jamie," I whispered. Surprisingly, she patted my arm—she probably felt sorry for me.

I faced Jamie. Since one maternal embrace was probably his limit for the day, I ruffled his hair. "Be good."

Moments later, Stephen and I climbed into the Toyota and he was backing down the drive. Trying to ignore my roiling stomach, I said, "I've something to tell you."

As Stephen pulled into the hotel car park, neither of us spoke. We'd already said it all.

Earlier, as we'd headed up the Ballydara road, I gripped the armrest for something to hang on to. "I'm keeping the farm and staying until summer."

Stephen's jaw tightened. "I told you, I'll get us a bigger flat in Vancouver, maybe somewhere near a park—"

"I don't want a flat of any sort, I want a farmhouse. And a farm. It's what I've always wanted." I saw Stephen clench the steering wheel. "I realize my decision puts us in a financial bind, and I'm sorry for that, but—"

"Forget the money," Stephen said tersely. "It's the least of our worries. Why can't you give Vancouver a go? It's a great city, with top-class museums, theatres, gardens—"

"So does Dublin."

"Kerry, think of us, all together." Hurt and exasperation edged his voice. "Jamie's keen on outdoor stuff these days—the pair of you can go cycling on the sea wall. There's hiking trails too, lots of wild places all over the city."

It could never be as beautiful as right here. On the road past Lough Corrib, I gazed at the small, fir-covered islands dotting the lake and the mist rising from the water. "Jamie will be busy with school and his friends and you know it. And trying to pressure me into going is only creating bad feelings between us."

"I won't say another word about it," he'd said, his voice clipped. As we entered the hotel drive, passing tall rhododendrons not yet in flower, the tension between us had been like a third person in the car.

Stephen turned off the engine, finally breaking the silence.

"Kerry, we're both exhausted, not thinking straight. Let's sleep on this and take another look at our options in the morning."

His business-speak infuriated me. "You're the one who got us into this fix, taking the job in Vancouver."

"Which I regret bitterly," said Stephen. "Does that make you feel better?"

"No, it doesn't! And there's the hypocrisy," I retorted. "You telling Jamie to make his intentions clear. Not 'spring things on people at the last minute.' But didn't you do the same when you took this job, and bang!—left Ireland two days later?"

"I learnt my lesson." Stephen was as stubborn as I'd ever seen him. "But can't you see, your place is with *us*."

"My *place*," I said hotly, "is being true to myself! So don't you play the duty card. My mind's made up." I crossed my arms, stiff and unyielding. "And nothing you say is going to change it."

Yet in a moment, I sagged in the seat. After my crying jag in the garden, I felt too wrung out to stay angry. And Stephen and I had only a few days left together. *I'm sorry* was on the tip of my tongue when Stephen said, "You know what's really ironic?"

I shook my head, meeting his gaze. His long-lashed gray eyes were red-rimmed.

"When you said you'd something to tell me, for a second, I thought you were going to say you were pregnant."

"Oh, Stephen." My eyes filled, and I reached for his hand.

"I thought there was some sort of fancy new test that could give an instant result." He drew his hand away. "Or it was intuition, that you just *knew* we'd started a baby. I'm a right eejit, aren't I?"

Dearest Stephen, you're not. I felt doubly sick at heart for turning him down, when he rarely pressured me about *anything*. Before I could speak he released his seatbelt with a snap. "Let's go inside."

Through check-in, I was convinced Stephen and I had ruined the passion and closeness we'd had last night. But as soon as we were in our room, he unzipped my anorak. "If we're going to live apart, let's make the most of being here."

The feel of his lips on mine broke the guilt and tension inside me, and I drew him close. When we paused for breath, I wondered dimly, *How can we even want to make love, in the middle of an argument?*

"Let's now row anymore, okay?" Stephen said if he'd read my mind. He kissed me again, his hands under my shirt.

I helped him pull it off. "What if we can't get past another…" *Separation.* I couldn't bear to say the word, twining my fingers through his hair.

Sitting on the edge of the bed, he put his arms round me and pressed his face against my breasts. "We might already have a baby started," he whispered. "This is all that matters now."

The next morning, any languor I'd felt after a night of lovemaking disappeared as soon as I opened my eyes.

Seeing the distant look Stephen's face, I knew it would be separate showers this time. We dressed in silence and headed to the car park, Stephen drawing out his mobile. As we climbed into the Toyota, he said, "Wait. I've a text from Jamie. From last night."

"So he and your dad made it to the pub." I sighed. "That means he got in touch with Con too." Jamie's Dublin friend had a way of stirring things up.

"You'll like this." Eyes on the screen, Stephen's face seemed to soften. "Jamie'll want it to be a surprise, though." He pocketed the phone and started the car before I could ask any questions.

He seemed preoccupied, probably thinking of his upcoming Dublin meetings. As soon as they were over, the three of us would visit Brian and Mary in Wicklow. I rubbed my forehead. We wouldn't have any time alone to resolve this rift before he left for Canada.

As he headed down Ballydara road, I suddenly said, "We *will* be all right, won't we?"

Stephen didn't answer. Finally, he took my hand and gave it a squeeze. "Of course. I'll drop you at the farm so I can run down to the pub—I've emails that can't wait."

Even on Sunday. As soon as Stephen let me off in the driveway, my head started to throb. I'd have to pretend everything was all right in front of my in-laws. And sooner than I thought, for there was Mary on the stoop, looking dour.

Checking to see if her son and I were on the skids again?

Or ready to give me a bollacking about keeping the farm?

I trudged toward the house. *Might as well get it over with.*

Fiona

12

*R*eally this had to stop.

Fiona jogged through the raindrops back to the village. So eager to hear his voice, she'd rushed to the Ballydara Country Club on a *Sunday*, forgetting her umbrella. Then stayed on the line too long. Now she'd be late getting lunch for her dad, and soaked to the skin besides.

"So, another mystery phone call?" the club manager had started to tease her every time she came in. Today, though, after she'd been using their public phone for weeks, he gave her a peculiar look. If she wasn't careful, it would be all over Ballydara: *What's that Fiona Whelan about, huddling in the links' phone box several times a week?* Dad would be sure to hear about it, adding to his worries...

So she'd finally given in to Colm's entreaties. "Can you get away from Dublin on Tuesday?" she asked him. "East of the village, you'll find the golf course—I'll watch for you at the top of the driveway."

He drew a sharp breath. "I'll make it work—anything to see you. We'll make a day of it."

"No. I'm only asking you to come so we can say goodbye. In person." Fiona's voice quavered. With Kerry busy with family, she hadn't had enough willpower to resist seeing him one last time.

"That's not possible and you know it," he said calmly.

After second-guessing herself about everything since she'd met Enda, she'd been drawn to his brother Colm's assurance. Not to mention his looks, which near struck her speechless every time she saw him. That was no excuse though, for acting like a teenager, ready to throw her self-respect under the bus.

"I mean it," Fiona insisted. "We've got to end this for good, before anyone else gets hurt."

"You mean, besides ourselves."

"There are so many reasons we can't be together." She was shaking with her longing to see him—and to make their final meeting swift and soon over, like a surgeon's cut. "And you know them all."

"Because I'll never have a steady job?" There was a hint of humor in his voice.

Fiona gripped the phone harder. "Don't try to jolly me along."

"You'll not give us another chance because of what my parents will say?"

Her eyes welled up. "Isn't that why you split with me last year?" *Because I hadn't the strength to do it myself.*

"I told you it wasn't meant to be permanent, that I only wanted to give my parents time to grieve properly before I told them I was in love with y—"

"Enda was your *brother*." Tears dripped down her cheeks onto her jumper. "And don't you *dare* say he'd want us to be happy because we'll never know."

Colm only said, "See you Tuesday." Unable to answer, Fiona had rung off and dashed out of the lobby.

Now, here on the road, she felt her hair getting wetter. Her dad would think she was losing it. And maybe she was—

"Fiona." A small pickup pulled up next to her, the engine rumbling. It was Davie Killeen. With no Gil.

Oh, God—I'm so not up for this... "Hallo," she managed.

"You'll want a ride back home?"

"But...you're not going that way."

"I'll turn around." As she hesitated, he opened the door and jumped out, rounded the bonnet and opened the passenger door. "Come on then."

"Where's your brother?" Fiona shivered.

"Gil and I may be twins but we're not joined at the hip."

"What are you doing in Ballydara? On Sunday?"

"I'm not allowed to have business here?"

"You haven't answered my questions." Fiona was determined to stand her ground.

"If you must know, Gil's taking the day off," Davie said impatiently. "And I just met with Bernard about a small project in Knockferry. So, get in, will you? Or do we both stand here in the rain like a pair of eejits?"

Chilled water dripping down her collar, Fiona gave in and climbed in the vehicle. It smelled of oiled metal, sawdust, and well-worn coveralls. Not unpleasant.

Davie banged onto the seat next to her. He drove a few meters, backed into the entrance to a field, and turned the pickup toward the village. "I won't ask what you're doing out in the rain at the golf course."

"I've taken up the links," she said defiantly.

"I've heard of golfing video games," said Davie, glancing at her. His eyes looked nearly black in the dim vehicle. "Haven't heard of any people can play on the phone, though."

Fiona crossed her arms and stared out the passenger window. "If you knew what I was doing there, why'd you ask?"

"I wanted to see what you'd say, that's all." She could feel him still watching her. "And what will you say to this? How about you let me take you to the city on the weekend?"

She'd been dreading this. Davie was a decent guy, for all his youth. "You mean...go out."

"You make it sound like serving time in gaol." His laugh sounded forced. "We can get dinner, listen to a session or something. Gil's playing at a pub on Quays Street."

"I can't," she said. Might as well make it clear. "I'm really not...available."

"Because you're looking after your dad? I wouldn't think he was the sort who'd want you to put your life on hold."

"I wasn't talking about my dad."

"You mean, there's another bloke." A pause. "If you were *really* unavailable you'd have a ring on your finger."

Jaysus, you're hopelessly traditional, Fiona wanted to say. Still, there was a sweetness about him...

"I can't believe your boyfriend would go for that kit you've got on, though—all gray and brown, like a country mouse."

Okay, you're not so sweet! Fiona couldn't summon the energy to be truly insulted. "What's wrong with my outfit?" Looking down at her damp, baggy trousers, she brushed at a streak of dust on the knee. "It's meant to be practical. For working at the shop."

"You're not working today, are you?" said Davie. "Looks like jumble sale leftovers."

Now *that* was an insult. "If you're trying to offend me, it's working." The village was another hundred meters ahead. "Stop right here."

Braking immediately, Davie didn't argue. "I'm not trying to put you off." Fiona glanced at him, seeing a vulnerable look on his face. "I'm trying to wake you up."

"What are you talking about?"

"You seem like you're sleepwalking most of the time," he said, staring through the windscreen. "But I know you weren't always that way."

She felt a start. Had Davie sensed something in her she thought had disappeared? When she didn't open the door, he put the pickup back into gear.

He drove through the village and up the hill without speaking, then stopped in front of her dad's driveway. "Better bring your umbrella next time." He reached one brawny arm across her and released the door latch.

Fiona drew in a quick breath. She couldn't help it—having his arm a scant inch from her breasts was...admit it...*erotic.* But she was meant to feel that only for Colm! "How do you know so much about me? That I used to be...different?"

He met her eyes. "Last month, up at Kerry McCormack's, your dad showed me a snap of you when you were at art college."

"You're having me on." Since when did her dad show people photos of his kids?

"You looked…I'll tell you another time."

"Tell me now." She was suddenly reluctant to leave him.

"You looked like a rainbow."

Kerry

13

"Hi," I said to Mary, keeping my voice neutral. "Stephen had to nip into the village. Work emails."

"While Jamie and his granddad are having a bite to eat," said Mary, shrugging on her gray raincoat, "I'll have a look round your garden." She stepped past me.

Oh, *great*. Mary's way of saying *I'll have a word with you.* "I'll grab a cup of tea first, and join you?"

Mary tightened her belt. "We'll not be long."

So much for the détente Mary and I had had before Christmas, when she'd opened up to me for the first time. Bowing to the inevitable, I zipped my jacket up to my chin. Following her into the front garden, I saw she was wearing new snow-white trainers. Not her usual sensible leather brogues.

"I'm afraid your shoes will get terribly dirty," I said before Mary could start lecturing.

"Never mind that," said Mary. "I can always get a new pair."

I could swear the world rocked on its axis. Then I pointed to the outbuildings across my overgrown lawn. "The chicken coop. And the barn."

"The next storm might peel that dodgy roof right off," observed Mary.

"I know, it needs replacing." I waited for her to say, *And that'll cost a packet.*

Instead, she pointed to the nearby square of dry stalks, surrounded by mid-sized stones. "Your perennial bed?"

"It's not much to look at now…" I felt I should apologize.

"In June, it'll be lovely, I'm sure," said Mary. "Now, did you say you've asparagus?"

I gave her a sidelong look. *Okay, I'll play along.* I led her past the rickety swing hanging from the big oak tree to my half-weeded vegetable plot, seeing the indentations in the earth where I'd wept yesterday. "Here."

"Looks like you'll have plenty of room for root crops too," Mary commented. "That is, if you're here to harvest them."

I tensed. *You mean, if I'm still being selfish and desert my husband and son through the summer?*

"Though I must say," she went on mildly, "Irish people worked hard to get away from digging in the dirt, to afford city comforts."

Okay, here it is. "I suppose they have." I shivered as the wind cut through my jacket.

Mary seemed to plant her trainers determinedly in the wet grass. "Farming's a harder life than I wanted. I made sure Brian didn't stay to work his da's place—that we both got secure jobs in the town. Stephen was hardly in secondary school before I was at him to go to university."

Stephen hadn't put it quite like that. "He never wanted to farm anyway," I said, too chilled to drag this out. "So I suppose you're going to try to change my mind about selling."

Mary only shrugged, which infuriated me.

"Well, you won't! I'm keeping this place even if I haven't a clue what I've gotten myself into. And if I *do* decide to go into farming, it just so happens that my great-aunt worked her small farm all by herself well into her seventies and there's no reason I can't do it too. Or better!"

Mary lifted her brows. "Are you done?"

Her expression, curious rather than forbidding, took the wind from my sails. "I guess so."

"This country life you want," she said slowly. "Stephen's choices. I've been having a think about them."

Now *that* was new. Mary had always been so sure—even bloody-minded—about her opinions. "You have?"

"I steered my son to the city," she said. "Pressured him to go for a high-end career, make a big salary."

"Looks like your dreams came true." I couldn't keep the resentment from my voice.

"Did they?" Mary asked. "If Stephen had taken over his granddad's farm, he would never have left Ireland. Or left Wicklow, come to that."

I'd done it again. Thought the worst of Mary and been wrong. "Perhaps he would've wanted that big career even if you hadn't encouraged him," I ventured. "I think it's his nature to strive."

"Stephen's nature," said Mary in a reflective tone, walking toward the apple trees that surrounded most of the house and garden. "It may tend more toward being a husband. And a father."

I nearly stumbled on a tuft of grass. "What are you saying?"

Mary gave me a straightforward look. I noticed for the first time—maybe because my eyesight wasn't clouded by my all-too-frequent negative feelings about her—that she'd lovely long eyelashes. Like Stephen's. "Maybe my son poured himself into his job because…" she swallowed.

Because he'd never had a child of his own? Or because he had only one child, when he'd so much love in him he should have had more?

Suddenly, I couldn't bear for her to finish. "Please—don't." I reached out blindly, and touched her arm. "There's a chance…" Should I really share this? The vulnerable look on her face made me keep going. "Jamie mightn't be an only child for long."

Her eyes went wide. "You're expecting a baby?"

"No. Well, I don't know." I quickly pulled my hand away. "I could be. It doesn't change anything, though."

"I'd say a baby would turn your plans upside down." There was a light in Mary's face I'd never seen before. "Sure, you and Stephen would drop this nonsense about living separately."

"I meant that my getting pregnant," I said carefully, "now or in the next few months, won't make Stephen's Vancouver commitment go away. Or this farm."

"Babies have a way of taking charge," said Mary. "Farm or no farm."

Was she actually *teasing* me? "All the same, I'm not turning back," I said firmly.

She only nodded. Strolling among the fruit trees, Mary paused to examine one or two. "Yesterday, Jamie and I noticed how your orchard trees make the place seem a bit like an island. An island of apples."

That was rather scarily poetic, I thought as we stepped over the pruned limbs and twigs I hadn't gotten around to cleaning up. "Having a proper orchard will come in handy," I said prosaically. "Pies and cakes—I can't wait."

"Cake, is it? When I was a girl, and my da lost another job, we were happy to glean the apples from the wild trees down the lane—if we got to them before anyone else did."

A lump grew in my throat. I'd forgotten, that as a child Mary hadn't always had enough to eat.

"If you decided to farm the place, these trees could bring in some money." She stared into the middle distance for a moment, then turned back to me with her usual wintry expression. "Or even supplement your groceries, if Stephen's job went dodgy."

"Dodgy…what are you talking about?"

"All that belt-tightening at his firm," said Mary.

Was that why Stephen had been economizing? I knew I should ask him about it, but I felt too guilty about the money we had tied up in the farm.

A few hours later, we were on the motorway, heading for Dublin. After my intimate conversation with Mary, I felt off-balance. Even…fragile.

Near Athenry, Jamie suddenly leaned toward the front seat as far as his seatbelt would allow. "Dad, you never showed Mam that text, right?"

"The one from last night, that's meant to be a surprise?" I asked, glad for the diversion. "Don't keep us in suspense."

"Have a look." Stephen pulled his mobile from his pocket and handed it to me.

I scrolled through dozens of Stephen's work texts—I couldn't believe how many there were, just from today—and finally found Jamie's.

> Hey dad i texted Con that we have a farm and he texted back that's totally brilliant and what's it called? i'm like it's not called anything and he's like every proper farm has to be called something. i was thinking of what granny and me talked about in the garden and i found this cool site, what do u think?

He'd included the link. "Nameyourbabywiz?" I read aloud. Jaysus, surely Stephen hadn't told Jamie we wanted to give him a sibling? "Jamie, what you are on about—"

"I Googled 'what's a name for island of apples' and I found out the Celtic name is 'Avalon,'" said Jamie. "You know, from King Arthur."

"Island of apples," I said wonderingly. "Oh, Jamie!"

"Don't forget my favorite book when I was a kid," Stephen put in. "'The Mists of Avalon.'"

At that, my emotions went haywire, tearing spurting from my eyes. "Avalon Farm—that's so…perfect!"

"Bernard was at the pub too," Jamie said, "and when I told him about the island thing he thought it was grand."

"Sweetheart, it is," I wept.

"Aw, Mam…" He subsided into his seat, pulling a pair of earbuds from his rucksack. "You don't have to cry about it."

Stephen stroked my cheek, catching a tear with his finger. I couldn't look at him, not when naming the farm—the farm that had come between us—made the place feel well and truly *mine*. Fishing in my bag for a tissue, I mopped my face. When I'd finally gotten control of myself, I said, "That's it, then. Avalon Farm."

"It's a good job you like it," Stephen said ruefully, "because Bernard's already put it all over the village." He glanced back at Jamie. "You've a right talent for names, son. When the time comes—" He stopped.

Had he imagined us asking Jamie for baby name ideas? A memory flashed in my mind, of the day Stephen had first met

Jamie, soothing my infant son like a sheep farmer caring for his lamb. As if on cue, I suddenly felt a cramp in the middle of my belly.

I knew instantly what was happening. Business as usual. No baby.

Fresh tears welled in my eyes, and I turned toward the window so Stephen wouldn't see. If I was pregnant, maybe he would have found a way to stay in Ireland. It was several minutes before I could trust my voice. "I need to stop at the next loo."

"There's a tourism spot just ahead." Stephen was already slowing down and pulling out his phone. "I've got to check in with the office anyway."

When I emerged from the Ladies, Stephen was pacing in the car park, his face like thunder. "Is everything all right?"

"No, it's not!" He opened the door and pitched his phone into the seat. "They're sending me back to Vancouver Tuesday, can you believe it?"

Two days from now. "What about our getaway this week?"

"We'll have to cancel—the same goes for visiting Wicklow."

"But your mother—"

"I know—she was really counting on seeing more of us." He paced the length of our car again. "And I was counting on us...you know." As he gave me a pained look, I knew what he wanted to say. *Trying for a baby.* "I feel sick about this, I really do."

My even-tempered husband rarely got this agitated. I glanced into the car to see Jamie watching his father. Frowning too, despite the earbuds he was wearing. I said to Stephen, "Do you want to ring you mam, or shall I?"

"Would you?" He rolled his shoulders and took a deep breath. "I'm not up for her disappointment just now. Or Dad's either."

I pulled out my own mobile and stepped away from the car to make the call. After telling Mary we couldn't visit after all, I didn't want to string her along. "You may as well know," I said in a low voice, "my...um...monthly visitor came." The old-fashioned term was entirely ridiculous, but this was Mary I was talking to.

"Oh," Mary said slowly. I heard a world of disappointment in her voice. "We wouldn't have wanted you all alone at the farm all spring anyway, if you'd had a baby on the way."

I rang off, touched. Climbing into the car, I knew it would be hours until Stephen and I were alone, when I'd have to tell him we hadn't conceived. As soon as we were on our way, he touched my hand. "Sorry—I really lost it there."

I brushed a lock of hair off his forehead. "It's okay."

"It's not," he said. "It wasn't only letting you and my parents down. Sometimes work makes me feel like…I don't know. Like I'm being sucked into a vortex. With all the time I've spent in stuffy conference rooms these last months, I could have used a longer break."

Although Stephen had always made it clear he hadn't much use for the country, I dared to say, "More fresh Galway air might've done you some good too."

"I would've liked that." He looked wry. "Have you heard about the new work thing? Instead of doing business over coffee, some people are doing it while they walk. I wouldn't mind swapping out my back-to-back Dublin meetings for a ramble up the Ballydara road."

"Really?" Feeling cheered, I was struck by one of those lightbulb moments: now that selling the farm was no longer hanging over my head (and to be truthful, feeling a bit less threatened at the thought of leaving it), wouldn't it be lovely if Stephen and I had some time together before my spring work began in earnest? "Stephen," I ventured, "with our cancelled getaway, what do you think if I came for a vis—" A blast of hip-hop made me jerk in my seat.

"Sorry," said Jamie, "I'm still getting used to these new earbuds."

As Stephen scolded him mildly about protecting his hearing, I thought, *Maybe it's just as well he didn't hear me.* Once Stephen had concluded his Dublin business, and he and Jamie were back in Vancouver, he'd be over the moon about what I had in mind.

Fiona

14

As Fiona approached the golf course, she saw a sleek, navy blue BMW idling not far from the driveway. She checked her step. This couldn't be Colm's car? She hurried forward to peer into the passenger window. A man with a shock of silver hair turned to meet her gaze.

He reached to open the passenger door, and she slid into the seat, drinking in the sight of him. She could spend hours looking at Colm—his wide-spaced, Nordic-blue eyes, aquiline nose, full mouth, and the thin scar that split one eyebrow into two. The dark stubble on his chin and the stud in one ear made him look even more rakish.

Their last encounter, all she'd seen of him was the back of his head, as he held his mother's arm at Enda's funeral.

His eyes smiled into hers. "Fiona..." His voice was husky as he leaned toward her, his work-roughened thumb stroking her wrist.

A thrill zinged up her arm. "Not here." She drew back against the door.

"Right," he said amiably and put the car into gear. "Where to?"

Instead of answering, Fiona asked, "This isn't your car?" A year ago, he'd driven a shabby little van with *Dwyer Engraving and Glass Art* painted on the side. The faint outlines of the previous owner's logo had still showed through.

"You like it?" Colm patted the dash. "I told you, I've come up in the world."

"But you never needed to look the part before."

"It's good business. We've more important things to talk about, though," Colm said.

Fiona dragged her eyes from his face with difficulty. When they'd been together, she could hardly believe a man with such striking looks would be interested in her. And despite his pursuing her all the way to Ballydara, she still couldn't *quite* believe he wanted her. "Like...what?"

He touched her hand. "On my way into the village, I saw a little woods on the other side of the links—we can be alone there."

Fiona squeezed her eyes tight, enveloped by the memory of lying in his arms, her head on his bare chest, their legs entwined. What harm, to be with him again before she said goodbye?

You are *mad*, a voice said in her head. *Think of what you're risking.* Opening her eyes, she tugged her hand away. "Going somewhere to be alone is *not* on. Because this—" and she gestured in the small space between them, "you and me—it'll never work."

Colm didn't answer. He drove a short distance, past the links, then pulled into a layby next to a field. His silences had often frustrated her, making her wonder, *what are you thinking*? Then he'd instantly disarm her by telling her—and she'd find herself falling even more deeply under his spell.

He shut off the engine and looked at her inquiringly. "You keep saying that. But it hasn't any effect on either of us."

"It would if you'd only...stop," Fiona said desperately.

"Stop what? Stop trying to see you?" He stroked the back of her hand. "Stop touching you? Stop loving you?"

He said *love* so easily. Her family had rarely spoken the word. And Enda certainly hadn't, not more than once or twice. His love had been more...assumed. She couldn't quite find the willpower to pull her hand away.

"I'll ask you again—come back to Dublin with me. There's plenty of room for us in my new place." His voice lowered. "Remember how it was for us before, round the corner from the bakery?"

At his bedsit in Galway City. "I haven't forgotten," she murmured. *You'd bring me a cup of tea in the morning, and once I was dressed I'd go out and fetch us warm buns, and we'd putter round your studio...* Feeling the undertow of his attraction, she struggled to be sensible. "But that's past now."

"We can have it again," said Colm. "You've so many talents going to waste. And this one-horse village hasn't anything to offer you—"

"It's Dad's *home*," Fiona said sharply. As long as she argued with Colm she could keep him at arm's length. "How many times do I have to tell you, I won't leave him?"

"So bring your dad to Dublin," Colm said. "We could find him a spot in one of those elders' housing places, he'd be looked after."

That made Fiona yank her hand away. "Living in the city would kill him." She was blunt. "He could never leave his farm."

"Well...what about hiring a carer to cook for him, spend a couple of days a week."

"I can't afford that."

"I can," said Colm. "You could jump on the bus every so often to see him."

"But he'd be so...alone." Although her dad had seemed in better spirits lately, he'd begun to sit by himself in the barn for hours, with only his cow for company.

"He must have neighbors, people who'd pop in."

She could feel herself weakening. Kerry would look in on her dad, Fiona knew she would.

With all this talk of being together, she felt an insane desire to fling herself at Colm. Once she touched him, though, once they kissed she wouldn't be able to stop, and he'd drive into the woods and it would be the pair of them in the back seat...

To stop it from happening, she said, "You haven't forgotten your mother?" At Enda's funeral procession, Fiona had had no choice but to walk at the back with the Dwyer's neighbors and friends, not at the front. Not with the family.

Colm looked crestfallen. "I'm sure Mum will come round."

"And if she doesn't?"

He brushed her chin with his finger. "Well…what if we were to give her a grandchild?"

Fiona drew a shocked breath. He'd never, *ever* mentioned having a family. "Kids aren't part of my plans," she said at last. "Besides, even if your mother has forgiven *you* doesn't mean she'll let me off the hook." The look on Helen Dwyer when they'd met face to face after the funeral Mass could've cut glass, better than Colm ever had.

When Helen had found out she and Colm had been seeing each other while her eldest lay in his sickbed, Fiona had gone from the family's inner circle to Outer Siberia. Of course she'd been summarily sacked too.

"It was only a thought," said Colm. "Still, I think Mum and Dad see me differently now, have finally accepted that I won't be joining the business—"

"What *are* you proposing, really?" Fiona broke in. "I go to Dublin, we keep it a secret that we're a couple? Let your parents know later?"

"Why not?" Colm's eyes darkened.

"You must *like* sneaking around—but I've no knack for it." Fiona gazed out the window without seeing anything. Had their meeting on the sly, before Enda's death, only heightened the chemistry between them?

"I *know* Mum'll grow fond of you again," Colm insisted.

The green blur in front of her focused into a low hedge, and beyond, the soggy pasture. "Let's be realistic—if she can't, it's not right for me to come between you and your family. Your mam's lost one son, she mustn't lose another. Mothers don't get over losing their children—"

"How do you know?" Colm said curiously.

Fiona couldn't say, *my art was my child, and when I gave it up it broke me in pieces*…She felt a jolt as Colm touched her hand again, lacing his fingers through hers. "Look at me."

Fiona slowly met his eyes.

"You remember that children's book project you were in the running for last year? Before…" he stopped.

Before Enda got sick. A sharp pain streaked in her chest. Enda's illness seemed to define every passage of her adult life. "Of course I do," she said dully. "They would have found another illustrator."

"Actually, the book was put on hold. But my...uh, associate...well, Pauline, you remember her, told me it's back on the table—and I want you to go after it."

Pauline? The name didn't ring a bell. Still, the thought of doing the book made Fiona's heart quicken. "I've probably been away from freelancing too long."

"I told you, I can't stand watching your talents go to waste," Colm said urgently. "Please—come to Dublin, talk to Pauline. The book's yours for the asking."

"My dad..." She couldn't go on, feeling torn in two.

"We've a duty to our families, I know that," he said. "But we've a duty to ourselves. To be happy. To do fulfilling work."

Fiona thought of drawing Judith's adverts. Those hours with her pens were all she had to look forward to, save for seeing Kerry. What would her friend think of Colm? And his proposal to come to Dublin to live on love? And art?

"Just imagine what we could do together," Colm urged. "Everything we've dreamed of."

Hope suddenly flared in her chest. Maybe she *could* resurrect the work she'd given up and mourned ever since. She suddenly remembered what Davie said, about the photo of herself in her artistic heyday. *Could I be that free, that creative again? Is trying to do the proper thing only an excuse in case I can't?* The sensations that had lain dormant in her body seemed to come back to life. "I'll think about it."

"That's my girl," Colm murmured. She could no longer resist him when his face lowered to hers, his stubble rough against her cheeks. The feel of his mouth was such a sweet ache, tears leaked from her eyes. And feeling *something* after the months of nothing was sweeter still...

Kerry
15

*A*pproaching Ballydara, I slowed down to a crawl. At dusk, the village's fairy lights were lit, a bright blur though the mist on the windscreen. I felt welcomed, easing the grief of my last glimpse of Jamie at the airport, how he'd briefly raised his hand in farewell. Such a grown-up gesture, instead of the flappy, childish wave he'd always done before.

My nose tingled. Determined not to cry *again*, I checked the dashboard clock. Half-five. Fiona would still be working. As I parked the car, my headlamps flashed past someone huddling against the side of the shop, near the back. I set the parking brake and clambered out, peering into the dimness beyond the lights. I could see someone in dark clothing, a long plait over one shoulder...

"Fiona!"

She turned a pale face toward me, straightening ever so slightly. She wore no coat.

"You must be freezing, love." I rushed to Fiona, shrugging out of my anorak, and wrapped it around her shoulders. She was trembling. "What on earth are you doing out here?"

Fiona mouth moved in a semblance of a smile. "I'm having a bit of a bad day," she said, and burst into tears.

I helped Fiona, weeping softly, into the warm Toyota. Turning up the heat, I grabbed my bag. "Be right back."

I hurried into the shop to find Judith behind the counter, her forehead creased. "Grand to have you back, so. Em…you haven't by any chance seen Fiona?"

"Actually I have," I said. "She's not feeling well so I'm taking her home."

Judith's face instantly cleared. "Thank the Lord—she didn't come back after her lunch break. While she was out Desmond phoned up to let her know Niall had rung all the way from America, and I said she was too busy restocking to get on the line. I felt right awful for deceiving the poor old fella."

Wondering where Fiona could have possibly been all this time, I said, "I'm sure she'll check in later tonight. I'd better run—"

"Before you go, I've been meaning to ask you something," said Judith. "Desmond's been going on about your lovely brown bread, and I'm hoping if the mood takes you, you'll bake a few extra loaves for us to sell here."

Fiona momentarily slipped off my radar screen. "I'd be very keen!" I'd no clue if I could actually make money selling bread, but to tell Stephen I'd a small income stream… "I'll have loads of time, now that I'm on my own." I remembered why I couldn't linger. "I'll be off—"

"Oh, speaking of yourself being alone," said Judith, "Bernard and I were having a think about you being up at Avalon Farm without Stephen and your boy, and he said, 'Kerry's got a chicken coop, such as it is,' and I said, 'If she can fix it up, she'll want hens, don't you think?' And Bernard snaps his fingers. 'Pat knows of a fella who has extra to sell.'"

"Chickens—that's a great idea!" I longed to ask her more, but not with Fiona crying out in the car. Casting my gaze over Judith's displays, I grabbed an oversized chocolate bar.

"Mind you get pullets, though," said Judith.

Pullets? "I'll do that." I pulled a five euro note from my bag, set it on the counter and headed for the door. "Cheers."

"Kerry, I've two euro for your change," Judith called. "Will you—"

"Keep it." Realizing my rush might make her more concerned, I glanced over my shoulder. "Thanks—if you like, put it on my account."

I ran back to the Toyota and climbed in. Fiona had stopped crying and was staring through the windscreen. I noticed her plait was half undone. "Where to?"

"H-home." Fiona gave me a watery smile. "Where else?"

Driving slowly, I made my way up the hill, biting the inside of my cheek to keep from asking, *What's wrong?* With one hand, I opened the chocolate bar and passed it over to her. "In case you didn't get around to lunch, this should keep you going until your tea."

She took a nibble. "I did forget about lunch." Chewing slowly, she took a bigger bite. "Thank you for rescuing me—I'm terribly sorry you had to see me like this."

"I've always been one to get over-emotional," I told her. "It's no harm to see what it's like on the other side."

Fiona bit off another chunk of chocolate. "If you hadn't come along, I'd probably still be skulking at the back of the shop."

I had no answer for that. Pulling into the Whelan's drive, I switched on the dome light. "Here you are." I watched her carefully out of the corner of my eye. By now she'd eaten most of the chocolate. "Have you something for your dad's tea?"

"Dad—" She winced and glanced toward the barn, where a dim light showed through a small dusty window. "He'll be in there, mourning. Again." Her throat worked.

I sensed more tears coming. "Anything I can do?"

She slipped off my anorak. Hands shaking, she bowed her head, slowly fitting together the zip of her cardigan. Her shirt was untucked, two buttons awry. "Fiona?"

She slowly drew the zip up, then looked at me. "Please... come in and have tea with us? I can't face Dad alone. Not with the state of me."

"I'd love that." I turned off the car. "If you start cooking, I'll nip into the barn to fetch your dad." Fiona still sat, not moving. "Fiona?"

"Before you do..." Fiona suddenly clutched my forearm, a

fresh sheen of tears in her eyes. "You'll never believe what happened while you were away."

I found Desmond standing next to his Jersey cow, illuminated by a single bare bulb. The scent that was barely discernable in my own barn was pungent here—a mix of cow, hay, manure, and dust. "I've brought Fiona home," I said cautiously, in case he was grieving like she'd said. "She's invited me for tea."

He only nodded, laying a gentle hand on the cow's neck. Chewing her cud, she accepted Desmond's touch easily. "This one's the last of them."

The only animal left from the herd he'd been forced to sell. "I've seen your cow before." Eyeing the animal warily, I stepped closer. "In the road, at least once. And in my pasture a couple of times."

He sighed heavily. "Maybe she's been looking for the other girls—the rest of the herd. Dairy cattle can be sociable animals..." He tightened his mouth and his nose turned red.

I tried not to notice. An Irishman showing emotion needed his space. "I can see why you kept her. She's very, um, pretty." Actually, she was. She'd large, gentle eyes, with the delicate bovine features that distinguished Jerseys. "I was very fond of my great-aunt's cows when I was young."

"She's full of mischief, this one." The tension seemed to leave Desmond's face. "Wanders round the neighborhood as she pleases. She's escaped from every fence I ever built too. I think Bets is part goat."

"'Bets'? You're having me on?"

"You don't like her name?" Desmond pretended to bristle. "Don't let on, she's a sensitive wee *cratur*."

"Oh, I like 'Bets' fine," I said quickly. "I didn't think you named your animals, if you're a proper farmer. My aunt didn't."

"When Fiona was young, she came up with names for all our animals, so I got into the habit," said Desmond. "She was always more fanciful than the rest of the kids."

Was that why, back in the car, Fiona had seemed so worked

up over such a little thing? "Davie gave me a ride Sunday," she'd said slowly.

"*Really!*" I gave her a wicked look. "That was fast—"

"Not *that* kind." Fiona's voice cracked. "You know I meant in his lorry."

I instantly regretted the joke. "Sorry. But I *knew* he fancied you."

"He wants to take me out," Fiona said. "Only I…can't."

"Is it because…" I hesitated. "Because of your fiancé? Enda?"

She stared into the middle distance. "I don't know," she finally said and clambered out of the car. "I'd better start some chops or something."

I'd headed for the barn, thinking, *If Enda's not the reason, why has Davie's attention got you so twitterpated?*

Now, I focused back on Desmond, stroking Bets with his knobby fingers. "Anyway, with only one cow," he said, "I'm no proper farmer anymore."

"You weren't interested in mechanizing your milking?" That sounded knowledgeable, I thought, preening a bit.

A corner of Desmond's mouth lifted. "I'd rather strip off and jump into Lough Corrib in the middle of winter. Besides, installing machines and all that lot would've hardly been worth the expense, for a dozen or so animals."

"Oh. Right." I reached out tentatively, and gave Bets' neck a pat. She blinked her long-lashed brown eyes, and kept chewing. "Would you teach me how to milk her?" I asked impulsively. I peeked toward her hindquarters to look for the swollen udder I'd seen on other cows, but all Bets had was four small teats up close to her belly.

Desmond chuckled. "She'll have to be bred first."

"Oh, right." I laughed, an embarrassed flush rising in my face. "But will you teach me?"

Desmond nodded. "I've put off breeding her—she was sickly as a calf, and she's still on the small side." He gave me a long look. "You like cows, then? Now that you're keeping your farm and you've a pasture…"

Could I buy Bets? I nearly blurted. Desmond seemed too fond of the animal to ever sell her. But to have my own cow! I'd be a *real* farmer then, have all the milk and cream and butter I wanted, and when I sold the extra I'd have more money to buy more cows, then of course I'd need to hire a farmhand, but the cows would pay their way—

Wait a minute—you are so ahead of yourself! And what would Stephen say about a cow? You're meant to stay at Avalon Farm only through the spring! Hearing footsteps outside, I pushed my farm fantasies away. "I'll look forward to learning, when the time is right."

Fiona opened the barn door. Although her face was still tearstained and mopey, she seemed more like herself. "Kerry, Judith rang up just now."

"For me?"

"She's been in touch with Pat Hurley—things are a go with the fella he knows with the chickens. You can pick them up Saturday."

"That was fast—I only spoke to her a little while ago." I was still trying to get my head around the idea of chickens. "So...I've four days to get things ready."

Fiona looked wry. "Ballydara folk have a way of arranging your life for you."

Desmond frowned. "I shouldn't have thought pullets would be ready in early spring."

There was that word again. *Pullets.* I wanted to ask Desmond what they were, but I'd already made an eejit of myself about milking cows. "I'll need to do some repairs on the coop first, buy a feeder and all that."

"You're not keen?" asked Fiona. "You'll need to decide soon, Judith said, and get the birds quick before they're sold to someone else."

"Well, I..." Chickens *would* be one step closer to my having real farm. "Okay, I'm in—Saturday it is." *They'll be easy enough to give away when I leave.*

Desmond stared at Bets for a long moment, then glanced at his daughter. "Saturday? Maybe you'd like to go along."

Fiona shook her head. "Chickens aren't really my thing." She turned to go. "The spuds and chops are almost ready."

"You liked hens well enough when you helped your mammy look after ours," Desmond told her reproachfully.

"I guess I did," said Fiona.

"You could use an outing, I think," said Desmond. "Kerry, I suppose you're fetching your chickens in that grand car of yours? You might consider borrowing a neighbor's farm lorry."

"My car will be fine," I assured him. "I don't mind a bit of dirt."

"A bit of dirt, she says," Desmond said to Fiona, with a very Bernard Hurley-like twinkle. "Kerry, you'll want some boxes to put your birds in. Else you won't recognize your car when you get home."

Fiona

16

"*I* can still hardly believe you're keeping your farm." Fiona was walking Kerry to her car after the meal. "Really, it's absolutely fantastic!" *It's kept me from falling apart.*

"I'm floating on air about staying longer myself," said Kerry, the gravel crunching beneath their feet. "And I'm to have chickens too! If Stephen and Jamie weren't so far away, I'd be in great form." Fiona sensed her friend's searching look. "Feeling any better?"

"I'm…getting there," Fiona said. The effort of holding in today's visit from Colm was a physical ache.

Kerry seemed to hesitate. "If you don't want to talk about Davie, I understand, but he seems like an awfully decent bloke."

"He is." Fiona thought of the look in Davie's eyes when he'd said, *You looked like a rainbow.* "Terribly decent." *And I'm so not, letting Kerry think it's Davie who's knocking me for a loop.*

"You could always meet him at Hurley's sometime," said Kerry. "Your dad did say you could use an outing."

"It wouldn't be right to see him," Fiona said slowly. "I mean, I'm not attracted."

Now that was an out and out *lie*. Davie did make her feel… *something*. Fiona's heart twisted. *What sort of woman does that make me?* Being committed to one man—and being drawn to another?

After not for the first time. What of being engaged to Enda, only to fall headlong for his brother? This afternoon, kissing

114

Colm, feeling his hands on her, she'd felt more real than she had for a long time, like she *mattered*...Until suddenly, she started to cry, desire and grief and longing swirling in her like a storm. She'd broken the kiss as Colm held her, his murmured comfort and promises making her weep harder...and want him more.

Now, Fiona heard the concern in her friend's voice. Kerry hadn't pressed for an explanation of her acting so unraveled, and had tactfully diverted her dad's attention all through their supper. As they reached Kerry's car, though, Fiona couldn't bear her shame and regret one second longer. "I've been wanting to tell you something, but I never had the nerve—I'm afraid of what you'll think of me."

Kerry touched her arm. "It can't be that bad—and God knows, I'm no angel." A shadow crossed her face. "Something to do with Enda?"

Fiona waited for the guilty ache she always got hearing Enda's name, but all she felt was an urgency to tell Kerry the truth. "Not Enda—it's about his brother. Colm."

Kerry went still. All the same, Fiona couldn't stop herself, and suddenly the words were tumbling from her. The secret— then not-so-secret—glances she and Colm had exchanged at his mother's Sunday lunches. The rare, stolen moments in his tiny flat. During Enda's swift deterioration, sitting beside his sickbed with Colm and the rest of his family, pretending she didn't know his younger brother very well.

And Colm's mother Helen finding out how badly Fiona had treated her eldest son. The same day Colm had split up with her.

"When Enda died, Helen came *this* close to disowning Colm," she finished shakily. Fiona couldn't bring herself to tell Kerry how she'd hardly spared a thought for her dead fiancé at his funeral, longing for the right to comfort his brother...

Kerry said gently. "I know this'll sound like something your priest or your granny would tell you. But if we can't forgive ourselves for what's already done, we could never go on."

"But falling for Enda's *brother* while the man was dying! And not having the decency or willpower to stop myself." Feeling shattered, she had to rest a hand on Kerry's car bonnet for support. "If that's not bad enough, coming between Colm and his mam—"

"Still. It's in the past now."

Fiona swallowed hard. She could *never* tell Kerry the rest— that she was seeing Colm again, even if her meltdown had ended their passionate embrace. And that she was actually considering his proposal that she throw over Dad and start over in Dublin. "I'm a right awful hostess, aren't I?" She tried to laugh but the tears in her throat nearly made her choke. "Invite you for tea, then force you to listen to True Confessions."

"I've been happy to stay, if it's helped." Kerry gave Fiona a quick kiss on the cheek.

Fiona didn't move for a moment, feeling a tiny bit absolved. Opening Kerry's car door, she said, "Away with you, now." Kerry might not want a friendship with such a needy article, who couldn't make up her bloody mind about anything.

Kerry climbed inside. "I see why you're in no rush to see someone else, but Davie could be...a friend."

Davie and his strong arms and intense dark eyes... "He deserves someone who really fancies him." *Not me, when I can still feel Colm's touch from this afternoon.* She swallowed hard. "I'll see you Saturday, for the chicken fetching."

Fiona returned to kitchen to find her dad scraping the plates. "I'll do that." She grabbed her mother's old apron. Not that her brown cardigan needed protection.

It hadn't been as horrible as she'd thought, telling Kerry about Colm. Fiona had watched her friend's face for some sign of distaste or judgment, but all she'd seen was sympathy. "Dad, you've already been on your feet a long while, in the barn."

"I don't mind washing up," said Desmond, slowly picking up another plate. "Have yourself a cup of tea." His gnarled hands seemed clumsier than usual.

Guilt struck her anew, that she'd even consider leaving him. "In a minute." Fiona turned on the taps to fill the sink, and squirted some Fairy Liquid into it. "I meant to ask you sooner—

what do you think of a city girl like Kerry running a farm?" She dipped a plate into the soapy water and began to scrub.

"Sure, she's ready to jump in with both feet," said Desmond. "I was thinking I should warn her about getting in too deep, but when we talked about having animals, her face was so bright I hadn't the nerve to put the lights out."

She handed Desmond a plate. "That's quite lyrical, Dad."

"When we first heard about her keeping the place," and he rinsed the plate, setting it carefully on the worn worktop, "I thought it would do as a hobby. But she has a spark in her, when she talks of farming."

"You could be a real help to her, Dad." Fiona's fog of misery lifted a little more. "More than you've been, fetching tools for Bernard and Gil and..." she cleared her throat. "Davie."

Desmond didn't reply. Was his hearing getting dodgy, along with his eyes?

"If you want to watch telly," she prompted, "I'll bring our cups in."

"Before you do..." Her dad stepped away from the sink to sit at the table. "I didn't tell you—your brother rang today."

Fiona followed him, perching on the edge of her chair. Dad bringing up Niall was never good. "To say hallo?" she asked, her voice caustic. "Or to apologize for not staying in Ballydara and taking over the farm like he promised?"

"Now, Fiona..." her dad began.

"Niall pulled a runner on you—on *us*. At Christmastime!"

The lines in her dad's face deepened. "On the phone, he seemed very torn up about going back to America, even after all these months."

"As he should be," Fiona said sharply. Her dad had often been too indulgent of his youngest, and look where it had got him. "He was here barely two days, the nerve of him. Then back to the West coast he goes!"

"What I mean is, he seemed a bit low. As if he'd returned to Washington State for some reason, but whatever it was didn't...come to pass."

Serves him right, Fiona wanted to say.

"He did put me in mind of…the farm here." Desmond brushed at a bit of sugar on the table, his hand trembling.

Fiona took a deep breath. *You're a rotten daughter, taking your own emotional turmoil out on him.* She softened her voice. "Yes?"

"I might've been in too much of a…rush. To get rid of the herd."

Desmond had never talked to her quite so openly. "Without Niall, what else could you do?" No reason to remind him they couldn't afford farm help. "I'm sure you miss the cows," she said gently, "but it's done."

Her dad nodded, looking pensive.

"And I shouldn't have slagged Niall either," said Fiona, trying hard to be more charitable. "He's as much right as the next person to live his life." Suddenly she heard Colm's voice in her ear. *Isn't it time you lived yours?*

"Say, Dad, I've been thinking…" Her throat went dry. "Of having a weekend in Dublin." There, it was out.

"Dublin," her dad repeated.

"I can see how Bronagh's getting on with her new job." Fiona swallowed, then said casually, "I might look in on an old friend too."

Her dad gave her an even look. "Anyone I know?"

"I may have mentioned him before." Keeping her voice casual was an effort. "Colm Dwyer."

"Enda's brother, the artist chappie?"

"That's the one." Fiona watched her dad carefully.

A crevice appeared between his bristly eyebrows. "When will you go?"

Was there a tremor in his voice? "Oh, I haven't decided," Fiona said. *I shouldn't have mentioned visiting Dublin—it's too soon.* "It was only an idea."

Desmond didn't reply. After a pause, he took her hand. He'd never done that before. "You've given up a lot to come to Ballydara, look after your old dad, so."

Mindful of his arthritis, she carefully squeezed his hand. "After I lost my job in Galway, living here at home made sense."

"But you haven't been…happy. Not out here in the country, working at the shop, and with losing your young fella…" His voice trailed away.

For a moment, she thought he was talking about Colm. "It's been a year, since Enda," she said. "Enough time to…move on. I've only needed a bit of a push to sort myself."

"Still, what's to become of you after I'm gone?"

Please don't talk that way, I can't take it tonight. "Dad, you've lots of good years left," she said firmly. "And haven't you already got Kerry looking to you for advice? You'll be keeping your hand in farming after all."

"Maybe." The worried lines in her dad's face seemed to ease.

"Now that I'm doing the adverts for Judith, my job's gotten a bit more creative."

"Ah yes," said her dad. "Judith tells me her customers are full of compliments."

"Never!" *Fake it till you make it*, Fiona told herself.

"Oh yes—Bridie O'Donnell, and Aislin up at the Lodge, and…let me think…that little friend of the Larkin girl." Her dad sounded more cheerful. "'Miles better than what you see at Supervalu or Tesco,' that's what they all say." He released her hand. "Maybe you could do something with yourself again."

Fiona was touched. Not one to pass on praise, Desmond had long fretted about her choice of career. *There's no security in art*, he'd said over and over. *You'll be living hand to mouth.*

It's worth it, she'd answered passionately, every time. "You mean, try for some design work?" she asked. "I'll keep it in mind." She rose to put the kettle on. "Why don't you look through the channels—'Father Ted' is sure to be on one of them."

Fiona put teabags in her mother's old flowered teapot as Desmond shuffled from the room. Yet as soon as he left she sank into her chair again. What *was* to become of her? She didn't see how she could start her life over, when she was needed here…

Bringing out the tea, she sat with her dad through two interminable episodes of the Father's high jinks while he dozed. When she finally escaped to her bedroom, she caught a glimpse of herself in the mirror. Her eyes were still pink from her crying jag. Her dad's sight must really be bad for him not to have noticed.

She shrugged out of her jumper. Opening the wardrobe to hang it up, she looked at it in disgust. *Jumble sale leftovers*, Davie had said. On impulse, she jammed the cardigan to the back, behind two pairs of practical trousers, then marched to her bureau and opened the bottom drawer. Beneath a pile of old shirts was a soft fold of purple-violet. Fiona drew out the mohair jumper. It had shiny purple buttons instead of a zipper, and violet sequins sewn onto the front. She grabbed a clean pair of knickers to lay out for work tomorrow, then defiantly, set the purple sweater on top.

"Need a hand?"

Saturday morning, Fiona stepped into Kerry's mudroom. She found her friend in an old jacket, wrestling with three large boxes crowding the small space.

"That'd be great—here, take one," Kerry said, then dropped the boxes and stared at Fiona. "Wait a *minute*—not in that outfit."

Fiona smoothed her rose-colored jumper, feeling self-conscious. She'd paired it with black trousers that actually fit and bright scarlet ballet flats, with a peacock blue ribbon tied round her plait and tiny green shamrock studs in her ears. She'd even worn a bit of peach-toned lipstick. Fiona had decided everything should clash. *Not* like a rainbow, though. "Dad insisted that I have a proper day off, so I brought out my holiday kit."

"You look simply lovely," Kerry said admiringly. "Just right for a country drive." She stepped into her Wellies. "So...no brown jumper?"

Why *had* she been dressing like a drab little mouse all this time? Mourning Enda? Or punishing herself for not being true to him? "I...um, retired it."

"Fair play to you, then." Kerry stacked the boxes. "Even if

you're my chicken wingwoman, you're only to be window dressing."

"That's what Dad said." He'd looked almost chipper when he'd seen her all dressed up.

"Desmond, that sweet old fella," said Kerry. "If it's a makeover you're after, though, the plait should go."

"Maybe next time." Fiona tucked a loose strand of hair behind one ear, and despite Kerry's protests, picked up a box. "I might even un-retire one of my long hippy-dippy skirts."

"I'll hold you to that," said Kerry, smiling. "Anyway, I can handle getting a few chickens into my car." She lifted the other two boxes and stepped outside.

"Speaking of makeovers," and Fiona closed the door, "you've gone from a city girl to a country one in record time." Suddenly feeling quite upbeat, she lifted her face to the sun, peeking behind billowy white clouds.

"I'm quite full of myself this morning," Kerry said. "Come and see my coop." Fiona followed her to the chicken run. "I fixed the holes in my poultry fencing yesterday. What do you think?"

Fiona peered dubiously at various patches of overlapping chicken wire. The fence would *probably* hold the chickens all right... "I thought Bernard was meant to help you."

"I did ring him," said Kerry, "and after some shameless hints, I came right out and asked him about the coop. But he's already moved on. 'I'm your man for quality interior work,' he told me, 'not jerryrigging farm repairs.' So I rang up your dad for advice. After he talked me through it, I discovered I like taking care of things myself." She glanced at the empty coop. "Desmond said Judith is terribly keen to sell my extra eggs— d'you really think so?"

"Absolutely," said Fiona. "Fresh farm eggs would be a massive hit—" She broke off as a small Isuzu pickup with a familiar logo pulled into Avalon Farm. Her wellbeing vanished. "What's *he* doing here?"

The lanky, dark haired driver climbed out, leaving the engine running. He wore paint-stained jeans and a worn jacket. "Hen taxi," said Davie, striding toward them.

Fiona muttered, "I can't believe it!"

"What?"

"No wonder Dad wanted me to look nice—he put Davie up to coming round!" Hot color rose to her cheeks.

Kerry giggled. "Desmond, that conniving old fella."

"At your service, Missus," Davie said to Kerry, then he looked straight at Fiona. "Yours too." His mouth quirked.

Still holding her gaze, he plucked all three boxes from her and Kerry. Shoving them into the covered bed of the lorry, he slammed the back shut, then opened the passenger side. "You don't look ready for chicken chasing."

"I'm not going to chase anything," said Fiona in a dignified tone. She waited pointedly as Kerry got into the cab, looking like she was stifling giggles. Then Fiona climbed in and closed the door.

Davie got behind the wheel. "Right," he said easily. "Myself, I don't mind a bit of a chase."

Kerry

17

"This is it?" I said faintly.

As Davie stopped the pickup, I stared at the tumbledown property, shrinking against the seat. Bits of toys littered the garden in front of a one-story cottage, green with moss. Half of the barn roof was caved in. Amidst piles of rusted equipment, plastic water containers also tinged with green, and chunks of fencing, a half-dozen enormous pigs were busily rooting in the unfenced yard.

Any exposed grass had been plowed up by the pigs, leaving divots everywhere and furrows of mud. A crew of mangy dogs yelped inside a broken-down run, two of them up on their hind legs. Chickens were *everywhere*, squawking and pecking at each other. The smell of manure seeped through the closed windows.

"Pat Hurley said Eddie Bolger's place," said Davie. "Everyone knows where Fast Eddie lives. Although the last I heard he's in gaol."

"I pictured something a bit different," I said in a small voice, taking in a nearby patch that was covered with what had to be pig droppings. "You know, a proper farm."

"Nothing proper about this train wreck," said Davie. "Changed your mind, have you? I'll take you home, no harm done."

I was tempted. But to risk my new standing as a village insider? "Pat would be sure to ask how my hens are. So…no thanks."

As Fiona made to open the passenger door, Davie reached across me and put his hand on her wrist. "Save your shoes," he said.

I glanced at Fiona's averted face, forgetting the derelict farm for a moment. Fiona had only said he'd asked her out. But what *had* happened between the pair of them?

Opening the driver's door, Davie clambered out. The stench of manure filled the cab, so strong my eyes watered. Turning my gaze back to the junk-filled barnyard, I told myself, *Just grab the chickens and get out.*

"Holy Jaysus," said Davie as I climbed from the cab. "Fiona, you'll want to keep the windows closed."

She didn't answer. Then, surprising me, she rolled down the window. "We'll all suffer together, shall we?"

Stepping away from the lorry, I eyed the loose pigs warily—weren't they known to attack people? Or was that only sows with a litter? To my relief, they paid us no attention whatsoever. Still, I was glad to have Davie alongside me—and to be wearing Wellies—as I picked my way through chicken droppings to the greeny-white farmhouse. When we reached the front stoop, the scratched-up door opened before we could knock.

A thin, careworn young woman, obviously pregnant, held a dirty-faced toddler on her hip. "You come for Eddie?" she asked in a heavy accent, resignation in her voice. Polish, I thought. The faded jeans and man's tatty tee shirt she wore added to her air of all-around weariness.

"Yes—can we talk to him?" I asked.

"He not here."

"Can we ring him?" I patted the pocket where I used to keep my mobile. Empty.

"No," said the girl, looking a bit lost. "My husband not *bek* for…awhile." The toddler laid his head on her shoulder.

I glanced up at Davie. His eyes said, *Didn't I tell you? Gaol.* I turned back at the woman. "But we've arranged to pick up—"

"Oh, you come for chickens," said the girl—Mrs. Fast Eddie. Her face brightened. "You catch, then. *Plez*, two hundred euro." She held out her hand.

I blanched. "For six hens?"

"Eddie sell twenty only. In job lot, he say." She hoisted the child higher on her hip and sighed, as if I was a thick. "Ten euro each hen, you take twenty hens, so you *gif* me two hundred euro. *Plez.*"

My coop wouldn't hold twenty birds. Nor did I trust myself to have more than a few hens to start with. Besides, after I'd blown nearly all my farm budget on the house remodel, two hundred euro suddenly seemed like a *lot* of money.

The toddler whimpered. "Shhh," said the girl, patting his back. Her hands were red and chapped. I looked at her tired face. *She clearly needs the money, but how will I pay for the feed and equipment I've ordered?* The manure smell seemed to intensify. I couldn't drag this out.

"Sorry," I said. "I'm here for only six."

"But Eddie say—"

"Eddie got it wrong," said Davie. "The Missus here wants six, and that's what she's—"

"Davie," I broke in. "I'll handle this." If I was going to be a farmer, I'd have to fight my own battles. Even if Mrs. Bolger was skint, I wasn't made of money either. "I wish I could take twenty, but I can't."

The toddler began to cry. *And here his mammy's going to have another baby.* I swallowed hard. "I've got only three boxes, so it'll be six birds," I said over the child's cries. "How much?"

She gave me a calculating look. "One hundred twenty." She patted the child again and he subsided.

"If each hen is ten euro," put in Davie, "it should be sixty."

"Ten is bulk price," said the girl. "Twenty each hen for smaller…orders."

I was positive she'd made these numbers up on the fly—this place couldn't possibly be a regular chicken operation. "I'll pay one hundred," I told her. "For six."

"Okay," she said instantly, and I knew I should've bargained harder. But the smell was so bad I couldn't think straight. She held out her hand again. "Cash only, *plez.*"

As I fished out my purse, Davie held up a hand. "We'll pay later," he told the woman.

"Wait—no chickens leave place before you *gif* money to me."

"We'll pay for the birds, no worries," said Davie. "But after we've caught them."

Fiona

18

*F*iona sat in the pickup while Kerry and Davie spoke to the farm owner. Why was the sale taking so long? The smell was starting to make her nauseated. Finally the woman closed the door. Kerry turned toward the farmyard, a helpless look on her face. To Fiona's dismay, Davie was heading back to the lorry.

She leaned toward the opened window. "Everything all right?"

"Grand." Davie opened the back of the lorry. "A bit of a misunderstanding, that's all."

Fiona glanced at the barnyard again. "These chickens seem almost…feral."

"They look wild, all right," said Davie. "Kerry's got her work cut out for her."

"You'll not be letting her catch them all herself, will you?" She hated asking Davie for anything, but for her friend…

"What d'you take me for?" asked Davie. "She forgot work gloves—Gil's got spares back here somewhere." He rummaged round the tools and Kerry's boxes for a moment, then held up two large leather gloves. "Got 'em."

"Um…thank you." Fiona shifted in her seat. "For helping."

Davie tossed Gil's gloves in the nearest box and pulled on his own. Lifting all three cartons, he gave her a grin that make her heart turn over. "You can thank me after we're done."

Fiona wanted to cover her eyes.

It was painful to watch, Kerry and Davie slip-sliding through mud and manure, squawking birds running hither and yon. Dodging round the pigs, the pair of them snatched at hens willy-nilly, only to have the birds race away, wings flapping, their frantic *buck-buck-buck-GAWs* growing deafening. A couple of roosters were chasing Davie, their tail feathers twitching madly.

The pigs were getting riled up too, squealing if Davie and Kerry got too close, adding to the cacophony. Finally Davie stopped and held up a hand, broad chest heaving. Kerry, red-faced, drew up short too.

"How about this," Davie shouted to Kerry. "You pick out one hen, herd it toward me, and I'll grab for it."

"Okay," yelled Kerry, advancing on a hen.

Their first few attempts were misses. I should be helping, Fiona thought guiltily. She glanced down at the pretty red flats she'd worn as a student. *And spoil my shoes without being all that useful?* Still, watching Davie, she felt a stirring of...something. He should've looked terribly comical, but instead he seemed entirely capable.

When Davie nearly fell over one the pigs, Fiona couldn't sit on the sidelines any longer. Jumping out of the lorry, she checked the back to see if Gil had a pair of Wellies. He did—a stained coat too. Before she could talk herself out of it, she flung on the coat and slipped off her flats. She jammed her feet into the big boots, tucking her trouser legs inside them, and joined the fray.

Davie spared her one surprised glance, then ran after another hen. Dodging clumsily in the oversized boots, Fiona tried herding one toward him. As the bird crossed his path, he snatched at it, both hands scrabbling. Holding the hen triumphantly, he said, "Victory!"

She stood back as he stuffed the chicken into one of the boxes he'd set nearby, using a short length of duct tape to create a tented closure. Within ten minutes, Fiona had chased enough hens for Davie and Kerry to catch and box five more birds. As the chickens thumped inside the cardboard, she and Kerry held the box tops as Davie taped them more securely.

As the pigs settled back into their rooting, Davie carried one carton to the pickup, the two hens inside squawking fit to raise the dead. Fiona trailed behind him, mud squish-squashing round Gil's Wellies with each step. While Kerry went back to the house and spoke to the woman again, Fiona watched Davie surreptitiously as he packed the box in the back and fetched the other two.

When he was done, he stripped off his gloves and swiped the sweat off his forehead, grinning. "If it hadn't been for you, we might still be trying to catch 'em."

Despite the state of him, she felt the pull of attraction. "Gil will probably be cross that I got his things mucked up." She handed Davie the coat and changed back into her flats, then set the boots where she'd found them. *I hope I don't look as wrecked as Davie does.*

"He'll get over it," said Davie.

As Fiona climbed into the lorry, Davie pulled a newspaper and two rain slickers out of the back. He spread the paper on the floor of the lorry and the slickers on the right half of the car seat, bunching part of one against her.

She managed not to shift away from his touch. "I suppose your brother won't like it if you bring the lorry back all dirty," she said over the squawking birds.

His face just inches from hers, he met her eyes. "I'd like it even less if the chicken sh—I mean, the stuff that's on Kerry, got on you. Or your pink jumper."

Before Fiona could reply, Kerry returned to the pickup and clambered to the middle of the seat. She wore a strange expression.

Concerned, Fiona asked, "You didn't get pecked by one of the birds?" Kerry shook her head as Davie settled behind the wheel. "You must be knackered, though."

Kerry leaned back and closed her eyes. The hens' noise subsided to a few clacks and moans. "Not as tired as that girl must be."

"Fast Eddie's wife?"

"Poor kid," said Kerry, "to be a foreigner with a little one, and another on the way."

"Having kids with that tosser Eddie," said Davie, shaking his head. "And him in gaol half the time. That'll be some life."

"Yeah." Kerry opened her eyes. "Well, that was *such* great craic, but let's get out of here. *Plez.*"

Davie chuckled and started the pickup. What's the joke? Fiona wondered. "I'm afraid your lorry will need airing out—for about a year," she said.

"So will we." Kerry sniffed the sleeve of her jacket, wrinkling her nose. "What do you think? A week? A fortnight?"

"As long as it takes." Davie flashed another grin at Fiona. Her lips curved, but she turned her head away before he could see. *I don't mind a bit of a chase,* he'd said.

So maybe you'll get one. She wondered what it would be like to kiss him, but she immediately pushed the traitorous thought away. Colm was the one she wanted. Yet he suddenly seemed... unimportant. What does that say about me? Fiona thought in despair. I'm in *love* with Colm! How can I be attracted to Davie?

She stared out the window as the lorry bounced down the potholed drive to the main road. Since her brother Niall had left in December, she was convinced she hadn't any options. Now, it seemed she had too many. *I've got to stop this. I'm not the sort who leads on one man, let alone two...*

"You've a knack for hen wrangling," Kerry was saying to Davie as he turned south onto the Ballydara road. "Were you a farm kid?"

Davie shifted the gears. "Actually, I've lived in Galway City all my life—Dad started a builders' firm there. My brothers and myself work with him."

Intrigued, Fiona asked, "But you do subcontracting work on your own? Like helping Bernard Hurley?"

"Now and then," Davie said. "But I'm no odd-jobs bloke. I'm part owner of our firm."

So he wasn't a handyman—more like Colm's equal. Then Fiona wanted to kick herself. *Stop comparing them!*

"So you're not available to be my farm helper," said Kerry with a mock-sigh.

"Sorry," Davie said. "We've got jobs lined up for the next year."

"I'd ask my husband, but it's not on," said Kerry. "Working on his granddad's farm when he was young made him go off farming forever." She still sounded jokey, but Fiona detected a bleak truth beneath her teasing.

Maybe Davie had too. "Kerry, I'd say you're up for running your farm yourself, no problem."

This could get complicated, thought Fiona as they neared Kerry's place. Davie being mates with her dad *and* Kerry.

"I wish my family could hear that," said Kerry. "They think it's a nutter whim or early mid-life crisis."

"They should've had a look at you back at Eddie's, catching chickens," said Davie.

As he turned into the drive, cutting the engine, the hens started their *buckGAW*-ing again. Fiona climbed out of the lorry, Kerry quickly following. "I want to pay you for helping me," she told Davie. "I'm...um, completely out of cash, but I can write you a check."

"I won't take your money." Davie clambered out too.

"Really, let me give you something," Kerry insisted. "You came all the way from the city, and gave up your entire morning."

"I did it as a favor," said Davie. "For yourself and..." Fiona felt his gaze on her. "Desmond."

"Will you at least let me give you lunch?" Kerry asked. "Fiona, you too? I'll need to put the hens in their pen, then shower, but I've plenty of soup and bread."

Fiona smoothed her hair. *Spend the afternoon with Davie? Maybe that'll help me sort myself.* "I'd love lunch," she said. "Chicken wrangling can give a girl an appetite."

"Is that so?" Davie murmured.

"Davie..." Fiona said under her breath. "Don't you—"

"I'll need to clean myself up," said Davie in his normal voice. "Before I do anything else."

"Then you can use my shower too," Kerry offered. "If you'd like."

Fiona felt a bit faint as the image of Davie in the shower, bare and brawny, entered her mind. And rather stuck there.

"I can't stay, no," said Davie. "I've some estimates to finish today. But once we unload those hens, I'll have a quick word with Fiona." He gave her a questioning look.

"All right." Was he going to ask her out again? Her voice shook slightly. "Kerry, I'll come to the house shortly."

Davie opened the back of the lorry. The squawking and thumping from the boxes intensified. "Really, I don't want you to do any more," Kerry said over the racket.

"Too bad," Davie said. He gave Kerry one carton and picked up the other two. Fiona watched his broad back as he and Kerry ferried the boxes to the chicken pen.

"I can't thank you enough," Kerry told him. "After I give Gil's gloves a wash I'll get them to you."

"No rush," said Davie, setting his two boxes down. He backed out of the pen. "I'll leave you to it, then."

As Kerry opened one box, Davie returned to where Fiona waited. "You're up for a bit of fresh air?"

Feeling a streak of anticipation, Fiona couldn't quite meet his eyes. *But am I ready for you?*

Walking alongside Davie toward Kerry's fir grove, Fiona said awkwardly, "Kerry couldn't have done this without you. She really wanted to say*, I'm really sorry about my dad's pushing you to help and his eejit matchmaking.*

"She'd have been all right," said Davie. "Catching those chickens might have taken her longer, that's all."

"It was so kind of you, too, to not let her pay you. I wouldn't be surprised if all the work on her house really set her back—"

"I saw you, you know," Davie interrupted.

She stopped, puzzled. "What do you mean?"

"Sitting in a posh car with some old guy. Last Tuesday."

The day she'd met Colm. Fiona blushed crimson. God help

us, how much had he actually *seen*? "You've been *spying* on me?"

"Not exactly, but I was—"

"Sounds like spying to me," Fiona said furiously. "Skulking about like that, following me around—" Sweat broke out on her upper lip. "It gives me the bloody creeps."

"I wasn't skulking." Davie shoved his hands into his trouser pockets. "I just happened to be taking that road, past the links."

"Just *happened* to take it?" Fiona asked sarcastically.

"All right, I was taking the long way in case you were getting caught in the rain again." He made a tiny shrug.

"Well, I'm a big girl, in case you haven't noticed. I don't need your protection!"

"So who's this bloke, your sugar daddy?"

"No!" Fiona took another indignant breath. "My...my friend Colm might have gray hair but he's not old—he's thirty-six! So if you think that's ancient then that makes me the same. And I'm perfectly free to see whoever I like, and do whatever I want, and if you don't like it you can bloody shove it!"

"Why so defensive?" Davie crossed his arms.

"I'm not!" Fiona clenched her fists, and turned on her heel. "Oh, go to hell—"

Davie caught her elbow. "You'll hear me out."

His composure made her want to scream. She jerked away from him. "I don't know why I should, I've done nothing wrong—"

"When I asked you to go out with me, I thought you were bluffing about having a boyfriend."

"I did say I was...unavailable," she said stiffly.

He regarded her silently, a dignity in his bearing despite the chicken manure on his boots and trousers.

"And Colm's not exactly my...boyfriend." Just the man who'd promised her freedom and the chance to do all the art she'd dreamed of.

Davie still didn't speak.

"He's...someone I knew in Galway, before I came to stay with Dad." Fiona gulped. "So why'd you come today anyway?

Letting my dad rope you into this horrible matchmaking thing after seeing me with Colm? And helping Kerry too, when you think she could've gotten the hens herself..." Fiona turned even redder. *You're babbling now, so just shut up.*

"Because...I like you." He shrugged. "Pretty simple."

Despite his offhand words, she saw the same vulnerability in his eyes she'd noticed before. Why *was* she giving out at him like this? "Really, I'm..." *I'm what? Attracted? Turned on?* "...I'm flattered," she said. "There are lots of girls who'd like to go out with you, I'm sure." Fiona took a deep breath, realizing she didn't want to think about Davie with other girls. "Besides, I've at least ten years on you."

"Eight." A slow smile curved his mouth. "And before you accuse me of poking into your business, your dad volunteered your age."

Fiona couldn't be angry any more. "*Farmers.*" She rolled her eyes. "They're all for checking the horse's teeth before they put their money down."

Davie's smile faded. "I assume your dad doesn't know about this bloke of yours, or he'd have never asked me to take you and Kerry up to Eddie's."

Fiona shook her head.

"So what's the matter with this Colm one? If I were him, I'd be a man about it, and go see your dad. Introduce myself properly."

"He lives in Dublin," Fiona said automatically. As if that was an excuse for him not meeting Desmond.

"If it was me, I'd want your dad to know I was your boyfriend," said Davie.

"I told you, Colm's not my boyfriend." *Even if we were snogging on a public road.* Thank God, thank *God*, she'd been in no state to take things any further...

"If he isn't," and Davie reached for her hand, his dark eyes intent, "then maybe you *will* go out with me."

Fiona couldn't help it. She laced her fingers through Davie's, desire rising in her, stronger than her longing for Colm and the chance to resume the life she'd loved.

She looked down, unable to meet Davie's gaze. Her red shoes caught her eye. A shocking thought struck her. Fiona tried to push it away, but the idea lingered, tempting her. Reminding her of the girl she'd once been. Daring in her art, in her life. *I could never do that. Could I?*

She lifted her eyes to meet Davie's. "I'll go out with you," she said before she could stop herself. "But you might as well know, I'll be seeing Colm too."

Shock flashed in his dark eyes, gone in an instant. He grinned carelessly. "Why not?" He released her hand. "But the minute you hop into bed with him, we're *done.*"

Kerry
19

$\mathcal{G}$azing at my little flock of six hens through the window, I made myself reach for the phone. "Ring him," I said aloud in the empty kitchen. "Before Fiona gets back. Tell him what you've gotten yourself into."

I lifted the handset to dial the international code, and glanced at my near-empty purse, sitting on the countertop. Abruptly, I disconnected.

I'd been keeping Stephen in the loop with the remodel costs—well, mostly. Now that I'd started the farm improvements, though, I'd have to own up to a whole new round of expenses. *Stephen,* I rehearsed silently, *you'll never believe how fast a person can spend two hundred euro...*

There was a rap on the back door. "Did I keep you waiting?" Fiona sounded breathless. She stepped out of her shoes and entered the kitchen, her color high. Her plait had loosened, and stray curls brushed her cheeks. She looked somehow...different. A more vivid version of herself.

"Not at all." The chemistry I'd sensed between her and Davie must be more potent than I thought. I was dying to know what was going on with the pair of them—that is, I *was* before I started thinking about money. Still, how out-and out-snoopy should one be with a new friend? *Do you think Davie will help you get over your man Colm?* I longed to ask her. Instead, I turned on the Aga with a casual, "You sent Davie on his way?"

"You got the hens settled?" Fiona said at the same time.

My curiosity could wait. "They seemed a bit crazed when I let them out of the boxes." I glanced at her as I set out a loaf of brown bread. "You must have heard them, down by the trees."

"What?" Fiona blinked. "Oh, the chickens? Screeching to high heaven, yes."

I hid a smile. "They pecked my hands, then scuttled off to the corners of the run, and pecked each other. But as soon as I gave them some grain, they were all over it. They seemed ravenous." I'd felt rather maternal as I watched them, thinking, *this lot's depending on you now.* "I thought a snack would keep them occupied while I filled their new feeder, but they practically started a stampede to get to their food."

As the hens punched their beaks into the feed, I'd knelt next to them, a motley collection of white, goldy-brown, and black birds with speckles, hoping they'd soon get used to me. All I'd gotten was pecked at. Almost instantly, however, the chickens ignored me to resume their frantic eating.

"Maybe they haven't had a proper meal for a while, poor things," Fiona suggested.

I no longer felt like smiling. "Or the competition for food was too intense at Fast Eddie's." I opened the fridge to retrieve a container of potato soup to heat. "That girl..."

"Who?" Fiona washed her hands and found a knife for the bread.

"Eddie's wife."

I didn't know whether to be glad or sorry I'd lingered on the stoop with her, after paying her for the hens. "You like chickens, yes?" she said almost eagerly, her little boy dozing on her shoulder. "You choose very pretty ones."

"Why, thank you," I said, although Davie and I had only "chosen" the birds we could catch. "You have a lovely little boy."

"My Peter." She pressed her cheek against the child's hair. How well I remembered the softness of Jamie's hair when he was small. "You *hev* kids too?"

"A son, Jamie," I said. "I'm called Kerry, by the way."

"Me, Beata." She actually smiled. "You have more kids maybe? With big tall husband out there?"

"He's not my husband," I said quickly. "He's a friend. My husband's abroad."

"Ah, *abroad*," she said. "Mine too. Eddie. Abroad."

A shame Davie was waiting at the lorry with Fiona—he would've had the laugh over the way Mrs. Fast Eddie described her man's incarceration. But really, her situation, alone on this wreck of a farm, was hardly funny. "You'll be…okay?" I glanced at her pregnant belly.

"You mean, with baby coming?" Her smile faded. "Euro from chickens will help. But miss home."

"Poland?" I asked.

She nodded. "My uncle come to Ireland, he ring home, say lots of jobs here. So I come to Ireland too, to clean. Lots of big house, office place, need cleaner. I work, get enough to buy little car. But then not so many jobs anymore. I wonder, I go back to Poland?"

"What made you stay?" I asked.

"I meet Eddie, we go out. I think he trouble, but he sweet to me. He say, *Plez* marry, you like farm, yes? I don't like so much, I say okay anyway, and my baby boy comes soon." She shifted the child in her arms. "Now new baby." Her face drooped even more. "My family, all back home. I miss."

"I'm sorry they're so far away," I said. If Stephen and I were having a baby, we would have plenty of money, family around to help… *Don't do it,* I told myself, but I couldn't help it. I'd pulled my purse out of my pocket again…

Now, Fiona asked, "What about the girl? Was she as manky as her farm?"

"She turned out to be quite nice," I said. "Polish, pregnant— and obviously terribly skint. Anyway, I did something I suppose I'll regret." Fiona raised her brows. "I told her I had to enlarge my coop first, but I wanted to buy more chickens and pay in advance. I ended up giving her every last euro in my purse."

Fiona squeezed my arm, then set the plate of bread she'd sliced on the table. "'Generous to a fault' is not a fault."

I ladled the soup into bowls and brought them over. As we sat down, Fiona looked down at the table for a long moment. I spooned up some soup, thinking she was saying grace to herself or something, then she met my eyes, a glint in her own. "I've just done something—something altogether reckless—that I *know* I'll regret. But right now I just can't."

Fiona

20

$\mathcal{F}$iona picked up her spoon, then set it back down again and pushed her bowl away. "Sorry—I'm too jumpy to eat."

Kerry grinned. "Davie?"

"It's that obvious?" said Fiona, disconcerted.

"I'm not exactly blind, you know. The electricity between the pair of you—well, it fairly zinged in the air." Kerry set back her chair. "Let's go outside."

As soon as she and Kerry stepped into the garden, Fiona knew she'd *explode* if she didn't let Kerry in on what she'd gotten herself into. "I have to tell you something."

"About you and Davie?" asked Kerry.

"About Colm." Walking alongside Kerry, she shared everything she hadn't had the nerve to mention before. That she and Colm had been talking on the phone for weeks. Only days ago he'd come to Ballydara, their first meeting in a year, and their feelings for each other were as strong as ever...

Kerry didn't interrupt her. "This past Tuesday, was it?" she asked finally. "The day I came back from Dublin and found you outside the shop."

"I was such a...a blubbering mess, I couldn't tell you then." Fiona stopped next to one of Kerry's apple trees. The flower buds were swelling, and soon the garden would be full of blush-pink blossoms. "Colm wants us to make a fresh start," she said, touching a bud. "In Dublin. He's making a name for himself, lots of commissions, and he's asked me to be part of it."

"What about Davie?"

"He says he…likes me. There's no complicated past between us, no big dramas. And when I told you I wasn't attracted to him…well, it was a big cod."

"Why shouldn't you be attracted?" said Kerry. "After being… um, celibate for so long."

Fiona met her friend's eyes, laughter escaping her. "It's been over a year, and I'm…well…"

"Still young?" Kerry's smile widened. "Not a dried-up spinster?"

Fiona laughed again. "Not yet." As Kerry led them toward the coop, she said, "I couldn't possibly leave Dad to move in with Colm. All the same, I do want to see him." She took a deep breath. "Here's my problem—I want to see Davie too." She searched Kerry's face. "Breaking out of a rut is one thing, but even I can see juggling two blokes is really teenagery. Or out and out mad."

Kerry seemed to go pale.

"Other girls mightn't think seeing two guys is a big deal," Fiona hastened to say, "but to me, after falling for my dying fiancé's brother, it feels like…I don't know. That my morals have gone missing. I can *feel* my mam rolling in her grave."

"You're awfully hard on yourself." Kerry's face tightened. "Having feelings for two men, though—I've a cautionary tale."

They reached the coop. The birds began squawking furiously, pressing against the fence as if straining to escape. *Like me*, Fiona thought. She suddenly remembered Kerry's first day back in Ballydara, and the cryptic remarks she'd made about the previous owner of the farm. "Something to do with young Mr. Power? You did hint that there was something narky about him."

Kerry didn't look at her. "There was something narky, all right, and not only about him. You see…well, I might as well confess the lot. He and I had a past."

Fiona's eyes widened. Seeing Kerry and Stephen after Christmas, looking so happy, so in sync with each other, she concluded they had an ideal marriage. Yet Kerry, her voice halting, told a far different tale. About her secret fancy for Will

Power when she was younger, that Stephen had sussed out and kept to himself, let it eat at him for years. About her silly emails to Will in which she'd all but admitted how she felt about him. And though she'd never sent the emails, Stephen had found them and assumed the worst. And that he'd had secrets of his own about Will, including loaning him a vast amount of money.

"We traded the unpaid loans for this place," said Kerry, her face drawn. "So I can't regret that." She reached for a sack of scratch outside the coop and tossed a handful of it over the fence. The chickens turned all at once, tripping over each other to get to the grain. "But the rest—my carrying a torch for Will, and what it did to Stephen and me—it makes me almost ill to think about." She clutched the fence. "I discovered the truth about Will, about myself, just when I thought my marriage was over. But somehow, Stephen still loved me, and we were able to find our way back to each other."

"I'm happy you did." Fiona squeezed her arm.

"Telling you this reminds me how much I miss him." Kerry's voice was strained. After a long moment, she released the fence. "Anyway, I trust you'll not muck up your life as much as I did."

"Almost did," Fiona corrected. "In your defense, a hunky bloke called Will Power—well, a girl's almost guaranteed have trouble resisting him."

"Maybe," said Kerry, with the ghost of a smile. "Still, here I am, apart from my husband by choice, loving this place too. And I've *got* to tell him about the chickens. It's funny, I've only had them for a few hours, but I feel…I don't know. *Committed.*"

They began ambling toward the front garden. "Now you've got to choose between your husband and your hens?" Fiona teased.

Kerry wore a rueful look. "Doesn't that make me a right eejit? If you told me about Colm to get some advice, my stupidity hardly qualifies me to give you any whatsoever."

"Still, I'd like to hear it," said Fiona. Overhead, the tattered oak leaves remaining from last autumn rustled in the breeze, and the swing hanging from the biggest bough shifted slightly. On an impulse, she moved to sit on the swing and grasped the ropes.

"Okay, you're not engaged, obviously," began Kerry, giving Fiona some room.

Fiona toed her red flats into the grass to push herself backward. "I've not promised either of them that I'll be exclusive either."

"Right," said Kerry. "So if you want to see two guys, why not go for it?"

"I don't know..." Fiona tentatively extended her legs. "What will people think?"

"Who cares?" Kerry grinned at her. "'Course, I'm biased toward Davie—I think he's grand—but if you feel like seeing both blokes, it's nobody's business but yours. And don't be ashamed. Own it!"

Own it. Fiona stretched her legs out a little more. *Do I dare?* "Okay, maybe I *will* go to Dublin."

"You're due for a getaway," said Kerry.

"It'll only be a weekend." Fiona put more *oomph* into her swinging. "I'll ring Colm as soon as I get home."

"You can ring him on my phone before you go," said Kerry. "Why put it off?"

Fiona swooped through the air, feeling her plait bounce on her back. *Maybe I'll ditch this hairdo too.* She pointed her toes and leaned back, feeling young and silly and altogether...free. "But Davie..."

"What about him?"

"He says he'll stop seeing me if I sleep with Colm. The cheek of him!"

"In a perfect world..." Kerry shrugged, her grin widening. "You could *have* both of them."

"You're meant to help me!" Fiona laughed again, almost losing her grip on the ropes. "So, what about..." She stopped pumping. *If you want to take chances, you'll need practice.* "Lemme try this."

Gathering her courage, Fiona let go and leaped off the swing. One of her shoes flew off, and she landed off-balance on the grass, falling onto her hands and knees. "Gah!"

Kerry was laughing helplessly. "Sorry," she gasped, and fetched Fiona's errant footwear. "You're not hurt?"

"Only my pride." Fiona scrambled to her feet. "What I wanted to ask you was…" She studiously brushed at the grass stains on her knees. "What about sex?"

"I can't help you there, Miss Red Shoes Whelan." Still grinning, Kerry handed Fiona her ballet flat. "That, you'll have to sort on your own."

"I look desperate don't I?" Fiona drew the ribbon from her plait and finger-combed her hair.

The sun was dropping in the sky as she and Kerry strolled down the hill toward her dad's place. "Dad will take one look at me and know I was herding chickens after all." Fiona pocketed the ribbon.

"I won't tell if you don't," said Kerry. "By the way, you've a smudge on your cheek."

Fiona grimaced and rubbed the side of her face.

"No, the other one," said Kerry. "Wasn't it a great day, though?"

"It was." Fiona decided she didn't care if her face was dirty. "The best part—I got my secret about Colm off my chest, *and* managed not to give Davie a clout after his ultimatum."

"What do you know?" said Kerry. "My best has to do with Davie too."

Fiona pretended to look alarmed. "You don't fancy him?"

Kerry laughed merrily. "Even if a ridey guy like him *does* have a way with my chickens? No."

Ridey. Fiona smiled, feeling her curls bounce against her shoulders. He *is* really ridey. "Then…what's your best?"

"We finally got Davie to stop calling me 'Missus,'" said Kerry. "And discovered he's willing to look like a complete gom to please you."

"I don't know, the chicken droppings on him were pretty sexy," said Fiona.

"Um, no comment," Kerry said. "Not to change the subject, but any second thoughts yet?"

Fiona's grin faded. "You mean…about ringing Colm today?"

"I think I pushed you a bit, to phone him up straightaway," said Kerry.

"Maybe that's what I needed," Fiona said. "Otherwise, having to wait until Dad went to bed—well, I might've lost my courage by then."

"You *will* tell your dad about Colm, though?" Kerry asked.

Fiona's steps slowed. Hearing the delight in Colm's voice earlier, she reproached herself for her lingering ambivalence about going to Dublin. "Of course—but first, I'll want to get used to all this…you know. Two blokes. So not yet."

"Say, in between all this romantic angsting," Kerry said, "I've been having a think about a housewarming party—asking my family to come up to Galway, and I'll want you and Desmond, of course." She gave Fiona a sly grin. "Naturally, I'll schedule it around your visit to Dublin."

"I'm sure I can fit your party into my soon-to-be-mad romantic life," said Fiona. As they turned toward the Whelan's, she stopped cold. Sitting in the drive was a bigger, shinier version of the pickup she'd ridden in today, right down to the sign on the door. A tall man stood near the stoop, talking with her dad.

"Your devoted swain isn't wasting any time, is he?" Kerry giggled.

"Davie—what's he doing here?" Despite herself, Fiona's pulse quickened.

"Pretty obvious, don't you think?" said Kerry. "Since I'll only be in the way…" Before Fiona could protest, Kerry had already waved to Desmond and was heading back up the road.

Her heart was beating far too fast, Fiona thought, for someone soon reuniting with another man. Buying some time, she leisurely strolled up the footpath. "Hi, Dad." She waited a beat to give Davie a careless look. "So…it's you."

"It was the last time I checked," Davie said. "Ready for an evening in the city, like we talked about?"

You've eyes in your head—I'm a mess! Ready to brush at her dirty cheek again, Fiona suddenly changed tack. Play it cool, don't fall all over him. "When I said I'll go out, I didn't mean tonight."

She swept a stray curl from her face, and realized that playing with your hair was one of those body language come-ons.

"My motto is, start as you mean to go on." Unabashed, Davie opened the passenger door of the lorry. "Everyone knows first one through the gate has the advantage. And I've brought better wheels for us."

Fiona didn't move. Still, why was she holding back? She wanted to spend time with him. Somehow, though, she'd have to keep the upper hand with this cheeky article. "You can close that door because I'm not going anywhere," she said. "But will you stay for tea?"

Davie volunteered to peel the potatoes—her least favorite chore—while Fiona washed her face and redid her ponytail. Returning to the kitchen, she felt her dad's approving gaze as she fried sausages. Over the meal of bangers and mash, Davie had her dad chuckling with the chicken action at Fast Eddie's.

"Your daughter here was a right corker, helping to catch birds—a proper farm girl, like that Bathsheba in the film."

Fiona nearly dropped her fork. "You don't mean the girl in 'Far from the Madding Crowd'?" *Only look what happened to poor Bathsheba, juggling blokes.*

Davie cocked at eyebrow at her. "We kids do watch art cinema now and then."

Desmond was shaking his head. "That Eddie is a right blaggard—imagine, that little girl all alone up there." He took a bite, chewing slowly, then made a big show of yawning. "I'm knackered," he said. "Think I'll turn in early."

"Dad." Fiona gave him a warning look. "You'll keep us company, watch some telly?"

"Not tonight." Avoiding her eyes, he disappeared into his bedroom.

"I've not seen him walk that fast in ten years," Fiona said, blushing. "Being subtle is not Dad's strong suit."

"I told you, I don't mind." Davie rolled up his sleeves and went straight to the sink.

You don't need to help, Fiona thought she should tell him, but it was a nice change. Colm hadn't been one to take over meal cleanup in his bedsit—in fact, was rather useless at housework in general.

Thoughts of Colm suddenly felt like so many flies that needed swatting. Fiona glanced at Davie's bare, brawny forearms, wet from the dishwater. "You seem to know your way round a kitchen." She turned red. *I suspect you know your way around women too.*

"I'm used to helping my dad." The plate in his hands slipped. "I mean, when I lived with him."

"And your mother?" After her mam's early death, Fiona didn't take a mother's presence for granted. "She's...gone?"

"Nothing like that, no." Davie rinsed the plate.

"She was away for her job?"

"She had her own place, that's all." Davie's tone said, *leave it.*

Fiona wanted to ask, *what happened?* But he clearly didn't want to elaborate. She said lightly, "An emancipated woman."

Davie began scrubbing the potato pot. "That's it."

Fiona couldn't tell if he admired that sort of woman or not. Still, she wished she hadn't brought up his mother. As soon as the last plate was dried, Davie unrolled his sleeves and grabbed his jacket. "I'll say goodnight."

Fiona walked him out, into the cool twilight. When they reached the big pickup, he opened the door. "We'll try for Galway another time."

"Wait." Fiona touched his arm. She didn't want him to leave with this uneasiness between them. "Your coming round tonight—you're not thinking you need Dad's permission to see me, are you?"

"I'm all for tradition," said Davie, smiling faintly, "but no."

In the dim light, she could make out his angular face and square, determined chin. Showing up tonight, Davie had proved he was no flirty guy who was after her because she'd resisted him, like she'd first thought. "By the way, you didn't have to do the washing up to get on my good side."

"I did it for the same reason I helped with the chickens."

"Which is?" She held her breath.

"Because I want you..." He paused. Reaching behind her neck, he slowly pulled on her hair ribbon, letting her hair fall around her shoulders. "To take me seriously."

Fiona slid the ribbon from his fingers. Her lips tingled. When she couldn't stand it any longer, she went up on tiptoe. "I do."

Kerry
21

*B*linking sleepily in the early morning gloom, I held my umbrella over my head as I approached the chicken run. With anticipation, I lifted the lids of all three nesting boxes attached to the side of the coop. Closing the third, I sighed.

As I stepped to the fence line, all six chickens, feathers drooping in the rain, rushed over to me, clucking madly. "I hadn't much hope I'd find any eggs, since it's your first morning here," I told them, "and you're a scrawny lot. But I couldn't help it."

The birds cocked their heads.

"Once you've sorted yourselves, though, bulked up a bit, I'll expect a couple of eggs every morning. My chicken book says young hens are really productive."

Three of the hens left the fence to scratch in the grass. "Bored, are you?" I asked. "Tell you what. Once you're laying regularly, as a reward you'll be allowed to free-range in the garden. Do we have a deal?"

One of the hens suddenly poked her beak through the poultry fencing and pecked at my jeans. "Must be a yes. And when we're better acquainted, you'll all get a name."

Despite the still-ramshackle state of the coop and pen, I glanced at my chicken set-up with satisfaction. One wall of the coop had a man door, although it hung awry in its frame. Next to the door was wee opening for the hens, accessed by a low ramp—a slightly rotted board I'd found in the barn. That wall formed one side of the run, an eighty square-foot rectangle formed by half-rusted fencing about my height. On the far side of the structure were the nesting boxes, cleverly built on the coop's exterior, so you wouldn't have to muck around inside to gather eggs.

I skimmed over my jerryrigged repairs—the fence gaps I'd patched with some wire, also from the barn—that I'd refine later. "I'm off," I told the birds. "I never got round to ringing Stephen yesterday."

Once inside, as soon as I changed out of my outdoor gear, I pressed his number. It would be right before Jamie's bedtime on the West coast. Surely he'd be home... As the tones clicked and the ringing began, I wound my fingers through the phone cord, a nervous flutter in my stomach.

"Kerry!" Stephen paused. "Uh...great to hear from you."

He sounded like he was talking to a colleague. I reminded myself that our voices were bouncing around God knows how many satellites. "Seems like a long time since we were together," I said, stalling.

"Does it?" he said. "It's been less than a week."

You don't miss me yet? If Stephen was going to be all business, I would be too. "A few things have come up, that I wanted to tell you about straightaway. About our...finances."

Another hesitation. "Yes?"

His tone was cool. What was going on with him? "I wanted us to keep tabs on our spending as a family, what with our recent..." I swallowed, "issues." I couldn't say, *after your secret loans to Will Power.*

"Things are grand on my end," Stephen said quickly.

"Actually, I was talking about here." I took a deep breath. "I'm planning a housewarming party. Which will involve some spending."

"You don't have to fill me in on a splurge now and then," Stephen said, sounding more like his usual self. "Unless you want me to spend two thousand on air fare for me and Jamie to come to your do."

"I wouldn't dream of it," I said, though I'd have been thrilled if he'd offered.

"Until then, you've enough to live on, right?"

"Oh, sure." For how long, though, I'd no clue. My index finger got caught in the cord and I wiggled it loose. "There's something else." A few hundred euro is not that big, I told myself.

"Are we still talking about money?"

Stephen *definitely* sounded strange. My stomach tightened even more. "I fixed the chicken coop this week, which didn't cost all that much but I had to buy some tools first since the ones in the barn were all rusted, and the new ones are rather high end," I burbled. "But you've always said you get what you pay for, which is why I went for the quality ones."

"You fixed the coop." Stephen no longer sounded smiley.

"Then this *other* thing came up and I gave a few euro to…" I gulped. A pregnant Polish girl. "A local charity."

"And this is related to your coop?"

"Um…naturally, I wouldn't have fixed the coop simply to make it look nice." I forced myself to go on. "Yesterday I bought some chickens."

Silence. The longest one yet. "Chickens," Stephen said at last.

"Hens. For eggs. I'm planning to sell my extras." I heard hoovering in the background. Stephen had gotten Jamie to help with housework? That was progress, even if Jamie was cleaning this late.

"Sounds like you're taking this farming business more seriously than you planned."

"I only bought six birds," I said defensively.

"Oh." Stephen sounded relieved. "They couldn't have set you back too much." Then he surprised me by actually asking, "So…the final tab for this chicken project?"

I swallowed. "Two hundred and sixty-five euro."

"Jaysus! For six bloody chickens?"

Stephen had never really given me a bollacking about money, all the years we'd been married. So why now? "You've spent the same taking a client out to dinner."

"On the company's tab, not ours!"

"But…" A lump grew in my throat. I couldn't cry on the phone, though, not over a little thing like this. "My eggs will be *organic*—they'll fetch a nice price at Judith's shop."

"Right." He was probably thinking, how many eggs, organic or not, do you have to sell to equal two-hundred sixty five euro? "You've a plan for what you'll do with your hens when you're back in Dublin with Jamie?"

"Of course," I lied. With Stephen thousands of miles away, I couldn't bear to argue any more, after we'd found such bliss together since our reconciliation. "Speaking of Jamie, is he around?"

"Not at the moment." I sensed a new, different tension in him.

"Then who's doing the hoovering?"

"Must be the neighbors," Stephen said.

"That must be a right pain, living next to people with such a loud machine," I said, trying to defuse this…whatever it was going on between us. "When will Jamie be back?"

"I'm…not sure." Stephen sounded odder and odder. "He's seeing a friend."

Must be a sleepover. "When he does get home, have him ring me, will you?"

"Look, I'm sorry about this—the money. I didn't mean to get all bent out of shape," Stephen said. "It's just that our being separated…" His voice trailed away.

So you do miss me. "It *is* challenging to sort out money things," I said with difficulty, "the way we're living." He'd gotten such a big raise to go to Vancouver, I thought money worries were far behind us.

"Frankly, everything about being here is a challenge."

My longing for him overcame my common sense. *It'll be hundreds of euro, but if you don't do it, you won't see Stephen until June.* And after the go-for-the-gusto advice I'd given Fiona yesterday, I made the snappiest of snap decisions. "I had a brainwave last week," I told him. "A rather expensive one, but I think you'll like it." I took a deep breath. "I'd like to come see you. You and Jamie."

He didn't say anything. If his silences before had been weighty, this one felt like lead. Had the line disconnected? Then I heard him breathing. "Stephen?"

"Visit Vancouver? That'd be great, but…" His voice sounded strangled. "I'm afraid it's just not…on."

Fiona

22

*F*iona rapped at Kerry's back door and turned the knob. "Kerry?" It was so lovely to have a friend you could just pop in on. *Especially when you're feeling rather amazing, and you have to tell someone about it—*

"Fiona?" A sniff came from the front of the house.

Quickly shedding her raincoat, she found Kerry in the sunroom, lying on her chaise longue. "Are you ill?"

Kerry shook her head.

Fiona took one look at her friend's red eyes. She retraced her steps to grab the kitchen toweling, bringing several sheets to Kerry. "I should have rung first."

"No—I'm glad you're here." Kerry mopped her face. "Even though I'm not being a proper hostess—" A sob broke from her. "I'm so s-sorry—the state of me—"

"Stay where you are," said Fiona. "I'll make tea." Her evening with Davie could wait. "You were there for me when I was a wreck last week."

"B-but I wanted to hear how you and Davie got on and I can tell from your face it was grand…" Kerry blew her nose.

Fiona couldn't help the tiny jolt of pleasure she felt just to hear his name. "Okay, but tea first."

Back in the kitchen, she drummed her fingers on the worktop as the water heated. She'd gotten used to her life being altogether banjaxed. So she felt a bit off-balance, to be the glowy one while Kerry was down in the dumps.

Within moments, she'd found a tray and carried in two cups, a small pitcher of milk and the sugar bowl back to the sunroom, setting it on a small round table. Kerry smiled wanly. "Look at me—I'd bought this loungy piece to make the room look nice for selling. I never expected to be lazing on it myself."

"Maybe it's time you gave yourself the luxury," said Fiona. After fixing a cup for each of them, Fiona sank into the easy chair next to Kerry. She sipped her tea in silence, listening to the rain pattering on the glass. Last night, a fine mist had softened the air as she walked Davie to his lorry, dampening his hair, his skin—

"I rang Stephen." Kerry lifted her cup to her lips, then set it on the table without drinking any. "To tell him I'd bought the chickens."

"It didn't go well?" Fiona would never have been so indelicate as to ask her friend about money, but given their big car, the major house redo, and Stephen's high-end job, she guessed the McCormacks hadn't any need to be thrifty.

"It did *not*," Kerry said. "Before he left for Canada in January, he told me to spend what I needed on the remodel. And I had. Then, on his recent visit, we were pretty much occupied with…um, being together." Her cheeks flushed.

Fiona pretended not to notice. "What did he say today?"

"He actually gave out at me, can you believe it? Over six hens!"

"Maybe he was only surprised," Fiona said.

Shifting, Kerry sat up. "Even so, his reaction seemed completely over the top. He did apologize right after, so I thought we were all right." She wiped her nose with the toweling again.

"Since I've never lived with a guy, I'm clueless about how couples share money," Fiona said, her thoughts going back to Colm.

He'd asked her to share his Dublin place, but she could hardly trade a painting or set of illustrations for her portion of rent, like she had when she was a working artist. Living with Colm was all theoretical anyway, with her brother settled in America. And there was Davie…

"Then Stephen really dropped a bomb." Kerry's eyes filled.

Fiona patted her arm awkwardly. What a crap friend she was, thinking about not one, but two guys while Kerry fell apart. "Tell me. If you want to."

"Yesterday I was so brash, giving you advice. 'Be adventurous! Get your feelings out there, live for the moment!' So I said to myself, you can do it too, and I told Stephen I wanted to fly to Vancouver for a visit. Just last week, he'd really pressed me to come—I thought he'd be *thrilled*." Kerry blotted her eyes.

"But he wasn't?"

"He made excuses—work was mad, Jamie's assignments were taking all his free time, air fares were super high at the moment, but they were all so *lame*. He really, really didn't want me in Vancouver. It was like a clout on the head."

"You know *men*," Fiona tried on. "They'll get their pants in a twist about one thing, when they're actually worked up about something else entirely."

Kerry looked unconvinced.

Fiona continued, "Whatever Stephen's going through, he's mad about you."

"You really think so?"

"When the pair of you came to see Dad and myself after Christmas, he couldn't take his eyes off you. And you said yourself things were great on his visit. He would've hardly gone off you after five days."

Kerry's mouth moved in a semblance of a smile. "I suppose."

"And when you're finally together, you'll sort it out in no time. Even have the laugh over it."

Kerry rested her chin on her clasped hands. "Thanks, love. You're very wise, for someone who says she hasn't known many blokes."

That's about to change, thought Fiona. "So, you're feeling better?"

"I am." Kerry picked up her teacup. "When you fall to pieces as easily as I do, you bounce back fairly fast."

"Is that how it works?" Fiona said ruefully. She'd somehow held it together while Enda was dying, then losing her job, and the split with Colm. But when he showed up last week, she'd gone completely off the rails.

Kerry sipped her tea, a faraway look on her face. "I know what'll really cheer me up—planning that housewarming do I mentioned. What do you think of May Day?"

"It's actually my birthday," Fiona admitted.

"Perfect!" Kerry set down her cup. "We'll make it a combination party. What do you think of doing something really festive? A wine tasting? Or a dessert bar."

"I feel I should say 'don't go to any trouble,' but really, either would be fantastic." It had been years since Fiona had celebrated her birthday.

"And you'll be back from Dublin, right?" Before Fiona could answer, Kerry's face brightened even more. "I almost forgot— Davie! How'd your date go?"

"We never went out." Seeing Kerry's face fall, she hastily added, "I did ask him for tea."

"That sounds...promising," said Kerry. "Even if your dad was there."

He wasn't in the pickup with us, though. Smiling to herself, Fiona admitted, "I completely forgot about our age difference."

"Which is not that big, mind," said Kerry. "You had a good time?"

Fiona hesitated. How long had it been since she'd gossiped about a man?

"Come on," said Kerry. "Give over!"

"Well...he dropped that flirty bit he'd been doing with me, with the double-entendres and all that—a perfect gentleman." *That is, in front of Dad.*

"Were you disappointed?" Kerry asked, her dimples showing.

"A bit." Fiona pressed her hands to her hot cheeks. "Okay, more than that. And would you believe when I walked him to his lorry he didn't kiss me goodnight."

"Now I'm the one who's let down," said Kerry. "I was sure there'd be some mad, passionate snogging."

"Um, after you and I talked about being adventurous..." *Come on, you can tell Kerry.* "I ended up kissing *him*."

She and Davie had climbed into the roomy cab for a snog, and he knew what he was doing, with kissing. But the utter *nerve* of him—he was the one to stop first, though she wouldn't tell Kerry *that*. And he'd said something she'd keep to herself too. "Goes both ways, you know," he whispered in her ear.

Dazed with longing, she murmured, "What does?"

"Once you sleep with *me*, you and that Dublin bloke are history."

Fiona had wanted to smack him, the cheeky brat. Instead, she'd kissed him again…

Lost in another daydream, Fiona blinked as Kerry said, "You're still going to Dublin?"

Colm again. Fiona concentrated on the connection she'd felt with him last week. "I am. Even if I can't leave Dad for good, I'm curious what a life with Colm could look like." *A life with my art again…*

"He'll expect sex," Kerry said baldly.

Flustered, Fiona wondered, *Am I ready to be intimate with him again?* "I'll ring my sister Bronagh—she'll let me stay at her place. That way, I wouldn't be lying to Dad about why I'm in Dublin."

A spark of amusement lit Kerry's face. "A girl can't tell her dad everything."

"Although I've no intention of exactly *lying* to Davie either, at this point I'm…" Fiona reddened. She wasn't used to this—deceiving people. "I'm not telling him about visiting Colm."

Kerry gave her a doubtful look. "You're sure?"

No reason to complicate things prematurely, thought Fiona. "Davie wants to take me to Galway City, and I really want to go. So, the way people talk in the village, let's keep Colm to ourselves, okay?"

Kerry

23

$\mathcal{G}$iving Fiona an encouraging smile, I waved at her, sitting behind the window. Then the Bus Eireann pulled away from the front of Hurley's pub.

Had I sealed my own doom? Encouraging Fiona to visit her former lover in Dublin? "It's all set," Fiona told me days ago.

"I didn't think you'd go quite this soon," I said.

"This weekend was the only time Colm had available," she replied. I must've looked worried, because she said, "It's only a couple of days. Luckily, Dad didn't seem fazed about my leaving on short notice."

Now, I stared after the bus. It was natural that she'd want to please the man she loved. She and Davie—well, it could simply be hormones, while she'd a history with this Colm. My throat tightened. What if Fiona decided to stay with him? What if I never saw her again?

You're catastrophizing again, love. Mam's scolding echoed in my head.

I took a deep breath. *Don't have a freaker before there's something to freak out about.* Anyway, with my housewarming party happening Saturday next, I had to get my act together. Summoning a smile, I opened the door to Murphy's shop.

"I can't extend any more credit to yourself," Judith was saying, her voice stiff. "I'm terribly sorry."

"*Plez*," came a familiar voice. I shrank against a shelf of boxed cereal. "I pay soon to you, I promise. I try find job, maybe."

"Until you do, perhaps you'd better go to another shop," Judith said. "I really can't—"

"The lady at Oughterard road shop say cash only. So I come back here. *Plez*. Only need milk for Peter."

I peeked over the shelf to see Beata Bolger in a tatty anorak, her child on her hip, her back sagging in defeat. Judith looked distressed. "Em...I guess we can do the liter of milk. And...I'll fetch you up a packet of oatmeal, shall I? For porridge?"

Before I could move Judith came round the counter and found me skulking in the aisle. "I feel simply awful," she whispered, looking close to tears. "She's such a sweet girl, but her bill—it's way past due. And I've been a bit...stretched lately. What else can I say, Kerry?"

I remembered Beata's thin, worn face back at her farm. "I'll settle her account," I said before I could stop myself.

"Oh! That's a lovely offer, but really, I can't let you do that," Judith murmured. "It's far too much money—"

"It's all right." I couldn't think of what Stephen would say, after giving me such a hard time about buying the chickens. "I'll give you a check as soon as she's gone."

I stayed out of sight while Judith returned to the counter. "I'm afraid there's been a mistake, Mrs. Bolger. About the bill. You go ahead, love, and pick out whatever you need."

"Really?" I looked over the shelf again. Beata's back looked straighter already. "Then I get meat and vegetables too. Maybe cake!"

The joy in her voice made me well up. Had she and the little boy gone hungry? Scuttling to the door, I managed to slide outside without the bell tinkling and found Bernard Hurley heading toward the shop. "So it's yourself, Kerry! How are those chickens of yours?"

I blinked back my tears. "Settling in nicely." Although if settling in equaled producing eggs, they were taking their time.

"Me brother Pat's been like a proud uncle," said Bernard, "to have organized a wee flock for you. Farm eggs—there's nothing tastier, wouldn't you say?"

I wouldn't know. "Hens are good company too," I told him. Each morning when I came into their pen to fill their feeder and change their water, they'd greet me with their vociferous clucking, clustering round my legs and pecking at my jeans and gloved hands. "They've each a personality," I went on, "and they act like seeing you is the highlight of their day."

"You're quite the doting mammy, so," said Bernard.

"Um...I try." Yesterday, though, they'd gotten a bit of a slagging. After I'd poured out their feed, as usual, the girls started pecking at it even before it hit the feeder, like they hadn't eaten in days. "You like it here, don't you?" I asked them. "I give you the best organic feed money can buy, and fresh bedding every couple of days!" I reached for the container of scratch grains. "And snacks every day too! So why haven't you given me any eggs yet?" Unimpressed, they kept eating.

I looked closely at Bernard, hoping he hadn't sussed out my secret. He only grinned. "You'll want to give them names, then?"

"I'm still deciding," I fibbed. I'd taken *Little Town on the Prairie* round to Desmond's last week, to show him where I'd gotten my inspiration. He didn't think I was barmy, though I was certain everyone else I knew would disagree.

"Well," said Bernard, "you've no time to waste, if you're adding fourteen more hens."

How did Bernard know I was meant to enlarge my flock? The village grapevine again? Before I could ask him, I heard Judith's bell. I turned to see Beata staggering out of the shop, toddler on one hip, a sack of groceries barely balanced on the other, pregnant belly straining against her jacket. Bernard and I leaped toward her at the same time.

"Beata, you mustn't carry all that!" I reached for the groceries.

Bernard got there first, plucking the sack from her arm. "I'll give you a hand."

"Kerry." She smiled tentatively. "And...Bernard? I *hev* name right?"

"That you do," he said. "And how's your young one?"

The little boy squirmed out of her arms. She set him down, and he started toddling off on unsteady little legs. Beata grabbed his hand before he could get too far. "My Peter want to explore, not let me hold all the time like before." She put a hand on her belly. "Not easy to chase these days." She pointed toward a battered Mini. "My car, there."

Bernard carried the sack over and I opened the back door. He set the groceries inside, and Beata strapped Peter into a child's safety seat. One of the straps looked broken. "Look after yourself, young Missus," said Bernard.

"Yes—try not to overdo," I said.

"Thank you." She looked even younger than she had that day at her farm. "Eddie home from…abroad soon, I think."

"That's great news," I told her. "He can help with Peter."

She shrugged. "We see." She closed the door and started the car.

I'd a sudden idea. "Wait!" She rolled down the window and gazed at me inquiringly.

"I'm having a party in a fortnight, May the first, and I'd like you to come." Then I remembered Eddie. Charming he might be, but did I really want him at my house without Stephen around? "It's a hen party."

She frowned. "You mean, chickens come?"

I chuckled. "Not chickens. It means a do just for girls. All the mammies will be bringing their kids too. Watch for my invitation in the post." I glanced at Peter, who grinned toothily at me.

"Bye-bye-bye," he said, flapping his little hand.

"Bye to you too," I said mistily, and waved back at him.

"I come, bring Peter then," Beata said. "Eddie not back anyway." She started to roll the window back up and stopped. "Oh, I forget to ask. Chickens okay?"

"They're great," I said. With Bernard there, I wasn't about to ask her for any hen-laying tips. "You'll see for yourself when you come to my house."

She laughed. "No, I don't look. I see plenty chickens every day at Eddie's place."

Eddie's place, she said. *Not mine*. I asked, "You get a lot of eggs?"

She shrugged. "Neighbor kids collect for me—I don't like."

Did she mean she didn't like to collect eggs, or eat them? Or both? "I'll look for you at my party May first." I waved as Beata put the Mini in gear, thinking of that tatty child's seat, and made a mental note to ask my sister if any friends of hers had a spare.

I turned to see Bernard's approving nod. "Your Stephen won't be back in time for the party either?"

Stephen's odd behavior during our phone call still weighed on me, but I kept my smile pinned on. "He won't be home until late June."

"When he does get home, the pair of you may want to enlarge your farm, eh?" He wiggled his bushy brows meaningfully.

It took me a second. So my wistful gaze at Beata's son had been that obvious? "You must mean those fourteen chickens," I said firmly. "Whatever happens, you'll be the first to know."

Back in Murphy's shop, Judith had her account book already open. "You're sure about paying this, love?" she said. "It'll be just between ourselves, of course."

"I'm sure." When she mentioned the amount of the Bolger's bill, though, I got a pain in my stomach. Trying to smile, I signed my check and handed it to Judith.

"I don't know how to thank you," said Judith. "It was fair breaking my heart to turn Beata down."

"I could see that," I said. "It takes a village, sometimes."

The worry lines in her face smoothed out. "That Eddie Bolger," she said, shaking her head. "A proper wastrel, he is, to leave his young wife alone in her condition."

I saw little Peter in my mind's eye. It's true, Stephen had seemed so keen to start a baby, but what if he'd changed his mind? And he didn't want me in Vancouver because I'd see he liked it a lot more than he was letting on? *Think of something else...* "Um, did those seed potatoes I ordered arrive yet?" That was one crop I was determined to plant—homegrown potatoes had a sweet delicacy that you could never find with spuds from the shop.

"I almost forgot! Without Fiona, my special orders sometimes fall through the cracks."

As Judith packaged up the potatoes, I asked, "You're able to come to my party?"

Judith looked torn. "I'm working on Himself to mind the shop." According to Fiona, her husband Padraig took retirement very seriously Although he did cook supper, he rarely deigned to help around the store. "While I'm thinking of it, Padraig loves fresh eggs. He's been after me to remind you I'm very keen to sell your surplus. You can bring them round anytime."

"Um..." I squirmed inwardly. "I'll keep that in mind." I moved to the baking supplies aisle. Feeling skint, I needed to downsize my party plans. "Do you think Fiona will go for chocolate cake? Or something fancier—a sponge with lemon curd?"

"Oh, our Fiona's easy to please," said Judith. "I'm that relieved, she's only going as far as Dublin for her holiday. A quick visit with her sister will be just the thing for her." She scratched some figures in her account book, then stowed it beneath the counter. "Although she mentioned looking in on an old friend too."

I felt a jolt. If Fiona was leaving hints about Colm, maybe she was taking this visit more seriously than she'd let on. I slowly reached for a sack of sugar.

"I only hope she doesn't get lured back into city life." Judith sighed. "I've come to depend on her. And not only to keep the shop ticking along."

"Me too," I said, feeling forlorn. I couldn't tell Judith what I'd done: carried away by Fiona's romantic possibilities, I'd all but talked her into going. Clearly, it would be on me if she left Ballydara for good.

Fiona
24

This couldn't be Colm's building.

Fiona stared up at the Georgian façade through the taxi window. "I must've given you the wrong address," she said to the driver. She'd envisioned Colm living in a bedsit above a shop, not this grand place.

The man sighed. "I can drive round the square again." As Fiona hesitated, he added, "Meter's ticking, miss."

"Thanks—I'll find my way from here." Fiona opened the door, grabbing her case before the driver could, and passed him the cash she could ill afford. She glanced at the vivid blue door in front of her, white stone pillars on each side, and the shiny brass doorknob and mail slot. *What do I do now?*

Feeling weary, she wished she could sit on her case for a while and get her bearings, but that wouldn't do, not in a tony place like Fitzwilliam Square. She was already disoriented at the way the city seemed almost transformed in the years since she'd last been here.

Traveling through Central Dublin, she'd felt like a country bumpkin, peering this way and that at the street improvements and construction projects. The April sun breaking through the clouds gave the cityscape an almost preternatural brightness, adding to the foreignness of it all.

Could it be she'd become accustomed to the quiet, unchanging countryside? But she couldn't loiter here forever.

She reached into her handbag for her ancient mobile—the one she'd never bothered to upgrade—and remembered she hadn't reactivated her service. She'd deleted Colm's number anyway. Why couldn't he have met her at the station? Was he too bloody busy?

The blue door opened. "You made it!" Colm hurried to pull her into his arms.

Nearly dropping her mobile, Fiona was too gobsmacked to return his kiss. "You really do live here?"

"Great place, isn't it?" He released her, smiling proudly.

Fiona gazed at the elegant entryway again. The cost of a flat in this neighborhood had to be thousands of euro a month.

Before she could answer, Colm took her case. "Wait'll you see the inside." He ushered her into the lobby. "By the way, I meant to pay for the taxi, but I didn't get down in time."

"It's all right," Fiona said, taking in the plush carpet and antique chairs. *Living here, you need the money more than I do.* As he asked her about her trip, she confessed, "I hardly recognized the city."

"Yeah—Dub's come a long way the last few years," said Colm. "Including the art world—there are massive opportunities out there." Tossing her a grin, he pressed the button for the lift. "Makes room for people like me to climb the ladder."

She'd always known Colm was ambitious, but it had never been about money. At least, not before. "You want to make your fortune then?" *So why are you spending it on a freakishly expensive car and flat?*

"Doesn't everyone?" He didn't wait for her reply. "Did you hear about the Dublin bloke who sold a photo of a potato? It was a bloody *potato* and he got over a million for it! God's honest truth."

Fiona couldn't wait to tell her dad and Kerry about the potato art—they'd fall about laughing. She gave Colm a covert glance. *You look the same, but please don't tell me your big dream is taking snaps of vegetables to sell to madzers.*

As for this flat... Weeks ago, Colm had asked her to live with him. Didn't he realize she'd never have the money to pay her share? "How do you afford this place?" she asked before she could stop herself.

"You're not to worry about that," Colm said. The lift door opened and he hustled her in.

"It's a reasonable question—"

He kissed the words from her mouth, then drew back, his light blue eyes warm with passion. "Let's just enjoy this—finally being together."

Together. She flushed with nerves. She'd told him she'd be sleeping at Bronagh's flat this weekend—so he would've worked out that she wanted keep things platonic. For now.

A bell chimed. "Here's my floor." As Colm guided her down a carpeted hallway, they passed a set of ornate, polished double doors. A short distance further, he stopped in front of a nondescript entrance. Setting down her case, he unlocked the door and turned the knob. Before she knew what he was about, he scooped her up in his arms.

"Colm!" Fiona squealed, clutching his shoulders.

He stepped inside, holding her easily. As he closed the door with his heel, Fiona's anxiety eased—carrying a woman over the threshold wasn't a gesture for someone playing about.

Kissing her hair, Colm slowly lowered her to the floor. "Welcome."

Fiona took in the one-room flat. A massive futon covered with a black duvet sat in one corner, a wardrobe next to it. Opposite was a tiny worktop with a microwave and an electric kettle sitting on it. Nearby, a door ajar showed a mirror and tile floor—obviously the bathroom. Another closed door had to be a closet.

She was accustomed to small places, yet here she felt almost claustrophobic. "It seems...comfortable," she said. *For one person.* "But how do you cook anything?"

"In a minute," Colm said. "First, you'll want to see—"

"What about your workroom? Your supplies?"

"You haven't forgotten what I promised?" He walked to the closet and opened the door with a flourish. "My—*our* studio."

Fiona rounded the futon to gaze through the doorway. Brightened by two tall windows, this room was spacious and airy. A wide, long shelf sat in front of the windows, and a large drafting table with two stools dominated the middle of the room. Strewn on both surfaces were the materials he'd once piled in a corner of his bedsit. Heavy sketching paper and pencils. Cutting tools. A long roll of semi-transparent paper propped against one table leg. Against the far wall was a small worn couch, and on a desk next to it, a high-end laptop.

"You like it?"

Fiona stepped inside the studio, hand outstretched, wanting to touch it all. She let her fingers drift over Colm's sketchbook and felt a quickening inside her—the way she'd felt years ago, when she was immersed in a project, lost to the world. Feeling like she was in a dream, she moved toward the drafting table.

"Wait," said Colm. He strode to a set of double doors she hadn't noticed before and flung them open. "You mentioned cooking."

Fiona peered into the shiniest, fanciest kitchen she'd ever seen outside of a magazine. The room held a modern cooker and Sub-Zero fridge, two built-in ovens, and granite worktops. A row of gleaming copper pots hung from an overhead unit. Late afternoon light shone through the windows, illuminating the expanse of polished wood flooring.

Fiona's mouth dropped open. "You're having me on." *The cost of this place must be double what I'd guessed.*

"Pretty great, yeah?"

Unable to picture herself preparing food in a kitchen like this, Fiona turned back to the studio table. She reached for a sheet of paper and grabbed the nearest pencil. Winding it through her fingers, she gazed through the window at the green of new leaves on the trees, and beneath them, the grassy park in the square. What a joy it would be, to wake up each day, go straight to this room, and know you were going to make art…

"I've my blast room in Temple Bar too, with all my heavy equipment and proper ventilation…Fiona?"

The voice seemed to come from a distance. Fiona turned toward the sound, almost resenting the interruption. Then Colm's face came into focus, the man who'd brought her to this wondrous place. Seeing the light in his eyes, she thought, I'll draw him first. She could already imagine the pencil strokes she'd make, to capture the strong planes of his face...

She hardly felt Colm's touch on her arm. "You can sketch later."

Fiona reluctantly came out of her daze. "Why not now?"

He slid the pencil from her hand. "We need to grab a bite, then we've got to leg it to Temple Bar." He clearly had that same restless energy. "I've another surprise."

But I don't want to go out. "What is it?"

"You'll see." Colm smiled mysteriously. "You brought something dressy, right?"

Less than an hour later Fiona stood in the bathroom, giving her reflection a critical look. *I look either eccentrically soignée or like a complete eejit.*

She wore a peacock blue silk sheath, a 60s-vintage frock she'd found in a Galway second-hand shop a dozen years ago, and a fringed paisley scarf in deep blues, greens and ruby red draped round her neck. A pair of red crystal earrings dangled from her ears. She'd let her hair down, plaiting the side strands with red ribbon. While fluorescent lights were no woman's friend after the age of twenty-five, she'd more color in her face than she'd noticed for a long time. Glancing down at her red flats, Fiona heard Kerry's teasing voice saying *Miss Red Shoes Whelan,* and wondered what her friend would think of Colm's new lifestyle.

After packing a tissue, lipstick and a few euro into a tiny satin evening bag, she found Colm waiting for her, dressed in an elegant gray suit she hadn't seen before. "I've gone full boho— you still want to take me out?"

"You look fantastic," Colm said, his eyes approving. "Let's go."

Once they were outside, Fiona searched for the blue BMW in the long row of parked cars. "Where's your car?"

"It's...uh, after your long day on the bus," Colm said, "I thought you'd be glad we're hoofing it tonight."

Fiona did feel weary, but maybe it was only Dublin and posh-flat culture shock. "I'm used to walking everywhere," she assured him.

Evening light bathed the buildings in a pink glow as Colm led them through the heart of the city: along Pembroke and Bagott Streets, past Stephen's Green, then up Grafton Street before turning onto Suffolk Street.

On the way, Fiona's gaze lingered on the restaurants. "Didn't you say we'd get a bite?" Fiona had been too anxious to eat much on the long trip, and now she was famished. "I wouldn't mind a curry, even a burger."

Colm frowned. "We did eat."

Nibbling on crackers, hummus, and a few olives as she changed had been supper? "Will there be any food at this place we're going?" Fiona asked.

"I'm sure there will." Colm pulled at his tie.

Seeing the tension in his face, Fiona tamped down her hunger pangs. As they passed the grounds of Trinity College, she wondered if Colm could make time to visit the library there. After another couple of blocks they were walking through a tangle of cobblestone streets—Temple Bar. *How much further?* she wanted to ask, her footsteps lagging.

As if Colm had read her mind, he said, "We're almost there." Taking her arm, he led her round a corner, then, "Close your eyes."

She obliged, letting him guide her, and short distance later he stopped. "Okay, open."

She found herself in front of a heavy metal door with a small sign above it. *Temple Bar Studios.* "Ready?" His grin flashed.

"Is this your new workroom?"

Opening the door, Colm's smile widened. "It's my surprise." He ushered her inside. "My first Dublin show."

Sipping another glass of white wine—her third? Fiona stood near the back wall of the crowded gallery, wishing she could leave.

Hours ago, she'd stepped into a high-ceilinged space filled with Colm's work. Stunned, she could hardly take in all that he'd produced in the year they'd been apart, each piece artfully displayed under spotlights. Before she could compliment him, a dizzying number of people surged around Colm, all gorgeously dressed, pressing congratulatory handshakes or kisses on him. He introduced Fiona to them, more faces and names than she'd ever remember.

A tall, middle-aged woman with cap of gray-blonde hair stood out from the crowd. Instead of the stylish frocks and high heels the other women wore, she was clad in a powder blue pantsuit that resembled upholstery rather than a garment. Stout, and shod in scuffed brogues, she looked more like a country veterinarian than an art fancier. She seemed to be drinking beer instead of wine like the others. Odder still, she seemed vaguely familiar.

While the woman didn't quite hover over Colm, she was never far from him. And throughout the evening, she was trying to catch Fiona's eye. Fiona kept her distance. Was the old girl one of those slightly daft people who go to events uninvited? But as Colm was swept up into the swarm of people, Fiona concentrated his artwork.

She knew she was biased, but each of Colm's pieces, whether functional or decorative, was distinctive—many inspired by nature or fantasy. Window panels etched with leaves or flowers hung on the walls, glass lamps perched on wooden pedestals cast a soft, aquamarine light into the room, and two door-sized pieces leaned against the corners. One, etched with a gigantic dragon, and the other with what appeared to be an oak tree, gave Fiona the sense that she could step through the glass into another world.

If the size of the crowd and the number of servers laden with trays of refreshments was anything to go by, the event was a success. Yet all too soon, she felt the evening turn into a blur. Sipping wine for something to do, Fiona was tired of making desultory chat. Her ears rang from the din, and her feet were killing her. And the more she wondered how Colm had bankrolled his uber-posh flat and the BMW, and who had paid for this fancy party with the drink flowing like the River Liffey, the worse they hurt.

Only there was nowhere to sit—the two armchairs in the gallery had been occupied all evening. Just as she was nearly asleep on her feet, Colm made his way to the front of the room. Someone tapped a glass to quiet the crowd.

"Thank you so much for coming," Colm began, and reeled off a long list of people who'd helped prepare the show. "But my greatest appreciation is for someone who's come a long way today, to be part of this." He reached for a brimming glass from a nearby server.

As his eyes searched the room, Fiona tried to meet his gaze. *Are you looking for me?*

Instead, he directed a smile at the stout woman with the cropped hair, towering over most of the people surrounding her. "Pauline!"

Pauline, thought Fiona. *I've heard that name before...*

Colm gave this Pauline an elegant bow. "I can't thank you enough—not only for sponsoring this event, and coming over from London to join us tonight. But for all the ways you've supported my art."

As the stout blond woman lifted a half-filled pint glass, grinning at him, Colm credited someone called Larry—or was it Harry? Then saluted Pauline with his glass. "*Slainte.*"

"*Slainte,*" the crowd echoed. As applause broke out, Pauline said, "Bottoms up!"

Fiona closed her eyes for a moment, wondering how much longer she could remain upright. She took another sip to wet her throat and the wine went down the wrong way. Eyes watering, she coughed into the crook of her arm. Barely catching her breath, Fiona nearly jumped when she felt a hearty pat on her back.

"Fiona, love, you're all right?"

Fiona cleared her throat and turned to find Pauline, the object of Colm's accolades. "I think so," she said. Not knowing what else to do, she extended her hand. "Hello, um, Mrs...." *Do we know each other?*

"God love ya, none of this 'Missus' business," Pauline said in a strong Northern accent. She gave Fiona a vigorous handshake. "Grand to see you again!"

"Thank you." Fiona wrinkled her brow. Was the woman really a nutter? Still, after the perfunctory interest of the other people she'd met, her friendliness was disarming. Fiona managed a genuine smile. "Not many artists have a mentor such as yourself—I'm sure Colm's lucky to know you."

"I should hope so!" Pauline's smile was uncannily like Colm's. "I used to change his nappies when I was the age of fifteen."

Fiona blinked. "Nappies?"

"Ah, you don't remember me," said Pauline. "I'm his cousin."

"S-sorry," Fiona stammered. "I think I've gotten myself a bit pissed." She set her glass down on one of the small high tables strategically placed around the room. "I'm not used to drink these days." She squinted at Pauline. "We've met before tonight?"

"Oh, yes." Pauline's expression sobered. "Twice, I think. The last time was at poor Enda's…"

"Funeral," Fiona whispered. She remembered Pauline now—Colm's fabulously wealthy cousin who'd married up, and lived in England part-time. She'd played hostess at the Dwyer's house after the funeral Mass, when Enda's frozen-faced parents seemed only capable of sitting upright.

How much did Pauline know about herself and Colm? That they'd become lovers before Enda… Fiona was suddenly queasy. "I need to sit down."

Pauline took her arm in a no-nonsense grip, and led her to one of the easy chairs. A young man in fashionably skinny trousers was perched on the arm, but Pauline said cheerily, "Take yourself off, lad." He hastily rose and disappeared into the crowd. She sat Fiona down, then signaled one of the servers. "Here, have one of these puffy shrimp yokes, won't you?"

The girl presented a tray of shrimp drenched in what smelled like hot pepper sauce, with a curlicue of lemongrass or something arranged on top. Fiona stared at it—the simple meal of bangers and mash she and Davie had cooked together last week was far more appealing. She shook her head.

"Fetch us some sandwiches, please," Pauline told the server. "And something non-alcoholic." The girl vanished.

"I'm not ill or anything," Fiona said, leaning her head on her hand. "Only a bit muddled—it's been a long day."

"You're not the sort who can be the life of the party until the wee hours, like Colm, eh?"

Fiona shook her head. In the short time she and Colm had been together, they'd spent quiet evenings at home. Not that she wanted to let on how little she knew about Colm's habits.

With another comforting pat, Pauline began nattering on about the opening, which Fiona knew was meant to distract her. Within moments, the server materialized beside the chair with a cheese sandwich and a small bottle of mineral water. "Lovely," said Pauline. "Fiona, soak up some of that drink."

Fiona nibbled at the sandwich obediently, and after three bites felt less like curling up in a fetal position. "If Colm's staying for the long haul, I should get a taxi."

"Taxi!" Pauline boomed with laughter. "None o' that. I've my driver waiting near Dame Street—she'll take you home."

"You've a chauffeur?" The rich really were different.

"My assistant." She drew a mobile phone from her pantsuit pocket. As Fiona sat limply, Pauline made a beeline for Colm and his crew of admirers, mobile at her ear.

As she reached his side, Colm met Fiona's eyes from across the room and broke from the group, only to have someone else grab his arm to drag him off. He gave Fiona a rueful smile, clearly his assent that she should go home.

Moments later, Pauline was back, taking Fiona's arm again. Fiona let herself lean onto the larger woman, feeling an odd kinship with her. "I must be more of a country girl than I thought."

Pauline chuckled. "Not a great one for hanging about with Dublin's...what do you call 'em? Glitterati."

Smiling at Pauline poking fun at the event she'd sponsored, Fiona stepped into the brisk night air, and they made their way out of Temple Bar's pedestrian streets. Pauline stopped as a dark blue BMW sedan pulled up. "This is *yours*?" Colm had been driving a borrowed car? But then, he'd never *exactly* said it was his.

"The one I keep in Dublin," said Pauline as a young woman with pink hair and a nose ring stepped out.

"An early night for yez?"

"Looks that way, Doraleen." Pauline helped Fiona into the back seat, then climbed in beside her. Doraleen slid behind the wheel.

"I shouldn't want you to leave the party," Fiona protested. *What'll I do now about not staying with Colm tonight?*

"Jaysus, I've had enough of all those artsy articles myself." Pauline yawned widely. "I'm ready to pack it in. Fitzy Square, love."

The BMW glided away from the curb. "Home it is then," said Doraleen.

Home...Fitzwilliam Square... Fiona thought blearily, then the realization dawned. "Colm's staying at *your* place?"

Fiona
25

"He didn't tell you?" Pauline rolled her eyes. "Artists, ya know—away with the fairies half the time."

The entire night was too much for Fiona to take in…The BMW, the flat in the grandest part of Dublin, the party in the upscale gallery…and not a word out of Colm about who'd laid down all the euro for it! *I've got to go back to the party*, *have it out with Colm.* But Fiona was too muddled with fatigue and wine to make the effort.

"So…" she began. *Does Colm pay rent?* "You don't mind having a…flatmate underfoot?"

"Lord love ya, not a bit of it," said Pauline. "Colm's like me little brother. He's mostly there in the little nook we did up for my son when he was at uni, and always welcome to nip into our kitchen or watch telly in the lounge with us anytime. That goes for yourself too."

Even in Fiona's woozy state, she could tell Pauline assumed they were a couple. Still, with Colm's lie of omission about his living arrangements, Fiona couldn't worry about his cousin's opinion. "Actually, I'm crashing at my sister's tonight—it's quite out of your way, I'm sure."

Pauline gave her a long look. "We've a comfy couch in our lounge," she said. "You could always sleep there."

Fiona realized that for all her hearty-matey kind of energy, Pauline saw more than you think she did. "Thanks, but my sister's expecting me." Feeling terribly awkward after Pauline's kindness, she tapped the front seat. "Um, Doraleen, if you'll drop me on O'Connell Street, I'll get a taxi."

"The Missus won't have it," Doraleen said without slowing down.

"That's right," said Pauline. "I like nothing better than a night drive—clears my head after these fancy-arse dos when my face is near frozen from smiling. Now then, the direction to your sister's."

Giving into the inevitable, Fiona provided Bronagh's address in North Dublin, then leaned back against the butter-soft upholstery and closed her eyes. She wondered dimly if Colm had been compromising his artistic integrity, letting someone underwrite his grand lifestyle. Or if Pauline had simply freed him to climb his career ladder a lot faster.

The social ladder too? Feeling disloyal, she was suddenly so tired she felt as if she could melt into the smooth leather seat beneath her. Not far from Bronagh's, Pauline said, "Colm's been after me to talk to you about something."

Fiona opened her eyes with an effort. "Um…yes?"

"It was my fault that the whole thing got bollixed up, after Enda…" Pauline heaved a great sigh. "Ah, well, water under the bridge."

"Sorry?" said Fiona, confused.

Pauline patted her hand. "Sure, I can see you're in no fit state for a proper discussion—we'll have a chat as soon as I'm back in Dublin."

What was Pauline on about? Surely not a pep talk about her relationship with Colm! *Oh, Jaysus…*

Seeing her sister's block of flats looming ahead, Fiona pointed to a bus stop near the entrance. "You can drop me just there. I can't thank you enough for the lift."

"Happy to do it," said Pauline.

"No bother," Doraleen affirmed. "Here you are."

Before Fiona could exit, Pauline kissed her cheek. "Keep well, love," she said. "I'm headed back to Knightsbridge tomorrow, but we'll have that chat soon."

Fiona blinked against the morning light penetrating the curtains. Her mouth was dry, her head pounding. For a second, she wondered frantically, *Where am I?* Then it all came back to her. Bronagh's place. In Dublin.

Last night, at Bronagh's door, Fiona was still reeling from the wine and Pauline's eye-opening revelations. She managed to find her sister's hiding place for the key and stumbled inside her flat, which was as plain and impersonal as an airport hotel. She found a note on the kitchen table.

Had to dash to London for a meeting, be back Sunday afternoon. Sleep in my bed if you like—it's a bit lumpy but the couch is the pits. By the way, I heard from Niall—he wants to talk to you.

What a relief, Bronagh being away—Fiona couldn't face anyone just yet. As for her wayward brother, whatever he wanted could wait.

She pulled off her silk frock, her brain swirling with the events of the last hours. Dominating everything, though, was meeting Pauline. Wishing it wasn't too late to ring Kerry, to tell her about Colm's cousin, Fiona suddenly envied Davie, having a twin to talk to.

Even if Bronagh had been home, though, Fiona wouldn't have confided in her. It wasn't that they'd never gotten on, they simply weren't...sisterly. Too different. Bronagh talked of little besides her job, and still regarded Fiona as a freewheeling, happily poverty-stricken artist. And like her other siblings, conveniently forgetting Fiona had left her career to look after their dad.

Wait—that wasn't true. Fiona slowly undid the ribbons in her plaits. She'd given up her art to be with Enda and work at the print shop. To have a safe life. As she crawled into bed in her bra and knickers, her last waking thoughts weren't about Colm, but Pauline. The way she made things happen. *I could use some of that energy myself,* Fiona had decided sleepily. *If I'm ever going to be a working artist again...*

Now, lying in bed after a fitful night's sleep, wishing it wasn't morning, Fiona heard a noise from the flat above. She rolled over and buried her face in the pillow. Were the neighbors practicing a bloody flamenco or something? With difficulty, Fiona lifted her head. No, the sound was at the door. Someone knocking.

And that someone could only be…Colm.

Groaning, Fiona crawled out of bed, fished a dressing gown from Bronagh's wardrobe and staggered to the front room. "One minute," she called, looking around frantically. Where was the bathroom again?

"It's me," said Colm from the other side of the door. "Open up!"

"Okay!" She found the bathroom door. "Give us a second!"

As Colm knocked again with an imperious, "Fiona!" she ignored him in favor of the loo. Then she forced herself to look into the mirror. She expected to look completely destroyed, but she was only pale, her eye makeup a bit smeared. Her hair was disarrayed too, but not a total rat's nest. She found some headache tablets and guzzled a half glass of water. Taking a swig from the bottle of mouthwash sitting on the counter, she swished and spat. Then she quickly splashed cold water on her face, blotted it with a towel, and hurried back to the front room.

Moving around had set off more throbbing in her head. Taking a deep breath, she reached for the knob. Colm would be angry, but he'd no right to be, she'd made it clear about taking things slow for this visit. She opened the door. "It's a bit early for dramatics, don't you think?"

For all Colm's banging, he didn't seem angry. He looked freshly showered, his hair still damp. The only evidence of his short night was more prominent lines around his eyes. "You're going to ask me in?"

"Oh." She stepped back, closing the door behind him. "Right."

"I'd have rung you first, but you left your mobile at my place." His smile looked forced.

"I was going to come back to your—*the* flat," she corrected herself. "As soon as I pulled myself togeth—"

"What are you doing here?" he interrupted.

"I…" she stared at him, confused. "I told you I was staying at my sister's."

"I thought you said that because your dad was in the room."

"No." Fiona tightened her sash. "I meant it—I don't want to rush things with you. With us."

"Fiona, love." He stepped closer, his pale blue eyes intent.

She could feel Colm's magnetism having its effect on her. Forcing herself not to move, she was surprised when he only took her hands. His were more calloused than she remembered.

"You don't need to stay here."

Feeling the urge to rub the hard spots on his fingers, she stiffened her resolve. "I need time."

"I thought that after seeing my place, meeting my friends and colleagues, you could envision the life we can have together."

"You mean *Pauline's* place," she said tartly. "And her car. You let me think they were yours."

A flush rose in his face. "I was going to explain, but the party—"

"It would have taken thirty seconds," Fiona said. Yet as Colm stroked his thumbs over her knuckles, she saw herself back in his studio. She could feel the pencil in her hand, the heavy paper sliding against her fingertips.

"Staying here…" Colm tugged gently on her hands. "You missed out on my bringing you breakfast in bed, like I used to." His voice was caressing.

"But you've nowhere to cook," she said weakly.

He drew her closer. "Pauline's got a kitchen, remember? When we get back to the flat I'll show you around properly. And show you…other things."

Warmth spreading through her, Fiona almost forgot she still had the sour taste of wine in her mouth, and hadn't showered yet.

"I'd have thought stuck out in the wilds of Galway like you've been," Colm went on, "you'd be eager to be part of the real world again."

That doused the embers. Fiona stiffened and pulled away. "Working at a village shop and looking after an elderly parent feels plenty *real* to me." She crossed her arms. "Your posh do last night—is that the real world, then?"

He ran his fingers through his silver hair. "C'mon, Fiona—you've come all this way so we can be together. Why are we arguing?"

She stared fixedly past him, itching to touch his curls but determined not to. "Because... I'm not entirely sure your lifestyle's for me."

"My lifestyle? Or myself?" His confidence seemed to waver.

"Colm, I..." She swallowed hard. She mustn't be guilty of dishonesty too. "Last week, I saw someone else."

"What?" His eyes suddenly bored into her like a laser beam. "You've another bloke? Are you bloody having me *on*?"

"It's not out of the realm of possibility, is it?" she snapped. "That another man wants me?"

"Who is he?" Colm's face went red. "How long has this been going on?"

"Not that you've any right to ask, but I met him a couple of months ago—"

"Did you sleep with him?"

"No!" *Other women do this, juggle two men,* Fiona thought wildly. *It shouldn't be this hard!* "I only had him round for tea, once, with my *dad*!"

"You and I ended up in bed the first time we went out!"

"That was different! We knew each other, we were already friends."

"Other people might share, but I'm not one of them!"

"I'm not other people either!" Fiona squeezed her hands into fists, her whole body hot with fury. She hadn't been this angry in a long time—and it felt good. "I've made him no promises, and I'll not make any to you."

His eyes changed. Seeing hurt in them, Fiona thought, *Is seeing Colm and Davie actually the worst idea I've ever had?*

Colm raised his hands in a gesture of surrender. "I'm sorry. But you can't blame me for being shocked, can you?"

Mollified, Fiona unclenched her hands. "No more shocked than I was to learn about Pauline." She wouldn't mince words.

"That you're the next thing to a kept man."

"Okay—I should have told you straight off. But I wanted you to feel I was…" He looked away. "Successful."

"Living like a high flyer on someone else's money isn't success," she said.

Colm rubbed his forehead. "I needed you to see I was finally on my way—not the black sheep of the Dwyers anymore. You can't have forgotten how I was living, in Galway City?"

Fiona shook her head. The tiny bedsit, his tatty van. "Still, you were doing good work."

"Yeah—in that manky communal studio." He stared into the middle distance. "My parents…with Enda being the fair-haired boy, taking on the print shop, well, they thought I was a real tosser."

"I can't believe that." Fiona hadn't realized he'd felt this way. "They knew you'd talent—"

"'Talent won't pay the bills,' they used to say." There was resentment in his voice.

"Every artist hears that," she said, her old sense of comradeship with him returning. "Believing in your work is what matters." Colm wasn't off the hook, though. "I still say you should've told me sooner about this set-up with Pauline."

Colm met her gaze again, entreaty in his eyes. "You'll not hold it against me?" Fiona shook her head, a bit undone to see him humbling himself. "I promise, there'll be no more secrets between us."

"Could we start the day over?" Fiona ventured. Her headache had disappeared. "Turn to a new page?"

Colm snapped his fingers. "I almost forgot! Pauline wants to set up a meeting about that book gig we talked about."

"Book gig?" Fiona's heart was suddenly pounding. "Oh my God, your cousin is the *book* Pauline?" She'd been completely clueless not to have realized it! Living in the country, maybe she really had lost her edge.

"I thought you knew it all along," he said. "She's been talking to her friends in publishing—they're keen to really go for it, and pull together a project team. She's ready to set up a meeting the next time she's in Dublin."

Was the project the "something" Pauline had referred to last night? "That would be beyond grand!" She flung her arms around Colm's neck, but quickly released him. *No leading him on.*

"After you get dressed, we'll get a coffee and play tourist," he said indulgently. "How about Trinity College Library? They've got a children's literature exhibit on. You could probably get tons of ideas for the book."

"I'd love that." Simply thinking of the book set off a streak of longing in her—to return to the art world, and work on a project that would challenge her...nourish her. *And wouldn't it be great to tell Davie I'm an artist again?* She said quickly, "How did you know that's exactly what I wanted to do?"

"Because we're made for each other." Despite his smile, Colm seemed entirely earnest. "After, we'll have the sort of weekend regular couples have." He looked rueful. "Except no sex."

Feeling much better, she had to laugh. "I'm shocked you'd want any part of being a 'regular' couple. It smacks of...well, *normal* folk." Although he'd proved he was too old-fashioned to go along with her seeing another man.

"I can be conventional," said Colm, smiling back at her.

"Is that so?" Fiona thought of Davie again. "Then I have a proposition for you."

Kerry
26

Stephen would be ringing any minute.

I set out flour, sugar, baking soda and a mixing bowl, trying to quell my anxiety about talking to him. Still trying to make sense of last week's distressing conversation, I peered through the rivulets of water trailing down the kitchen window, to watch my little flock scratching in the yard.

I sighed and pulled eggs from the fridge, feeling a familiar twinge of guilt. When I wasn't feeling torn in bits over my marriage, deceiving Judith weighed on my mind. I'd taken to buying eggs down at the Topaz near Knockferry, instead of at her shop, so she wouldn't realize the hens weren't laying. Given all the organic feed she was special-ordering for me, she had to know they were perfectly healthy. How much longer could I put her off? The phone rang.

I grabbed the receiver. "Stephen?"

"I rang earlier—you were in the garden?"

"I was at Desmond's, fixing him an early tea." I returned to the fridge to fetch buttermilk.

"Oh."

To fill the silence, I said, "Fiona's away in Dublin, so I've been looking in on him. I didn't want to work outside anyway, in the pouring rain."

I glanced at the vegetable plot I'd spent the last weeks digging out. I hadn't told Stephen I'd be raising potatoes. Else he'd know for sure I was getting even more emotionally invested in Avalon Farm.

"Fiona…right. She'll be back for that party you spoke of?"

"Yes—we'll be celebrating her birthday too." I latched onto the neutral topic. "Mam and Suz and Gwen—you remember Gwen, from Smy—" Better not mention Smythe's either. "Anyway, they're all coming and bringing the babies, and so is another local girl, Beata. Even your mam is driving over from Wicklow."

"She…uh, mentioned it."

This stilted conversation made me ache—yet there was so much I couldn't bring up. *You've never explained why you don't want me to come to Vancouver. And why is Jamie never home? Or doesn't he want to talk to me?* At night, when I crept into bed, I'd rest my hand on the empty pillow beside me. *What's gone wrong, Stephen?*

"I'm just now making a Railway Cake," I remarked, carefully *not* saying *I'm doing my own baking for the party to save money...* Suddenly, I couldn't pretend any longer. "Stephen, will you tell me what's going on?"

"What do you mean?"

I swallowed past the lump in my throat. "We're talking like strangers."

"I'm sorry," he said automatically.

"Don't be sorry!" I snapped. "For God's sake, be honest—has something happened?"

"Not at all. Things are just…the usual here. Mad." His tone was reassuring, but there was something else beneath.

"You'll be taking some time off in June, when you bring Jamie home?" I hated the pleading in my voice, but I couldn't help it. "We've got to get his school organized again, and find a temporary spot for us. Until you're back to stay."

I could hardly bear the prospect of leaving Ballydara. In fact, I'd avoided thinking about it pretty much altogether. The truth was, I couldn't quite face moving house while Stephen and I were still living apart.

"Right—my holiday," he said. "I'll make a note to talk to the partners about it."

"Make a note," I repeated. *You should already be planning it.*

"So, then, how are those girls of yours?" There was Stephen's fake-hearty voice. The one he used when he was trying to smooth over a situation. "Mary and Laura and...Grace, isn't that what you're calling some of your hens?"

I frowned. "How did you know?"

"You told me." Stephen sounded bewildered.

"No, I didn't." I'd been careful not to breathe a word to Stephen about naming the chickens, not wanting him to know how fond I was of them. "You and Desmond haven't been in touch?" I asked suspiciously.

"Why would we?" Stephen said patiently.

Desmond wasn't *that* big on gossip, but he did chat up plenty of folk in the village, like Judith and the O'Donnell ladies and the Hurley brothers... It hit me. Stephen's visits to Hurley's pub. "You and Bernard—you haven't been talking to him, have you?"

"Uh, well, every so often we email," he admitted.

"Why?" I asked baldly.

"You know how he is, so friendly and outgoing, likes to keep up with people—"

"You've had Bernard keeping tabs on me!" I paced the kitchen, the long phone cord swaying back and forth.

"I wouldn't call it that, but—"

"What *would* you call it? I can't believe this was his idea!"

"All right, it was mine," Stephen said slowly. "I wanted... needed someone there to keep an eye on you. He emails me now and then, so I know for certain you're all right."

I felt knocked for a proper loop. "I can't believe this."

"Come on, Kerry." Stephen's voice roughened. "How d'you think I feel, you up there on the farm, alone?"

"I haven't a clue, because you don't tell me!" The more I paced, the angrier I got. "How *do* you feel?"

"I didn't want you to think *I* thought you couldn't manage the farm yourself—"

"I mean, how do you *feel*? About me?"

"I...well, can't we talk about this later?"

"Here's what I've worked out. You're too busy to keep up with what I'm doing, so you've outsourced that job to Bernard. You don't have time for me to visit you and Jamie either. And since I haven't spoken to our son for weeks, you obviously can't be bothered to get him on the phone! Where is he, anyway?"

"He's actually with his friend Griffin—"

"Are you even looking after him properly? You're so devoted to your work you've made no plans about coming home. But you've plenty of time to exchange emails with Bernard! That's rich!"

"It's not like that—I can't get into it now, but I'll fill you in when I see you—"

"Don't bother." I rang off and burst into tears.

Sobbing noisily, I swiped the back of my hand against my nose and stepped to the worktop. Swirling around my mind were all the things that were too painful to ask him. *Are you deserting me? Or did I emotionally desert you first and you've never forgiven me?*

To stop my thoughts, I spooned flour into a measuring cup and whacked a knife across the top of the cup to level it. Flour flew everywhere. Then the phone rang. Of course it was Stephen. Crying, I ignored it. He gave up after seven rings, then immediately was at it again, letting the ringing go on interminably. When I couldn't stand it anymore, I lifted the handset and banged it down again.

As I tossed the flour into the bowl a cloud of particles rose to my face. I sneezed and wept harder. Stephen cared enough to check up on me, but there was something else going on...and he intended to wait two whole months to explain? Could it be he wanted to stay at the Vancouver post permanently? Jamie wanted to stay too? Or...my blood ran cold. Stephen had had an affair with a colleague?

The phone rang, *again*. I sniffed hard and picked up. "What! What have you to say for yourse—"

"Please, let's don't do this. I love you."

Stephen wasn't a great one for *I love yous*. Instantly contrite, I said in a watery voice, "I-I love you too."

"We're too far away to argue like this—it's just too bloody hard." He spoke in a rush. "After what we've been through the last year, we just *can't*."

The year we nearly lost each other. "I know." I bent my head, rubbing a knot forming between my brows. A marriage can take only so much, and we'd probably gone over our limit already.

"So come on then, don't cry. We'll sort everything, I promise. When we see each other." Stephen's voice was shaking. "If I could come home this minute, I would, but my hands are tied. Can you bear with me, just a bit longer?"

I sniffed again. "I'll try. Really, I will."

"Then…we'll talk soon, right?"

He sounded so unsure I felt a fresh spate of tears building in my chest. "Yes. I'd better go, since Desmond's coming round," I lied. I didn't want him to know I was crying again.

As I returned to baking, teardrops ran down my face to drip into the bowl. I stared down at the tiny impressions in the mound of flour. Years ago, I'd seen a lovely mystical film about a girl who was an extraordinary cook, and her emotions would be transmuted into the food she prepared. How would Fiona take it if all her party guests started crying as they ate my cake?

I grabbed some kitchen toweling and wiped my eyes. I'd no clue how things were going for Fiona this weekend in Dublin, but I was determined to make a happy day for her. Yet what I couldn't tell my friend, or anyone else, was this: even if Stephen and I loved each other, our marriage seemed to be hanging by a thread.

Fiona

27

*F*iona strolled with Davie through the Spanish Arch in Galway City. As they stopped to enjoy the view of the River Corrib in the waning evening light, she could see the green-gray dome of the Galway Cathedral across the river, and the reflection from the streetlamps shimmering on the water. The soft cotton of her long skirt brushed her legs, and the thump of Gil Killeen's bodhran still echoed in her ears.

"It's been ages since I played tourist," Fiona said as they began walking again. "In Galway, that is." *So when do I tell him about seeing Colm?* Deciding she was having too lovely a time to worry about it now, she gave Davie a teasing glance. "I have to tell you, it felt a bit surreal, there in The Quays while Gil played."

"How's that?" said Davie, threading his fingers through hers.

"Watching your double while you were next to me." The Killeen twins were identical in every sense of the word—maybe Gil's nose was a little longer, his eyebrows a bit thicker. And he'd a guardedness about him that Davie didn't. "Your brother didn't look surprised to see me."

"We don't have many secrets, Gil and myself," said Davie.

"A twin thing?"

"A friend thing," Davie said. "We've always been best mates, since we were small. I get along with my other four brothers, but not like with Gil."

"Holy Jaysus—there's six of you?" said Fiona. "Your mam had her work cut out for her."

Davie's hand tensed. "Yeah."

All right, if you're going to go narky when I bring up your mam, I won't mention her. "When I was a student," Fiona said, trying to diffuse Davie's baffling vibe, "I used to wander all over this part of the city, sketching madly. The tourists, the river and swans, the angels in the Cathedral—I must've filled dozens of sketchbooks."

As they turned into the little passageway near St. Augustine's, Davie's steps slowed. "Where are they?"

"My sketchbooks?" Surprised by a rush of grief, Fiona struggled to keep her voice even. "They...got lost." Colm's mother would have thrown them in the bin after sacking her, if not before. "If my mam was still around, she'd have saved them—" *Jaysus, there I go talking about mothers again...* "But Dad's no good at that sort of thing."

"Wait." Davie suddenly tugged on her hand, to encircle her loosely in his arms. "There's something I want you to know." In the shadows, his face was grave. "About my mother."

Fiona looked up at him, resting her hands on his broad chest. "She *is* all right?"

He nodded. "When I told you she had her own place, I didn't mention that she left our house the day after Gil and I turned fifteen."

"Oh." Fiona smoothed the front of his jacket. "Your parents—they're not divorced?" She didn't know any divorced people, even though it had been legal for years and years.

"Mam didn't believe in divorce. She wouldn't tell us why she left, and when I finally got up the nerve to ask my dad about it, he said it was none of my business. Anyway, she didn't go far— she lived in a little bungalow down the lane."

Fiona reached up to touch his cheek, picturing a much younger Davie missing his mother. "How did you take it?"

"My brothers and I were in and out every day, and often stayed there nights, in our sleeping bags. Gil and I were a right pair of eejits—we used to skulk about, trying to listen in on her phone calls, and sometimes we'd even follow her to the shops. But we never heard about or saw any other fella, or evidence of one coming round," Davie said soberly. "So we were sure it wasn't another man."

A frisson of alarm shot through Fiona. She dropped her hand. "That must've made her leaving easier."

"There was nothing easy about it." Davie's voice was rough.

Fiona's heart lurched, thinking of what he must have gone through. Even if his mother hadn't died, the rending of his parents' marriage had to feel a bit like a death. "I'm sorry— wrong thing to say."

"It's all right. Gil and I don't talk about it anymore, but I didn't want to shut you out every time someone's mother comes up." His arms tightened round her. "I don't want to have any secrets from you."

You've got to tell him about Colm right now—and our plans... "Davie," she began, but before she could speak, he dipped his head. The heat she'd felt kissing him in his truck flooded through her, with a new intensity.

As his mouth grew more insistent, she pressed herself against him. Davie drew her closer, sliding his hand to her hip. Overwhelmed by sensation, all Fiona could think of was how she wanted him, wanted to open to him, and hardly cared that they were snogging on a public street. She whispered against his mouth, "Oh God, Davie..."

He broke the kiss, breathing hard. "I...I've got to have a word with Gil."

"Now?" Fiona murmured. "Why?" *I want to stay right here and kiss you for...like, forever...*

"It won't take long." Davie released her, still keeping her hand in his, and led her purposefully toward Quay Street.

Dizzy with lust, Fiona struggled to keep up. *I'll kiss him just one more time—*then *let him know I've seen Colm.*

Kerry
28

The party was just as I pictured it. Well, almost.

My entire tribe of mammies and babies and grannies filled the sunroom. Gwen's newborn Drew dozed peacefully in his baby carrier, and my niece Ailish toddled from Suz to Mam, while Beata's little Peter seemed content to watch the action from his mother's lap. Munching on ham salad sandwiches and fruit salad, my guests seemed in great form, the hum of voices softened by the light patter of rain on the glass windows. And yet...

I'd awakened that morning with an odd ache around my heart I couldn't explain. And Fiona, the first to arrive, didn't seem quite all...there. Dressed in a skirt printed with tiny violas, she wore a vague smile as she hugged me. "You're a proper dote, to give me a party."

I tried not to cling to her. "Happy Birthday! It is happy, isn't it?"

"What?" Fiona had a faraway look. "Oh...yes. Very."

When she didn't elaborate, I asked, "Have you heard from Judith? She promised to nip in once she got her husband organized at the shop."

"I'm sure she'll turn up," Fiona said absently.

She *was* distracted. Pale too, with purple shadows beneath her eyes. When I'd seen Fiona at the shop two days ago, she'd volunteered very little about her weekend in Dublin. Her sister was grand, and so was her *friend*, with a career that was taking off in a big way. I'd wanted to ask, *but did you sleep with him?*

With Judith and her customers within hearing distance, however, *that* wasn't on. "We'll catch up after the others go, shall we?"

"Right," said Fiona. I could tell she was back to thinking of something else.

Before I could wonder what it was, in trooped Mam, carrying Ailish, with Suz brandishing a bottle of wine in each hand. "How's this for luck? I got Ailish weaned in time for your party."

I was passing around seconds of birthday cake as Suz drained her glass of wine. "Isn't May the first some kind of significant holiday? Besides May Day." She licked icing off her fingers, shooting a mischievous grin at Fiona. "And your birthday, of course."

Fiona was staring into the middle distance. "Fiona?" Suz prompted.

"Your birthday, is it, Fiona?" Mam put in. "Happy day to you."

Fiona looked startled. "I keep forgetting."

"Not keen on getting older?" Gwen looked sympathetic.

"You're a bit young for that worry," said Stephen's mother, with one of her rare smiles. Mary had been quiet through much the party, and her expression—lips pursed, brows drawn together—wasn't out of the ordinary for her either. Yet she seemed to come out of her shell around little Peter. She'd even taken Beata under her wing after a fashion (which I would have never believed if I hadn't seen it myself), fetching her a piece of cake, and a clean fork when Peter dropped the one his mother was sharing with him.

"Back in Poland, my babcia—my grandmother—she say, you never too old to *hev* good birthday," said Beata, feeding another bite of cake to Peter. "So nice to be at party for girls, dress up." She smoothed her yellow cotton frock over the curve of her stomach. "Not wear dirty jeans, like when I feed pigs."

I pulled my gaze from her tummy. "Suz, you mean Beltane, the traditional version of May Day?" Mindful of Mary's presence, I said carefully, "It's the old Celtic festival meant to encourage…um, fertility."

"That's it." Suz smiled wickedly. "Isn't that the one where couples nipped off to shag in the hedgerows?"

"Suz!" I choked on my drink. "Beltane is a celebration of *nature*."

"What's more natural than that, I'd like to know?" Suz said.

"Sure enough, there'd be a crop of babies born around the first of February," Mam put in.

"Whatevs." Suz refilled her glass and took a swig. "I'm all for going natural. What do you girls think of going outside, stripping off and doing some mad fertility rite?"

Gwen coughed on her mouthful of cake.

"Shut up, Suz!" I hissed as Mam giggled. "What will Mary think of us!"

My mother-in-law seemed unperturbed. "I think I'll pass on your Beltane dance," she said. "It's turned right filthy outside."

Fiona wore a dreamy expression. "What's that about dancing?"

Beata looked dubious. "Dance in rain? I don't like."

Mam said, "Beata, my daughter is having us on."

"Ah," said Beata, smoothing her little boy's blond head. "You all *hev* the joke."

"I'm serious," said Suz. Aislish toddled up to her mother for another bite of cake, then fell abruptly onto her nappied bum. "Come on, girls!" Suz helped Ailish back on her feet. "No one's out in this downpour—all the privacy we need."

Mam giggled again. "You lot," she nodded at Suz, Gwen, and Beata, "hardly need any help in the fertility area."

"I'd rather not be too fertile for another two or three years," said Gwen. Setting her plate aside, she took baby Drew from his carrier and put him to her breast.

Watching Ailish and Drew, the ache in my chest intensified. "The tradition would be a *little* more authentic with some men about," I said without thinking. Stephen came to my mind's eye and suddenly my face felt like it would crack.

Suz didn't respond, peering through the sunroom window. She suddenly jumped off the lounger, deftly stepping around her baby daughter. "Who says there's no blokes around? Here comes a very promising specimen."

Fiona
29

She'd been in a daze all day.

After the late evening in Galway City, Fiona managed to arrive at the party on time. She found herself daydreaming though Kerry's lunch, until Suz's *promising specimen* jolted her back to the present. She craned her neck to look outside. Davie's Isuzu! She tensed in her chair.

A decisive rap sounded at the door. "I'll get it!" Suz dashed out. Seconds later, she reappeared in the doorway with Davie. His jacket was damp, and raindrops sparkled in his brown hair.

Fiona drank in the sight of him. "Hi." She had to cling to the seat of her chair to keep from rushing into his arms.

Davie met her eyes, the warmth in his making her tremble. Holding a large parcel wrapped in brown paper, he swiped at the moisture on his cheeks. "I've a little something for Fiona's birthday."

A *gift*? "For me?"

"I think Kerry said no presents, *plez*." Beata sounded mortified. "I should go now, come back with one?" Her little boy yawned.

"No, no," Davie said, his voice kind. "It's not a proper gift anyway."

Fiona thought he'd be awkward in a room full of women but he looked entirely at ease. "No one else brought presents, Beata."

"That's right," Kerry said quickly. "Davie didn't know he wasn't meant to bring anything. Fiona, you'll take him into the kitchen?"

Fiona rose to her feet, not sure if she could trust herself to be alone with him. "Davie?"

He followed her, setting his parcel on the worktop. "I know, the timing's not great, my interrupting the party, but this afternoon was the only…uh, chance I'd have to see you."

Touched and nervous at the same time, Fiona made no move toward the parcel. "You shouldn't have gotten me anything." *Because I haven't been honest with you, and you don't deserve that…*He hadn't mentioned Colm since the day they'd fetched Kerry's chickens. Surely Davie hadn't forgotten about him?

"It's not much," said Davie. "C'mon, then, open it."

The entreaty in his dark eyes made Fiona feel all melty again. "My family's not big on birthday gifts," she admitted. "So this is a right treat." She began tearing at the cellotape, but her short nails were useless.

Davie covered her hands to still them. "I've an ulterior motive."

Longing streaked through her, simply feeling his hard palms on her hands. "What—you want to get into my…good graces?" She blushed. *Jaysus, if that's not a come-on I don't know what is.*

Removing his hands, he held her gaze a moment longer, a smile lurking in his eyes. "I hope so." He eased a penknife from his pocket, opened it, and neatly slit the butcher paper. "Okay, have at it."

Feeling more self-conscious than before, Fiona began unwrapping his offering, then swallowed hard. "Oh, Davie…" It was large sketchbook, the high quality sort found only in art supply shops.

"There's more," said Davie.

Fiona tore at the bottom of the parcel to find a box of drawing pencils in dozens of colors. "Not a proper gift, you say? It's perfect!" She laughed joyously, wanting to hug the sketchbook. "I've so missed just messing about, drawing."

"I thought maybe you did." Davie extracted the box of pencils. "I actually saw you once, working in the back of the shop."

"Putting away stock?" Fiona was confused.

"No," said Davie. "You were drawing. Carrots or something, but you'd a…a *different* look on your face."

"What kind of different?"

"I don't know. Like you were dreaming. In another place entirely."

Now she *really* wanted to kiss him. "Probably wishing I was somewhere *not* having to make adverts of carrots."

"Well," said Davie, "now you can draw whatever you like."

She stepped closer. *Just a thank you kiss—no one will see, from the sunroom…* Then it struck her, what this gift really meant. That he wasn't only out for a good time, that she was important to him. And that she'd better rethink the whole two blokes thing. "What do you see in me anyway?" She made her voice light. "You could snap your fingers, have your pick of sweet young things—"

"I don't want a sweet young thing," he said simply. "I want you."

His sweet, earnest passion tore at her heart. Still trying to fake her way through this, she said, "Aren't you eloquent, now? You'll really turn a girl's head—"

"Don't." He put his hand on her arm, his dark eyes intent. "Don't make sport of me, all right? I'm not a kid, and I'm not playing about."

Instantly, horribly sorry, Fiona stared down at his strong hand. How could she want him when Colm could give her a bigger life? A perfect life? She said a little despairingly, "I don't know what to…to *do* about you. You deserve someone younger, someone who will…" *Commit to only you…*

"And you deserve someone who wants to make you happy." His Adam's apple moved. "Which is myself."

Fiona couldn't help it. She reached up to kiss his cheek. "You have."

They stood for a moment, neither of them moving. Then Davie gently set her away from him. "Then maybe you'll go out with me again next weekend," he said, a gleam in his eyes.

Before she could answer, he left the kitchen to stop in the sunroom doorway. "Grand seeing you all." Without another glance at Fiona, he let himself out.

Overcome with bittersweet emotion, Fiona didn't want to face the others. She dallied in the kitchen, wiping stray crumbs off the worktop. Postponing telling Davie about Colm, about next weekend, was only making her feel more ambivalent.

Only this morning, she'd been filled with misgivings about her proposition to Colm—inviting him to Galway. Should she put him off? But the date was set, and she'd have all week to sort out if she wanted to stop seeing him. As Desmond finished the breakfast she'd been too agitated to eat, she said, "My f-friend Colm Dwyer would like to meet you—take us to dinner in the city. Saturday next all right?"

Desmond took a long time to answer. "These days, I've nothing in the way of leaving the farm."

He was talking about the animals, of course. "Great," said Fiona. She felt selfish, not wanting to deal with her dad's grief, but lately her own emotions were so all over the place. "Colm's already got it on his calendar."

"Ah, yes. Those busy city blokes have full calendars, don't they," her dad said.

"Colm *is* running a business, Dad," she said evenly.

He fiddled with the sugar bowl. "You're sure you want to do this?"

Fiona looked at her father more closely. He didn't mean, *be with Colm?* "You don't want to have dinner with him?"

"He's all right, I'm sure, but there's his family—they didn't treat you well, Fiona-girl."

"Colm says they'll come round," she said automatically. *Jaysus, I've really stepped in it now. Why should I want the Dwyers to accept me if Colm and I aren't a couple?*

"But Davie—" He checked himself.

Her stomach twisted. "We're just friends, Dad." *God should strike me dead for that one.*

"Didn't you say it was Colm you were friends with?" said her dad, looking troubled.

Why did I ever think I could manage this? She'd no honest way to reply. "It's all right—Davie knows about Colm." *Sort of...* Unable to meet her dad's eyes, Fiona had said, "Oh, look at the time—I'd better be off to Kerry's."

Now, Fiona stepped back into the sunroom, feeling self-conscious. "Sorry to have interrupted things."

Suz's gaze was curious. "So...who's your man?"

"Um..." *Boyfriend? Or boytoy?* Fiona tried not to blush. "A friend."

"Davie very nice," Beata spoke up. "Piece of house fall down, he come over with Bernard and fix for me."

"That's a lovely big parcel he brought for you," Suz observed. "For a *friend*. Give us a look, won't you?"

"Suz, stop teasing Fiona," said Kerry. "She said he's a friend, so please shut your gob."

"He bring gift to party," Beata said, "to show us girls he your man."

"He's not my man." Fiona could feel heat crawling up her neck. "Is that bottle of wine around? I'll top up everyone's glass—"

"Kerry used to have a guy friend I thought was ridey," said Suz. Fiona saw Kerry wince. "But this bloke's got him beat all round. Anyway, I've always thought a girl can't have too many friends—"

"There's someone out in the road," Kerry's mother-in-law interrupted, gazing through the window.

Fiona said, "It must be my boss Judith driving up?" Thank God—she couldn't talk about Davie any more.

"Not in a car. It's a girl," said Mary. "She looks soaked to the skin."

Kerry
30

I rushed from the sunroom, relieved. Suz, mildly scuttered, was being more outrageous than usual. I was happier still, *not* to be watching the three contented mammies and their little ones. I opened the front door for a better look. A young woman, her auburn hair plastered to her head, stood on the side of the road. "It's one of my neighbors."

I grabbed the umbrella I kept by the door and hurried down the drive. My hen Laura, the most curious of the lot, was quickly at my heels.

"How'd you get out of your pen, you rascal?" I quickly sidestepped to avoid tripping on her, then broke into a run as the girl sank onto the low stone wall next to the road.

"Mrs. Carpenter—Aislin?" I called over the *whissht* of the leafed-out oak tree. I was nodding acquaintances with Aislin Carpenter, who lived at Ballydara Lodge, up the road. "You're not ill?"

Aislin shook her head, her pretty features drooping. Approaching her, I saw she was shivering, her lips blue with cold. "Please, come inside."

She made no move to rise. "Not…quite up to it," she said. "Feeling a bit pukey, actually."

She did look rather green around the gills. I turned toward the house, waving at the sunroom window to summon help. Mary of all people was already rushing out of the farmhouse, her unzipped raincoat flapping in the wind. Reaching us, she took Aislin's elbow. "Kerry, take her other arm."

"Sorry about this," Aislin mumbled as Mary and I trundled her up the footpath. "It wasn't raining this hard when I left my house."

Now two hens had got underfoot. Opening the front door, I pushed them firmly away with my heel as Mary got Aislin inside. Making sure neither chicken was trying to sneak in, I shut the door.

Aislin's wet clothes dripped puddles on the floor. "Oh, look at the mess I've made."

Mam, Suz, and Fiona crowded around, Beata looking uncertainly from the sunroom doorway. "You'll have some tea?" said Fiona. "I'll make a fresh pot."

"She'll want wine," Suz diagnosed. "Mam, you'll open that third bottle?"

"She needs to get out of those wet clothes first," I said. "Aislin, let's get you upstairs, to my bigger bathroom."

As I set aside the umbrella, Mary shrugged out of her coat. She actually left it on the *floor* to help me escort Aislin up the stairs. "Before you catch your death, Miss," she said firmly. We waited outside the bathroom door while Aislin undressed, then I handed her my spare dressing gown through the door, along with a towel for her hair.

A moment later Aislin opened the door, her head swathed in terrycloth. "I'm so terribly sorry, intruding like this."

"It's no bother," said Mary, leading the way downstairs.

"Kerry, I've been wanting to meet you properly," Aislin went on, carefully descending the stairs, "but I've really mucked it up. Ben always teases that I'm a terminal klutz, and now I've become a social disaster."

"Don't be silly," I said. "And mind the hem of my dressing gown, it's a little long for you."

"Thank God you were home," she said, grasping the railing. "My mind's a right sieve these days—I don't know how else I could have forgotten to bring an umbrella."

"You'll stay for a bit, have a rest?" I asked. "I'll find you some dry things."

"Lovely," she said. "You'd think after a year in Galway I'd be prepared for the weather, especially with being—"

Aislin broke off, letting Mary and me guide her onto the sunroom chaise. Fiona fetched a throw for her lap. "Really, I'm not an invalid," Aislin protested.

Suz said, "Have a glass of wine."

"I think she'll want tea," said Mary and poured her a cup.

"You're spoiling me," said Aislin, accepting the tea. "No wine for me, thanks."

"Come on," said Suz, "it's medicinal. Besides, we're celebrating Beltane. The fertility yoke, you know."

"I think we've all the right props," said Gwen. "There's eggs." As she gestured toward the hens outside, I didn't mention I'd yet to see an egg. "And lots of babies."

"With another on the way," said Mam, smiling at Beata.

"Then I've come to the right place." Aislin glanced uncertainly at all of us. "Because I'm pregnant too."

My nose tingled. Yet another happy young mammy, another new baby on the way. Swallowing past the lump in my throat, I saw Mary watching me, her gaze keen.

"Congratulations!" Suz exclaimed, already topping up wineglasses. "Beata, have another lemonade, won't you?"

My smile wobbled as I joined the well-wishing and toasts— even Mary chimed in, holding a full glass.

"Ben's over the moon, but we haven't told anyone yet, not even our little boy," Aislin confessed. She pulled the towel off her head and swished her fingers through her damp hair. "You never want to put the news out too soon."

Feeling a wrench, I knew exactly what she was talking about. Gwen and Suz had both waited to share their pregnancies until their third month in.

"Anyway," said Aislin, "can you keep my news to yourselves?"

I was no stranger to secrets, especially about babies, but I could hardly mention that. "No worries," I said, trying to sound upbeat. "It's a good job Judith wasn't here though, because Bernard would somehow worm it out of her."

"And the Ballydara grapevine would be off to the races," said Fiona. She seemed less spacey since Aislin's arrival. "Your son would be hearing about his new sibling from the postman."

"Unless your neighbors find out by osmosis," said Suz. "There's enough estrogen emanating from this house to shout the news from the rooftop."

"The rain's eased up, I see, and I'm feeling tons better," said Aislin. "I'd better get along so I can nab Ben the second he and Kevin get home. Let him know it's time to spill the beans."

"I'll not even let you *think* of walking," declared Mam. "We'll give you a ride home, and leave as soon as you're dressed, shall we?"

After Aislin had changed into one of my skirts and a warm jumper, she and Beata exchanged morning sickness stories. I pretended not to listen, but really, who was I kidding.

Beata yawned. "Time for afternoon nap, I think." She smoothed her little son's hair. "Peter very good when I have a sleep, stays in playbox—no, what do you call?"

"Playpen?" supplied Suz.

"Yes." Beata slung Peter onto her hip. "Eddie's mother give to me. He play with toys, I have lie-down."

At least Beata wasn't entirely alone, but I felt her isolation as if it were my own as I got out my umbrella again. I held it over Beata and her son as we walked to her Mini.

"Thank you for *hev* me and Peter. I feel like part of..." Beata wiggled her hand at the house. "You know, so many nice peoples."

"Thank you so much for coming," I managed, tension and anxiety thick in my chest. I didn't know why, only that I was feeling so much, too much, that I couldn't put into words.

I returned inside to find Fiona slipping on her coat, frowning. "I'll pop down to the shop," she said. "Find out why Judith didn't make it."

I gave her a hug and whispered, "You seemed not quite yourself today. Is it...Davie?"

Fiona returned my hug, then fussed with her zipper. "We'll have a chat later."

Suz appeared. "Fiona, you've forgiven my cheek? About your man."

"He's not my—" Fiona's face relaxed. "You're incorrigible, aren't you?"

"Oh yeah," said Suz, laughing. They exchanged a quick hug, and Fiona headed for the kitchen, presumably to fetch her gift. I heard the back door close.

Beata's and Fiona's departure seemed to signal the end of the party. "It's been grand," said Mam, embracing my mother-in-law.

Surprisingly, Mary didn't shy away. "Such lovely babies here today," she said, giving Ailish and Gwen's baby another grandmotherly look. "Puts me in mind of when our Jamie was a wee one, doesn't it, Anne?"

Another wave of emotion rolled through me. Suddenly I was missing Jamie so badly I could have wept. I somehow pulled myself together, following Mam as she shepherded her small flock to Suz's car. "I'll drive," she told Suz.

Handing Mam the key fob, Suz hiccoughed. "I wasn't going to push to get behind the wheel." She buckled Ailish into her safety seat as Gwen secured Drew in his, then the two of them somehow wedged themselves into the car.

Aislin slid into the front seat. "Kerry, I don't know how to thank you. I'll return your things as soon as I can."

Suz shifted uncomfortably, squished up against Gwen for the short drive to the Lodge. "Put your pedal to the metal, Mam, to get to Aislin's as soon as you can." She lowered the window. "Gwen and I can't breathe."

"Save the oxygen for the babies." With a tremulous smile, I waved to all of them.

Suz looked up at me. "I always thought Mary was such a dragon," she said in a low voice. "But she's not really, is she?" As I shook my head, my sister gave me a significant look. "In case you're thinking of the future, she's very promising granny material for your second round."

Stepping back, I let my eyes linger on my niece's little face. Then it hit me. My baby, the one Stephen and I had lost, would have been due right about now. Watching Mam painstakingly turn the car around, tears blurred my vision. Grief came over me in waves, and I wanted so badly to weep, but there was Mary, waiting for me. I wished if anyone had stayed behind, it would've been my own mother. Maybe I would have found the courage to tell her what I'd kept secret from her all these months.

My life had been so full lately I'd hardly thought of the miscarriage. Yet as I trudged back to the house, all I could think of was Ailish's proud grin as she stood by herself, Drew's newborn grunts and sighs, and Peter's small arms clinging to Beata's neck. *You've got to pull yourself together, at least until your mother-in-law leaves.*

I found Mary in the kitchen, leaning against the worktop, her mouth in a straight line. Dread filled me—I knew well that wrath-of-God look. "Is…everything okay?"

"It's about Stephen," she said. "And Jamie. I couldn't leave without saying what's on my mind."

My chest, already clenching with grief, tightened even more. "Has Stephen said something to you?" *That he hasn't shared with me?*

"Not…straight out, but I'm hardly sleeping nights, I'm that worried."

I clenched my hands. Whatever it was, I would've wanted to hear it from Stephen—but his mother would have to do. I was desperate to ask if he'd hinted that he wanted to stay in Vancouver. Or was Jamie ill? Was that why Stephen wouldn't put him on the line? "For God's sake, Mary, please!"

"Stephen's very troubled, I think." She clasped her hands, her knuckles showing white. "It's nothing he's said, but I'm his mam, I know when he's not right."

I was really frightened now. "What does his dad think?"

"Brian's worried too, but he can't get an answer out of Stephen either." She looked more vulnerable than I'd ever seen her. "Maybe he'll tell you what's on his mind. I know it must be early in Vancouver, he might be sleeping, but if you'd ring him…"

I was already reaching for the phone, my hand shaking. So I hadn't imagined Stephen's stonewalling last time we'd talked. Pressing the multi-digit number, I kept hitting wrong keys and having to start over.

Mary sidled beside me and actually took my hand. I gave hers a grateful squeeze as the line picked up. "Kerry!" Stephen's voice was raspy. "This is a strange time to ring—what's wrong?"

The tears building in my throat suddenly threatened to explode. "I can't bear it!" Mary's grip on my hand tightened. "I can't stand living this way any longer—I want you and Jamie home. Right now. So we can start fresh." I gulped. "Start a bab—"

"Call you right back." The line went dead.

Fiona

31

*T*he rain had dwindled to sprinkles by the time Fiona left the party, carrying her new sketchbook tucked inside her coat. *As soon as I'm home, I'll draw...oh, who cares? Mam's teapot! I'm going to create again!*

Her mind spinning with ideas, she was nearly home before noticing the pickup in the drive. What was Davie doing here? She hurried into the cottage, tossing the sketchbook onto the kitchen table. "Dad, are you okay?"

She stopped in the front room doorway. There was her dad, watching telly with Davie on the couch, as calm as you please. Desmond glanced at her, confused. "What are you on about, girl? We're grand, just watching a bit of sport."

Davie didn't take his eyes from the screen. Fiona looked at him uncertainly. "You said you'd things to do today."

He finally shifted his gaze to her, but there was no trace of his ardent expression at Kerry's. "Did I?" He yawned, covering his mouth with the back of his hand.

"It's why you stopped by Kerry's, you may recall," she said.

He rose to his feet, making the room seem smaller than usual. "I'd better get to it, then. Cheers, Des."

"I'll walk you out," said Fiona. *Sort this odd mood of yours.*

"Don't bother." Davie brushed past her to the door.

He seemed a different man entirely from two hours ago. Fiona banged outside after him. He was already climbing into his pickup. "Wait!"

"What for?" He slammed the door.

Fiona rapped on the driver's window so hard her knuckled smarted. "What's with you?" Finally Davie rolled down the window. "If you want to give me a bollacking for something I've done, get it over with!"

He stared through the windscreen as if she wasn't there. "I don't want to give out at you."

"Then why are you acting like such a childish brat?"

He turned to her, a somber look on his face. "Maybe because that's what I am. Just a kid, right? Compared to that Colm bloke."

Fiona could've bitten her tongue out. Trying to backtrack, she said, "Really, I didn't mean to say that, we can work this out—"

"No. I realized you want a different kind of life than I do. So it's a no-go."

"You mean…seeing me?"

"Come on." His voice was rough. "It won't work, not when you've another bloke."

Dad, how could you have told him? "Did my dad say something about Colm coming to Galway?"

"He obviously didn't know your big date was meant to be a secret," Davie sneered.

"You were the one who said Colm should meet my dad properly!" Fiona rounded the bonnet and without an invitation, climbed into the passenger seat. "You can't leave like this, not after—I mean, without explaining."

"You want an explanation?" Davie asked curtly. "After I went to Kerry's, I stopped in at Murphy's shop. Turns out, you'd gone to Dublin last weekend. To see him, right? And now he's visiting you."

Fiona was stricken. *Why didn't I tell Davie sooner?* "I was g-going to mention it," she stammered. "I promise."

Davie squeezed the steering wheel, hard. "I'm not sure your promises mean anything."

"Nothing happened," Fiona rushed on. "I stayed at my sister's—swear to God."

"'Swear to God,'" Davie repeated. "I'm sure my dad must've done that when he married my mother."

"What have your parents to do with anything?"

He was silent for so long it was like he'd gone into a trance.

"Please," Fiona said. "Tell me."

"I told you my mam left." He didn't look at her. "A couple of months later, my dad took me and Gil with him to the pub. He'd had a few too many pints, and some bloke started singing 'Carrickfergus' or something. Dad got all morose—sloppy even. I'd never seen him so jarred."

"I imagine he was devastated," Fiona murmured, for something to say.

Davie didn't seem to have heard her. "When I told him it was time to go home, he says, 'No—not until I tell you about your mam.' Turns out, Mam left because she discovered he'd a woman on the side, and had for years. Eileen."

"I'm...I'm so sor—"

"I wanted to hit him, call him a gobshite, though he's a massive bloke. For all I knew he might smack me three ways to Sunday right there in the pub. Not that he ever really hit us, but how could he have done that to my mother? Hurt us all?"

Fiona's heart clutched. "Davie, if only you'd told me..."

"Dad had tears in his eyes." Davie suddenly looked years older. "He told me he didn't blame Mam for leaving, that he still loved her. 'But I love Eileen too,' he said. 'You won't hold this against your old dad, will you?' I still wanted to hit him. But I felt sorry for him." A muscle tightened in his jaw. "Maybe now you'll see I'll have no part of being pissed about while you play with your backdoor guy."

"He's not my backdoor—"

"Yeah?" A short, mirthless laugh broke from him. "I'm the one you want to sneak around with?"

Fiona felt torn in two. "Why did you keep seeing me when you knew Colm was in the picture?"

He didn't answer.

"Please, Davie...I'll ring him, cancel his visit—"

"I wanted you too much to stay away, can you believe it? What a bloody eejit I was!" Despite his sharp words, he looked defenseless.

"But you weren't—you aren't." Fiona wanted to touch him but she was afraid he'd recoil from her. "Please believe me, I never wanted to hurt you."

"I thought I could wait it out until you got this other guy out of your system. Then there'd be no holding back. Jaysus! I can't believe I was so pathetic." Before she could speak, he turned toward her, his face like stone. "Now I'll ask you to leave my lorry."

Fiona knew then it was too late. She'd spoiled everything. Wanting to weep, she quietly lifted the latch and slid out. "Maybe you'll want your gift back."

He turned the ignition. "Keep it. A goodbye present." He leaned over and pulled the door shut. Then he backed out of the drive so fast he nearly hit the fence.

As Fiona watched in shock, Davie turned onto the road, rocks spewing beneath the tires as he tore out of sight. To keep from bursting into tears, she savagely kicked a stone in the footpath. *I knew I wouldn't be any good at juggling two men, but I'd done it anyway! What the hell is wrong with me?*

If she hadn't already turned her life to crap, Dad had put his oar in. Clenching her fists so hard her nails bit into her palms, Fiona marched into the cottage.

Whatever he's told Davie, I'll have it out of him right now.

Kerry

32

$\mathcal{I}$ dropped the handset in shock. "Stephen rang off on me." Pulling my hand from Mary's, I sank into a chair.

Mary replaced the handset with a *clack*. "The line must've gotten disconnected, those satellites can be terribly dodgy—"

"No." I began to cry. How could Stephen be so *heartless*, just when I'd gotten the courage to mention a baby? "Just—bang! No goodbye."

"It's not what it seems." She patted my back awkwardly. "It can't be."

Detecting her uncertainty, I buried my face in my hands, my sobs loud in my ears. Before long, though, I grew too embarrassed to be caterwauling in front of Mary. Snuffling, I could hear the soft tick-tock of the kitchen clock, ticking down the interminable minutes since Stephen had ended the call. If it had been a mistake, he would've rung back by now. Clearly, whatever was going on with Stephen had to be worse than I'd ever thought.

"There now." Feeling Mary's touch on my shoulder I lifted my head, feeling like it weighed far more than my neck could support. She handed me a tea towel. "A woman can't face things with a wet face."

I blew my nose, bemused. *Stephen always said you never cry.* "Mary, you'd better get on the road," I said dully. "If you leave now you can get to Wicklow before dark."

"I'm not going anywhere," she said. "Not until we find out what's wrong with Stephen."

"It seems that he's made a decision about me—about us." I swallowed down another spurt of grief. "Without saying exactly what he means to do. Which is so *typical*," I added bitterly. That was Stephen's specialty—keeping himself to himself.

"But he can't have meant—" The phone rang.

Mary lunged for it before I could move. Her eyes actually grew red. "Stephen! What have you to say for yourself? Is your work so important that you disrespect your own wife—"

She stopped abruptly, her eyes going wide, and held out the phone. "He wants you."

Oh, if only he still does. I reached for the handset, my fingers stiff. "Y-yes?"

"Listen to me." Stephen's voice was terse. "I love you. Things aren't...good here. It would take too long to explain, but—"

"Try, anyway! I can't go on, not knowing."

"I will, as soon as I see you. I've just phoned up my boss, sent out a round of emails for a meeting first thing with the whole team."

"What about?" My voice quavered.

"Whatever happens, I'm coming home. *We're* coming home."

It's all right, my heart sang as I wheeled my bike out of the barn. Everything's all right.

Late afternoon sun peeked through the clouds, making rainbows of the water still dripping from my apple trees and the big oak out front. Cycling down the Ballydara road, I couldn't wait to tell Fiona my news.

Mary left soon after Stephen's phone call. Her step seemed as light as mine as I walked her to her car. "Did Stephen give you a definite date for leaving Vancouver?" she asked.

"Not yet—he'll ring as soon as he knows." I touched her arm. "Thank you for staying. I could never have gotten through this without you."

She stopped as we approached the oak tree. "That's what...mothers are for."

She seemed so different from the intimidating presence she'd been my entire married life. So...approachable. It was almost absurd that she knew more of my secrets than my own mam. Suddenly, feeling blotto after all the careening emotions of the afternoon, I wanted to tell her the only one I had left. "Before you go—there's something I want you to know. I think Stephen would too."

My voice halting, I told her how we'd longed for baby, only the years had flown by and we still hadn't tried to conceive. "Then last summer, while my mam was dealing with her cancer, I'd fallen pregnant."

Mary's face blanched.

"I was so stressed, looking after her, that I hadn't realized it. Two months on, I miscarried. I took it hard. But Stephen was absolutely shattered."

"And he buried himself in his work, didn't he." Mary grasped the rope of the swing as if for support. "You and Stephen—what you've been through." Her chin trembled. "It feels a small miracle that you've sorted yourselves."

"It won't be all smooth sailing, Mary." Saying it, I felt a tiny blot on my happiness. "Moving house back to Dublin, getting reestablished there."

Mary released the rope, and we continued on to her car. "They're only details."

Don't they say the devil is in them? I thought, and the small blot seemed to expand. As Mary and I said goodbye, I wouldn't let myself think about what would happen to Avalon Farm. Instead, I let myself anticipate sleeping in Stephen's arms, sharing our lives again.

Reaching the Whelan's, I leaned my bike against the fence, rejuvenated by the fresh air. When I knocked, no one answered. Perhaps Desmond was napping? And Fiona had gone out with Davie? I'd turned to leave when I heard a shuffling noise. Desmond opened the door.

"Fiona's left." He looked defeated.

"She's not with Davie?"

"He was here when she came home from the party, and they

must've argued. Because he drove away like the wee man himself was after him." Desmond seemed even more distressed. "When she came back in, face like a thundercloud, I thought I was in for it. But out she stormed, taking Davie's present with her. I hope she'll not fling it into the bin."

"That doesn't sound like Fiona." I was genuinely concerned now.

"Sure, I put my foot in my mouth. I thought I could make things right for her, but..." he spread his hands in a helpless gesture. "I should've stayed out of her affairs."

Had he mentioned Colm to Davie? "Fiona was going to check on Judith. I'll let you know."

Cycling down to the village, I went straight to the shop, hardly looking at Fiona's posters of rosy rhubarb stalks. I found Judith behind the counter staring down at her open account book. As she raised her head, I saw her perm was rather lopsided, as if she hadn't brushed her hair that day. "Kerry! I'm sorry I missed the party. Today of all days, Padraig's dodgy heart decided to act up."

"He's okay?" Judith had mentioned her husband's angina before, though Fiona had privately told me he was a bit of a hypochondriac.

"Just a spell, thank God," said Judith. "He has his tablets."

I made sympathetic noises, and told her she'd been missed. "Is Fiona about?"

Judith shook her head. "Might she have gone round to Hurley's with Davie?"

So Davie's pursuit of Fiona was common knowledge. "Thanks, I'll try there." It wasn't for me to say the pair of them were on the outs.

I popped my head into the pub, in case Fiona had been troubled enough to have a one-off drink in the afternoon. No. Then I peeked behind the shop, to see if she was hiding out for a weep like she'd done two months before. I even walked up to St. MacDara's in the super-unlikely event she'd gone up for Saturday confession. Still no sign of her.

I cycled back up the hill, pedaling past the Whelan's, then

stopped at the foot of my drive, biting my lip. If I didn't keep searching I'd only fret.

The road was steeper past Avalon farm, the reason I'd never biked this far. The sight of the greening pastures and the wild fuchsia in the hedgerows full of buds made me wish I'd come sooner. In the distance, downslope, I saw what looked like a peat bog. My own plot of turf would likely be there, but with Stephen coming back I'd never get to harvest any.

I rounded a curve to find a herd of golden-brown Jersey cows grazing contentedly. On the low stone wall bordering the road sat Fiona.

Fiona

33

"*I*'ve been hunting for you *everywhere*," said a familiar voice.

Fiona jerked up her head, her hand stilling to see Kerry clamber off her bicycle. She swiftly closed the cover of her sketchbook. A shame she'd no way to hide her face. "Dad sent you to fetch me, I suppose?"

"I came on my own." Kerry leaned her bike against the wall. "Your dad was rather beside himself, though."

Fiona sighed. "He would be, after seeing Davie take off like a bat out of hell." She fidgeted with her charcoal pencil. "I'm sorry I've worried you both."

Kerry sat beside her and touched the sketchbook. "Davie's gift?"

Fiona nodded, reaching into her coat pocket to show Kerry the box of pencils. "These too."

"Gorgeous," Kerry commented, and waited a beat. "You've been crying."

Fiona searched her friend's face. Her eyes were swollen. Had she been having a weep too? Before she could ask, Kerry said, "You and Davie—you had words?"

"More than that," said Fiona, an ache building in her chest again.

"Your dad implied it was his fault."

Fiona slung her sketchbook onto the wall and jumped to her feet. "Oh, I wanted to blame him. He let Davie know that Colm would be visiting Galway next week." She kicked at a tussock of grass. "So of course it's on him, that Davie's gone off me," she said sarcastically. "As soon as Davie left I was set to royally give out at Dad for interfering."

"I think he meant well," Kerry said.

"With my brother Niall not coming home, I knew why Dad had palled up with Davie, going for this matchmaking bit, the likes of which he'd never done for my brothers or sisters. I wanted to accuse him of throwing me at Davie so I'd want to stay at the farm and look after him." Her eyes *would* keeping filling with tears. She dashed them away impatiently.

"I wouldn't have thought your dad could be quite that…well, Machiavellian."

"Dad hasn't a selfish bone in his body. I had to face that it was *me* who'd ruined everything—I should never have gone out with Davie, started…liking him, when I was involved with Colm. It was just so *wrong*."

Kerry twisted her hands together. "I feel responsible—it was me who led you astray, encouraged you to see both of them."

"Please don't," Fiona said immediately. "You've helped me…I don't know. Be braver. More true to myself." She was silent for a moment. "Still, when Davie showed interest in me, *and* Colm wanted me back, I was so bloody *full* of myself. 'C'mon Fiona, embrace being free, take chances, be a wild artist girl again!' But you know what I was? Full of shite!"

"You're not—"

"I am. I knew in my heart I wasn't the sort who could deceive people, keep track of what lies I told who and when."

"I'm sure you haven't really *lied* to anyone," Kerry said.

"Lies of omission are still lies. All I've done is hurt everyone involved." Fiona thumped back down on the low wall and bowed her head. "Davie hates me now."

"Oh, Fiona." Kerry put her arm round her. "I'm so sorry."

Fiona sniffed hard. "I've been trying to tell myself it's for the best—now I'm free to be with Colm. No more of this eejit 'torn between two lovers' and all that. But I can't make myself believe it."

"Still, if Colm loves you…"

"Why isn't that enough?" Fiona raised her gaze to Kerry's. "Only weeks ago, I was sure I loved him too. But Davie..." She leaned her head onto Kerry's shoulder and let the tears come.

Kerry patted her back. "I'm sure it'll be all right, in the end."

After a few minutes, Fiona straightened, lifting her skirt to eyes to dry her eyes. "Davie makes me feel like I did when I was younger, like I should grab life with both hands—it's too short to wait for what you want."

"A grand way to live," said Kerry.

"I should say, he *made* me feel. Past tense." Fiona's heart squeezed with grief. She wondered how she could feel so bereft. One date was hardly an epic love affair.

"And Colm?"

Fiona took a deep breath. "For so long I was sure he was the *one*—that we were completely right for each other. And if only we could be together, my life would be complete."

"Rather like a good marriage," said Kerry.

"Then along comes Davie, and suddenly I'm doubting every feeling I ever had for Colm." Davie's face rose again in her mind's eye. "After knowing Davie, the prospect of a life with Colm feels...tame. Comfortable." She dabbed her face with her skirt again. *When I want sparks—fire.*

"But you're young, you can still find—" Kerry broke off. "There I go, sounding like someone's granny again. What I mean is, you never know what's around the next corner." She gave Fiona one more comforting pat and stood up. "So, what's next?"

Fiona forced a smile and rose too. "I'm taking Dad to Galway Saturday next for dinner with Colm, just three of us. Then...we'll see. Maybe I'll spend another weekend in Dublin. And be with Colm, properly this time. Nothing's stopping me."

"Why not?" Kerry said lightly. "But I'd better go. I promised your dad I'd let him know when I found you." She stepped toward her bike.

"Kerry—wait."

Her friend looked at her inquiringly. "I noticed before, that your eyes are a bit red," said Fiona, shamefaced. "I was too full of my own dramas to say anything."

"I'm surprised I can see out of them," said Kerry wryly. "I had a cloudburst after the party—I rang Stephen."

"The pair of you are okay?" Fiona asked.

"Much better." Kerry wore a tender smile. "He'll be home in a few days."

"Now there's a new development—you can tell me about it on the way home." She gazed at the pasture with an odd reluctance to leave. "Earlier, I felt I'd been such a cow it was only right to spend some time with our old herd."

Kerry glanced at the animals. "These were yours?"

"Some of them," Fiona said. "I still miss them, a bit."

"I thought the country wasn't your thing," said Kerry.

"So did I." *Maybe I'd have been happier here, if I'd been creating instead of denying myself.* "Back to the cows—I'd never tell Dad I was rather fond of them. He grieves for his girls enough for both of us."

"Could be," said Kerry, "that he'll feel better if you show him your drawing. Was sketching the cows therapeutic?"

"I wasn't drawing cows." Fiona hesitated, then picked up the sketchbook and lifted the cover.

"Oh." Kerry examined the drawing. "Did you...?"

"Yes," said Fiona.

Kerry
34

$\mathcal{I}$ paced the corridor outside the customs hall at Dublin Airport, practically hyperventilating. Mam, sitting on a nearby bench holding Ailish, watched me sympathetically. "Try to settle down, love," she suggested, though I could see the tension in her own face. "You know how long these queues can be."

I'd asked Mam and Suz to come with me for my reunion with Stephen and Jamie. If something really narky was going on with my husband, I didn't want to face it without reinforcements. Even if Suz was hardly worked up—she'd taken a table in the open seating section not far from Mam, had a coffee and was now madly thumbing her phone screen. Not quite the support I'd hoped for.

"Kerry!" Suz called over. "Pull yourself together, will you? They'll be here any second."

I scanned the crowds of people streaming by, partially silhouetted by the light from the nearby windows. "How do you know? I can't see them."

"Crikey." She waved her mobile. "You've heard of texting?"

Then suddenly, there was Stephen, looking straight at me, a quizzical smile on his lips. He dropped his case in the middle of the crowd and held out his arms. I ran to him, not caring whose way we were in, and wrapped my arms around his neck. "I can't believe it," I whispered. "You're here—you're finally home."

Releasing him, I saw how haggard he looked. I wanted so badly to kiss away the fatigue and stress in his face. Then I noticed the tall boy at his side with a huge rucksack slung over his shoulder, mobile phone in his hand.

"I was wondering when you'd get round to noticing me," Jamie teased.

I released Stephen to fling my arms around Jamie and the backpack, then suddenly Mam and Suz were pressing hugs on the new arrivals, Ailish getting a bit crushed in the scrum.

"Here," said Stephen, picking up his briefcase to usher our little party off to one side. "Let's get out of the way."

I stood back to gaze at my son. Jamie seemed even taller than he had in March, his hands and feet no longer so out of proportion. His complexion was clear and tanned—all that outdoor sport in Canada? His brown hair curled round his ears and neck, with some light streaks mixed in.

Suz flicked one of his blond locks. "Don't tell us you've gone to the salon?"

Jamie pushed his hair behind his ears self-consciously. "Did it myself—lots of blokes at school put color in their hair. Dad wasn't too happy, though." He exchanged a grin with Stephen.

"I can see how upset your dad was," said Mam wryly, Ailish on her hip. "But it could've been worse, if our lad had gone for purple."

"Yeah." Jamie plucked Ailish from her arms. "So Ailish, Lish-lish-lishy." He gave her a big smacky kiss on the cheek. "Didja miss me?"

She grabbed his ear as my gaze met Stephen's, the light in his eyes telling me we were thinking the same thing. My heart beat faster. "You missed Ailish, then?" I asked Jamie casually.

He shrugged. "I got used to being around babies, a bit. My mate Griffin has a baby bro." He pried Ailish's death grip from his ear. "Just because you want my ear," he said to her, "doesn't mean you can have it."

I lifted my hand to touch his cheek, then patted Ailish's back instead. Jamie might like cuddling his little cousin, but that didn't mean I would be allowed to do it. "I'm sorry you had to leave school and all your friends before the term was up."

"Aw, it's all right." Jamie handed Ailish to Suz. "Things were getting like, *totally* intense with Grif, we were hanging out so much when I was staying at—"

"Let's not catch up here," Stephen broke in. His voice seemed strained.

"That's some North American accent you've got, love." I smiled at my son.

"Staying where, Jamie?" Suz asked.

Mam frowned, then suddenly linked her arm with Jamie's. "Suz and I will take you home with us. I think your parents would like a mini-getaway."

I gave my mother a grateful look. She and I had planned this ahead of time—we'd brought two cars to the airport, and I'd actually booked a room at a little B&B in Howth, on the seashore not too far away. I'd been prepared to cancel it if things were too awkward with Stephen and myself, but after that look in his eyes just now…

"Sure," said Jamie, his cheeks flushing.

I could see marital romance and raising a teenager could get really thorny, only I couldn't care about that right now. "We'll be back at your granny's tomorrow to pick you up," I told him.

"Or the day after," said Stephen.

"Can I get a latte before we go?" Jamie pulled out his mobile. "Then I've got to text Con, tell him I'm here."

"A latte," Mam repeated. "Looks like you've been living high on the hog."

"Wait a sec," said Suz. "Jamie never got to tell us where he'd been staying?"

Jamie gave me a surprised look. "Didn't Dad tell you? At Griffin's house."

After the quick goodbyes at Mam's car, Stephen and I walked to our Toyota without speaking. I felt the sting of betrayal. *How could you have kept Jamie's living arrangements from me? And what else have you been hiding?* He opened the back, and slung his case inside as I slid into the right-hand side. "I'll drive," I said to break the silence. "I'm sure you're destroyed with jet-lag."

He climbed in beside me, staring through the windscreen. "I said I'd explain everything—and I will." He sighed heavily. "I haven't a clue where to start, though."

He sounded so worn out, even defeated, I couldn't give out at him about his secrets. Instead, I leaned over to kiss him. "Then don't," I said against his mouth. "Not now."

I lay with my head on Stephen's shoulder, my hand on his chest as he slept. Through the lace curtains of our room, I saw the evening light turn red-pink. Moving carefully, I rose from the bed and padded to the window, pushing aside the curtains to watch the waves undulating onto the shore.

Our coming together had been hungry and wild and fast. "There'll be more of it where that came from," Stephen murmured afterward. He dozed off almost immediately, but an hour later he'd roused and we'd made love again, slower and sweeter this time. Then he'd fallen back to sleep.

Wide awake myself, after our long cuddle I got up to shower. Dressing in the silk bra and knickers I'd bought for the occasion, then a skirt and top, I went downstairs to the B&B's tearoom to fetch sandwiches for us. Eating mine back here, I gazed out at the sea, then at my husband's sleeping face.

Stephen's mobile suddenly vibrated, loud in the quiet room. I grabbed it off the table and saw Jamie's ID. "Everything all right, love?" I whispered. "I thought you'd be fine at your granny's."

"It's great," Jamie said. "I wanted to tell you I've been texting Con, and we've already made some summer plans."

That could have waited, I wanted to say, yet I was pleased he wanted to connect with me. "I'd love to chat," I said low, "but your dad's asleep."

"The other thing—Dad said I was to ring the McElligott's straightaway and sort out a visit with them. I promised I would— do I have to do it today?"

"I'm sure tomorrow or the next day would be okay. Do you...want me to make the call?" I didn't want to push him to be responsible, not when he'd just gotten home.

"I'll do it, Mam," said Jamie confidently. "Grif actually thought it was cool, that I had a mystery dad."

After we rang off, I carefully set down the mobile. My son was quickly turning into a capable young man. The desire for another child rose in me, as powerfully as the day of my party. Listening to the swish of the sea, as soothing as a lullaby, I suddenly pressed my hand to my stomach. Had Stephen and I started a baby? "I'm ready now," I whispered.

"So am I," Stephen said sleepily from the bed. I turned to see him pull back the covers. "Care for another go?"

"You're not seri—" I saw a muscle move in his jaw. "Oh. We'll talk now."

"I want to hold you first," he said.

I pulled off my skirt and top and slipped in next to him. Stretching out on my side, I propped my head on my elbow so I could see his face. "Let's get it over with."

He carefully arranged the covers over my shoulder. "You already know my first mistake—taking the Vancouver job back in November."

It had gone wrong almost from the start. The firm's initiative to open a Vancouver office had been conceived on the fly, or close to it, he told me, and the subsidies and the tax breaks looked so good that the top brass jumped on it. "After that disaster with Will, I was so ready to drink the kool-aid I hardly read the contract before I signed. I was in that much of a rush to get away."

The company was wildly overextended, and when the subsidies were delayed, the bonuses he'd been promised fell through. "And here I'd let this flat—in the city, housing costs are unbelievable—leased a big car too, and I was so busy working Jamie and I went out for meals or had takeaway. Before long, the pressure at work ratcheted up even further. A couple of our biggest clients did a runner, and several more followed. Like rats deserting a sinking ship."

To think he'd kept so many worries to himself! "Why didn't you say anything?"

"I couldn't let you in on my financial problems. Not after

you'd left your job, and you were so keen on the remodel and keeping the farm."

The hints about economizing and belt-tightening that Jamie and Stephen had dropped back in March—hints I'd never asked my husband to explain—suddenly made sense. Guilt struck me. "Stephen, if only I'd known! I'd have worked out some way to help."

I dropped my eyes. Would I *really* have done anything differently? Sold the farm to make up the money Stephen had lent Will? Stayed in Dublin and the soul-sucking job at Smythe's?

He drew me closer. "I had my pride. I wanted to show you I was still the big power broker at work, even if I'd turned our family life to crap. How could I admit the job, the move, everything had all been for nothing?"

I was having trouble absorbing all this. "Jamie—what was he doing at his friend's house?"

Now Stephen was the one to look away. "Our flat had a short-term lease. Before it ran out I hadn't had time to find something cheaper. When I started seriously looking for a place, I discovered rents had skyrocketed in only a few months. Jamie and I were bunking at an apartment the company keeps for visiting executives, but our stay there was meant to be only a fortnight or so, because the firm was letting go of the place."

I touched his face. "The walls were closing in, then."

"Jamie asked to spend a weekend at Griffin's while I had a big project to finish. I was ready to book a hotel, despite the cost, when I asked myself, why not crash on the couch in the break room at work. The cleaning staff was grand—they didn't give me away."

Well, *that* certainly explained why I'd heard someone hoovering in the middle of the night. "I'm trying not to be judgmental here, but this gypsy lifestyle must've put a lot of strain on our son."

Stephen nodded unhappily. "He seemed to be taking it all in stride, but he must've said something to Griffin's mam. She rang and invited Jamie to stay with their family until I got us a flat. That was the weekend you'd asked to come visit us. You see why I had to put you off—I was dreading that if you were to find out the state I'd put myself and Jamie in, you'd tell me to stay in Canada and not come back."

I was silent. He'd been stuck in a pressure-cooker, while I'd been living in my little dream world in the country. "Are we completely skint?"

"Of course not." Stephen looked surprised. "I've still got my salary coming in, but it's tied to the company's performance. I'm going to do whatever I can to get the firm back on its feet, but I'll be working flat out for weeks..." His voice trailed away. "They're expecting me in first thing Monday."

He'd always been so decisive, so in control about his job. It hurt me now to see him struggle. "What a crew of slave drivers," I said indignantly. "That's hardly long enough to recover from your trip."

"Yeah, well, it's the reality. I won't have time for house-hunting, so that'll fall to you." Stephen rubbed his brows tiredly. "Finding something affordable won't be easy, but we'll have to do it soon, with Jamie having another month of school."

Now was not the time to tell him about the state of my own bank account. "Will we be able to see each other at all?"

"I wish I could say, sure we will, that's why I came home, but I...can't." He looked dejected. "I forgot to ask—you've someone to look after things, there in Galway?"

"Not yet." Pondering how we'd handle the expense of moving house and the cost of living in Dublin, I suddenly sat up. "Can we try something for a few weeks? What if you and Jamie stay with Mam and Dad so we can regroup a bit?"

Stephen's expression lightened. "Would your parents be up for that?"

"I think so." Mam would probably be *thrilled*. "While the firm's got you in its clutches I'll go back to Ballydara and go flat out myself—do everything I can to make it pay. Nothing's ready to harvest of course, but I'll have produce to sell by midsummer."

"It's a grand idea," he said dryly, "but a few eggs and vegetables won't make a dent in our bills."

"Actually, organic eggs fetch a nice price," I countered. At least my eggs *could* once the hens started to lay. "When term is over, Jamie can spend the summer with me, and we'll visit you in Dublin on weekends. Or you can come up to Galway."

"It sounds workable," he said slowly. "But I never thought I'd be coming home only to have a commuter marriage."

"Okay, it's not ideal," I admitted. "Jamie will probably resist leaving all the action in Dublin."

"Jamie may surprise you," said Stephen. "He's been talking about taking a bus trip to Galway—learning how to travel independently."

"Really." Living in Vancouver may have broadened Jamie's horizons more than I thought. "Maybe we'll not have to twist his arm, then?"

"I hope not. And by the end of the summer, I'll have a better idea where things stand with the firm."

Once Stephen had his job back on track, maybe *then* I could face leaving Avalon Farm. "Let's talk to Mam and Dad as soon as we can."

"Right." He shifted toward me, his eyes intent on mine. "You've not forgotten, have you, what we were about the last time we were together?" He trailed his hand from my throat, between my breasts, down to my tummy. "Or what you said on the phone last week?"

"You remembered that, did you?" I teased.

"If we're going to live a bit madly for a while, let's go all out, throw caution to the winds. Or keep throwing it." He grinned. "I'll come to Galway at the weekends. I don't want to have baby-making sex down the hall from your parents."

I smiled into his eyes. "I'm all for that." Still, I had a sobering thought as I slid my arms around him. Once we conceived, we'd want to experience my pregnancy together—not miss a moment of it living apart. Then I really would have to leave Ballydara.

Fiona

35

*C*olm reached across the dark wood table at the King's Street Pub to squeeze Fiona's hand.

He'd seemed distracted, even agitated, when she and Desmond arrived. As the brother of her dead fiancé, had Colm felt awkward about meeting her dad, showing he was serious about her?

Whatever he was feeling, now that he'd met Desmond, he was smiling and confident again. He wasn't wearing his earring tonight—Fiona guessed he'd wanted to make a good impression. Not that Desmond would criticize, but he'd think a man's earring was nonsense. Meeting Colm's eyes, she mouthed, *Thank you*, and tugged her earlobe with her free hand.

"What do you think, Desmond?" asked Colm. "Finding something that looks good?"

Seeing her dad's beetled brows drawn tight as he perused the menu, Fiona said anxiously, "I know it's a lot later than our usual tea at home." After Desmond had liked Davie so much, she so wanted him to enjoy the evening with Colm.

"Your old dad hasn't had supper in the city for a long time, that's all." Desmond finally set down his menu as a server approached. "So many choices—not like Hurley's."

While Desmond painstakingly ordered his food, Fiona gazed around the familiar Galway City landmark. Over the years, she'd been in here dozens of times. The upstairs dining area still had the same medieval vibe, with the sturdy wood beams, the stag's head on the far wall, and the curved wooden chairs with purple-pink upholstery.

The random notes of a fiddle drifted up from the bar downstairs, and suddenly, the lurid pink turned to a blur.

Spending an evening in the city again, only a week after her date with Davie, was…painful. The memories of being with him were still vivid—the feel of his big hand wrapped around hers as they'd strolled through Shop Street, listening to his brother Gil's session in a nearby bar, the sensation of Davie's mouth as they'd kissed in the passageway around the corner…

She pressed a knuckle to the corner of her eye, and glanced across the table as Colm spoke to the server. "Will the fish be grilled or broiled? And what's in the marinade?"

Does it matter? Fiona didn't remember Colm being so… particular. He would never have gone for running through a filthy farmyard to catch chickens for Kerry, that's for sure. Fiona thought impatiently, I have *got* to stop thinking of Davie. Colm's the one who's right for me.

Tell yourself that enough and maybe you'll believe it.

Colm suddenly straightened. "Sorry," he interrupted the young woman. "Come back in ten minutes?"

As she left, his gaze went over Fiona's head, and he waved. Surely he hadn't invited a friend to join them, when he was meant to get acquainted with her dad? She turned, summoning up a polite smile.

Her face froze. Not a friend—far worse.

The two people approaching their table were all too familiar, though Fiona hadn't seen them for over a year. "Surprise!" said Colm. "You remember my mum and dad, don't you?"

Fiona looked daggers at Colm, but he was already standing up to greet his parents. "You made it!" He kissed his mother's cheek and shook hands with his father. As Desmond rose uncertainly, Colm introduced him to Helen and Dennis Dwyer. "And here's Fiona—it's been ages since you saw her, hasn't it?"

How could you spring your parents on me like this? Swallowing her ire, Fiona forced a smile. *Oh, yes, it's been ages since you sacked me. And barred me from coming back to the shop to collect my things.* "Lovely to see you."

"And you," said Colm's mother, her smile strained. "When Colm said you were…part of his life, of course we'd want to get to…know you."

Know me *again*, you mean, Fiona thought. Seeing the anxiety in Helen's face, Fiona didn't think this was her idea. Still, for Colm to give her no warning…

As everyone sat down, Dennis observed, "I see you've got rid of that eejit earring, son."

Colm adjusted the table settings that she'd assumed were extras. "Right, Dad."

So much for thinking Colm had removed his earring for *her* father. Fiona itched to take him aside, give out at him for forcing her into an impossible position. Yet with Dennis' implied criticism—and the discomfort on her dad's face—she decided she'd deal with Colm later.

Fiona's cheeks ached from smiling.

To Helen's credit, she kept the chat flowing over dinner, most of the conversation centering around Colm's career in Dublin. "You've seen his new work then?" she gushed. "Isn't it brilliant?"

"Brilliant," Fiona repeated.

"And he's turning a profit already, with all sorts of commissions flowing in." Apparently the Dwyers were done pressuring Colm to join the family business.

"Mum, you're making a show of me," protested Colm, not too vigorously.

"Maybe," said Helen, "but that's a mother's prerogative."

"Not many new businesses do so well right out of the gate," Dennis said. "Sure, not in the arts."

Fiona had to bite her tongue. *You could have told Colm you were proud of him years ago.*

She joined in the conversation as best she could, trying to see beyond the Dwyers' polite smiles. Helen looked well, her hairdo stylish, makeup meticulous and carriage erect. Not the gray-faced, slumping woman Fiona had seen at the funeral. She wished she could ask, *You're coping with losing Enda? And does your being here mean you've gotten over my affair with Colm?*

As for Dennis, he'd never been matey with her at the print shop, though he'd tried to stand up for her when Helen sent her packing. He seemed too busy quizzing Colm to worry about her. "Have you all your accounts in a software programme yet, like a proper business?" he asked as the server arrived with the food. "Your efficiencies will go through the roof once you've got all your systems up to speed."

"No worries, I'm working on it," Colm said as the young woman put a steak in front of him.

"What are you using now?" Dennis pressed.

Colm smiled ruefully. "I've currently got my financials scribbled on bits of paper, so I'll be hiring someone for data entry." He glanced at Fiona with a tiny eye roll. *Fathers!* "I'll join the modern age as soon as I can."

Picking up his fork and knife, he turned the charm on Desmond. "My guess is, from the fine work Fiona did at the print shop, you're one to keep your farm accounts tidy."

Desmond looked pleased. "Yes, yes, ever since I took over from me old dad. Paper never needs a plug socket, nor a fancy machine."

Relieved to see her dad tackle his burger with relish, Fiona ate her salmon mechanically. All through the meal, Colm went on about his workspace in Temple Bar and the commissions that had come in after his debut show. As if it was an afterthought, he said, "Pauline was good enough to come."

"That Pauline." Dennis chuckled. "Helen's cousin landed on her feet, marrying that Larry—captain of industry! I still can't believe it."

When Dennis nattered about Pauline's Dublin apartment and her car, Fiona could sense Colm's tension. Did his parents have a clue to what degree Pauline was supporting him? Or maybe they did and thought it was grand, as long as he was successful.

By the time the server cleared their plates, Fiona felt suffocated by everything she couldn't say. She stood up, nodding toward the Ladies. "Back in a moment."

Moving swiftly toward the hallway, she dodged into the stairwell and dashed downstairs. Passing the musicians warming up in one corner, and two massive, ancient hearths, she stepped out the front door. Fiona took a few fortifying breaths, hardly noticing the Saturday evening crowd surging up and down the street. Colm bringing their parents together—it had to mean he really *was* serious. She'd have to decide soon, if she was going to be with him…

Slipping back inside the pub, she saw a tall man with dark hair and an angular face in the corner of her eye. She nearly staggered. Davie? Bracing herself against the metal fireplace across from the bar, she did a double take.

It was Gil. As he recognized her, she nearly asked, *What are you doing here?* Then stopped herself just in time. He'd every right to play a session in whatever pub he liked. "Hallo, Gil."

He stared at her for a long time. Finally, he shifted the bodhran he was holding. "Fiona," he said coldly.

So Davie had told him they were no longer seeing each other. "I'm here with my dad and some…friends."

"Friends." He gave her a scornful look. "I'm sure you've lots of *those*."

She felt tears behind her eyes again, wanting to defend herself. *I didn't mean to lead Davie on, it was your brother's decision not to see me anymore…* Before she could reply, Gil rudely turned back to his mates, setting his drum under his arm.

Yet his expression was nowhere as forbidding as Davie's had been when he'd split with her. She tried to swallow the lump in her throat. It had been far too soon for this dinner with Colm, she realized, moving shakily toward the stairs. I should have put it off—

"Fiona. I wondered where you'd got to." Helen stepped off the bottom stair.

Could the evening get any worse? "I stepped out for some fresh air."

"Now that you have," Helen said in an almost friendly tone, "might I speak to you?"

Entirely unprepared for a private chat with Helen, Fiona inched toward the fireplace, trying to create a small island of privacy. *Gil, start your session, will you?* But save for a plunking note here and there, no one started playing.

"This isn't easy for either of us," Helen began. "Colm putting us on the spot."

"No," Fiona managed, praying Gil couldn't hear them. But he probably could.

"Still, I hope we can put a good face on it."

Fiona bristled. "On what?" Gil's snub made her want to lash out. "Tolerating each other?"

Helen's composure seemed to crack a bit. "What I-I mean to say is, I want Colm to be happy, and if he's chosen you, it's up to me to accept it."

"*If* he's chosen me?" Fiona lifted one eyebrow.

The older woman's face crumbled. "Fiona...after what our family has been through, I'm just now g-getting on with...you know." She choked. "Sorting things..."

Feeling cruel, Fiona dropped any urge she ever had for payback, remembering the closeness she and Helen had shared at the print shop. As for her affair with Colm—falling desperately in love was an excuse that only took you so far. "I...imagine so."

In a moment, Helen had her expression back under control. "What I should have said is, Colm's been a good son, and he's been working very hard." As she paused, Fiona added silently, *Even if he didn't take on Enda's job.* "And *since* Colm wants you to share his life, surely a mother ought to be...supportive."

Helen hadn't exactly pleaded forgiveness, but after losing Enda, reaching out like this seemed like a large concession. Fiona tried on a smile, her first real one since Colm's parents had shown up. "I appreciate that. Shall we join the others?"

Fiona ignored Gil as she walked past, sensing that he was just as pointedly *not* looking at her. *All right, so I was awful to your brother, but I hardly deserve a scarlet "A" across my front.* It was a balm to see Colm's broad smile as she and his mother returned to the table. Maybe, thought Fiona, I won't give out at Colm about his "surprise" after all.

Soon after, outside the pub in the fading light, Helen and Dennis' farewells were warm. "You'll be good for our Colm, I think," Dennis said.

Helen said, "You'll have us visit in a fortnight or two?"

"That'd be great, Mum," said Colm. "We—" He glanced at Fiona and took her hand. "At least I very much hope it's both of us in Dublin in the near future."

Gil's contempt flashed in Fiona's mind. Suddenly, she was struck by an overpowering urge to get as far as she could from Galway. Davie was lost to her. But Colm wanted her—why shouldn't she try for a different life? Still, there was her dad... "Helen...Dennis—I've told Colm I've no plans to live anywhere but Ballydara."

Desmond spoke up. "Maybe it's time you changed them."

Fiona glanced uneasily at Colm's parents. "We'll talk about this when we're home."

"We've the Dwyers right here, waiting for your answer," her dad said. "You might find some new opportunities for your art, there in Dublin."

"But Dad, it's not right for me to—I mean, you'll be on the farm by yourself."

Colm put in, "I wouldn't want Fiona to come unless you were completely comfortable with it, sir."

Desmond slowly took his handkerchief from his pocket and dabbed at his nose. Replacing it carefully, he said, "Fiona, why not give Dublin a go? I can try my hand at being a bachelor again."

She detected a flash of anxiety in his eyes, but she knew he was sincere. Her dad was so much better these days, maybe he *could* manage living alone. And two days ago, Kerry mentioned that Beata might be interested in caregiving.

No more drawing bananas on cheap newsprint, thought Fiona. *Here's my chance to really start my life. If I dare...* She glanced at Colm. "If I *did* decide to come, I'd have a lot of arrangements to make."

"Of course." Colm reached out to shake Desmond's hand. "Thank you, sir. Desmond."

He *is* a good man, Fiona reminded herself. And he loves me.

Helen reached up to kiss her son's cheek. After a glance at Dennis, she gave Fiona a kiss too. "Since it seems you'll be in Dublin, when we come to visit, we'll have something for you."

Bemused, Fiona watched the couple head up Shop Street, her heart already lighter. She didn't see herself and Helen ever being friends again, but if Colm's mother was trying to do the decent thing, she could do it too.

"Crikey," said Fiona, climbing out of her dad's little Ford a week later.

A tote bag in one hand, her sketchbook under her arm, she pasted a smile on her face and joined the small crowd gathered under Judith's pale pink awning. Her dad accompanied her, carrying her case. "I'm only going across the country, not Timbuktu."

"And what sort of friends would let you leave Ballydara without a proper send-off?" said Judith. Standing next to her was Pat and Bernard Hurley, along with Beata, her son slung on her hip.

Kerry was pacing in front of the pub, scanning the road. "No sign of the bus yet." Stephen and Jamie were coming in on the same bus Fiona was departing on.

Seeing her friend's agitation, Fiona wondered if Kerry was dreading their goodbyes as much as she was. Her dad hadn't said much about her going until a little while ago, on their way to the village. "That'll be a posh life you'll have in the city," Desmond said, not looking at her. "You'll not forget where you came from?"

"Never," Fiona had said. She wanted to tell him, *I wish I was more certain about living with Colm, trying to restart my career*, but to share her doubts might give him false hope. That her living in Dublin was only temporary.

A rumble sounded in the distance. Bernard checked his watch. "Ah, right on time," he said. "Fifteen minutes late."

As Kerry approached the little group, Fiona gazed at the faces around her. "Thank you so much for all you've done, for myself and Dad," she said, then there was a flurry of goodbye kisses for Judith, Bernard and Beata. Pat held out his hand, but she ignored it and kissed his cheek too.

"The place won't be the same without your lovely posters," said Judith.

"Or yourself," Bernard added.

"And here you are," said Pat, "off to the big city when I'm after working up a new menu."

Fiona turned to Beata and Peter, and touched the little boy's rosy face. "Dad's looking forward to having a little pal up at our house, for sure." Beata had seemed delighted when Fiona sounded her out about looking after Desmond a few hours a week.

Beata beamed. "Very happy to *hev* nice job. Peter and I take good care of your papa, we promise." She smoothed her round stomach. "Until baby comes."

Fiona glanced at Beata's tummy. Before long, she'd have to sort something else for her dad, but she'd cross that bridge later. As the bus rounded the curve approaching the village, she held out her arms to Kerry. "Right, this is it." As they hugged, Fiona said, low, "Part of me doesn't want to go, but Colm and myself—it feels meant to be." *Almost.*

"I'm a great one for soulmates," Kerry said, her smile bittersweet. "So if he's yours, there's no question—you should be with him."

Drawing away, Fiona couldn't quite agree with the soulmates bit, and she felt a stab for all she was giving up. "I'll miss you."

"I'll miss you more," said Kerry, sounding jokey, yet there was a sheen of tears in her eyes. "I mightn't have stayed in Ballydara, if it hadn't been for you."

Close to tears herself, Fiona nodded toward her dad. "Your keeping an eye on things means the world. Whatever happens, we won't lose touch."

Then it was one last kiss for her dad. Fiona resisted the urge to press her face against his wrinkled cheek. It would only embarrass him. "Keep well, okay?"

He looked troubled. "I'd have thought young Davie would call round to say goodbye."

Fiona didn't want to think of how many times she'd wished it too. Her split with Davie meant Desmond had lost a friend as well. *Why does changing your life have to hurt so many people?* Gently, she pried her case from his gnarled hand. "I'll ring after I've settled in."

With a long groan and the hiss of brakes, the bus pulled to a stop in front of Hurley's. Judith said hopefully, "Last chance to change your mind?"

"Ah, now, Judy, we've got to let her go," said Bernard.

Fiona gazed at them fondly. They all saw her as one of their own—and she was. Determinedly, she made for the bus, stopping near the door as Jamie McCormack bounded down the steps, Stephen right behind him.

"Fiona!" Stephen said, shaking her hand. "You're off to Dublin, Kerry says. Good luck and God bless." His eyes went straight to his wife.

Jamie was taller than Fiona remembered. He gave her a self-conscious "hi" as his father hurried away. With hardly a nod to the group of well-wishers, Stephen took Kerry in his arms and kissed her like they'd been apart for ages, not a fortnight. Fiona found herself watching them a second longer than she should have. The involuntary thought hit her. *Oh, to have someone love me like that...*She quickly reminded herself that Colm did love her. Of course he did.

Jamie said behind her, "In Canada, my mates'd say, 'Get a room, will ya?'" He hooted self-consciously. "Aren't my mam and dad too old for that?"

"You're never too old, actually," Fiona said around the lump in her throat. That night in Galway with Davie, she hadn't cared a fig if anyone had seen them snogging madly. "Cheers, Jamie."

"Back at'cha," said Jamie. He turned to help the driver extract a mud-speckled mountain bike from the luggage compartment.

As the driver stowed her case, Fiona dropped onto a seat. Across the aisle, a young, fleece-clad backpacker was frowning at his phone. "My call won't go through," he complained, glancing at her.

"Mobile reception's extremely spotty around here, I'm afraid," she told him. She and Kerry had shared a retro sort of pride about Ballydara not being in thrall to technology. Which made her sad all over again.

Fiona took one last look at the village and the clouds scudding along the hills above it. Suddenly, her gaze was caught by a small gray Isuzu bouncing down the road, slowing as it approached Hurley's. The vehicle had hardly jerked to a stop before the driver climbed out.

Fiona's heart stopped. Had Davie come to say goodbye after all? Or to ask her to stay?

She half rose in her seat, but as the bus lurched into motion, she sat down with a thump. Within moments, Davie—and her last chance to change her mind—slipped from view.

Kerry
36

A theatrical *harrumph* came from Bernard's direction.

"We're making a spectacle." I blushed as Stephen drew away. "What'll our neighbors think?"

"They'll think what they like." Stephen grinned at me. "By the way, I've brought something for you…us—Right, hallo!" He looked past me as Bernard approached.

As they shook hands I looked at Jamie, standing next to his bike. "How was school this week?"

He allowed me to give him a kiss. "Okay."

"And how'd you like riding the bus?"

"Fine. Can I go to the pub and text Con, at the hotspot?"

I sighed. Conversation with a teenager—like pulling teeth. "Didn't you see your friend yesterday?" I glanced around for Desmond, to see how he was dealing with Fiona's departure, but he'd disappeared.

"Yeah." Jamie pulled out his mobile. "I'll be quick."

Bernard piped up. "If it's all right with yourselves, I'll take the lad in."

"That'd be great," said Jamie.

Stephen thanked him, then said, "Jamie, this'll be your one and only chance on your mobile all weekend."

"Then I'll text my new mate Donal too," said Jamie, already parking his bike outside the pub. "Bernard, let's get a plate of chips or something. I've got money."

"All right?" Bernard asked me. As I nodded, he said, "Then how about I run Jamie and his bicycle home in my van, after he's done with his mates. Save you a trip back to the village."

Was that a twinkle in Bernard's eye? I tried not to blush. "Stephen does look knackered."

"Right, I'm overdue for a little sleep." Stephen actually faked a yawn. "We'll see the pair of you back at our place in an hour or so."

My heart warmed. That was the first time I'd heard Stephen call Avalon Farm *ours*. As the two entered the pub, Bernard was saying, "Make way, make way, our lad needs the hotspot."

I watched my son disappear inside, feeling a bit like a cipher, then glanced toward the shop. At least I could keep Jamie fed, if nothing else. "Stephen, I'm a bit low on milk, and we're right here..."

"We'll get it tomorrow." As he prodded me toward our car, Stephen's weary air vanished. He leaned close and murmured suggestively, "If we hurry, as soon as we're home we can jump into—"

"Stephen!" I grew warm. "What's got into you?"

"Stephen McCormack!" From the shop's doorway, Judith waved vigorously. "Sure what a treat to have you and young Jamie back in Ballydara."

Stephen sighed. "Might as well get that milk after all."

"I was saying to Bernard this morning," said Judith as we approached, "it used to be every day in Ballydara was the same as the day before. But since you McCormacks arrived, the village has been hopping." Holding the door open, she followed us inside. "Before I forget, Kerry, how's that wee flock of yours getting on? Young hens like that, you must be fair buried in eggs."

"Oh, buried," I said faintly.

"I'm still *very* keen to sell whatever you can spare, even a few dozen."

Still unable to admit to Judith that my laying hens were a non-starter, I managed, "That's so kind." I stepped toward the dairy case and reached for a liter of milk.

"Having a local source of eggs would be grand," Judith told Stephen. "The wholesaler fella wants large orders, coming to an out-of-the-way little shop like mine."

"Farm eggs are very big in Vancouver," said Stephen.

Returning to the counter, I muttered something about baking a sponge that had used up every last egg in the fridge. I opened my bag, hoping my face wasn't red. "I'll bring eggs as soon as...I've a free moment."

"I've got this." Stephen drew a five-euro note from his wallet. "Sounds like a win-win," he said to Judith. "With Jamie and me here weekends, Kerry will have more time to catch up with the farm."

I frowned. Cooking and cleaning up after the three of us instead of just myself would be more work, not less. And with Jamie's appetite, he was more like two people.

"More hands make light work, my mammy always told me," Judith replied. "As I was saying, with your house remodel, the Killeen boys and delivery folk were in here every day. When the job was done, I thought, well, that's that, back to normal."

I could see Stephen trying not to check his watch.

"Then this week," Judith went on, "I discovered Beata and her little fella will be keeping Desmond company and doing his shopping. And Aislin Carpenter says she's going to start a yoga class here in the village, can you credit it? If that's not all, both girls are *expecting*!"

Stephen took my hand. I saw Judith's gaze drop. "Ah..." she said slowly. "Maybe there'll be a third village baby soon?"

"You never know." My husband grinned.

"We really can't s-say." What in the name of God was Stephen about? I couldn't look at him. "I mean, who can predict it."

"Yes, such things are up to...you know," and Judith cast her eyes upward. "Of course, I'll be as silent as the grave."

"We'll be off now," I said hastily. "See you later!" Grabbing the milk, I almost pushed Stephen out the door. "What's gotten into you?" I hissed and practically dove into our car, Stephen plunking into the driver's seat next to me.

"You," he said sheepishly and gunned the engine.

Hanging onto the armrest, I said severely, "Propositioning me on the street? And all but going public that we're trying for a baby? How will I ever face people?"

"I couldn't help it. I'm going round the bend for wanting you."

"Really?" I forgot to scold him. "Prove it."

He started telling me all the things we were going to do before Bernard and Jamie showed up. And by the time we got home and hustled ourselves up the stairs, I couldn't have cared less if he'd personally told everyone in the village we were having it on.

Afterward, still breathless, I borrowed in the covers for my knickers. "We've made a shocking mess of ourselves." I gave Stephen a poke. "Come on—Bernard could be here any minute!"

"Before he does..." Stephen rolled toward the edge of the bed to grab his trousers. "You remember the surprise I mentioned?"

"You didn't need to bring me anything."

"It's for both of us." He dashed out of the room. A moment later he was back upstairs. He sat on the bed and pressed on my shoulder. "Lie back."

"Not again." I resisted. "We've got to get dressed."

"It'll only take a minute." As I complied, he set a small package on my bare stomach. "Is it too soon to give it a go?"

It was a pregnancy test kit. I looked at the anticipation in Stephen's face. And the anxiety I could see behind it. "Oh, love." I reached for him, the package sliding onto the sheet. To think, Stephen had actually gone into the chemist's to buy such a thing. Still, this baby-making had gotten awfully real, awfully fast. "It's a bit early," I said carefully. "Two weeks isn't *quite* long enough for the pregnancy hormones to develop."

He drew away to look into my eyes. "Can we try it anyway?"

"I...the test mightn't be accurate." His face fell. "But I have to tell you," and my whole middle tightened, "I'm...scared."

I hadn't thought of the miscarriage since my party. But with all our unprotected sex, and a pregnancy confirmation only a

241

small plastic stick away, the possibility of things going wrong loomed in my mind.

Stephen pulled me close. "It'll be all right."

"But what if I got pregnant, and…it did happen again?"

"*When.*" Stephen kissed the top of my head, his voice quietly confident. "*When* you get pregnant."

"Okay, *when*. I know chances are everything will be grand, but still, it's possible, and what if—"

"*If* it does, we'll face it then." He leaned in to kiss me, then drew away abruptly as the front door clattered open. "Mam, Dad—I rode my bike home!"

Jumping up, I yanked on my jeans and buttoned my shirt. "Hurry, will you?"

"Wait." Before I could rush out he reached for my hand. "Let's promise ourselves something." He kissed me one more time. "Starting now, good or bad, we face things together."

"Shop eggs?" Jamie closed the fridge the next morning, holding a carton of eggs I'd bought at the Topaz station. "What's wrong with ours?"

Stephen, sitting at the table, was seemingly absorbed in yesterday's edition of *The Irish Times*. "I haven't gotten to collecting eggs the last day or two." I watched the newspaper for any sign of movement.

"Why not?" Jamie wrinkled his nose. "Won't they spoil, sitting in the coop?"

"I've…um, had so many things to do lately." Despite the hours I'd put in trying to control the spring weeds, the garden beds were a right disaster. And in honor of Stephen and Jamie's return to Avalon Farm, I'd spent an entire afternoon cleaning the chicken coop, to make up for its somewhat ramshackle appearance.

"Freshly-laid eggs will keep all right for a few days without refrigeration," said Stephen behind his newspaper.

"Your dad's right," I said quickly. Trying to look super-efficient, I rushed through filling the kettle, getting bread and butter out, and laying the table. "Since the morning's half gone, let's get on with breakfast."

Stephen lowered a corner of the newspaper and winked at me. Heat rose to my cheeks. We'd had a lie-in—but not to sleep.

Jamie cracked eggs into a bowl, whisking them with a practiced arm. I watched my son admiringly, until he said, "I'll go get them after we eat."

"Get what?" I switched on the kettle.

Jamie rolled his eyes. "You forgot already? The *eggs*."

Eggs. How do I get out of this?

The newspaper rustled. "Watch the tone, Jamie," Stephen said pleasantly.

"Sorry," Jamie said. "I just want to see what chickens are like, up close."

Getting out the frying pan, I searched for an excuse. "The hens are…used to me. You can collect eggs on your next visit." Please God they'd be laying by *then*.

"They can't get used to me if I'm not around them." Jamie's chin squared stubbornly, and he suddenly looked like Stephen. "Why can't I have a go?"

Who knew I'd be arguing with Jamie over something like this? "Because… I might have other things for you to do today." I set a big pat of butter in the pan, wishing he'd focus on video games like a normal teenager. "Will you do the toast now, please?"

Stephen set his newspaper down. "Your mam's certain to have chores. You've a list, Kerry?"

Surprised, I said, "In my head." *Clean coop, thin apples, finish weeding, finally muck out the barn…* Sometimes my ever-expanding mental list drove me bats.

As the kettle boiled, Stephen rose to pour the water into the teapot. "How about over breakfast, you write it down? It'll be more efficient."

Who was he to swan in here and tell me how to run my place? "Efficient for whom, may I ask?"

Stephen looked puzzled. "For myself and Jamie—so we'll know what to do."

"You mean...farm jobs?" I asked, confused. "I assumed you brought work with you, and that you'll be down at the pub to do emails." As the butter sizzled, I poured in the eggs. "And Jamie, haven't you schoolwork?"

Stephen set the kettle down. "Jamie and I agreed we aren't coming all this way on weekends to be layabouts." He kissed the top of my head. "And I've had my fill of meetings and emails for a while."

I gazed at him. "You're serious about helping?"

"We live here too," said Stephen.

"We can't have Hurley's special booth all afternoon anyway," Jamie added.

I had to laugh. Before I could come up with the most pressing tasks, Stephen let go of me to fold up his *Times*. "I still say Jamie could be a champion egg man, given the chance."

Jaysus. Frantically trying to find more excuses, I heard a loud sputter outside, then a long mechanical wheeze.

Saved.

An hour later, I surveyed the various farm implements in my barn with Stephen, Jamie and Desmond. My neighbor had driven his elderly tractor up the hill to bring us an extra pair of Wellies he'd had at his place. "Like most things on a farm," Desmond said, "they're happier being used." It hadn't taken much persuading to get him to park his machine and join us for breakfast.

I glanced nervously at the piles of rubbish strewn about. I'd seen plenty of rodent droppings in here, and odds were good if Jamie saw a rat he'd leg it away from the farm, never to return. I didn't want Stephen to think Avalon Farm was a pest-ridden wreck either.

"Your mower there," said Desmond in his slow way. He nodded at one of the many rusty contraptions. "You'll want to cut your pasture fairly soon, I'm thinking."

That was a mower, then. Good job I hadn't gotten rid of it.

Stephen bent to examine the piece of equipment. "It's in pretty rough shape."

"Ah, it just came back to me," said Desmond. "Two years ago, the Powers' renter fella mangled the thing when he scraped it against the wall."

"Looks like a baler over there," said Stephen.

"It's banjaxed too," Desmond said. "The fella used to borrow mine."

"Whoa, catch this Grim Reaper yoke," said Jamie, pointing to the wall. "A scythe, right?"

"It'll want sharpening," Desmond said.

As if Jamie, Stephen or I would cut a pasture by hand. "So...no mowing today," I said brightly, still thinking about the rats, and ushered the three back outside.

Under a sky full of puffy clouds, Desmond headed for his tractor. "If you're not inclined to replace your mower, Kerry, maybe you'll consider Mother Nature for the job."

"Sorry?" I asked.

"Jeez, Mam," said Jamie. "You call yourself a farmer? *Sheep*."

"Oh, right." Too much sex and too little sleep last night must've addled my brains.

"We didn't plan to have sheep," Stephen said quickly.

"A shame," Desmond said, with a philosophical shrug. "They'd have a grand feed with that tangle of gorse you've got there."

"What if we wanted a proper pasture?" I envisioned tall grasses and wildflowers waving in the breeze.

"Well," said Desmond, "you'd want to plow it up, overseed with some rye grass. A bit of white clover too."

"I didn't see a plow in the barn," Stephen put in.

"Mother Nature can help you out there too." Desmond's eyes twinkled. "Get yourself some pigs."

"I'm not really a...pig person," I said. *On the other hand, a cow will do me*, but I couldn't say it in front of Stephen. He actually seemed rather fond of Avalon Farm at the moment, and I didn't want him to go off it.

"A shame," said Desmond. "Pigs'll have your field rooted up quick as a wink."

"Fertilized too." Stephen sent me a teasing glance. "Though we've no plan for pigs either," he added hastily.

"You could consider animals in the future, though," said Desmond. He nattered on about productive pastures and forage and silage and he'd be happy to loan us his equipment, while Stephen's face grew more alarmed.

"Desmond," I broke in, "I don't think that's exactly...on."

"Ah yes," he said, looking deflated. "You'll not be living here, to properly run the place."

"No," I said unhappily. "Not full time."

"Well, then." Desmond stared into the middle distance, then gave his tractor a fond pat. "Since you don't know how long you'll be in the district, maybe young Jamie would like a go on my old machine here. With your permission, of course."

"A ride?" I asked. Jamie might've liked that at the age of six, but now?

"In a manner of speaking," said Desmond. "At ten years of age, I was driving my da's. Jamie, isn't it time you learned?"

"You mean it? Drive your tractor?" Then Jamie shifted his feet, assuming a bored expression. "That'd be okay."

I could tell he *really* wanted to do this. "But you're not..." *Old enough.*

"I was driving at that age myself," Stephen volunteered. "Kerry, what do you say?"

"All right," I said weakly. I had to get used to this.

"So, I guess I'll learn to drive then." Jamie couldn't maintain his cool for long. "Wait'll I tell Con!"

As much as I wanted to watch—okay, *hover*—I knew Jamie would want this to be a man thing.

After Desmond coaxed the tractor back to life, he drove it to the pasture as Stephen and Jamie followed on foot. To stay out of sight, I visited the chicken pen. The hens rushed to the fenceline, with their funny little drunken-sailor gait. "I know you've gotten used to having your run of the place, but you won't be getting out for a while." I took the lid off their grain container and tossed a handful of scratch over the fence. "We've a new driver on the premises."

All six dove for the grains. After a moment or two, though, the novelty wore off and they abandoned the bits still on the ground. Returning to the fence, all six of them cocked their heads as if to say, *That's all you've got for us?*

"You may as well know, you've got one week, a fortnight at most, to sort yourselves," I told them. "If you don't produce some eggs we'll all be in big trouble." Four of the girls wandered off, but Laura, my dark brown hen, and Carrie, more golden-brown, lingered at the fence. "I mean it this time. Now if you're good, I'll bring over some greens."

I fetched my garden gloves and headed for the vegetable beds. I couldn't help peeking at Jamie in the distance, bouncing in the high seat as he took the tractor along the edge of the pasture. He sat straight, looking impossibly grown up.

Starting on the carrot bed, I set to some serious weeding. Before long, I'd a modest heap of thistle and thick-rooted buttercup, ready to move to the parsnips, when the tractor engine slowed. A few minutes later, Jamie was ambling toward me.

"So." I squinted up at him and clambered to my feet. "How'd it go?"

"All right." His bright eyes belied his tone. "There's a bit of a trick clutch, and Desmond said he's always had trouble with it, but I was able to slip it into gear, no bother." He nattered on about how he'd know everything by the time he took driving lessons, and wouldn't Con be madly jealous. He went quiet for a moment. "Um...Mam?"

I paused in the middle of brushing off my jeans. "What's that, love?"

"I wanted to tell you...uh, Con's asked me to come on holiday with him and his family. In July, I think. Dad didn't say yes or no, only that I had to ask you first."

I sighed. Jamie was ready to leave when he'd hardly just arrived. "It sounds lovely. Maybe his mam could ring me, let me know more details?"

"When I see him Monday I'll ask him." Jamie looked away.

I knew then that the Con holiday was only a warm-up. "There's something else?"

"Well..." Another long pause. "It came up this week, sort of a last minute thing."

"What thing was that?" Some other scheme of his and Con's?

"I...I saw the McElligotts this week—my granny and granddad. I...um, hope that was okay."

My heart clutched. I'd so wished we were done with that pair, but Jamie getting together with them had been bound to happen sooner or later. "Of course it is," I said carefully.

"Dad was working so I asked Granny Anne drive me to Bewley's to meet them. She went shopping while my granny and granddad gave me tea."

"I'm sure that's fine." I was dying to ask, *How was it? Did they pressure you for more visits?* "Will you see them again?"

"I didn't tell Dad, but I asked them when I'd see my other father."

I looked over at Stephen and Desmond. They were lingering in the pasture, near the idling tractor. "You don't want your dad to know about it?"

"That's not it." Jamie stepped over to a weed-filled row and dropped to his knees. He began tugging at some greenery.

I swiftly knelt, and stopped his hand. "That's a parsnip." I pulled at the buttercup growing next to it. "These are the weeds."

I knew he was helping me so he wouldn't have to talk. Still, it was nice to have company and we weeded in silence for a while. When I couldn't stand it anymore, I said, "You'll let your dad in on this soon?"

Jamie set another chunk of weeds on the pile we'd amassed. "Every time we talk about the McElligotts, Dad gets a funny look on his face."

I'd seen that look myself. "You've more plans with them?"

"They asked me to come to their house in a fortnight. If Granny Anne can't bring me they said they'd pick me up."

"Oh." He hadn't asked permission, so I didn't feel I should give it. And he'd every right to see his grandparents if he wanted. "And..." I swallowed, "when will you be meeting your..." I couldn't call Mike *your father*, because that was Stephen. "I mean, the McElligott's son?"

"Granny McE said Mike's getting some time off this summer, and he'll be back in Ireland. Will you tell Dad for me?"

I lay next to Stephen, listening to his slow, regular breathing. Jamie had been heavy-eyed all evening, and turned in early. After Stephen and I made love, I'd meant to bring up Mike McElligott's visit, but he dropped off before I could summon the nerve.

I didn't want to mar what had been the loveliest day we'd spent together at the farm. Jamie, seeming eager to drop the topic of the McElligotts, had volunteered to thin the apples. Stephen, to my great surprise, had actually taken out the dull scythe to whack at the grass around the fir grove. I watched him settle into an easy rhythm. He seemed to be entirely at peace.

As Desmond walked over to say goodbye, Jamie returned from the orchard to meet him. "Jamie lad, if you'd like another go on the tractor, I'll bring it round on your next visit."

"That'd be brilliant!" Jamie grinned. "Mam, you could learn to drive it too."

"I'd like that," I said. Although opportunities to operate Desmond's machine would be few and far between, once we returned to Dublin.

"I'd another thought, Jamie," Desmond said. "If you're to be spending time here this summer, you'll likely want to go to the pub now and then to use your fancy phone. You're still underage, so?"

"Yeah. I won't be fifteen for three more months."

"Well, then, if we don't want Pat Hurley to toss you out on your ear, when you want to phone up someone I'll nip down and meet you there."

"Wow, Desmond, what a *totally* bomb idea," said Jamie, his face one big smile. "Then I wouldn't have to bug Mam to come with me."

"That's so kind," I said gratefully.

"Before I leave, though," said Desmond, "maybe I'll have a look at your birds? Stephen thought they haven't been as productive as they could be."

Stephen apparently *had* been listening this morning. I faked nonchalance as Jamie sauntered alongside Desmond and me, laughing like a little kid as the hens ran over. Before he could ask about collecting eggs, I showed him the grain bucket. "Here—they'll expect a snack."

Desmond peered at the chickens, watching as they attacked the grain. "You give them lots of scratch, do you?"

"They love it." I didn't mention I used the grain to supplement their expensive organic feed.

"You'll not want to give them too much," Desmond cautioned, and Jamie paused in the middle of grabbing more scratch. "It's like candy to them."

"Like chicken junk food?" Jamie dropped the grain back into the container.

"That's it, lad," Desmond confirmed. "Their feed's got vitamins and proteins and such for good laying."

So I'd been feeding them wrong! "Thanks for the tip." What a relief! If I cut back on their scratch, the hens would be producing for sure in another week or two.

Now, I watched the rise and fall of Stephen's chest. He'd been wonderful all day, not only cutting the grass, but acting very keen on the farm overall. I was grateful for it—yet I knew all our baby-making sex was the reason he was being so accommodating.

I also guessed that this second honeymoon-ish stage of our relationship wouldn't last long. Stephen would soon revert to his workaholic ways, bringing work on weekends. Doing fewer chores. Even visiting less often. Then it would be fall term for Jamie, and we'd be in Ballydara only for visits.

In his sleep, Stephen reached for my hand. As I twined my fingers around his, he rolled toward me and kissed me. I tried to form the words to tell him about Jamie's plans. *He's set to see his biological father, and we've got to be supportive...* But with a sigh, he relaxed again.

No reason to wake him, to talk about Mike McElligott. I'd tell him for sure tomorrow.

Fiona
37

$\mathcal{S}$he still hadn't had sex with Colm.

Fiona sat at the table in Pauline's gleaming kitchen, staring down at her bowl of soggy cornflakes. She'd been in Dublin for a fortnight, but she wasn't any closer to working out how she felt about living here. And she would soon have to act like the devoted partner she came here to be, and play hostess to—

"You're up early again." Colm strode in.

She jerked her head up as he leaned to kiss her hair. Her head banged his chin. "Ow!" they said at the same time. "Sorry, did I hurt you?" Fiona asked.

He chuckled and rubbed his chin, the stubble dark before his morning grooming. "Only when I laugh." Dressed in boxers and a tee shirt, he reached up to stretch, exposing his trim stomach. Fiona's eyes dropped to his bare skin. A year ago, the sight of his naked torso would have made her weak with desire. Now, she thought, he's doing it on purpose. Trying to lure me into bed.

"So then." Colm opened the big fridge. "No cooked breakfast?"

She pulled her eyes from his bare skin without much difficulty. "Not today." Fiona shoved a spoonful of mushy cereal into her mouth. Who'd decided she should cook breakfast for him?

"Didn't you make your dad a big fry every morning?" Colm took out the milk, giving her a teasing smile over his shoulder.

Which she ignored. "You haven't forgotten? We're to get ready for our dinner party tonight."

They were putting on a welcome home do for Pauline and her husband Laurence. Their hosts had been away since Fiona had arrived, and Colm's parents were driving over from Galway City to join them. But if Colm's blithe disregard for most domestic chores held, she would be the one doing the cleaning, shopping and cooking.

"As if I'd forget I've new pieces to show them," said Colm in mock reproach. He picked up the empty carafe from his espresso machine. "No coffee either?"

"I never make coffee," said Fiona, her annoyance growing. "Why would I?" She never drank it. A fact that also seemed to have slipped his mind.

Colm didn't answer, measuring coffee and water and twisting the various knobs. When the hot liquid was hissing into his mug, he turned to face her. "With Pauline and Laurence home, we'll have to…sort ourselves. You know what I mean?"

Fiona looked away.

Her first night back in Dublin, Colm had shown her the note from Pauline, cellotaped to the double doors leading in the larger apartment.

Fiona, it's a right treat to have you staying with us! Have your run of the place, and we'll see you sometime in June. —P.

"I couldn't possibly make myself free in their home," Fiona said. "I hardly know Pauline!"

"She's *family*." Colm chuckled. "And we can't do much cooking with a microwave."

Fiona stuffed the note in her bag. "Then we'll have to do takeaway."

"Whatever you like," Colm said with a quizzical smile.

They sat on the lumpy studio couch to share a curry over a bottle of wine. Fiona was collecting the cartons when Colm took her hand. He pulled her gently toward his bedroom.

"Not…tonight." Fiona tugged her hand away. "I'm a bit jarred."

"On one glass of wine?"

"Um…I'll be more comfortable here." She patted the couch.

Colm seemed nonplussed. "On this old wreck?"

"I'll stay here anyway," she said stubbornly.

He frowned for a second, then he smiled, charmingly, Fiona thought. "There's always tomorrow." Colm gave her a brief peck on the lips. "And we've the rest of our lives."

The thought rather alarmed her. As Colm had predicted, she'd lain awake for hours on the cramped couch. *It's the energy of all the art in the room*, Fiona decided. She itched for daylight, so she could do some sketching.

The next day, unpacking, organizing the studio to give her some workspace, and trekking to Temple Bar so Colm could show her his blast room left her no time for sketching. After another takeaway supper, they watched a film on Colm's laptop, about a conflicted artist who never seemed to eat but drank wine constantly. Halfway through it he yawned. "Sorry, love," he said. "I'm knackered. Let's have an early night." He nuzzled her neck.

Fiona was exhausted herself, after sleeping so poorly. "Wait." She put her hand on his chest. "I've an open invitation at my sister's—I'll stay with her tonight."

"What for?" Colm looked hurt. "Didn't you move house here so we could be a proper couple?"

"But sleeping together feels..." *Wrong*. No, that couldn't be. "Too fast," Fiona improvised. "We've been apart for over a year. We'll want to get to know each other again before...all that."

"We can't regain our closeness, if you're not here." Colm caressed her back.

Even if she wasn't ready to make love, catching the bus to Bronagh's this time of night was daunting. And Colm was right— they couldn't strengthen their relationship if she was away half the time. "I'll stay." Resigned to the prospect of another sleepless night, she added firmly, "On the couch."

Colm's eyes narrowed for an instant, then he gave her an indulgent look. "There's a massive sectional couch in Pauline's lounge. Her son's mates would always camp out there. She'd want you to use it."

Fiona thought longingly of having a comfortable place to sleep. "I couldn't—it would be presumptuous—"

"Pauline invited you to use her apartment as you like," said Colm. "In writing."

"If you really think she won't mind..."

Smiling, he ran his finger down her nose, then lightly touched her lower lip. "She won't. So off you go, even though my bed's much comfier."

"I'm sure it is," said Fiona, refusing to take his bait.

Colm kissed her goodnight, his mouth opening on hers, and she'd been stirred. But not enough to spend the night with him. She'd slept on the huge couch ever since.

Now, Fiona idly mashed her cereal. If she and Colm were sleeping separately, Pauline and the others would wonder what was wrong. As things stood now, Fiona was feeling no better than a freeloading mate of Colm's.

Setting down her spoon, she rubbed her forehead. Watching Colm stir his espresso, she said, "I'm not sure I'm..." *Ready to give up on Davie.* The thought startled her so much she nearly fell from her chair.

"Steady on, love." Colm gently clasped her shoulder. "You haven't a headache, have you?"

Fiona shook her head. She'd tried to force Davie from her thoughts, yet when she least expected it, she'd picture his smile, the look in his eyes when he'd given her the sketchbook, remember the feel of his mouth against hers...

Colm released her and knelt next to her chair. He looked deeply into her eyes, his own crinkling with humor. "You're not waiting for a ring on your finger?"

She felt another jolt. Marriage? She waited for a surge of tenderness for him, but all she felt was...curiosity. "You're not serious."

"I didn't expect we'd want to tie the knot, but if you were keen..." Taking her hand, he grinned crookedly. "Maybe we should give it a go."

"If this is your idea of a marriage proposal, I'm afraid it's a bit wanting." Fiona yanked her hand away.

His smile disappeared. "Well, I'm on my bloody knees, aren't I?" He clambered to his feet.

She shoved her chair back and stood up too. "You're thinking that if we were engaged, I'd be up for sex?"

"You were engaged to my brother, so obviously you were up for marriage. And you slept with *him*." He sounded aggrieved. "So will you?"

Suddenly, Fiona saw the humor in Colm's behavior. "Will I have sex, or will I marry you?"

"I don't know!" He threaded his fingers through his silver hair, and pulled her into his arms. "I just want to be with you. Right now." He kissed her, drawing her hips against his.

Fiona kissed him back, but *still* wasn't tempted to have it off with him. She broke the kiss. "Stop."

"What is it now?" Colm looked like a little boy denied a treat.

Fiona stifled a giggle. "We've our do tonight—we can hardly lie in bed all day, then run to the chipper's for dinner."

"Right." Colm sighed theatrically. "But don't think we're done with this conversation," he warned.

"Oh, I won't," said Fiona, keeping a straight face with an effort.

"I mean it. I can't go on much longer like this."

Now she really wanted to laugh. "What, will your bits come to grief if you go without sex too long?" Before, she would never have dared to mock Colm. It was rather freeing.

Colm only gave her an irritated look and turned on his heel. Fiona watched him leave the room. *If I'd made sport of Davie that way, he would've laughed.*

"Have you seen my good white shirt?" Colm shouted from his bedroom.

Six hours later, Fiona was in Pauline's kitchen again, her amusement with Colm's petulance long since gone. He had a habit of yelling from wherever he was, instead of coming to find her. "No," she called back. *Since when am I your laundress?*

"My other good one's dirty! I thought you did the laundry yesterday."

Fiona didn't answer him. *I did* my *laundry.*

When she'd first arrived, with no outside job, she felt she should take care of the household. Colm's work involved a lot of physical labor—once his projects were past the drawing stage, there was hauling around massive sheets of glass, and the noisy, dirty task of carving into them with abrasive grit in his blast room. When he wasn't actually blasting, he'd need to maintain his pressure pot, vacuum, and protective gear. He often came home with cuts on his fingers, reeking of burnt oil from the compressor.

Despite his absorbing job, she'd soon worked out that she actually had one too—as Colm's assistant.

This morning, she'd been hoping to finally get some drawing done, have some new material to show Pauline if her hostess brought up the book project. Before she could settle in with her sketchbook, Colm asked her to help him tidy the stacks of paperwork nearly falling off his desk. "It's no bother, is it?" he'd said with a winning smile. "I'm simply desperate at filing."

She turned on the oven light and stared balefully at the roast for tonight's party. She'd have been all for making a dish from her usual repertoire, say, chops and colcannon, food her dad liked. But Colm had insisted on the best cut of meat she could find.

In her mind's eye, she could see Desmond's gnarled hands making tea. A pang of homesickness hit her. She missed him, missed Kerry. She even missed Bets' lowing out in the shed when her dad went too long between visits. Her throat went tight.

She swiftly got out the potatoes to peel, perplexed at her sadness. *You left home nearly fifteen years ago—what's wrong with you now?* She wished she could tell Colm how she felt. But he'd probably get offended. Again.

Dennis set down his fork, patting his ample stomach. "The roast was grand, Fiona." He winked at her.

Fiona smiled back absently, sitting across from Colm's father at Pauline's massive dining table. She'd been furtively watching Pauline and her husband—the oddest pair she'd ever come across. Pauline's ruddy face, booming voice and sheer robustness were a stark contrast to Laurence Smurfit's pale gentility and quiet demeanor. Yet the affection between them was obvious, in the way they touched hands and exchanged smiles.

"You did a bang-up job on this potato thingummy too," Dennis went on. "Colm's other girlfriends were useless in the kitchen—"

"Denny!" Helen's color was high.

Pauline laughed. "That gob of yours'll get you in the doghouse, Dennis."

"What?" said Dennis. "It's the God's truth, none of them could so much as boil an egg! Fiona here is far more sensible—"

There was a thump under the table. Dennis winced and reached for his wineglass. Helen whisked it away. "I think you've had enough."

"Really, it's all right," Fiona said. It was hardly news that Colm had known a lot of women. *I was so grateful he'd chosen me.* She went still. Had that changed too?

As Dennis leaned down, no doubt rubbing the bark on his shin, Colm said, "Fiona's made dessert too." He smiled approvingly at her—even though he'd been in high dudgeon most of the day, after she'd made the crack about his bits.

"I imagine your dad misses your good cooking," Helen remarked. "He's keeping well, with you away?"

"He is, actually," said Fiona. "A helper comes in a few hours a week." Her dad was already fond of Beata—Fiona tried not to mind that she'd been the one to persuade Desmond to finally go to the eye doctor. "My friend Kerry looks in on him too."

"Right." Colm pushed back his chair. "Before the evening's gone, I'd like you all to come up to Temple Bar, to my blast room—I've a couple of new projects to show you."

Had she never noticed before that Colm had a tendency to direct the conversation back to himself? Tamping down her annoyance, Fiona said, "I've seen them—they're quite gorgeous."

"Sounds like great crack," said Pauline. "But Larry's got phone calls to make."

"Yes, I'll have to pass," said Laurence, rising from the table.

"Lovely dinner, Fiona." He kissed his wife's brow and headed for his office.

"Bye, *muirnín*," Pauline called after him, then she gave Fiona a meaningful glance. "Since Larry'll be tied up for hours, Helen, you and Dennis go on. Fiona and I have a tête à tête that's overdue."

Fiona's spirits soared. Pauline had to be talking about the book. "I'd love that."

"Pauline, I'd *really* like you to come," said Colm. Was he actually *pouting*? "You might have some display ideas."

"A patron of the arts' work is never done, eh?" Pauline looked ruefully at Fiona. "We'll have that chat over pudding, as soon as we get back."

Later that evening, after Fiona had stayed home to do the washing up, she settled gingerly on the poufy sectional with Colm alongside her, and Helen and Dennis kitty-corner. She glanced around the lounge, hoping she'd left no evidence that she was spending her nights here.

"Mum and Dad liked my new pieces." Colm took her hand. "Still, you deserve credit for freeing up my time to finish them." Before Fiona could reply, he told his parents, "She's become my business manager."

"Really?" Fiona said involuntarily, pleased. Even if Colm had invented her title on the fly for his parents' benefit.

"Fair play to you both," said Dennis. "Takes the business up a notch."

"I thought so," said Colm. "Fiona pays suppliers, gets invoices out, and she even keeps up with my email, all sorts of things. I don't know what I'd do without her."

"Like I always say, you can't make money if your paperwork is a muddle," Dennis pronounced.

Helen smiled at her. "Fiona has lots of practical talents."

"Fiona?" Pauline shouldered in with a tray laden with dessert plates and began passing them around. "Oh, she's the sort who does a bang-up job with everything."

"A hard worker," said Dennis. "But so is our Colm here!"

"I do worry about you accidently inhaling that grit you use, Colm," Helen fretted. "Getting that lung condition…what do you call it?"

"Silicosis," Fiona said. It was an all-too-real risk with Colm's profession. She worried about it too.

"I take every precaution, Mum," said Colm as he, Dennis and Pauline started in on the tart. "Fiona frees me up from office work so I'm super-focused when I'm blasting."

"Don't I know you're a right treasure, Fiona," Helen said with a relieved smile. "The way you kept things running smoothly at the shop…" Her smile turned fixed.

Fiona tensed. *Only you sacked me anyway.* She saw Colm exchange a look with his father. Were they thinking the same thing?

Pauline said, "About that chat, Fiona—the evening's gotten away from us. I'm turning in as soon as I polish off this lovely tart of yours."

"C'mon, Pauline, the night's still young," Dennis protested.

"I'm not one to stay up half the night in front of the telly like some I could mention." Pauline reached over and gave Dennis an affectionate jab. "Not with the loads of meetings I've got coming up."

"Didn't you say you're seeing some media people?" asked Helen.

"Oh yeah," said Pauline. "Watch for this kid of yours in the papers. A rising star, he is." She looked at Colm fondly, and turned back to Fiona. "So then, love, what's your schedule for next week?"

"I'm open," Fiona said quickly. She'd happily postpone the invoicing and filing that Colm seemed to think was so urgent.

"We're still working on our daily routine." Colm glanced at his father again. Dennis paused, then dug into his tart again.

Pauline took her last bite. "The pudding was delish, Fiona."

"She could open a bake shop, if she wasn't running Colm's show." Dennis was already scraping his plate. "This girl's a keeper."

Helen dropped her fork.

Pauline frowned, then rose from the couch. "Fiona, we'll make time in another day or two," she said. "'Night," she said over her shoulder and disappeared.

Helen set her plate aside. "Now that we're alone...Fiona, I've—*we've* something for you." She left the room and reappeared a moment later holding a new portfolio case of royal blue leather. It looked hand-stitched. "I was going to send it by post, but isn't it so much better to give a gift in person?"

"This is...for me?" Fiona's voice was tremulous.

Helen carefully set the case on the coffee table. "Your things."

Hands shaking, Fiona opened the large, elegant portfolio. Inside were the art supplies she'd left in the print shop's storeroom last year. Her pencils and chalk, her watercolor set. Pages and pages of sketches. And the stack of practice pieces for the book gig that had been put on hold. Eyes smarting, she felt like the part of her life, of *herself*, had finally been restored.

She looked at Helen, blinking back tears. "Thank you—I've so missed having my work with me."

"It's fantastic, Mum," said Colm.

Dennis cleared his throat. "Fiona, I hope you know, what's past is past."

"Yes," said Helen, her voice strained. "I so regret...well, I hope we can put all our...difficulties behind us. Start fresh."

Fiona sensed they were not only asking forgiveness for sacking her, but for cutting her out of the family. "I'd like that," she murmured. The weight of guilt she felt over Enda lifted a bit.

"Mum, Dad—this means more than you'll ever know." Colm leaned over to kiss his mother.

As Helen squeezed his hand, Dennis said, "We're a family again, right? And now that Fiona's got her things, she can get back to her noodling."

Noodling?

"Fiona's a serious artist, Dad," Colm corrected.

Warmed by his parents' gesture, she smiled at him and dug into her dessert, ready to overlook his pettiness this morning. As for Colm's odd glances with his dad the last few hours, she'd let those go too. She *could* try harder, to make a go of this relationship.

As Colm collected empty plates and brought them to the kitchen, Fiona drew out one her of practice drawings, then realized it was nearly bedtime. Even if Colm was being so sweet and supportive, was she ready to make *that* much of an effort? She stuffed the paper back into the case as he returned.

"Mum, you're probably ready to turn in."

Helen hid her yawn with a genteel hand. "More than ready."

Not looking at Fiona, Colm switched on the telly. "I know you're still a night owl, Dad. What channel?"

Oh, *Jaysus*. Of course Colm had planned this—to keep his dad on the couch so she couldn't sleep in here. All the same, as he gathered up her new case, Fiona decided not to make a fuss. She'd gotten her portfolio back, after all. And why shame Colm in front of his parents, when he'd recognized her efforts with an actual title, *and* she'd finally reconciled with them? She followed him into his little flat.

"There you are," said Colm, propping her case against the studio desk. "All you need now is inspiration." He faced Fiona, eyebrows lifted. "So...bed."

She glanced at the lumpy couch. She *could* sleep there—in a manner of speaking—but there was always the risk the others would find out. The drawings for the book project crossed her mind. *Oh, what the hell.*

She headed for Colm's bedroom. "I'll sleep in here, no bother," Fiona said blithely. "Although nothing's changed."

"You think?" Colm said playfully and pulled back the black duvet. "I'd say it's a whole new game."

Kerry
38

"For heaven's sake, Stephen, stop pacing." Mam patted an open space on the big blanket Dad had spread on the grass at Phoenix Park. "We're all of us on tenderhooks too. Come and eat."

Stephen glanced at my mother's picnic meal. "Thanks, Anne. I'll go see what's keeping Anthony." He strode toward the playing field some distance away, where Suz's husband was watching a rugby scrimmage.

"A likely story," Mam muttered darkly. "And here I made him a lovely turkey sandwich, just as he likes it."

"Leave Stephen be, Mam." I popped the last of my sandwich into my mouth and opened a packet of biscuits, the crackle of cellophane made me hungry all over again. "He's been a nervous wreck. The pair of us have."

I'd come to Dublin for the weekend, to be with Stephen while Jamie was visiting the McElligott's. Mike Junior was apparently ready to do the decent thing and meet his biological son. Ever since I'd heard that Jamie was to see him, I'd experienced nearly overwhelming spikes of anxiety—and the only way I could calm myself down was to eat.

"Even if Stephen hasn't any appetite, it was sweet of you to organize this outing, Mam." I grabbed a handful of biscuits and ate the first one in two bites.

"Ailish'll have a biscuit too," said Suz. "If you can spare it." I pulled a face at her and handed a biscuit to Ailish, who crammed it into her mouth. Bits crumbled all over her and the blanket beneath her. Suz leaned back on her elbows, gazing at me speculatively. "I see *your* nerves haven't exactly put you off your food," she observed.

Dad reached for another sandwich. "That's enough out of you, Suzie." He took a big bite. "I shouldn't wonder Kerry likes to tuck right in, with all that gardening and looking after her hens. Aren't you cycling down to the village too?"

So he thought I was doing it for the exercise. "That's right, Dad." I smiled at him, though I was sure he'd risen to my defense so Mam wouldn't go on at him about how much *he* was eating.

"Right, Kerry works so hard," said Suz. "Isn't it me who's got a toddler to run after? You don't see me devouring biscuits by the dozens."

"I'm raising *food*," I told her loftily. "I'll be picking carrots soon."

"Huh. If you'd a proper farm, you'd have a cow." Suz grinned. "Or at least a half-dozen sheep."

I threw a biscuit at her. "One of these days, I will!" I conveniently forgot I wasn't staying in Ballydara long-term. "What do you know about farming anyway?"

"Enough to know you need animals," Suz said.

"Oh, stop it, the pair of you," said Mam. "How can you joke at a time like this?" She sounded close to tears. "We've come out to take our minds off Jamie and have a good time. So for God's sake let's have some *craic*!"

I glanced at Suz, brows raised. *Wasn't that what we were doing?*

Ailish gave Mam a long, considering look, then picked up the biscuit I'd tossed and solemnly gave it to her.

Mam sniffed and started to chuckle. "Oh, look at us! You'd think we were worried Jamie'll like *that guy* better than his own dad!"

"That guy" was what Stephen and I had started calling Mike McElligott when Jamie wasn't around—neither one of us could bring ourselves to say his name aloud. It had caught on with the rest of the family.

"Better than Stephen? As if!" Suz said as Stephen headed back toward us, Anthony in tow.

My husband looked even more anxious, like a permanent wince had settled on his features. I said, "I'll walk with Stephen for a bit."

"Don't be long," said Mam. "I've some lovely sparkling wine to go with our pie."

I struggled to my feet, all that lunch weighing me down, and made my way to the two men.

"Hey," said Anthony, a sport-mad bloke of few words—he generally let Suz do the talking. "Got a bit caught up with the game there." He thumbed toward the scrimmage, then shambled off to where the rest of the family was sitting.

I took Stephen's hand. "It's going to be all right."

"You know, I've always wanted to meet *that guy*," he said a reflective tone. "Have a proper go at him—punch his bloody lights out. If I cruised round to the McElligott's, do you think they'd let me in?"

"You're never serious?" The closest I'd seen Stephen to any sort of violence was the previous autumn, when he'd gone toe-to-toe with Will Power, a head taller and half again as broad. "It's not that guy's fault he didn't know about Jamie," I said, in case Stephen was getting any ideas. "You know that."

"He's a bloody tosser anyway," growled Stephen. "He should've done the decent thing, asked you to marry him—"

"No, he shouldn't have," I said. "Else you and I wouldn't have gotten married."

"Then he should've—hell, I don't know!"

I bit my lip. "I'm more worried about that guy wanting more time with Jamie." Something new occurred to me. What if Jamie developed some kind of hero-worship for Mike, and wanted to visit him more often? It would *kill* Stephen. "What'll we do then?"

Stephen's face grew so tight I had to look away, and saw my dad beckoning to us. As we joined the family, Mam was packing up the picnic. "What's up?" I snagged the packet of biscuits and stuck them in my bag.

"Hoarding food, I see." Suz gave me a cheeky grin. "Maybe you need therapy."

"Don't you start again," warned Mam. "Kerry, I just got a text from Jamie. It sounds like something's come up at the McElligott's and he needs me to fetch him straightaway."

Stephen narrowed his eyes. "Kerry and I will go."

"We will *not*," I said firmly. "Jamie's expecting Mam and Dad to pick him up—if you showed up..." I didn't need to finish. *Jamie would know something was wrong.*

"We'll rendezvous at our place, then," said Dad.

"Bye, then, you lot." I kissed Suz and Anthony, and Ailish twice.

"I'll break out the wine for the four of us," Mam added. "We'll celebrate getting this whole thing over with."

Back at my parents' house, I was the one pacing. The possibility of Jamie taking a real shine to Mike had my stomach doing somersaults.

Stephen was scrolling on his mobile. "Weren't you going to try connecting with Fiona this weekend?"

Poised to ask, *how can you check messages at a time like this?* I noticed his hand was shaking. "Um...yes."

Fiona hadn't returned my calls for some weeks now. Last time we talked, I'd teased her about having her mad, boho life back. She'd made a tinkling laugh. "Oh, sure, my days are jam-packed with art, 24/7."

On my parents' phone, I pressed the number where she was staying—I'd stopped using my mobile altogether—and waited impatiently through five rings. Up came the same message, delivered in a crisp, prep school accent. *You've reached Smurfit, Limited. We're not available to take your call but if you leave your name and number...*blah, blah, blah.

I quickly rang off. Fiona had given me Colm's mobile number, "but only for absolute emergencies, mind." This weekend would be my one chance to see her, which hardly constituted an emergency. I couldn't help thinking, was she too taken up with Colm and her new life to keep in touch?

The front door rattled. Forgetting about Fiona, I almost collided with Stephen as my parents came in. Mam gave me a tiny shake of her head, and she and Dad went straight through to the kitchen. Jamie was clumping up the footpath, head bent to his mobile.

Stephen said from the doorway, "How'd it go, son?"

Jamie looked up and shrugged. "All right."

Once he was inside, I couldn't hold it in. "You meet your...Mike McElligott, which you've been thinking about for months, and that's all you can say? Tell us, what'd you think? What's he like?"

"I told you, he's okay!"

"Jamie," Stephen warned. "I won't have any of that."

Jamie shifted uncomfortably. "Uh, like I said, he's all right. Granny McElligott put on a big lunch for us. Her food's not as good as yours or Granny's, though."

"Anything else?" I held my breath, imagining Jamie saying, *I can't wait to see him again.*

"Actually, I've this long text from Con," said Jamie. "Remember, he asked me to go on holiday with them? His mam's ready to buy tickets and all that."

"We'll deal with that later," I said. "First, Dad and I would like to—"

"I'll be upstairs," Jamie broke in. "Got to answer this text."

I waited long enough to hear a bedroom door close, then flew into the kitchen, Stephen at my heels. "Mam, Dad—what do you make of it?"

Mam raised her brows. "You mean, Jamie keeping such a big thing to himself? I raised three teenagers. This is normal."

"But we've always been so close," I protested. "At least, he and Stephen have been."

"He didn't want to talk to me either," Stephen said gruffly.

"Teenagers are like wild creatures," Dad pronounced.

"Honestly, Tom," said Mam. "I'll get out that wine."

"What I'm saying," Dad continued, "if you chase them, they'll run. Or fly off."

"Righty." Mam rolled her eyes. She pulled the bottle from the fridge and poured out four glasses, topping one to the rim.

"Don't change the subject, Anne," said Dad. "You've got to let the young people come to you. Food helps, in most cases."

Mam looked a bit thunderstruck. "You might be on to something. Now, let's have that celebration. And remember, the next time Jamie sees that guy it'll be easier."

"Next time?" echoed Stephen, a deep line between his brows.

Mam handed him the fullest glass. "Your children will make their own choices, love."

Stephen only looked bleaker. If I couldn't bear to think of going through this Mike thing on a regular basis, I knew Stephen would be feeling three times as bad. Think about the farm, I told myself. My small potato and carrot crop growing in the garden's rich soil, apples swelling on the trees. The hens *finally* laying. Everything moving forward.

I raised my glass of wine, wrinkling my nose at the smell. "This isn't a bit off?"

"I bought the bottle last week," said Mam. "Now drink up!"

I took a cautious sip and nearly gagged, then hastily set down my glass. "I'll go up and check on Jamie."

"Let them come to you, mind," said Dad.

"I can't wait that long," I said. Spying a bag of Taytos from the picnic, Jamie's favorite, I grabbed it. "Maybe this'll help." And if Jamie wouldn't talk to me, I'd at least have something to eat.

That night, I nestled in Stephen's arms, obsessing about the light still showing under the door of Liam's old room where Jamie was sleeping. Or rather, *not* sleeping. When I'd knocked on the door earlier, Jamie opened it a crack.

"Will you come down? Granddad's got the football on." I offered the crisps.

Jamie didn't even look at them. "Later, Mam." He avoided my gaze. "I'm still finishing my text."

That's some long text, I wanted to say, since you can probably thumb sixty words a minute. "Okay," I said instead, trying to keep my voice from trembling, and returned downstairs. Now, as I pictured Jamie lying sleepless, my heart ached.

"So what do we do now?" I whispered into Stephen's chest.

If we'd been back at the farm, Stephen would have said, "This," and drawn me closer. Here at Mam and Dad's, though, with Jamie in bad form and my parents down the hall, I wasn't remotely tempted.

Neither was Stephen. Twenty minutes ago, as he undressed, he said, "Maybe we'll take a break tonight? Let my little swimmer blokes build up their strength."

Normally I'd have giggled at a remark like that, but I couldn't manage even the ghost of a chuckle. "I know you're awake." I gave him a poke. "What are we going to do?"

Stephen sighed. "You mean, about Jamie?"

"What else?"

"I think all we can do is sit tight until he asks to see the McElligotts again. Then go from there."

"That's very sensible, but I'm going mad with worry." I shifted away from him. "I'll try those crisps again."

"Pestering Jamie won't help."

"I've got to do *something*."

"I've an idea," said Stephen, his voice sounding less tense than it had all day. "Why don't you take that test we've been waiting on?"

The test. The one Stephen had diplomatically not mentioned for an entire fortnight. *That* was enough to take my mind off Jamie. "I...um..."

"I suppose you left it at home." That's what Stephen had started calling our Ballydara place. As if he was living there properly, instead of only at the weekends.

"I can do it when I get back tomorrow night," I said. *Maybe.*

"Let's wait until we're together. Friday next, okay? Jamie's sure to be feeling more himself by then too."

"It's a date." I kissed Stephen's neck in secret apology for my reluctance to take the test. Even if he was calling the farm "home," it wouldn't be our home much longer. Not if I was pregnant.

The family had gone to Mass without me. I'd been so wrung out after yesterday's anxiety I couldn't drag myself out of bed in time. But after eating a couple of pieces of wholemeal bread, I felt rejuvenated—even fired up again about the farm tasks awaiting me. My homemade bread was much better than this shop stuff, I thought smugly. Once I was home, I'd make another batch of loaves to bring to Judith.

Hearing voices, I jumped up from the table and found Stephen and Jamie coming into the house. Right behind them was a boy a bit shorter than my son, with bright red hair and oversized ears. His freckles competed with a crop of spots.

"Look who we ran into at the church," said Stephen. "Con's having lunch with us, okay?"

My heart sank. Just when I wanted to have it out with Jamie... "Hi Con, it's been ages, right?" I gave him a quick hug.

As Con stiffened, I realized I should have rethought the hug. Backing away from him, I saw relief on Jamie's face. *You can't avoid me forever,* I vowed, and put on a smile for my son's friend. "So...how are your parents?"

He mumbled, "Ah, you know, the usual."

"What's for lunch?" Jamie said at the same time.

As the boys trooped into the kitchen, I asked Stephen, "Where are Mam and Dad?"

"They went to a film matinee," he said, and lowered his voice. "I think they wanted us to have time as a family this afternoon. Then Con showed up with his parents."

"We ought to come up with something fun for the boys before Jamie and I leave for Galway," I said. Actually, I wanted a nap. Preferably with Stephen.

"Yes." Stephen sighed. Maybe he'd hoped for a *nap* too. "I'll have to check my messages before I take the afternoon off."

"It *is* Sunday," I pointed out, but he'd already taken out his mobile. I joined the boys, hoping there were enough leftovers from yesterday's picnic to feed everyone. "Mam?" Jamie said.

"Hmmm?" Opening the fridge, I spied a packet of sandwiches and a tub of salad.

"Guess what? Con and I have a fantastic plan. His parents said it was okay."

Reaching for the packet, I paused. Con and the word "plan" didn't bode well. I pulled out both items and quickly closed the fridge. "What's going on?"

"I asked Con to come back with us to Galway."

"Today?" I set the food on the counter. My visions of working steadily through my baking and gardening chores vanished. "What'll you boys do with yourselves?"

Con said, "Jay wants to show me around."

Jay?

"You mean, around Ballydara?" I was a terrible mother. I should *want* Jamie to see his friends, not hang out by himself at the farm. Still, I couldn't help saying, "You realize, Con, that the village is very small. And we haven't Internet."

"It's no bother," said Con cheerfully. "Not when we can use our mobiles at the pub. Jay says there's a signal at the back."

I'm sure your parents will just love you hanging out at a bar all day. "Right," I said, resigned, and opened the sandwiches.

"We're going to do some country cycling too," said Jamie. "Can we bring Dad's bike?"

"No, we cannot," I said. "Your dad needs it." I was still a bit flabbergasted that Stephen often commuted by bicycle—in the not too distant past he would have regarded cycling as a waste of time. "We'll have your bike and my old one."

"But yours looks *desperate*," Jamie complained.

"Lucky for you, *Jay*," I said, "it works perfectly fine."

"Okay," said Jamie with a martyred look. He got out four plates and set them on the table, along with the tub of salad. "Mam, you remember I'm to go on holiday with Con?"

Actually, I had forgotten. "Holiday. Right."

"It's going to be great," said Con.

"Massively great!" Jamie's face grew animated. "You'll never guess where we're going—London!"

"Oh," I said carefully. London prices were *insane*. Stephen and I hadn't had a chance to sort out our family finances yet. How much cash would we need for this expense? "Con, as I recall, your holidays are later this summer?" At least we'd time to come up with the money. "Next month?"

"Nuh uh," said Jamie. "Next week!"

Fiona
39

*F*iona glanced at the digital clock on Pauline's fancy cooker. As she dished up two plates of eggs and toast, she knew her hostess would be in soon to start her own breakfast—so it was now or never. "I've started looking for a job." She set Colm's plate in front of him.

"Hey, I'm working on this." Pencil in hand, Colm nudged his plate off the Sudoku page of *The Irish Times*. Then he jerked up his head. "Did you say a *job*?" He dropped the pencil. "What are you on about? You have one."

Fiona sat down. "Do I?"

"Of course." He caressed the top of her hand. "Running my business. Keeping our life ticking along."

Fiona gave his plate a considering look. She'd relented about cooking breakfast, but she wouldn't on this. "I want a *job* job. Sliding her hand away, she picked up her fork. "A proper one, that pays actual money."

"What for?" Colm set both elbows on the table. Resting his chin on his laced hands, he gazed deeply into her eyes.

He had a way of doing that, looking at her like she was utterly fascinating. And since last week's article about him in the *Times'* "Weekend" he seemed to have gotten better at it. She refused to get distracted. "Isn't it obvious?"

"Not at all," said Colm, his eyes crinkling. "I've the house and groceries taken care of, and whatever else we need."

"You mean, Pauline's taking care of them," Fiona said. Something flickered in his face. Before he could answer, she added, "And you'd better eat your eggs, if you want some tomorrow."

Colm's crinkle un-crinkled. He picked up his fork and took a large bite. "Come on, Pauline's grand. She's made it clear I'm...*we*...are to stay here as long as we like."

"So you can focus on what you're best at," Fiona said, deadpan. "Just like I can, as your faithful Girl Friday." Her pleasure at Colm calling her his *business manager* hadn't lasted long, even if it showed Pauline she was pulling her own weight. Especially since her job duties seemed to include forever having to search for this or that yoke Colm had misplaced—the car keys or his mobile or his favorite blue tie.

"That's right." Colm actually sounded serious.

"While Pauline may feel it's an honor to support you," and Fiona took a bite of her wholemeal toast, "living off someone else doesn't do it for me."

Colm looked perplexed. "It's not like that." He picked up his toast, then dropped it. "Say, have we any white bread?"

"I don't buy white bread," Fiona said. "And here's what it *is* like. I can't afford service for my mobile. Among other things."

"You're welcome to use my phone," Colm said. "You know that."

She forked up some eggs. "It would be cheek to use it for international calls."

"Why would you need to..." Colm's eyes narrowed. "That bloke you went out with—he's not abroad?"

Fiona set down her fork, her appetite gone. She'd had plenty of time to get over Davie—so why did any thought of him still hurt? "I'd like to ring my brother. In *America*."

"Well. Right." He didn't look embarrassed.

"As I was saying," Fiona continued, "if I haven't any income, when I'm at the shops I feel I can't afford even little things—a bun, or hand cream."

"I'm sure there's extra in the grocery kitty," said Colm, smiling again. "For all the sweets and cosmetics you'd ever—"

"Or women's products," she went on relentlessly. Colm blanched. Enjoying his look of man horrors, she asked, "Have you priced tampons recently?" She watched him get his expression under control. It was almost funny, when he'd swallow down what he really wanted to say.

"Obviously you need a small stipend." He started eating again.

"A stipend that Pauline will cover?"

Colm ignored that. "Eventually, we can turn that into a proper salary, as our income grows."

It sounded a lot like what his mother had said when Fiona, after two years at the Dwyers' print shop, had asked for a raise. Before Enda's symptoms. "Custom still hasn't bounced back after the downturn," Helen had told her. "When it does, you'll see something bigger in your pay packet."

Fiona studied Colm across the table, resentment building in her chest. "I missed an important appointment the other day." She'd been invited to join Pauline and her friend Sarah Gallagher from *The Gallagher Post* for lunch. "Because one of your clients had a massive meltdown and only I could sort it."

"And you did," said Colm. "Beautifully."

Pauline promised to set up a new time, but Fiona had learned their hostess had her finger in so many pies she wasn't easy to pin down. If she had a job, she'd at least be in control of her own daily schedule. "That's laying it on a bit thick," she said. "Anyway, I'm not waiting for 'eventually.' Once I'm working, we can start saving for our own place."

"All your day jobs have been at shops," Colm said mildly. "Which wouldn't bring in much anyway."

That was a low blow. "I don't care," she said stubbornly. "I want more independence. And if you stopped turning up your nose at those job lot commissions you've been offered, we *could* afford to get our own flat."

"Doing assembly-line sort of work?" Colm looked horrified. "Look, can we just drop this?" He had apparently reached the end of his saintly patience. "I keep telling you, Pauline's family! She wants us to consider this our home!"

"Whatever she says, we can't stay here indefinitely. It's taking advantage. And keep your voice down."

"I'm sorry." Colm pulled a face. "I got a bit heated there." He scraped the last bite of eggs from his plate. "We won't be here much longer—with your help, I'll only need a few more months to build my inventory and line up commissions."

"I'm critical to your success, then."

"Ab-so-*lute*ly," said Colm, seemingly deaf to the irony in her voice. He reached across the table to take her free hand. "You keep me grounded, you know that." He gazed earnestly at her. "Keep me creative. I couldn't do without you."

Fiona felt herself weaken. She knew every artist needed someone to believe in them. And as much as she hated to admit it, he was right about her earning power. Yet there was something in his eyes, in his words, that seemed so...*practiced*. "I'm happy to hear it." She drew her hand away. "You won't talk me out of it, though. My job hunt."

Kerry
40

"*I* do have a proper farm, no matter what Suz says," I told the chickens as I replenished their feeder. "At least I *will* have a farm, once you lot start giving me some eggs."

Inside the hen run, I breathed deeply of the fresh country air, mixed with a hint of chicken droppings. After being in Dublin all weekend, I'd checked the hens' nest boxes first thing—and found them as empty as they'd been the last two months. "I know you're pretending you don't hear me," I said, "but I'm getting impatient."

They ignored me, diving at their feed. "And now that Jamie's expecting farm eggs to show off to Con, the pressure's really on."

The boys were still in bed. I would've liked a lie-in too, especially with my dodgy digestion this morning. Still, I wanted to at least *try* to act like a farmer.

I glanced over at my apple trees. I was still disappointed that only one tree would bear much of a harvest. "Did I tell you?" I said to the birds. "Judith would like to carry my apples at her shop too." Laura, the brown hen, stopped pecking to cock her head at me. "So I'll be selling bread and apples, *and* eggs as soon as you sort yourselves."

My eye was caught by another hole the birds had dug along the fence line. Laura and Nellie were the worst culprits, scratching out hollows at the edge of the run. Making a mental note to plug the gap with rocks as soon as possible, I turned at the sound of footsteps on the drive. "Desmond—Hallo!"

He crossed the garden to join me. "So, back from Dublin," he said, his eyes owlishly large behind the thick lenses. He'd offered to feed the hens while I was away, but I told him the feeder would hold enough for two days. "I thought maybe young Jamie would be on chicken duty while he's here."

"He brought a friend back from Dublin," I told him. "So probably not this week. Don't be surprised, though, if Jamie asks to drive your tractor so he can show Con how it's done."

"I'm more likely to be asked down to the pub, so they can use their mobiles," said Desmond ruefully.

"You're probably right." I grinned and leaned down to shake the feeder, to redistribute the powdery bits. As I straightened, I felt a spurt of nausea. I reached for the coop wall to steady myself.

"All right there?" asked Desmond.

"Nothing that time won't cure," I said. "Last night, the three of us went to Hurley's for supper, and I discovered Pat's taken to putting hot peppers in what used to be perfectly good pub grub. They don't quite agree with me." Stepping out of the run, I opened the gate wide to let the chickens out. They burst out of the enclosure like they'd been incarcerated for years. "Mind the girls," I told him, though Desmond seemed unfazed by all of them underfoot. The glasses, maybe? "I like your new look, by the way."

He adjusted his glasses self-consciously. "Feel like a bit of an eejit, you know. Thinking I was going blind and Fiona wringing her hands over me, when all I needed were these." He hesitated. "I don't suppose you were able to see her while you were in Dublin?"

"I...um, got caught up with Jamie and Con." I couldn't tell him Fiona hadn't returned my calls.

"Last time she rang, she mentioned she was looking for a job." Desmond sighed heavily.

"A job," I echoed, hurt that she hadn't told me herself. "Sounds like she's staying." I felt bad for Desmond too. But at least she was talking to *him*.

"That it does. Although I'd been so sure she'd make a go with Dav—" He looked distressed.

I didn't know what to say. "Would you....um, have time to take a look at my carrots? I think they'll be ready to harvest soon."

Desmond smiled faintly, and looked down at the hens. "Ah, don't mind this old fella. Beata's good company, she and little Peter—" He suddenly leaned down to peer at Nellie Oleson. "What's this?" He bent closer, nearly eyeball to eyeball to the chicken until I worried she'd have a go at his shiny new glasses.

"What?" The hen didn't look any different, as far as I could tell. "Is she sick or something?"

He straightened up slowly. "Have your birds here given you many eggs?"

"Not one," I confessed. It was a relief to get it off my chest.

Desmond took off his glasses, polishing them on his sleeve, then put them back on. "In the spring, when you got your chickens, didn't you take my advice then? To get yourself pullets?"

I frowned. "I did buy pullets. Bernard Hurley said that Pat said Beata's husband Eddie would have pullets for me. I paid top price for them too."

"Pullets are young chickens," Desmond said patiently, as if I was thick. "Just starting to lay. You wouldn't have gotten any eggs from this crew of old grannies."

"My hens—they're *old*?"

He patted my shoulder. "Too old to produce eggs, I'd say." Giving the hens a good look-over, he said, "See there, how their combs are pale? And on the legs and feet, those leathery-looking scales. That shows they've a few years on them."

I was crushed. "My birds aren't fit for more than the soup pot?"

"I'm afraid so," said Desmond, his brows knotting. "I'm surprised at Beata though."

Beata. I wanted to cry. How could she have...*betrayed* me like this? Now that we were friends, she could have said something about the hens being old. No matter how skint she was, didn't she have a conscience? And here I'd paid her overdue bill at the shop! Even if she didn't know about it.

Given Beata's circumstances, I could hardly demand my money back for the hens. And now I hadn't any spare funds to buy more chickens. I couldn't help it—tears started to my eyes. Even if I'd ended up with the oldest hens because they were too ancient to outrun Davie and myself, she'd still cheated me.

"There now." Desmond patted my shoulder. "What's done is done. Best to start over."

"You mean, with chicks?" I dashed my tears away. Normally I'd be embarrassed to cry in front of Desmond, but I felt quite broken up. "Won't they be harder to source, this late in the year?"

"Very likely," said Desmond.

Even if I could find some chicks, I didn't have money for a separate coop and run, warming lights and a chick-sized feeder, and everything else I'd need to raise them properly. I looked over my small flock, back to scratching again. I couldn't see having them butchered, much less eating them. So they'd be pets? What kind of a farmer was I anyway?

"Kerry?" Desmond was giving me a searching look. Rather odd, for an elderly Irishman. "With another youngster to look after this week, you'll try not to overdo?"

I sniffled. "I'll be fine."

"As you said, time will be the cure." Desmond patted my shoulder again. "Ah, well, look at the pair of us, in the same boat—we've a cow and chickens, and none of them earning their keep."

Desmond left soon after, to tidy the house before Beata came round. Once inside, I changed out of my outdoor gear in the mudroom, my stomach churning. How would I face her after what she'd done? Ballydara was a tiny place—I couldn't be on the outs with a neighbor. So...what to do? Keep pretending Beata was my friend, that I didn't know the hens would never lay? Or treat it like a joke, and act like having chickens as pets was grand?

I slumped into a kitchen chair, suddenly exhausted, and wondered if I'd any antacid tablets in the house. I pressed the heels of my hands to my forehead. The boys would be down soon, and they'd want something to eat—

"Hey."

I lifted my head as Jamie and Con came in. "I didn't hear you come downstairs."

Jamie went straight to the fridge. "What's for breakfast?"

I started to rise, then decided it was too much effort. "Porridge?"

Con pulled a face but didn't say anything. Jamie had no such reservations. "*That's* not on." He grabbed a carton of eggs. "Have we rashers? We need protein if we're going cycling."

"Protein," I repeated, thinking of my rapidly diminishing bank account. "I think we've enough meat for today's breakfast. I'll get more next time I'm in the shop."

"Con and I will cook," Jamie said, getting out the frying pan.

Con stuck his hands in his pockets, looking helpless. "I...uh, can't, really."

"Any eejit can crack eggs," said Jamie, pointing to a unit. "Bowls are in there."

Con jabbed him with his elbow, but fetched a bowl and started in. As I watched Jamie arrange the rashers in the pan, my mind ran in circles. Beata cheating me was bad enough, but I'd need to confess to Judith why I wouldn't have eggs for her, only how to do it without incriminating Beata? Of course I'd have to tell Stephen about my hen fiasco too. He'd have something to say about the hundreds of euro I'd spent, and it wouldn't be good.

As for my quasi-farm plan—the one I'd scribbled on the old yellow tablet in the kitchen drawer to show Stephen—I'd be taking the hoped-for egg income off the ledger. But at least I'd have a few euro from selling my extra produce—

Splat. Con had let an egg roll off the worktop onto the floor. I sighed, resigning myself to another run back to the Topaz to buy more overpriced eggs. After Con cleaned up the mess and both boys inhaled their breakfast, they were ready to cycle to the village. "We're going to the shop for some crisps, Mam," said Jamie. "And chocolate."

"You're hungry again?" Taking my last bite of eggs, I tried not to be disconcerted. It was costing more to feed this pair than I'd planned.

"Well, no, but we will be," said Jamie.

"We're going to stop in at the pub too," added Con. "If that's okay."

"I'll meet you in the village, then." I didn't want Desmond to feel obligated to accompany the boys to Hurley's *every* time they wanted to go. This way, I could see Judith and tell her about my neophyte farmer's mistake. And if the boys were going to sit in Pat's special booth to use their mobiles, it would be only right if I bought a few burgers in return. Dodgy budget or not.

With Jamie using my old bike, and still feeling too crushed about the hens to take a long walk, I drove down to the shop. "Judith," I called over the tinkling of her bell. "Have you a moment?"

Silence. "Be right there," she called from the back, not sounding at all like her usual cheery self. She seemed to be taking her time, but finally she emerged. "What can I do for you?" Judith said formally. Her hair was newly permed, making her face look tighter than usual.

"Just that..." Was she angry with me? "I'm terribly sorry I haven't been round with that bread I promised you," I began. Her expression didn't change. "I've Jamie and his friend here this week, so I haven't gotten to my baking..." My voice trailed away.

"I'm sure it won't hurt Bernard to go easy on his breakfast toast," she said. "Now if you'll excuse me, I'm quite busy."

I dimly heard the bell chime but Judith's coolness was making me feel teary. Again. "I'm actually here because of my eggs," I forced myself to say. "The extras you wanted to sell for me."

Her face became even more aloof. "I'm sure it's all the same to me if you want to get a better price at another shop."

My stomach turned queasy again. "You thought I've selling them to somebody else? But I never had any eggs at all!"

"No eggs..." Her face lost that stern look.

"I've been a complete eejit—thanks to Desmond, I just discovered the hens are as old as the hills! They're not laying, and they're never going to."

"Old hens!" Judith's face eased into a smile. "And here I suspected you'd been selling your eggs in Knockferry!"

"No, I'd been *buying* eggs there," I confessed, relieved we were still friends. "I'd been putting you off so you wouldn't find out what a failure I was with—"

"Kerry, here you are then." Bernard emerged from the sweets aisle.

I froze.

"Have you been skulking in here? Eavesdropping?" said Judith severely. "For shame!"

I flushed. Bernard would have it all over the village about that eejit Kerry McCormack and her ancient chickens. And everyone would know too, that I'd been swizzed by Beata.

"So then, those hens of yours have been eating their heads off with organic feed?" He chuckled. "And all for nothing?"

I felt more heat crawl up my neck. "That's right."

"You'll keep this to yourself, Mr. Bernard Hurley," Judith told him. "Seeing that it's your brother's fault for lining Kerry up with that worthless Eddie Bolger and his worthless birds."

"I wouldn't dream of telling anyone," said Bernard with an injured air, but his eyes were twinkling. "As long as Kerry starts turning out more bread from that Aga of hers."

"Kerry, before I forget," said Judith, "you'll want to know I'm keeping a spot for your new potatoes, once you harvest some." She pointed to her small produce section.

"I hear potato bread's quite good," said Bernard. "Puddings are always welcome too."

"Speaking of puddings," Judith said, "myself and some of the girls round the village would like to organize a summer harvest festival. Can we put you down as co-chair in charge of refreshments?"

As I entered the pub, in such good form after my egg confession *and* being asked to be part of a village do, I felt almost mellow. I could make some desserts with my farm bounty, I thought dreamily, winding my way to the back booth. Carrot cake, for sure… I found Jamie and Con had already settled in. "You should've waited outside for me."

"Aw, Pat's back in the kitchen," said Jamie.

Don't be cheeky, I considered saying, but I was already segueing into apples. A tart for the party?

Con added, "Besides, we've loads of texts."

"I'll wait while you finish." I set down my bag. Maybe I could till up more garden space. It wasn't too late for another sowing of carrots, was it?

Jamie looked alarmed. "You're not going to sit here, are you?"

Teenagers. "No," I muttered, leaving them to go up to the bar. When Pat appeared, I celebrated coming clean with Judith by ordering a burger for myself too. "That's with *no* peppers," I told him, then took a table near the door. Considering carrot cake, I knew I'd need two or three large carrots. Should I pull up one to check if they were ready? I thought idly, resting my chin on my hand. I'd risk wasting one if they weren't—then I jerked in surprise as someone slid into the chair across from me.

Beata.

Her usually sweet face was pale and strained. "Kerry, I *hev* to make apology to you. About old chickens."

I wasn't at all ready to face her. "Desmond shouldn't have said anything," I told her stiffly. "You don't have to explain."

"But I do." She settled into the chair, bumping the table with her round belly.

I couldn't help looking at it. *She's pregnant. Do the decent thing and hear her out.* "Well then?"

She smoothed her hand over her stomach. "You so kind to me and Peter, everyone so kind, I ask Desmond to look after Peter so I can see you, tell you truth."

"O-*kay*." For all I knew, she and Eddie were two of a kind.

"I did not know nothing about chickens. I sell, like Eddie tell me to do. But I did not look after them. I stay away."

"How is that?" I said, unconvinced. The birds were all over her farmyard.

"See, I make deal with neighbors. They feed, water chickens. In return, they get all the eggs. They don't tell how many they find, and I don't ask."

That seemed far-fetched. "If some of your hens have been laying, you've been missing out on making a bit of cash," I pointed out. And thinking of the eight eggs Jamie, Con and I had eaten for breakfast, I said, "And yummy, home-grown food."

She wrinkled her nose. "Egg—I don't like. They give Peter tummyache. I think, maybe he aller...allerg...what is word?"

"Allergic?"

"Yes. So I don't know if chickens lay or don't lay. *Hev* no idea if old or young."

I was beginning to understand. Sort of. "So...the chickens were more your husband's project?"

She shuddered. "I scared of chickens. I tell Eddie, 'no problem, I take care of things' but I afraid, terribly. My babcia back in Poland had many, many chickens when I am small. They chase me, peck me. Rooster, he worst of all, he come after me, jump on me." She showed me a small pink scar on her arm. "I tell myself, when I grow up, I will be city girl. Never *hev* to face chickens again. But then..." Her face turned resigned.

"You married Eddie. With his farm."

"That?" she made a dismissive gesture. "Eddie's place a...what do Irish say? A kip. Not proper farm, neat and tidy like yours. Or Desmond's."

I was so disarmed by that I forgave her for the entire hen disaster. Including all the euro I'd never see again. Pat approached with my burger, still sizzling on the plate. It smelled delicious. I could already taste it...then I saw Beata glancing at my lunch with longing. "I'm not really all that hungry," I said to Beata, lying through my molars. "Will you have it?"

"Well..."

Pat looked from me to Beata. "Girls, where do I put the plate, then?"

"We share, yes?" said Beata. "Bring extra plate, please."

Over our shared burger, Beata told me she was fixing up her place. "I am not sure I stay."

"You're not leaving Ballydara?"

Shrugging, she took another big bite. "I don't like my childrens in shambly house. I already tell neighbors, come take hens. I don't want." She hesitated. "Maybe I move house, take Peter to Galway City. Many jobs there, my uncle say. Then I..." She shifted in her chair. "I start to pay you back for chickens."

"Please don't worry about that," I said. "If you don't mind my asking, though...does Ed—your husband know?"

She shook her head. "I hear someone say, if you want something, lots better to do it first, make sorry later."

It was exactly what I had done, deciding to keep the farm. "Still, fixing up your place seems like a really big job, when you're expecting." I glanced at her baby bump again, and felt a new, powerful surge of envy.

"I *hev* helpers. My uncle, he comes from Galway City to fix roof. And other...young fellas come too. The Killeen boys."

"Killeen boys?"

"Gil? You remember, yes? He work on your house? Well, he help." Color came into her cheeks. "And his brother."

Kerry

41

⟨T⟩hree days later, I was lying in bed, still seeing Beata's tender expression at the pub. She seemed ready to dump that tosser Eddie, and good riddance to him. But to hook up with none other than Davie Killeen!

Did Fiona know about the pair of them? Would she *want* to know? Beata herself had provided proof of how serious things were. "Davie Killeen, he say, 'When you leave farm, I will buy your pigs.' I know he does to help me, but…I don't know."

What fickle bloke he'd turned out to be, transferring his affections in no time flat to the next pretty girl. Pretty and pregnant. And *married*, for God's sake! Okay, so Fiona had made her choice. But how could Davie have gone off her that fast?

It was a good job she'd reunited with Colm. Yet I couldn't help thinking that Fiona and Davie had had something…special. More than a spark. An electrical fire, maybe, the kind you can't throw water on. You have to go full out with a fire extinguisher.

Their failed relationship is *so* none of your business, I told myself, and heard the shower running. Which only reminded me of my next worry. Stephen was in Germany, and neither he nor I had remembered to get cash for Jamie's travel expenses before he'd left. Ringing the night before last, he said, "With any luck, I can cut my trip short."

"Will you be home in time to say goodbye to Jamie?" I asked.

"It's a long shot," he said. "I can't *wait* to finish this round of meetings, though—our investors are really turning the screws. At least Jamie's good about keeping in touch."

I'd worked out he was texting Stephen from the pub. I hated to ask, but I had to. "Um…what about Jamie's travel cash?"

"Can you cover it?" Stephen asked. "Until my next paycheck gets deposited."

With my own bank account looking skinnier than Desmond's cow Bets, I could hardly get my head around Stephen not having plenty of ready cash. I wondered if his firm was now requiring him to pay for his travel expenses up front and reimbursing him later. So where did that leave Jamie and me? Living off my garden carrots?

Okay. I was being ridiculous. Yet now, I curled into a ball, unable to stop fretting. Jamie hadn't breathed a word about Mike McElligott since seeing him. But when he wasn't talking to Con, I'd often see a downcast look on him. Had Jamie liked Mike far more than he'd let on? Maybe that why he was so keen to go to London with Con, thinking he could connect with his father there. I broke into a sweat.

If I didn't have enough worries, Jamie had gotten a hold of some hot peppers from Pat Hurley's cooking experiments, and last night, he and Con had made their version of a Southeast Asian feast. My son had looked so pleased with himself I couldn't *not* eat it. Now, I could still taste the peppers in the back of my throat.

There was a knock at the door. "Mam?"

I swiped at the moisture on my upper lip with the sheet, and struggled to a sitting position. My stomach rolled a little. "Come in."

Jamie let himself in quietly, unlike his usual banging from one room to the next, his hair damp from the shower. "You'll be ready on time, to take us to Dublin? Con's packing now, but I'm done."

I'd seen Jamie's duffle bag—everything neatly rolled up, even his pants, in separate zipper compartments, passport on top, just like his dad always did. *His dad.* The thought pained me. "Of course."

"But you haven't given me...um..." Jamie avoided my eyes.

"Money for your trip?" He'd obviously been worried about it. "I'll stop at the bank when we get to Galway City."

The anxious look didn't leave his face. "Can we leave a bit earlier, then, like noon? Con's mam is expecting us for tea, and yesterday Dad mentioned that Dublin traffic is a disaster with all the summer tourists and stuff."

"We'll be okay." Wondering what else he and Stephen discussed in all those texts, I pushed the covers aside. "Now go on, so I can get dressed."

Jamie turned to leave, then suddenly sat on the bed. "Mam..." He swallowed hard. "There's something..."

"You haven't changed your mind about your holiday?" Was Jamie concerned about getting homesick? A sinking feeling hit me. How could he? He hadn't had a proper home for months. Feeling guilty, I reached out to smooth his hair.

Jamie moved his head just enough to keep me from touching him. "I'm still keen." He suddenly looked red around his eyes. "I've been wanting to tell you," he said in a rush. "About last weekend."

So Jamie *had* been thinking about *that guy*. "When you met...Mike?"

"Yeah. Granny McE made a nice tea for us, but as soon as he started talking...I dunno."

Let them come to you, my dad had advised. "I'm sure it was a bit...awkward."

Jamie looked down. "The thing is...when I got my brainwave to see him—you know, last autumn—I thought it was a great idea."

Actually, it was Con's idea, I wished I could say. "And...?"

"So all the months I waited to meet him, I like, built him up in my mind. Into this fantastic bloke."

"Lots of people would do that." I'd pretended Mike was a great guy myself, the whole time we'd gone out.

"I was so sure he'd be really cool, really bomb, and think I was too." Jamie looked back at me. "So I get to the McElligott's and we shake hands and he says, 'Tell me about yourself.' I start talking about studying physics at school, and how I want to see that Hadron Collider in Switzerland, but he says, 'I don't get any of that boring science stuff.' *Boring*!"

"Unbelievable," I said.

Jamie's cheeks flushed. "Then I told him about living in Vancouver—all the outdoor sport and stuff. He interrupts me, and starts nattering on about Manchester United! Seriously?"

I wanted to touch him, but fearing another rebuff, I joked, "He's not for our lads, then?"

"He doesn't follow the GAA either!"

"That's pathetic," I said. "I can't believe I ever went out with that tosser."

"Jeez, Mam—ewww!" said Jamie.

Wrong thing to say. How could I forget teens didn't want to believe their parents had sex, even to conceive them. "So. Mike wasn't so cool after all."

"Cool? He knew about me for months, and he could've nipped over to Ireland any time to see me, only he didn't. So why should I try to get on with him, go and see him, if he doesn't really care about me?"

I tried to look noncommittal, but the tension in my stomach began to uncoil. "That's up to you, love." I hesitated. "Does your dad know how you feel?"

Jamie shook his head. "Like a total eejit? I couldn't tell Dad—I mean, I made such a big deal out of meeting Mike, though I knew it bothered him a lot."

"Your dad's a big boy," I told him. "Sometimes you have to do what seems right at the time."

"But I made Dad feel bad," Jamie said, his eyes shiny. "All for nothing."

I couldn't help stretching out my hand to smooth his hair. This time he let me. "Think how happy he'll be," I teased gently. "Not wondering if you like this guy more than him."

Jamie digested this in silence. "That *gom*?" He suddenly grinned and bounced off the bed.

Clearly, his disappointment over Mike McElligott wouldn't scar him for life. I rose too, jostling my stomach, and abruptly sat back down. "Oh—got up too fast." I couldn't tell him his supper had made me sick.

Jamie frowned at me. "Mam, we're going to be way behind schedule…"

"Really, I'll be organized in time." I took a deep breath and stood up carefully.

Jamie gave me an odd look. "Great," he said briskly, sounding a lot like Stephen. "I just remembered—I've got to cycle down to the village. Con too."

"What about breakfast?"

"It won't take long," he said over his shoulder. "We'll eat when we get back."

As I dragged myself through a shower and getting dressed, the prospect of driving to Dublin felt as overwhelming as a trek through the Amazon jungle. But I could rest up at Mam and Dad's, I decided, sitting down with a cup of tea. If I stayed a day or two, maybe Stephen would be back in Ireland by then.

The phone rang. That could be him—had he been able to cut loose from his meetings? I lunged to pick up.

Mistake. I had to sit down. It was four rings before I was able to reach for the handset. "Stephen?" I said automatically.

"Sorry," said a young woman, "It's Robin. Robin Keane?"

"Robin?" I drew a complete blank.

"The estate agent," she said in a chirpy voice. "We met in March, about listing your property."

"Right, right." I so wasn't up for this. "Can I…ring you tomorrow?"

"I would've emailed you," she said quickly. "In fact, I did email your husband and he indicated you were in charge of the place. Since I knew you didn't have Internet up there, I decided no harm, why not check in."

"I…um, appreciate it." The timing and sheer unwelcome-ness of her call made my stomach go sour again.

"It's such lovely little farm, isn't it? I'm just getting in touch to let you know the market's had a bit of an uptick—a rather robust one, actually—in case you have any further thoughts about selling."

"We're very happy here," I said. "In fact, I'll be harvesting my first crop of vegetables soon."

"Right," she said, as cheery as before, but I could hear her disappointment. "Still, if there's anything I can do for you, you've my card."

I thanked her and replaced the handset, breathing deeply to settle my tummy. If I was going to be away for a few days, pepper-pukey or not, I'd want to take a look at my carrot crop.

When I felt steady enough to move, I grabbed a trowel from the mudroom, trudged out to my vegetable patch and climbed over the poultry fencing I'd strung to keep the hens out. Kneeling next to my carrot rows, I brushed the soil away from the one with the tallest foliage and pushed the trowel into the soil. Savoring this significant moment, I tugged gently. Out came a modestly-sized carrot.

Or something that used to be a carrot. I blinked stupidly at the orange article dangling from my hand.

It had a carrot top, and an orange shell, but it was like…hollowed out. I quickly dug out its neighbor. This carrot had big chunks missing. I yanked out a third. Same thing. "Dear God," I muttered. My little crop—what had happened? Insects? Some kind of…carrot disease?

Frantic now, I pulled out two more, then scrabbled round my patch, wrenching at another dozen carrots. I found a couple of shorter, skinny ones that were intact, but the rest were damaged. Completely ruined, in fact.

I sat back on my heels, weeping helplessly. My lovely dreams felt completely spoiled—baking with my carrots, selling them, my small place being a real, productive farm… Then I heard the boys' voices. I swiped my arm across my face, and gathered the carrots I'd pulled. Uncaring of the garden soil clinging to them, I cradled the vegetables in my jumper, against my stomach. Desmond. Desmond would know what the problem was.

Jamie and Con rode up the driveway, my son dismounting first. "Mam!" he called. "We've got to get breakfast—"

"We've less than an hour," broke in Con.

"I have to see Desmond." Still snuffling, I walked past them, clutching my carrots.

"What for?" Jamie frowned. "Mam, you're acting really weird." He whispered to Con, "She is, isn't she? Acting really weird. It's a good job I…."

I didn't hear the rest. "I can't talk now," I said over my shoulder and headed for the road.

"You're *walking* to the Whelan's? Come on, Mam, we don't have time, can't you take the car?"

"Not with these." I hefted my dirt-covered carrots. "Be right back."

I walked as fast as I dared, fixating on the damage to my crop. The hens couldn't have caused it—they'd scratch up every square inch of ground they could get to, but they didn't dig to eat roots. Still, what did it matter? Ruined was ruined.

Reaching Desmond's drive, I gathered my carrots closer in my jumper and rushed toward the house, feeling ready to keel over. You can collapse later, I told myself. Even throw up. Only not now. I banged on the door. "Desmond!"

Moments later, Beata opened it. "Kerry! Something is wrong?"

"Yes! I need to talk to Desmond, right now—"

"Shhh," she said in a crooning voice. "Shush, *plez.*"

"I can't!" I was shaking. One of my carrots slid to the stoop.

"Peter *heving* a sleep." Then she looked at the carrots, quivering in my unsteady arms. Her smooth brow wrinkled. "Vegetables for Desmond?"

"Yes! I mean, no, I just have to see him!" I was beyond pleasantries.

"Desmond is at pub." She blushed prettily. "Mr. Killeen, he come here, he take Desmond to watch match."

So. Fickle Davie was back in the neighborhood. And pursuing

Beata publicly. Desmond was okay with that? Yet *another* thing I couldn't worry about. I turned to go, but caught by another wave of dizziness, I had to lean against the door. Closing my eyes, I heard Beata say, "Kerry, you are all right?"

I mumbled, "I've got to get to the pub." *First, run back home, get into the car...* I pried my eyes open, but couldn't seem to move.

"You do not look okay." She chewed on her lip. "I think you stay here, yes?"

"I have to see Desmond! It's an emergency."

Beata looked at me, frowning. "Then I drive you," she said. "I wake Peter. He not happy, but I wake him."

"I can drive," I protested. "I only need to fetch my car."

Beata said, "No drive for you, Kerry. I drive. My car *hev* seat for Peter."

By the time I'd shuffled to her Mini with my carrots, she was leaving the house, a sleepy Peter on her hip. Despite the state of me, I noticed how his legs tightened her shirt around her protruding stomach. I was being an awfully demanding friend, but that was something else I couldn't seem to help right now.

As she strapped Peter in, I practically fell into the passenger seat, hugging the carrots closer. As the little car bumped down the hill, I leaned back and closed my eyes. It was lovely to let someone else be in charge. Maybe my real problem wasn't a tummy upset—a panic attack? I did feel overwhelmed with worry—Jamie's travel money, Robin's ill-timed phone call, driving the boys to Dublin, Davie forgetting Fiona...but most of all, my carrot disaster—

The car jerked to a stop. I opened my eyes to find we were in the village. "Thank you," I muttered, and heaved myself out of the car with my armful of vegetables. Opening the pub door, I slumped in the doorway. There was Fiona's dad sitting at the bar, Bernard too, and a dark-haired young man on the stool between them. "Desmond!" I croaked.

Davie Killeen, who I'd *thought* was a friend, barely glanced over his shoulder. *You should be uncomfortable, you faithless gobshite.*

"If it isn't Kerry!" said Bernard, as his brother Pat called, "You'll have a burger?"

I shook my head. "Desmond!" I said louder.

Desmond slid off his stool and scurried toward me, at least as fast as a septuagenarian could scurry, Bernard on his heels. "What is it?"

I tried to rearrange my arms to pull out a carrot, but dropped three instead. Beata appeared at the door, holding Peter. "Is emergency, she say."

Davie did turn to look at *her*, then he was back to the telly.

"We take Kerry to shop, yes? Judith *hev* couch in back."

"But my carrots!"

"Got 'em." Bernard checked his watch, then with his big workman's hands, picked up the ones on the floor. Desmond took my elbow.

I mustered the strength to walk across the road. We were no doubt an odd procession, Desmond, me with my jumper full of carrots, Bernard with his handful, and Beata leading the way— actually, more like waddling—with Peter. As the two men got me inside, the shop bell clanging, Judith's anxious face appeared in my line of vision. "Kerry, love, what's happened?"

"It's horrible!" I said tragically. I shook off my escorts, and let my entire armful fall. "Look! A disaster!"

Desmond slowly leaned over and picked up a handful of carrots by their tops, gazing at them for a long moment. "No, it's bank voles."

I stared at my carrots and suddenly the damage took on mythic proportions. I burst into tears again.

Desmond was saying something about digging creatures but I wasn't listening. "Look at them," I sobbed. Part of me realized I was acting like I'd lost my wits, with my dirty hands and jumper, bawling about vegetables, but I was beyond caring. "I was going to sell my crops, and maybe do a farm-to-table thing I'd read about!" I babbled. "What'll happen to my farm now? I've let Stephen down too, in fact, he'll probably say we have to..." I trailed off.

They were all watching me, Desmond, Bernard, Judith and Beata, sympathy and something else in their faces. Even little Peter glanced at me uncertainly. They obviously thought I was completely away in the head. I hiccoughed, but I couldn't quite stop crying.

"There, there," said Judith, giving me a pat. "You'll upset the wee one."

Confused, I sniffed hard. Jamie would always be my little boy, but he was hardly *little*. "It's okay," I managed, tears leaking from my eyes. "He's st-still up at the house."

They all exchanged another strange look, then Bernard fetched a chair from the back and brought it out. Judith pressed me into it. "No, the *baby*," she said slowly.

"What baby?" I choked. A snort came from Desmond as the shop bell tinkled again.

"Yes, what baby?" said a familiar voice. I turned my head carefully to see Aislin Carpenter, accompanied by a pretty brunette girl I'd run into several times, Deirdre O'Donnell.

Beata hoisted Peter higher up on her hip and pointed at my stomach. "That baby," she said.

I stopped crying as if someone had turned a switch.

"That's the one," said Desmond. "So, have you told Himself then?"

Kerry
42

Oh. My. God. How blind could I have been?

The fatigue, the over-the-top appetite, the nausea. Add my aversion to drink, and my careening emotions, how could I not have guessed? It was textbook. It was a…baby.

My eyes welled up again, but this time in a good way. I rested my hands on my tummy, taking in the wonder of it. "A baby," I murmured softly.

I finally looked up, at the circle of amused faces around me. I could tell Bernard was trying not to laugh. Deirdre had no such compunction. "Jaysus, it must be something in the water here, Ash," she said merrily to her friend. "Thank *God* I'm leaving the village before I catch it."

"You're not seeing a bloke these days, are you?" Aislin asked her.

"Actually, I'm going out with someone new tomorrow." Deirdre giggled. "Though you know very well I never do *that* on a first date."

Aislin rolled her eyes, then gave me a once-over. "Kerry, you seemed a bit pale last time I saw you. I wondered if…you know, you'd joined the crowd." She patted her round tummy, and smiled at Beata.

"Desmond, how did you work it out?" I asked him.

"Ah, you know." He shuffled his feet. "When a cow is pregnant, her udder—" He turned deep crimson. "What I mean is, her mammary—" His gaze slid over my chest then he turned away. Even the back of his neck was brick red.

"Right, right," I said hastily.

"I noticed too," Aislin said, gesturing at her own round bosom.

"Yeah," Deirdre put in. "The size of them!"

I'd noticed my bra was tighter—and thought it was from the weight I'd put on from my recent snack-fests. "Pregnant or not, I've got to get Jamie and his friend to Dublin today."

I started to rise from the chair. Desmond gently pressed my shoulder. "Now then, you can bide another minute."

Bernard looked at his watch then sidled away, making for the door. "Bernard!" said Judith. "You don't breathe a word of this, do you hear me?"

"I've some important business to take care of," Bernard said quickly, and left the shop. I only hoped he wasn't going to bring in a few more villagers to enjoy the show.

"Does Stephen know?" Judith asked.

I shook my head. "I was going to take a...a test," I stammered. "But I didn't." I wasn't ready. Or I was ready, but I was too scared...

"Then you're in luck," said Judith, and scuttled behind the counter. She brought out a small package and beamed. "I did a special order."

I gaped at the pregnancy test kit she held. At this moment, with my friends working out that I was pregnant before I'd even had a clue, I couldn't quite get out, *I already have a test.*

"Off you go then," said Judith, and nodded toward the back room. "Loo is to your right."

I gazed at the expectant faces, hysterical laughter bubbling up inside me. They didn't really think I'd go to the shop toilet and wee while they waited for me, then emerge flashing my stick and official announcement? "I'll take it later, thank you," I said, trying to gather the tatters of my dignity. "When I see Stephen."

Desmond was shaking his head. "I'll say again, it's as plain as the nose on your face."

Deirdre was checking her mobile. "Holy crap, the bus will be here any minute."

"The driver will wait for *you*," Aislin told her. Then to me, "Do you have to postpone your test? We so want to know *now*."

"The sooner you are sure," Beata coaxed, "the sooner baby will seem more real."

"Kerry, why not get on with it?" Deirdre said. "I'd love to know the result before I leave."

Desmond snorted again. "What does the girl need a test for? Anyone can tell that—"

He broke off as the bell tinkled yet again. Holy Mother of God, I thought. Who else is going to know my secret? I jerked my head toward the door, which made it swim worse than before, and closed my eyes again.

"That she's pregnant, sure," said Judith. "Still, these days expectant mammies take the test."

The door closed. A man said, "I thought so too."

I felt myself pitch forward. Then everything went black.

Fiona

43

*C*olm came in with a takeaway sack as Fiona sat at Pauline's kitchen table, drawing. The aroma of fried fish filled the room. "Do you mind shifting your papers?" he said pleasantly.

Actually, I do mind. Intent on the elven figure she was sketching, she didn't look up.

"I've been to the chipper's—we're due for a celebration." Colm sounded quite proud of himself. As if he'd really gone above and beyond to fetch them lunch.

"Thanks," she murmured. Fiona had given up trying to claim a spot in the studio for sketching, so most mornings she staked out the roomier table in here. "I'm not hungry just yet." She added a flourish to the elf's cap with a red pencil. "I'll finish this series of drawings before I eat."

"I'm famished myself," said Colm, "but you've left no room on the table."

Fiona lifted her head to see a flash of irritation on his face, quickly masked. "I have, haven't I?" She surveyed her untidy papers, gazing with satisfaction at the drawing she'd been working on. Her elf looked mischievous, sly, and wicked at the same time.

"Since this isn't the first time, maybe you can plan to organize your materials in time for meals, all right, love?"

These days, no matter how contrary she was, Colm would only smile and make some sort of soothing reply. She'd been deliberately acting more—well, there was no other way to put it—bloody-minded, to see if he'd crack. His annoyed look hinted that she was finally getting to him.

"You know, Colm, you're right." She glanced at her sketchbook and colored pencils, and the other drawings strewn about. "I shouldn't want to spoil any more of *your* meals by having my things in your way." She scooped up the loose papers and strode past him into his studio, heading for the drafting table.

She heard a rustle of paper packaging, then his footsteps behind her. "Fiona…"

"Since you never got around to making room for my work in here, it's apparently up to me." Fiona swept a pile of his pencil sketches aside, some drifting to the floor.

"Hey!" Colm dove for the papers. "These are for my new commission!"

"Are they?" Setting down her own drawings, she waved carelessly toward the long worktable by the window. "They can go over there."

"But I'd got them properly organized, with my works-in-progress in order of priority—you know that!" He straightened the papers, not doing a good job of it. "Anyway, what the hell's gotten into you lately? You *know* I made a space for you." His handsome face reddening, he jerked his finger toward the small desk in the corner, where the laptop sat. "There!"

"Right," she said. "A spot for 'my' invoices, and 'my' list of businesses to ring to see if they'll display your work. And look! I've room for 'my' applications for shows too."

"You don't have to be sarcastic." He took her hands, which she immediately jerked free. "Okay—you're obviously having a bad day."

"*Bad day*?"

"I get you're disappointed that you haven't found a job yet, but don't take it out on me." He smiled at her, but something in his expression seemed…what? She couldn't work it out. "We're a team, aren't we? Isn't this the life we dreamed of? Once I sell a few more big pieces, we can focus on your work."

"I'm not willing to wait until then." She crossed her arms

over her chest. "And this life you're so keen on? You've envisioned it. I haven't."

"What are you talking about? Didn't I ask you to marry me? *Marry* me! D'you think I'd do that if we weren't sharing this dream?"

"You have odd ideas about being a couple—living off someone else, staying in their flat, letting everyone else do for you so you can live your perfect life with your work completely uninterrupted."

"I don't know how you can say that. We've been happy here, even if you've been stringing me along—"

"*You've* been happy here," Fiona snapped. "I've been going round the bloody bend—"

"Kids!" Pauline appeared in the open double doorway. "Is that fish and chips I smell?"

"Pauline!" Looking comically dismayed, Colm scurried around Fiona into the kitchen, and gave Pauline the package from the chippers. "Sure, sure, help yourself—there's plenty."

"I will." Pauline reached into the sack and drew out a handful of chips. "Larry won't touch fried food." She smacked her lips. "By the way, can you tone it down? I could hear the pair of you from my bedroom."

"Sorry!" Colm looked horrified. "We didn't mean to disturb you—it's nothing really... Fiona? It was nothing, right? Tell her."

Fiona tightened her lips.

"It's all the same to me if you want to have a donnybrook," said Pauline, munching her chips. "A lovers' spat now and then is good for a relationship. But I'd rather not have a front row seat." Dropping the sack of food on the table, she stepped into the studio, Colm following her like a puppy. "Since I'm here..." Pauline studied at Fiona's papers on the drafting table. "Fiona, you're up for a chat?"

Did that mean Pauline had an update on the book project? "Of course." Fiona glanced at Colm. *See, my work is important.*

"Maybe you can talk some sense into her." Colm perched on the edge of the worktable.

"Colm." Pauline waved him away. "I'm speaking to Fiona in private."

"But Fiona and I—we share everything—"

"I doubt that," Pauline said wryly, and jerked her head toward the kitchen. "Go on."

"My lunch is getting cold anyway." Colm marched out, banging the double doors.

Leaning against the drafting table, Fiona contemplated the closed doors. "I'd like to slam a door or three right about now."

"For all his silver hair, Colm acts like a right little boy sometimes." Pauline wandered toward the window worktable. "He's a bit too used to getting his way."

So Pauline *wasn't* going to talk about the book. "I should've expected you'd make excuses for him," Fiona said bitterly.

Pauline looked amused. "Blood's thicker than water, eh?" She thumbed through a stack of Colm's layout paper.

"If you want to give out at me for not treating Colm right, have at it." Fiona was so *done* being the polite guest, keeping the peace by going along with what Colm always wanted. Except that one thing. "If you're here to try talking me into marrying him, save your breath." She was spoiling for a fight—and since Colm wasn't available, Pauline would do.

Pauline was watching her, her jolly look gone. "I was a lot like you, once," she said unexpectedly.

"Oh?" Fiona said, suddenly deflated.

"Hard to believe, yeah?" Pauline examined one of Colm's preliminary designs. "I was a pretty country girl who was mad for art. But not drawing, not anything you could market. I was into creating these bizarre, avant-garde yokes with wire and bits of rubbish. Drove Mum and Dad bats." She chuckled. "They thought I was completely unraveled."

"Another name for nonconformist." Fiona suddenly felt more simpatico with Pauline. "Myself, I'd hide in the barn, drawing, instead of doing my chores."

"We were two of a kind, then." Pauline dropped the paper to fiddle with one of Colm's mechanical pencils. "Anyway, I left the farm to go for an art degree. Caught the eye of a lot of blokes too, can you believe it?" She ruffled her cropped hair. "Back then, I'd long blond curls down to my waist."

Fiona fingered her plait. She'd stopped wearing her hair down soon after she got here.

"Had some great crack, but I gave 'em all up—the blokes, I mean—when a toff like Larry went for me. We were an odd pair—my parents were hardly scraping by, and the whole crew of Smurfits had money coming out of their...ah, you know. Still, I was under no illusions about why he wanted me."

"Your...artsy free spirit?" *Davie had liked mine.*

"There's that—I did exactly what I wanted. No kowtowing to family or social pressure." Pauline put two fingers up, thrusting out her big hand. "*That's* what I thought about acting properly."

Fiona grinned at her gesture. "Seems a strange reason for a man to marry."

"Oh, I worked it out. I represented the freedom Larry didn't have, running the family business. His way of walking on the wild side."

"I can't quite see..." Fiona's voice trailed away. She couldn't reconcile this middle-aged matron with the reckless girl Pauline described. "What happened to your art?"

"Gave it up. Quit uni too. I was smart enough to realize I'd no real talent," Pauline said frankly. "That it's hard enough for gifted artists to make even a semblance of a living." She picked up Colm's X-Acto knife and lightly touched the tip. "I loved Larry to bits, but my head wasn't completely in the clouds. Since I'd no way to earn my crust, his money would free me up to do anything I wanted. So there you are."

"Why are you telling me all this?" Fiona asked suspiciously.

"Why not?" said Pauline. "You're a practical girl. I've seen how you get things done. Colm admires that, tremendously." She chuckled. "Why'd I say that? You told me I could save my breath."

It was impossible to be angry with Pauline. "Okay, I am a practical sort." Not thinking, Fiona traced a small heart on the table with her index finger. "I don't crave hearts and flowers from a bloke, but once in a while you want to know your man is dying of love for you."

Pauline's smile turned bittersweet. "Artists will always love their work more. You know that. But Colm does love you, in his way."

"In his way," Fiona repeated. "I don't want lukewarm love." *I want to burn with it.* The thought shocked her so much she dropped onto the stool.

"Why have you stayed, love?" Pauline asked. "If you're not mad for Colm either?"

"Because I…" A lot of reasons, all of which shamed her. *Because I didn't want to go back to Dad's as a failure. Because I'd invested so much time and emotion in Colm, loving him all this time. Or thinking I did.* "I may have made a mistake."

"You're not the first woman." Pauline set down the knife. "I may be Colm's Lady Bountiful, but I want to see you happy."

"I…appreciate that," Fiona said slowly.

"You're not entirely like I was." Pauline waved toward Fiona's papers. "Besides your talent. You see, marrying Larry, becoming his helpmate, I got to enjoy my cage. And his family loved me for it."

Family? A dim light flickered in Fiona's mind. Before she could work out what it meant, a slow burn started in her middle. She'd left her dad, left Kerry and all the people who cared about her to start over with Colm. But to be a dabbler, *a noodler* while he grew his career?

She wanted to fly at him for putting her in this position. Yet as wrath filled her, Fiona knew she'd done this to herself. Working so hard for Colm because she felt guilty—

The double doors blew open, banging on the walls. As Fiona jumped from the stool Colm bellowed, "Just what the holy hell is *this*?"

He held out her sketchbook. It was open to the page she knew she should have destroyed.

Fiona yanked the sketchbook from his grasp. "*This*," she said, "could have been my future. But I gave it up for you."

Kerry
44

*F*eeling a tiny breeze against my cheeks, I struggled to open my eyes. The first thing I saw was Stephen's face close to mine, his smile tender. "She's okay," he said over his shoulder.

Stephen was cradling me in his lap, his arms warm and tight around me. Aislin hung over our chair, fanning me with a piece of cardboard. "You were only out a minute or two, but you gave us a proper scare."

Deirdre was grinning. "You would've keeled to the floor, if your man here hadn't caught you. He's grand in an emergency."

"Don't I know it." I touched Stephen's face, smiling mistily. "I'm feeling better already. How on earth did you turn up here?"

"Left my meetings late yesterday, booked the first flight to Dub, and hired a car at the airport," Stephen said. "Yesterday, a little bird had told me—actually, not little, and it was by text—that his mam hadn't been feeling well all week."

"Jamie?" I struggled to sit up. To think, he was so worried he contacted his dad... "Oh, my God, he's waiting for me up at the house—Con too! I've got to get them to Dublin—"

"Hold on," Stephen said. "You're in no state to go anywhere."

The shop phone jingled. Judith reached under the cash desk to answer it, only saying, "I'll tell them." Replacing the handset, she said, "That was Bernard. Turn out, the boys walked to the village, and he's met them at the pub."

"Jamie mustn't see me like this!" Stephen helped me rise from the chair, but kept his arm round me. "I don't want him to

305

know..." I took in the concern on my friends' faces. "Please, don't tell him. About the baby, I mean."

"Of course not," said Judith.

"Our lips are sealed," Aislin promised.

Stephen said, "Jamie's leaving on holiday today. I'm thinking we don't want him to worry about anything like that while he's gone."

"You know teenagers." I was finally steady enough to step away from the chair. "He'll be embarrassed to have a pregnant mam."

"Yeah, completely mortified," Deirdre confirmed. She glanced at her mobile. "Okay, the bus'll be here any second and I can't miss it."

I looked at Stephen helplessly. "I've got to get myself together—we've the long trip, and the boys haven't had breakfast."

"You didn't eat either, I'll bet," said Stephen, looking torn. "Or course, I'll drive them, once I know you won't be passing out again."

Judith frowned. "Stephen, you'll not want to leave when Kerry's feeling so dodgy. Why don't you put the boys on the bus?"

"Oh, I couldn't," I said. "Not without an adult."

"Will I do?" Deirdre asked. "Though Ash is always telling me to grow up."

Judith looked thunderstruck. "Why Deirdre, how lovely! Stephen, you'll ring the boy's mam and get her permission?"

Stephen took his mobile from his pocket, then looked at me. "I'll just pop into the pub."

"You'll do no such thing." Judith pushed her phone toward him. "And if you're thinking of the charges, the call's on the house."

"Deirdre, that would be wonderful." I lowered my voice. "But Stephen, Jamie's travel money..."

His face creased with worry again. "There's no way round it, I've got to drive them. We'll need to stop at our bank on the way."

"If it's cash you need," said Judith, opening her register drawer, "I think I've enough here to cover the basics. That way, Stephen can stay here with Kerry."

Tears filled my eyes. "Judith, that's so kind, I don't know what to say…"

"Say, 'I'll write you a check,'" Stephen said, his face wreathed in smiles. "Judith, it looks like we've a deal."

As she counted out a pile of euro, Stephen was already phoning up Con's mother. While he was talking I looked around for Beata and Desmond, to thank them, and finally noticed they'd disappeared. Beata was probably keen to see Davie. Surely Desmond wasn't trying his luck at a second round of matchmaking?

I forgot about them as Stephen rang off, looking less than easy. "Con's mam is fine with the bus, but she's stuck at work until six at the earliest."

"Deirdre," said Judith, "might you stay with the kids until the mother gets to the station? Jamie'll have all that cash on him."

Deirdre looked dismayed. "It would be no bother, but I promised my sister Mags I'd look after her kids tonight."

My brain, admittedly on holiday all day, suddenly kicked into gear. "Wait—maybe Fiona could meet the boys at the station. But…" I felt tragic again. "I haven't her emergency number on me. It's up at the farmhouse."

"I have it," said Judith, ferreting under her cash desk. As she waved a scrap of paper, in walked Jamie and Con, each with a duffle bag and a bulging sack with grease marks.

"Bernard stood us for cheeseburgers and chips—" As Jamie caught sight of Deirdre, his face turned bright red. So did Con's.

I stepped toward Judith's phone, rather amazed the boys had not only walked to the village, but carried their luggage too. "Your dad and I are making arrangements for your trip to Dublin."

My son paid no attention, his eyes glued to the vision before him, all curls and dimples and laughing dark eyes.

"Hi, I'm Deirdre," she said, smiling. "Apparently you blokes are taking the bus, and I'm to be your seatmate. That's okay?"

"Oh *yeah*," said Jamie. Con was too busy staring to answer.

"Great," said Deirdre. "I hope you'll share Bernard's goodies, though, because I'm absolutely famished." Con nodded vigorously.

She was clearly up for escorting two boys gobstruck by her charms. Dialing the phone, I glanced at Jamie, feeling bittersweet. My son might not mind spending more time in Ballydara, if he'd a chance to see this goddess. Still, I was determined to say our goodbyes before Jamie could catch even a whiff of my pregnancy.

Fiona

45

*F*iona gazed at the sketch that had finally made Colm blow his cover.

She'd drawn Davie from memory, lying on rumpled sheets, torso bare, drowsy satisfaction in his face.

"Well?" Colm stood in the doorway, rigid with outrage. "This is the guy you *said* you only had tea with?"

Fiona clutched her sketchbook to her chest. "It's none of your bloody affair what I draw." She stared back at Colm, daring him to contradict her.

A mobile phone rang, coming from his pocket. And rang and rang. "You're going to pick up?" asked Pauline.

"What's more important than *that*?" Colm pointed at the offending sketchbook. The phone finally stopped.

Feeling too wrought up to speak, Fiona made to leave the room—and realized she had no space to call her own. Nowhere to be alone.

The phone began ringing again. Not taking his gaze from Fiona, Colm pulled out his mobile and barked, "Yes?" His eyes flickered. "Now's not a good time."

"Is someone ringing for me?" Fiona asked.

"Sorry," Colm was saying into the phone. As he took it from his ear, Pauline warned, "Colm!"

Dropping her sketchbook, Fiona lunged for the mobile. "Hallo?"

"You're not easy to get a hold of," said Kerry.

"Kerry!" Fiona ignored Colm's dagger-eyed stare. "It's been ages!"

"I'm at the shop, and can't really talk, but is there any chance you could meet Jamie and his friend at Connolly Station this afternoon? It would only be for an hour or so, until Con's mam gets there. I realize it's terribly short notice."

Giving Fiona an encouraging smile, Pauline disappeared into the kitchen. "It's no bother," Fiona told Kerry. "Tell Jamie I'll be watching for him."

"Super! The bus should arrive around five. I've tons of news, but things are frantic here—I've got to say goodbye to Jamie. Can I phone you right back?"

"I'll be here," Fiona promised. Disconnecting, she stared at Colm, resentment and regret at her own folly making her chest hurt. *Not easy to get a hold of...*

Colm held out his hand. "I'll have my mobile back."

"Not yet," said Fiona, pushing past him into the kitchen. If it took the last euro she had, she was getting service for her mobile.

Pauline was pouring hot water into three mugs. "Cuppa for you?"

"Please," said Fiona. As Colm followed her, Fiona dunked her teabag in the water so vigorously liquid splashed onto the worktop. The phone she held rang, and instantly, she had it to her ear. "Kerry?"

"I wanted to let you know straightaway—I'm pregnant," Kerry said in a low voice, tremulous joy in her voice. "Well, ninety-nine percent sure, anyway."

"How wonderful!" Fiona choked out, feeling both elation for Kerry and a sense of loss.

"I'm still at the shop, in the back. I wanted to tell you before anyone else did, because...well, it's a long story, but everyone in the village knows."

"Isn't that Ballydara for you," Fiona managed, suddenly missing the place more than ever. "Stephen must be over the moon."

"Oh, way beyond that," said Kerry. "Both of us are."

Fiona imagined their delight in each other at this moment.

Had she and Colm ever been that happy? "I admit it's not quite a shock."

"Your dad dropped some hints?" Kerry asked ruefully.

"Very subtle ones," said Fiona. She realized between job-hunting and dealing with Colm's prima donna routine, she'd rung Desmond only rarely, and Kerry even less.

Colm was talking to Pauline in a loud voice, obviously trying to disrupt her conversation. Still, paying him no attention gave Fiona more satisfaction than telling him to shut his gob. She hesitated, then asked the question she couldn't avoid. "Does your pregnancy mean you'll be moving house to Dublin soon?"

"I guess it does," Kerry said, not sounding joyful at all now. "But knowing you'll be there makes it much easier."

What'll I do now? Fiona thought despairingly. I can't live here... With difficulty, she said, "I'd love to chat but I'd better go."

"Wait." Kerry sighed audibly. "I wish I didn't have to...well, if your dad hinted about my being pregnant, then maybe he might've also mentioned...um, Beata."

"She's still looking after Dad, right?"

"Yes. I don't want to gossip." Kerry's voice caught. "But it seems only right you should know that..." She dropped her voice again. "Davie Killeen's been coming round to see her."

"*Beata*?" Fiona felt a stab of pain behind her breastbone. When she could speak again, she said, "That's no surprise."

"But it is," said Kerry. "He seemed so mad for you—"

"He wasn't," Fiona interrupted. "Of course a bloke like him would find someone new."

"This fast?"

"A sweet young thing like Beata is perfect for him. He likes rescuing people." Fiona hated the cynicism in her voice but she couldn't help it.

"I could hardly believe it," Kerry said. "And her still married! Only when Davie offered to buy her pigs, I knew that..." Her voice trailed away.

Pigs? "It had to be true love," Fiona said, aiming for irony but failing miserably. "I've moved on, anyway," she lied.

If she concentrated on her ire at Colm, it would keep her from dwelling on Davie. And how very lost he was to her. "Before you go," Fiona made herself say, and stared at Colm, not caring if he was listening, "What did you mean, that I'm hard to reach?"

"Oh, I've caused enough trouble telling you about Davie."

"Tell me," Fiona insisted.

"Well," Kerry's voice was reluctant, "I've rung the house phone there—the Smurfits'—and left messages. Or a man will pick up and say you're out, but he'll tell you I rang. Only I never hear back from you. I'm sure you're busy, though."

"Not that busy," said Fiona, her slow burn growing into white-hot rage. How could Colm be so underhanded! "Anyway," she got out, "I'll have Jamie ring you right after he gets off the bus. And congratulations again."

She ended the call, letting her anger give her strength. "Colm," she said coldly, despite Pauline's presence. The woman knew everything about their relationship anyway. Her hand tightened around Colm's mobile. "You've been screening my calls."

He slowly turned from Pauline. "I wouldn't say *screening*—"

"What would you call it?" She carefully set down the phone. Otherwise she'd have slung it at him like a grenade.

"Well, you know how I am in the middle of a project, dropping balls all over the place…I'd forget my own head if it wasn't—"

"What utter *shite*."

"It's true! I intended to pass on the messages, only I didn't want to distract you from your work."

"Biscuits with your tea?" Pauline said desperately.

"You mean, *your* work," Fiona snapped. "Are you such a control freak you want to keep me from my best friend?"

She expected him to give her an icy glare and stalk from the room. Instead, he said, "It wasn't that—at least, I…didn't *mean* to."

"Stop, will you?" Fiona clenched her fists. "Jaysus, I cannot *believe* I was so taken in! All that sweet talk and patience and bloody I love you's!"

"Please." Colm's eyes were pleading. "I wanted to be the one you depended on. And there was that Galway bloke..." He glanced at Pauline, his ears red. "When you didn't want to...I mean, I thought we could be...close again, if only—"

"*What*?" Fiona couldn't believe what she was hearing. "Are you saying you thought I'd have *sex* if I didn't have any friends?"

"No, n-not that," Colm sputtered. "I mean, I d-don't know..."

Fiona stared at him. She'd thought Davie was too young for her? Colm had acted like a complete infant. "I have to go."

"Fiona," Pauline interjected, "you're not leaving? Please think about this—we're a family, we can sort this—"

"A family?" Fiona went still, her mind cycling through the years since her career had disintegrated. How she'd put her art aside to take the job at the Dwyers' shop. Then sleepwalking right into her relationship with Enda, and before she knew it, helping him and his parents manage the business on a minimal salary.

If that wasn't bad enough, she'd glommed onto Colm like her lifesaver, letting her attraction for him mask what she was doing to herself. She saw Helen Dwyer's conciliatory words and her eagerness to see Colm get serious about her in a new light. Everything was suddenly so *obvious*.

Colm *and* his family wanted him to be successful. And she was meant to be his helpmate, like Pauline was for her husband, and Helen was for Dennis. "Sorry, Pauline," she said, "The price of being part of this family is too high."

"But what'll I tell Mum?" said Colm.

"I'll handle Helen," Pauline said.

Without answering either of them, Fiona marched into the studio, snatched her handbag off the desk and retrieved her sketchbook.

Following her, Colm tried to reach for her arm. "Please, don't go—"

"Don't." She slapped his hand away. "Don't speak to me." Fiona grabbed her sketches from the table and stuffed them under the sketchbook cover. "I've an important appointment this afternoon."

"Where? Who are you meeting?" Ignoring him, Fiona stomped to the bedroom, Colm still at her heels. "Please, let's talk about this, I love you…"

Fiona slowly turned to look at him. When Colm split with her last year, she now knew why she'd wallowed in her heartbreak. Because she'd felt so little of it when Enda died. But she was done letting Colm take up space in her head. "I won't hear one more word of your utter rubbish."

Fiona swept a handful of knickers and nightgowns from a drawer, tossed them on the bed, then yanked her case and tote bag from the wardrobe. Glancing over the small space allotted for her things, she plucked up her red ballet flats and stuffed them in the tote. Something shiny caught her eye. Her violet sequined sweater. She set it in her case, then jammed her shirts, trousers and lingerie on top of it, draping her peacock blue silk dress over the lot and zipped the case shut. Where she'd go after meeting Jamie and his friend she'd no clue. But she had to get the hell out.

Colm sat on the bed, hard, as if his legs no long supported him. "This is goodbye, then."

"You guessed it." Fiona returned to the kitchen to find Colm's cousin waiting for her.

Pauline wore a regretful look. "Sorry you're leaving us, love."

"You've been good to me," Fiona said. Even if Pauline would always be on Colm's side, she *had* been an ally. "So I'll be honest. The biggest reason I stayed in Dublin—stayed with Colm—was also the worst." She took a deep breath. "I've been afraid you wouldn't recommend me for the book commission if I left."

Pauline chuckled wryly. "Why would I do that? I've seen your sketches." She leaned down to give Fiona's cheek a kiss.

"I wouldn't blame you if you decided to work with someone else," Fiona said.

Pauline only said, "I'll be in touch."

Hefting her luggage, Fiona didn't look back as she exited the flat. Seeing her name on a book cover would never be worth staying with Colm. And even though she'd nearly given them away, she still had her art. And her soul.

Kerry
46

Stephen drove us home in the hire car in record time. I went straight upstairs to the bathroom and retrieved the test kit. Moments later, Stephen knocked on the door. "Well?"

"Give us a minute!" I called, trying to sound normal despite the massive lump in my throat. I binned the package and stick, and washed my hands, leaving my jeans in the bathroom.

Opening the door, I nearly crashed into my husband. "It's pink!"

"Pink!" Stephen grasped my shoulders. "What the hell is pink?"

"Positive, you eejit!" I fell into his arms, laughing and tearful and altogether carried away. We barely made it across the hall before we collapsed onto our bed, kissing madly.

"I can't believe it's really happening," Stephen said wonderingly, curving his hand reverently over my belly. There was a sheen in his eyes. "After all this time, hoping and praying too…"

"You did, really?" I kissed him again.

"I did," he said, and I lost track of time amidst our murmurs of baby hopes and plans. I was imagining showing the baby Desmond's cow when Stephen touched my cheek. "Amazing, how things work out." He sighed. "Just when life seems like a proper train wreck…"

I didn't want to break the spell of babyland and ask him what he meant. I shifted to pull off my shirt. "Say, before I start feeling pukey again…"

Hours later, I roused from a nap to find Stephen beside me, half-dressed, very unromantically checking his watch. "We should be hearing from Jamie soon."

Thank God Stephen was keeping track of these things, I though muzzily, because I seemed to be in the throes of that baby-brain thing...I dozed off again, waking when the phone rang.

"That must be him now." Stephen drew away, and snatching his shirt, ran down the stairs. "Jamie?"

I should get up, I told myself, say bon voyage, but before I could move, I heard Stephen say, "Have a grand trip, son." He called up, "The boys made it to Con's, and they're all set."

Forcing myself out of bed, I dressed in my pajamas and padded down to the kitchen. As I reached for the fridge, the phone rang again. I rolled my eyes Stephen. "I hope that's not Jamie ringing back to say he needs more money."

Stephen grabbed the handset. Seeing him frown, I felt a clutch in my chest. "What's going on?"

He held up a hand. "I'll put her on," he said, holding out the phone. "Desmond."

The old man rang so seldom it had to be important. "Is everything okay?"

"It's the veggies," he said.

I squinted into the middle distance. "I'm sorry, I haven't a clue..."

"You left your carrots at the shop," he said patiently, and my baby euphoria instantly drained away. "I brought them back to my house."

The last thing I wanted to see was my heap of mangled vegetables. Hit by a wave of sadness, I managed, "We'll come round in the morning and fetch them."

"Ah, sure," he said, "but I wanted to make certain you knew what you were in for. With the bank voles."

I dimly remembered the word "voles" from earlier, but I'd been too off my head to pay attention. "They're the culprits, you said?"

"I showed your carrots to Bill, the farmer up the road, and he agreed, it had to be voles."

"But what are they? Where'd they come from?"

"They're small rodents that live in the woods and meadows, and feed underground," Desmond said. "Your situation's ideal for them."

Ideal. My stomach sank even further. "How?"

"Well, your place is surrounded by trees and overgrown brush and such," he explained. "Voles thrive there, especially because the ground isn't tilled. With you raising the only food crops in the area, the little bast—er, *craturs* have made a beeline for your vegetables. They especially go for roots—"

"The potatoes!" I dropped the handset and ran for the mudroom.

"Kerry!" Stephen said behind me. "What is it?"

"Tell Desmond...I don't know, anything—" I jammed my feet into my Wellies and banged out the back door.

"Gardening? But it's getting dark—"

I was already running to my biggest vegetable bed. Kneeling, I dug with my bare hands and finding a solid roundness, drew it from the soil. Despite the dim light, I could see half the potato was gone, gnawed clean away. The second of the same hill was even worse. I moved onto the next row, scrabbling into the earth to find a few undersized potatoes still intact, but the rest... It was wholesale destruction.

I bowed my head. In the perfect world I'd imagined, living off the land, these potatoes were meant to be my staple crop. Then I felt a hand on my shoulder. "Kerry," Stephen said gently. "Desmond told me. I'm sorry, love."

I had a flashback of kneeling in my garden back in March, and my father-in-law comforting me. With my decision to keep the farm, I'd felt all the promise of early spring, picturing the food I'd raise. Now, my dreams of farming crashed around me.

Patting my back, Stephen was going on about an idea of Desmond's, building structures lined with wire mesh to prevent further damage. "It would take some prep work, but they're not complicated."

"What's the use?" I said wearily, curling my hands around a half-eaten potato. "Fancy raised beds won't help this crop." I didn't dare look at my rows of parsnips. If I dug in there, I knew what I'd find. And I couldn't take it right now.

"Let's go inside." Stephen cupped my elbow.

Before I could move, a new wave of queasiness hit me. The baby. *I'm sorry, little one.* Suddenly feeling dampness on my knees through my pajamas, I realized I was acting like a madzer *again* over this place, when I'd my baby's future to think of. My husband's and son's too. "Oh, Stephen," I cried softly.

He crouched next to me, there in the dirt. "We'll come back out in the morning, see what we can save."

"It's not that—it's…the baby. We need to be a proper family again."

"Yes," was all he said.

In the silence, I heard a rustle near the coop. One of the hens, rousing. Odd—by nightfall, they were usually dead to the world. As Stephen helped me to my feet, I sensed something moving nearby, a brownish streak gone in an instant. I dimly wondered if it was one of those bloody voles, a rat, or only my imagination. Either way, I was too dispirited to care.

Once we were inside, I'd the presence of mind to wash my hands and change into clean jammies. As soon as I came back downstairs, Stephen sat me on the couch. "I'll make us sandwiches."

"Oh, but I couldn't—"

"I could," he said.

His face was drawn. I'd forgotten he'd rushed back from abroad, and my stab of guilt added to my dodgy stomach. How I'd taken Stephen for granted! Treating him so cavalierly while I played the farm drama queen.

Not only today. For months I'd been indulging myself, thinking only of what *I* wanted.

Listening to the kettle boil and the homely sound of crockery from the kitchen, I braced myself to do the right thing. When my husband entered the room, I patted the cushion next to me. "Stephen." I had to get it out before I lost my nerve.

Before I could speak he said, "I got an interesting text from Jamie, on my way to Ballydara."

Relieved to delay my moment of truth, I asked, "Besides the one he'd sent to bring you home?"

"It was about Mike McElligott—what really happened when they met."

"Jamie told me. We can be pretty certain he won't ever like Mike more than his *real* dad."

"Yeah," said Stephen wryly. "One less thing to worry about." He rubbed his forehead.

No more selfishness, I reminded myself. "Will you tell me the other things you're concerned about? Your job?"

He met my eyes. "When I got the text from Jamie about you being ill, I didn't think twice. I walked out of my meeting."

"That's not quite...um..."

"Done?" said Stephen. "Not for people at my level." Coming from anyone else, it would've sounded boastful. Not for Stephen, though. "Especially when you're in the middle of some crucial negotiations."

"You didn't get the sack?"

"I thought I would," he said. "Although people like me don't get *sacked*—you 'resign because of family reasons.' But part of me wished I *had* been given the boot."

I stared at Stephen, nearly having a freaker to hear him say that. "There must have been...repercussions."

"I got a call from the boss before my plane took off. He thought my doing a runner was brilliant—a power play, can you believe it? The company we were talking with caved right in on the buyout price. Now he wants me to head up the new division."

"*More* responsibility?" I said faintly.

The line between his brows seemed to deepen. "I won't be able to manage coming to Galway on weekends. I'm already pressed to the limit." He looked at me, pain in his eyes. "But now that you're pregnant..." He gently touched my belly.

I covered his hand with mine. "Of course I'll be coming to Dublin. Besides finding us a place, I'll need to start antenatal care." As if in protest, my stomach flopped over. "Could you give me a fortnight?"

"Do we have to wait that long?"

Thinking of my fatigue the last few days, I said, "So far, it feels like having a baby in your thirties is much more taxing than in your teens."

"Let's get you some food then." Stephen rose to bring in the sandwiches.

As he set two plates and two mugs of tea on the coffee table, I said, "I'll feel stronger for house-hunting when I'm closer to my second trimester—over the worst of the nausea." Which was true, even if I hadn't *quite* intended to make a shameless ploy for sympathy. And since Stephen had been so supportive about my ruined crops, I couldn't put *it* off any longer... "I have to t-tell you—about the chickens."

He set down his sandwich. "They're not laying."

"Oh! Bernard told you, the wretch." I should have *known* you couldn't keep a secret in Ballydara.

"No, he didn't, but I suspected something was up. All the years my granddad and granny kept a few chickens, they'd have a fridge overflowing with eggs."

"I...see." With the price of organic eggs at the Topaz, I'd never bought more than a dozen at a time.

"Farm eggs come in all sorts too—brown, beige, cream-colored." His mouth quirked. "At least Granddad's did."

My shop eggs were uniformly brown. "Why didn't you say anything?"

He smiled ruefully. "I knew you'd tell me eventually."

"I didn't mean to deceive you," I said, shamefaced. "I kept hoping they'd start laying, at least I did until Desmond worked out how old they were. But the money—"

"Let's forget about it. I've laid out a *lot* more on...non-essentials."

Was he thinking of the diamond ring on a saucer in the next room? Biting into my sandwich, I realized I had to woman-up. Do my part. "So on to Dublin," I said resolutely, knowing I'd have to get rid of the hens straightaway. "Maybe we can find a place with a garden." Giving Stephen a beseeching look, I asked, "We can still visit the farm for an occasional weekend, though?"

Stephen swallowed. "With the baby, you'll have your hands full…"

"Then we can spend our holidays here." I tried not to think of the deserted coop, the farmhouse lying empty for months at a time, weeds filling the grounds I'd worked so hard to maintain.

"Our holidays?" Lifting his mug of tea, he didn't look at me. "Sure. We'll do that."

Fiona

47

$\mathcal{S}$tanding in the queue at Griffin's Bakery on Shop Street, Fiona fingered the euro in her pocket. Buy a loaf of bread to take back to the hostel, or a bun to eat on the go?

A bun, she decided, trying not to think of her dwindling cash. Leaving the shop with her treat, she made her way through the crowd of summer tourists toward Eyre Square, a fine mist dampening her hair. She averted her eyes as she passed the King's Head Pub, the mullioned windows bright red despite the gray day. She'd nearly gone inside a dozen times, hoping to find Gil Killeen to ask after his twin. But how pathetic was that, now that Davie had found someone new?

She'd come to Galway City because it was here she'd always felt most at home. Yet after arriving over a week ago, prowling the same streets she and Davie had strolled along, she felt an unrelenting regret. And she was no closer to working out what to do next. Getting mobile service was progress, though, and hungry for a friendly voice, she'd rung Kerry as soon as she was settled. "It's me—are you one hundred percent sure yet?"

"Fiona! You mean, that I'm pregnant? Oh, yeah—I've taken two home tests already."

She said something about Judith and stocking pregnancy test kits at the shop, but Fiona couldn't wait another moment to tell her. "I've left Dublin," she said baldly.

"And Colm?" Kerry sounded perplexed. "Where are you?"

"Galway City. I'm staying at a little hostel." She faked a light laugh. "Although it's rather grim after the splendor of the Smurfits' place." Fiona had been too proud to contact any of her old college friends for couch surfing. After feeling she'd taken gross advantage of Pauline, her freeloading days were so over.

Kerry was silent. "This seems so sudden," she replied at last. "I thought you loved Colm."

"I did too." Back at the print shop, she'd felt invisible. Colm had made her feel real again. *Only not as real as I could be.* "I'm so sorry I won't be in Dublin when you move house there."

"I am too. More than I can say." Kerry's voice held an ache. "But I would never have wanted you to stay there if your man didn't make you happy."

"I seem to have fallen out of love with Colm even faster than I fell in," Fiona admitted. "The thing is, I discovered he wasn't the man I thought he was."

Kerry suddenly giggled. "Isn't that what people say when they find out a bloke is gay?"

Fiona had to laugh. "All I can say is, he turned out to be a right diva. I can't talk long—I'm on a bare-bones calling plan— but Dad's keeping well?"

"He's grand," said Kerry. "He seems a bit bereft when your name comes up, but Bea—I mean, I hear he's eating well, and gets outdoors every day. He's even been looking after my chickens."

"Kerry, I hate to ask, but don't tell him I've left Dublin, will you? I don't want him to worry."

"I shouldn't want to deceive him—he's been such a good friend, now that..." Kerry didn't finish.

Fiona guessed what she meant to say. *Now that you're gone.* "I'll tell him soon—I'm still finding my feet, getting ideas for a new project." She'd bought a small tablet for on-the-go drawing, but so far hadn't even opened it.

"I'm not feeling so great," said Kerry, "but as soon as I'm better, I'll come to the city and take you to lunch."

A lump grew in Fiona's throat. "I'd love that." She'd rung off soon after, feeling like she was in limbo. Going no place and belonging nowhere.

She'd hoped to hear from Pauline about the book commission, but not a word from her. Fiona had nearly phoned her up several times, yet couldn't go through with it. I've lost my nerve, she thought. How can I ever freelance again if I'm too afraid of rejection?

So Kerry was the only person she'd been in touch with. The day before, when Fiona rang her, Kerry admitted she'd been flattened with nausea. "I haven't been up for house-hunting, like I promised Stephen."

"I'm sorry you've been under the weather, love," Fiona told her. "Though I can't help being glad you're still in Galway."

"Just between you and me, I am too. And happily, morning sickness won't last forever," said Kerry. "I've an appointment with a local GP, so no worries."

"And everyone's keeping well? Dad and Judith?" *Davie?*

"Oh, sure," Kerry said. "'No complaints,' they say. And yourself? Living the free, artistic life again?"

Fabricating some rubbish about the big project she'd started, Fiona couldn't wait to change the subject. "How's your garden?"

Her friend's laugh seemed hollow. "That's a story for another day. But how about that windstorm last night? Very strange, a summer gale like that."

"Um...I guess it was pretty breezy." Fiona hadn't paid much attention.

"It blew something terrible here—I was sure the wind would tear the hen run to bits but the whole lot held together."

Anxiety struck Fiona. "What about Dad's place?"

"It's all right," said Kerry. "A few tiles blew off the roof."

Fiona pictured her dad, alone at night during the storm. Kerry wouldn't be up the road much longer to see how he was doing. "Thanks for letting me know." Fiona wound up the call, feeling worried and more bereft than ever. *I'm nearly out of money, and Dad needs me.*

Now, stowing her bun, she dodged the tourists clustered around the Browne Doorway in the square and headed for the nearest park bench. I'm still going round in circles, she thought despairingly, feeling more alone than she ever had in her life. If only I had a little more time to sort myself...

"Hey," said an unfamiliar voice right behind her. She stiffened. A pickpocket, trying to distract her? Like she had anything worth picking! She clutched her bag tight to her side, and strode past the bench.

"Fiona!"

Turning, she froze at the sight of a rangy, dark-haired man. Davie—

It was Gil. Wearing his usual scowl. "What is it?" Her voice actually sounded normal.

"I've seen you in Shop Street the last week—I thought you lived in Dublin."

"I left," she said shortly. She'd never forget how rude he'd been to her when she'd run into him at the King's Head. "If you've been spying on me, you've seen I'm minding my own business. You should try it."

"I'm not spying," Gil said loftily. "I've only kept an eye out for you. Now and then."

"Why?" *Then you've seen that I haven't a proper life, or purpose...* "Actually, I really don't care." *So piss off.* She couldn't say it aloud. It would only show how hurt and angry she was.

"I only wanted to say if you were keen to ask after my brother, all you had to do was come to the pub before a session."

"Well, I'm not," she said. "I couldn't care less what Davie does." Fiona's throat tightened. She was terribly afraid she'd start crying in front of Gil.

"Too bad," said Gil. "Because he's mad about you. Why else would I let him take you to my flat?"

Gil's flat? "I'm not listening to this!" Why was he lying to her? Revenge for his twin? "Your brother and his bloody pigs can go to hell."

She turned away, hurrying toward the bus station. Without looking behind her, she climbed on the first bus she saw. The fare was worth the quick getaway.

Seeing Gil brought back her longing for Davie, that she'd tried so hard to quash—and the incandescent evening they'd spent together. As the bus got underway, Fiona rubbed her forehead with a shaking hand. Shame clawed inside her, that Gil knew—and Davie soon would too—that her life was one big disaster. Not hearing from Pauline only confirmed it.

Fiona opened her handbag to find her bun had smashed, leaving an oily spot on her new tablet. Slumped in her seat, she clasped the unused sketchbook and stared out the window at the familiar streets. The tarnished copper dome of the Galway Cathedral caught her eye, reminding her how much she'd loved sketching the iconic Celtic imagery inside. Especially the angels poised just under the rotunda. You'd get the sense that if the dome opened up, they'd break away and fly heavenward. *If only I could escape this half-life I'm living...*

"...Cong first thing tomorrow," said a nearby voice.

Fiona blinked. In the seat ahead of her were two older women. Tourists, she guessed, who had to be well into their seventies, nattering about sightseeing. Distracted from the awfulness of running into Gil, Fiona couldn't help watching the pair of them, seeing their vibrancy despite their wrinkles and graying hair. She clutched her tablet. *I'm young! Why am I acting like my life is over, my art played out?*

Was she waiting for someone to give her permission to make something of herself? Suddenly fired up, Fiona opened her tablet. As she pulled a pencil from her bag her mobile rang, and she glanced at the screen. *I should pick up...* But with only a few more days before she'd have to leave the city, she hadn't a moment to lose.

Kerry
48

*F*our days after the big windstorm, I pulled on my Wellies and headed out into the breezy late summer afternoon, feeling like a new woman. Or close to it.

This morning, I'd awakened late, hungry for my first proper breakfast in weeks. Once I'd eaten—and rested from eating—I felt strong enough to take on the chores I'd neglected. Cautiously making my way to the barn, I realized it was past time to tell my family about my pregnancy. Yet with Jamie still in the dark and on holiday, I couldn't risk him finding out about the baby from anyone other than his dad and me.

My first priority, after letting the chickens out for a roam, was to harvest my apples. In the barn, a quick rummage rewarded me with a couple of baskets. I eyed the wooden stepladder near the door. Stephen would have my head on a platter if I tried to lift it. Instead, I tied a rope to one of the rungs and dragged the ladder outside, stopping every few paces to catch my breath. Eyeballing the distance to my one bearing apple tree, I felt my energy seriously wane.

"Need some help?"

I turned to see a familiar dark-haired girl, a bit younger than myself, stride up my driveway, the hens dogging her steps. She was tall, with shoulders like a man's—but in a good way. "I could actually." I racked my brain, but couldn't remember her name.

"You're Kerry, right? The girl who discovered she was up the pole right there in the shop." The young woman grinned, her striking golden eyes warm. "I know, I've a terrible cheek, but I hear the local folk haven't been that entertained since...well, ever."

I couldn't hold it against her. "I made a complete spectacle, I know."

Her face was suddenly pensive. "Being pregnant, you seem to be joining every other girl under thirty in this village."

"I'm not under thirty." I yanked on the ladder. "Anyway, I'm sure I would've found the whole bit hilarious if it hadn't been me."

"Say, that's rather vigorous of you." She gestured at the ladder. "For a girl in your condition. I do like the rope yoke you've gotten up."

"I wish I did. The ladder feels like it's made of lead."

"I'm just the woman for you, then." She picked up the ladder easily. The way she hoicked it onto one broad shoulder reminded me of Gil and Davie pirouetting round my sunroom with chunks of wall. "Which way?"

"To the only tree with fruit on it." I pointed to the back garden. With the hens underfoot, I trailed her long strides as best I could, a bit envious. *If I'd your muscles, Miss, I'd have whipped Avalon Farm into shape long ago.*

"Seems early for apples," she remarked.

"They're a summer variety," I told her. "'Irish Peach,' I think." As we approached the tree, I said, "Thanks so much, Miss...I'm sorry, we've run into each other before, but I've brain fog something terrible."

"I'm called Grainne—Grainne Larkin." Setting down the ladder, she added, "It may be too soon to thank me. Take a look."

Peering around her, I stared in horror at the ground, littered with apples. Most of them were scarred with big gashes, the flesh starting to decompose. I could have puked. Or cried. Not that I'd dare either in front of this Amazonian. "That wind the other night..." My voice cracked. "Then my hens must have got to them..."

"Probably," she said, sympathy in her voice. "The ones on the tree got nailed too."

I looked up at the remaining fruit. Many apples had conical-shaped divots in them. "D'you think robins would've done that?" I asked weakly. I'd never seen my hens fly, save for a low jump over the garden wall.

"Crows, maybe," she said. "Look at that blagger now." She pointed to a large black bird settling on one of the lower branches of my oak tree. Yanking a mangled apple off the tree, she fired it at the crow. "Close," she said, scowling, "but no bulls-eye. I'd stay to help you fight 'em off, but my family's expecting me."

Trying not to look at my ruined crop, I said, "I shouldn't keep you, then." With the part of me that wasn't broken-hearted over my apples, I tried to picture her with a husband and children. And failed utterly. "You've kids?"

"Not yet." Her gold-brown eyes suddenly gleamed. "But I'm working on it."

I could hardly ask if she was referring to having lots of sex, or going for in-vitro fertilization. "Um…good luck to you then."

"Today I'm meant to help my friend Justine put on a special dinner at my mam's. I'll be in for a right bollacking if I'm late."

"You're celebrating something?"

"Not exactly," said Grainne. "Justine's testing some recipes for a mad idea she's got, about doing a pop-up restaurant. Problem is, she's also invited my…boyfriend." She said "boyfriend" like she was just getting used to saying it.

Why is that a problem? was something else I couldn't ask. As another damaged apple suddenly dropped off the tree, I got a tell-tale ache in my throat. "I hope everything works out."

"Oh, it will. In the meantime, a long walk is a socially acceptable way to avoid people." There was her cheeky grin again.

"I'm glad you came this way," I said. "By myself, I probably would've had a complete meltdown." I tried to say it carelessly, but my eyes started tearing.

I felt her penetrating glance. "You'll want your ladder back in the barn?"

*Leave it where it is, I don't car*e, I almost said, but a proper farmer would take care of her equipment. "Yes, please."

Once the ladder was secured, she gave me another appraising glance. "Apples aren't worth bawling your eyes out over," she said kindly. "If I've learned anything lately, it's to save your tears for bigger things." Before I could answer she was on her way, her long legs soon taking her out of sight.

I stumbled to the back stoop and sat down with a thump. With Grainne gone, my farm fiasco hit me hard. Resigned to not having any eggs, I'd been trying not to think about my misbegotten vegetable crop. Yet with the loss of my apples, the math in my head buzzed away. So many apples per kilo…each kilo worth so many euros… I drooped in defeat. Now Stephen would have to know my last hope for an income was gone.

I finally clambered to my feet, heading for the chicken pen, where I saw the sack of scratch I'd missed before. It was lying sideways in one corner of the run, grains spilling out onto the ground. The hens were all over it. "Girls!" I swatted at them. "Get away from that!"

Desmond must've forgotten to stow the sack. Instead of trying to lift it, I rolled it to the plastic bin where I'd been storing the grain. "I supposed you've gorged yourselves." I tipped the bin on its side, pushing the sack into it, and managed to right the bin. "Bad enough you got to my apples! Do you lot ever stop eating?"

Laura cocked her head at me, while the black hen, Nellie Oleson, pecked my legs. "If only you'd been young enough to lay eggs, maybe I could've made a go of things here." My eyes teared up again at the thought. "All right, I can't blame you for being old. Or that I'm expecting a baby so I'll have to leave." Sniffing, I gazed at them affectionately. "What'll I do with you?"

Nellie had already lost interest in me, but Laura still hung at my feet. I picked her up and cradled her in one arm. "It wouldn't be right to palm you off on someone who wants layers. But I'm terribly fond of you girls, you know that." Laura tried to flap her wings. "And clearly I'm a complete nutter, talking to birds."

Setting her down, I left the run, wondering where I'd left my baskets. At least I could salvage the few edible apples and make a pie for Desmond. On my way to the barn, I heard the phone ring. I rushed inside, relieved not to be facing my apple mess, and grabbed the handset.

"Hey, Mam."

"Jamie!" My sadness dissolved. Quite heroically, I managed not to say, *it's about time you rang!* "How's your holiday?"

"It's been great. We've done the Eye, and the Underground and the wax museum—you know, the one with all the celebrities."

"Madame Tussauds?"

"Yeah. We're in Derby now, visiting Con's aunt and uncle. He and I were wondering, though…once we're back in Dub, can I stay at Con's house a few extra days? I texted Dad, and he said to ask you."

I sighed. More time with Con—the kid with the *amazing* ability to complicate our lives. "I wouldn't want you to wear out your welcome, love."

"We already asked his parents and they said I could."

"Okay then. I'm hoping to be in Dublin soon—your dad and I will fetch you."

"Only if you're feeling…you're all right, aren't you, Mam?" He actually sounded anxious.

"Of course I am…" A suspicion crept up on me. "Is there some reason I wouldn't be?"

"Well, the…um, baby."

49

I want to talk to you. Ring me.

*F*iona shifted in her chair at the Chat & Net, a prickle running up her spine. Again.

For days, she'd had the strangest feeling of being watched. Yet a nervous glance around the Internet café confirmed there was no one who looked even remotely suspicious—mostly students and tourists—nor anyone showing a jot of interest in her. And she hadn't seen a trace of Gil Killeen since she'd blown him off.

She turned back to the computer screen. After getting two phone messages from her sister Bronagh, that Niall had been trying to reach her, Fiona knew she'd put off contacting her brother long enough. Logging in to the account she hadn't checked for months, she'd found three emails from him. He'd sent that first, terse "ring me" message right after she'd first visited Dublin. Then he'd emailed again while she'd been staying with Colm.

> Bronagh says you're living with some artist bloke in Dublin. If you're still not on your mobile, email me. I've news.

She tensed. *Please don't tell me you're moving to yet another organic farm at the ends of the earth.* With trepidation, Fiona opened his third email, dated from last week.

> Have you gone completely underground? I'm ready to leave here and come back home—

Fiona stared hard at the screen, hope streaking through her. Did he mean return to Ballydara?

> Before I do, I want to make sure there's still a place for me at the farm.

Fiona immediately closed the email and logged out. Pulling out her mobile, she stepped outside and pressed Niall's number, not caring how much it cost.

"Fiona! You took your time."

She felt a rush of emotion at hearing her younger brother's voice, realizing she was no longer angry at him. "It's my fault, I know—but you're not having me on, about coming home?"

"I've had my fill of working for other people," said Niall. "I want to run Dad's farm."

For one glorious moment, Fiona thought, *I'll be as free as the air*. Then reality descended. "Oh, Niall, there is no farm, you know that." Her heart ached. "Your being there would give Dad a new lease on life, but without the animals, what could you do?"

"I mean to build the farm back up somehow," Niall said. "I've been researching all sorts of farm programmes, saving madly, too. It might take months to get started, but I think I can do it."

"You're serious." Fiona could hardly believe what she was hearing. Seeking a quieter spot, she ducked into a small passageway, and realized it was where she and Davie had snogged like they'd just invented it. She practically ran back to the street. "Dad will be in absolute *heaven*."

Niall didn't say anything for a moment. "There's something you should know first."

Fiona's delight evaporated. "You're not entirely sure about coming?"

"That's not it—before I leave here, I've a few things to work out with...someone." He laughed self-consciously.

Fiona recognized that laugh. "A *girl*? Your girlfriend's coming with you?"

"She's...uh, not really my girlfriend. Not yet, anyway."

Fiona suddenly wished she could hug away Niall's worries

like she had when he was small. "Would she be up for living on the farm?"

"I think so," said Niall. "I hope so."

"Well, after the pair of you sort things, let me know."

"If I actually got her to come, would it be awkward at Dad's?" Niall asked. "Bronagh told me about that little Polish girl who's been helping out."

"Beata's not little." Resentment surged in her throat. "She's the mother of two. Well, almost two."

"A *mother*? And pregnant? Jaysus. I'd feel like a right gobshite, to ask Dad to sack her."

"You mean you'll be looking after Dad?"

"Of course." He sounded surprised. "Besides, we'll need every spare euro to get the place going again."

"She needs the money too, I'm sorry to say, with that useless husband she's got," said Fiona. "Although I heard she might be leaving him." Even if having a new guy lined up didn't exactly put Beata in clover. It would take her years to obtain a divorce, which might not sit well with an impetuous bloke like Davie... She shoved *that* thought away.

"A *single* mother." Niall sounded genuinely concerned. "Now I *really* couldn't ask Dad to let her go."

"You can't worry about that now. Just come. Work things out with your girlfr—your friend from here."

"Right." Niall cleared his throat. "I meant to ask, how are you, there in Dublin?"

"Bronagh's behindhand," Fiona told him. "I split with Colm a fortnight ago." Saying it aloud should have made her sad, or at least nostalgic for what she and Colm could have had. But all she still felt was relief.

"No way—Bronagh gave me the impression you really fancied him."

"I did once," Fiona said shortly. "Anyway, I've been in Galway City ever since, playing tourist. I haven't told Dad—I knew he'd worry." *I didn't want him to know—or the rest of the family either—that I'd made such a hash of my life.*

"You're okay, then?"

"I am," she lied, and suddenly felt creeped out again. "Look," she said in a rush, "why don't you phone up Dad, tell him what you've in mind." She began hurrying toward the Spanish Arch. There would be lots of tourists in the area, and she could go to the museum. "I'll plan to see you at the farm, hopefully soon."

"What about Dad? You've got to let him know where you are."

"I'll ring him in a day or two." As she said goodbye, Fiona wondered, So what do I tell Dad? That I'd been avoiding going home, or that now I've a bigger problem on my hands?

Fiona left the Galway Cathedral, pausing under the high, arched entryway. For the last couple of hours she'd felt transported—the violet light from the rotunda had been perfect for her last series of drawings. But now that she was outside again, she clutched her small sketchbook closer, glancing furtively at her surroundings.

After speaking to Niall two days ago, her passion for her dream project had mushroomed. She felt like her old self again—bursting with promise and creative ideas. At least she did when she wasn't having that nagging, almost constant feeling of being followed. Fiona was nearly out of minutes, but as the afternoon shadows lengthened she sat on the shallow steps of the church and rang Kerry. "You're feeling better yet?" She forced a breezy tone.

"Oh, hi! I am, a bit—some setbacks here and there," said Kerry. "Just hearing your voice is like a shot of energy, though. And yourself?"

"I've actually had a couple of breakthroughs." Feeling a new rush of elation despite that unnerving sensation, she had to share. "The biggest one is my brother Niall coming home to run the farm—Dad's big dream."

"Holy God," said Kerry. "That *is* big. The world's your oyster now."

"If I don't need to stay home with my dad," Fiona said, "it certainly could be." *If I've the courage to venture out of my shell, that is.* "Niall's already looking into some expansion programmes—he should be back in Ireland in a few weeks."

"How wonderful," said Kerry. "Your dad must be thrilled to *bits.*"

"I…um, imagine so," said Fiona.

"You haven't spoken to him yet?"

"I will," Fiona rushed to say. *Any day now.*

"So…" Kerry went on, "did you say you've another development?"

"It's far less earthshaking," Fiona told her, "but I've finished a set of drawings for that book project I mentioned."

"Fair play to you," said Kerry, "doing something you love. And it looks like you'll be free to see it through."

Fiona heard wistfulness in Kerry's voice. "I decided that if my contact doesn't want to hire me for illustrating, I'll find a writer and do a book myself."

"You absolutely should," Kerry said stoutly. "You could work from Galway, or…or wherever you end up, no bother."

Fiona felt the awkwardness of their lives going in different directions. "I never did tell you, it was grand seeing Jamie in Dublin, even for that short time. His friend's a dote too. They're having a good holiday?"

"Great crack, I think. Jamie finally rang me a few days back," said Kerry. "Turns out, he guessed about the baby."

"Never!" Sounding chirpy helped ward off that disturbing sense of being watched.

"Yeah," said Kerry. "I was so droopy while he and Con were visiting he actually Googled pregnancy symptoms. Do you believe what kids get up to?"

Fiona faked a chuckle. "What does he think about having a sibling?"

"When I asked him, he didn't answer right away," said Kerry. "I wondered if he was jealous or something. Then finally he says, 'It's brilliant!' He did give me a bit of a hard time, though—that he wasn't a kid and we didn't need to keep important things from him." She sighed. "Say, if you're going to be in Galway City a while longer, on my way to Dublin we could meet for that lunch date we talked about."

"I'd love to see you sooner rather than later." Fiona couldn't help admitting, "I've missed you."

"Me too," said Kerry. "But I didn't want to pressure you to come back to Ballydara for our goodbyes if you weren't... ready."

Fiona knew what Kerry was alluding to. Ready to face Beata. Or see her with Davie. Suddenly, that eerie sensation grew stronger. "Lunch in the city would be f-fantastic." Her voice wobbled.

"Fiona," said Kerry, "is something wrong?"

"I'm okay," Fiona managed, her voice tight.

"You don't sound okay," said Kerry. "What's going on?"

"Well, I didn't want to tell you—it's probably my imagination..."

"Tell me what?"

"I think someone's been following me." Fiona saw her minutes were dwindling fast. "I'm sure it's nothing, though."

"Nothing! Where are you?"

"I'm actually at the Cathedral, there's loads of people around. But I've got to ring off—"

"You'll do no such thing—go to the Garda station!" Kerry ordered. "I'm not letting you off the line if you're being stalked!"

"I...I'm sure it's not *stalking*—" She broke off as the church doors opened.

"Ring the Garda! Now! Don't make this pregnant woman have an anxiety attack—"

"Wait!" In shock, Fiona took the mobile from her ear and pressed it to her heart. Then, hand shaking, she lifted the phone again. "The...um, stalker? I know him."

Kerry
50

*S*till recovering from the scare I'd gotten over Fiona—and trying to get my head around the hurt I'd caused her, jumping to conclusions—I was outside the chicken run, shivering in the evening's chill. Shooting my mouth off about people before I was in full possession of the facts was like taking my catastrophizing to a whole new level. From now on, I vowed, I'd take a deep breath, make sure I knew what I was about before letting my hair-trigger emotions run the show.

As the hens meandered into their enclosure for the night, I pulled my jacket around me more tightly, watching them with another sort of regret. Ma ventured up the ramp first and disappeared through the little coop entry, Baby Grace behind her, as Carrie, Mary and Nellie Olesen followed more leisurely. After I'd shared my baby news with Mam and Dad and Suz, and heard how over the moon they all were, the pressure was really on—not only to start house-hunting, but to get moving on sorting the girls. Even if I couldn't bring myself to put them in my stew pot, they'd surely end up in someone else's.

Laura still hovered next to me. "You're always last to go in, aren't you," I said fondly, and opened the pen gate wide. She cocked her head. "It'll be warmer inside," I coaxed.

A car turned into the drive. "That'll be Stephen, so goodnight." With three steps she'd crossed the threshold. "That's it, in you go! I'll be back to check on you."

I closed the gate without fastening it and headed for the driveway. Seeing Stephen climb wearily out of our Fiesta, I rushed to embrace him. His face seemed even more haggard than the last time I'd seen him. "Long week, love?"

"Interminable." His arms tightened around me. "Meetings and more meetings."

We stood for a long moment as the light deepened, the twilight silence broken by the lowing of Desmond's little Jersey cow. A sound I loved. "I was tucking up the hens for the night," I said. "I'll need to secure the pen before we go in."

"I'll come—stretch my legs a bit." He took my hand, leading me the roundabout way. As we strolled along the ring of apple trees I finally told him what had happened to the crop.

He shrugged philosophically. "There's always next year."

"How can you say that?" I heard an odd, subdued squawk from the direction of the chicken pen, but I was too indignant to pay it any attention. "I lost nearly a whole tree's worth of fruit! You *know* I was counting on it for an income."

"When you're a farmer," Stephen said, "you have to be able to let some things go. Or the 'if onlys' will drive you mad."

I opened my mouth to protest, then remembered what his father had said to me last spring, about Mother Nature, and knew Stephen was right. I squeezed his hand in silent apology, then we sauntered behind the barn and back toward the garden. Reaching the chicken run, I let go of him to step toward the gate, straining my eyes to ease the wire loop over the post. I heard a flap of wings, which had to be Laura, finally settling herself on the roost, and listened to the other birds' sighs and coos as they slept. Suddenly, a thump. And a rustle.

I clutched Stephen's arm. "What was that?" A streak of darkness shot from the far side of the chicken pen, gone in an instant. "Something's there!"

"An animal?"

I stumbled to the opposite side of the run, but the creature seemed to have vanished. "Do you think it was a mink, or a marten?" I bent to poke the ground along the fence line, trying to feel for any holes.

"Whatever it was," said Stephen, "it's long gone—no sense trying to chase it."

"Wait—there's a gap here." The animal must have enlarged one of Laura's or Nellie's digging spots next to the fence. Jogging to the back door for the torch I kept in the mudroom, I hurried back and aimed the beam around the run, then along the ground until I found what I was looking for. "I told you—a hole!"

Stephen leaned down to peer at it. "Okay, but there's obviously no predator here now. If there *was* something—"

"There was!" I insisted. "I saw an animal a fortnight ago, but didn't realize it. Now it's back."

"You probably caught it before it could do anything." He straightened. "Come on—we'll do the repairs in the morning."

"No way," I said. "I'll fix this now."

Stephen sighed. "We'll need some stones."

I was already striding toward the pile of rocks I'd pulled from my garden beds. In his business suit, Stephen helped me ferry a dozen or so to the chicken run. Together we stuffed the stones into the crevice. "It's not enough," I fretted.

"I don't know what else we can do in the dark." Stephen sounded more weary than annoyed. "In the morning, we can bury the fencing a few inches and pile more stones on."

"This won't wait until morning. You can go to bed. I'm staying."

"Outside with the chickens?" Stephen said, aghast. "You need your rest—"

"It's only one night."

"You're pregnant!"

"I'll be all right." Afraid for my girls, I could feel adrenaline rushing through me. "I can't leave them."

Stephen said forcefully, "For God's sake, you've no business pushing yourself like this—"

"I don't care!" Hot tears sprang to my eyes. I was being stubborn and horribly selfish, but I had a fierce, mother's love for this land, that Stephen would never understand. I'd sown more than seeds on my farm—I'd put my heart and soul into my little crops and this small flock. Whatever the cost, I would protect them. "This animal is *not* going to have another go at my girls!"

"Kerry, love, this isn't rational, losing sleep when you're expecting a baby," Stephen said more calmly. "These birds aren't even...well, you know what I'm saying."

His soothing tone only made me more determined. "I *know* the chickens aren't laying, or worth saving, but they're part of this farm—part of me!"

I was acting completely crazed, I knew that. I ran to the house anyway, toed off my Wellies and grabbed a kitchen chair. After I hauled it to the back door, I tore Stephen's old work coat off the hook in the mudroom and slung it over my jacket. A woolen hat next, and a stick I'd found under my oak tree after the windstorm. Pulling my Wellies back on and donning work gloves, I dragged the chair outside.

Stephen met me on the stoop, and I walked alongside him as he took the chair to the pen door. Then he loped back to the house. Clearly, he was taking my advice and going to bed.

Yet a moment later he reappeared in his winter overcoat and the boots Desmond had brought us, carrying a second chair toward me. Without saying anything, I opened the pen gate and plunked my chair in front of the little ramp leading up to the hen's coop entry. He followed me, setting his chair next to mine as I closed the gate behind us, my stick within reach.

Then we sat. "If that creature wants a chicken dinner," Stephen remarked, "it'll have to get past us."

As the stars began winking in the sky, he crossed his arms over his chest and soon fell into a doze, head nodding. I was wide awake.

For hours, I stared into the darkness. The knowledge that I'd be leaving Avalon Farm, probably within days, brought a lump to my throat, the memories of my months here in Galway taking on a sharp poignancy. Chasing the chickens with Fiona and Davie...Jamie bouncing around the pasture on Desmond's tractor…Fiona sailing through the air on my swing…And the most cherished, coming to after fainting in Judith's little shop, to find myself safe in Stephen's arms. All the moments I'd never forget in this beloved place.

It was longest night of my life. Longer, even, than the night here at the farm last November, when I'd lain next to Stephen after Will Power's betrayal. At least that night, I'd been warm…

I must have dropped off, because the next thing I knew I was blinking against the faint light warming the horizon. Stephen was fast asleep, his chin on his chest. He'd been done for, yet he'd stayed with me. And the hens.

I looked at him more closely, and noticed his long lashes casting half-moons on his cheeks, making the shadows beneath his eyes more pronounced. Suddenly, I felt a pain in my ribcage, like the wind had been knocked from me. I realized the enormity of all I'd asked of him these last months.

To forgive me for what had happened with Will. To go along with my dream of living on the farm. Most of all, to trust me enough to start fresh, with this new life inside me.

What was I doing? Risking his health—maybe the well-being of our baby—for a half dozen birds? I *was* mad. Pregnancy hormones or not, I had to cop on to myself. Stephen had been there for me…always. Waiting for him to awaken, I knew I *had* to stop putting the farm first. Be the wife he deserved.

The hens began to stir. Instead of their usual low clucks, the flap of wings, they made very little noise. I struggled off the chair, my limbs stiff, and cracked the man door of the coop. The hens were cowering against far corner. In the dimness, I counted five heads. Perplexed, I backed out, peering at the area Stephen and I had shored up with stones, and saw it.

A clutch of brown feathers a short distance from the run.

Tears spurted from my eyes. Laura, my favorite, was gone. "I'm not having it." I nearly collapsed against the fence. "I'm not having it!"

"Kerry!" Stephen jerked awake. "What is it?"

"I just can't bear it!"

He was off chair in an instant, slinging his arm around me. "What's happened?"

My tears warm against my cold face, I couldn't answer. Had the creature killed my girl after I'd dozed off? Or snatched Laura earlier, while I'd gone to greet Stephen? Whenever it had happened, I'd been utterly insane to stay outside—*and* to guilt Stephen into joining me.

Suddenly my hen's death and our family separations and the way I'd nearly ruined our marriage seemed all of a piece. All I could do was weep helplessly against Stephen in the chicken pen, his wool coat rough against my face.

He didn't say anything, only patted my shoulder. Finally, my sobs dwindled. Trying to gain control of myself, I saw the chickens were finally trailing out of the coop. They approached me, curiously silent, picking at the stray threads on my jeans.

Tears dripping off my chin, I forced myself to move. "They'll want to eat," I said and filled their feeder, the dawn cold penetrating the two coats I was wearing.

Stephen went outside the run and examined the ground around the feathers. "It must've been a fox."

I didn't say anything. What did it matter? Dead was dead. Yet Stephen was trying to help. "How..." I swallowed. "How do you know?"

"I remember my granddad saying a fox will kill just one prey—a mink or a marten can take out an entire flock in one go."

I could hear what he wasn't saying. *It could've been worse.* As he fetched scraps of wire fencing from the barn, I looked more closely at the feathers. In the early morning light, I could make out the pieces of what had once been a hen.

It was the sign I needed.

When Stephen returned, I helped him pin down the wire with the biggest stones in my pile to reinforce the gap we'd filled last night, and any other weaknesses along the fence line. It would do. For now.

Then came the sorry task of burying my girl's remains. Stephen found a piece of ragged burlap in the barn and I wrapped what was left of Laura in it. Carrying a shovel, he led me past our circle of apple trees, perhaps to keep the bad luck at the far end of Avalon Farm. After he finished digging, I placed the sad little corpse in the hole, and covered her with the dirt Stephen had shoveled. "I'm sorry," he said simply.

I took his hand, and for a moment neither of moved. All I could hope was that nature had been merciful, and my hen's death had been quick. Then I said a prayer, as penance for letting her down. And for not knowing, until this moment, how much I loved my husband.

We stumbled into the farmhouse together. Stephen put the kettle on as I took the hottest shower I could stand. I stood under the steaming water, the prospect of tea the only thing keeping me from crumpling into the tub. When it was his turn, as soon I heard the water running I dug in my jumble drawer for the business card I'd stowed there last March.

It wasn't hard to find. *Robin Keane, Estate Agent. Call Anytime.* I reached for the phone.

I made eggs and toast, and laid the table, placing the business card in front of Stephen's plate. In silence, we slowly ate our breakfast. After he took his last bite, he picked up the card and studied it.

"It's the right choice," I said. "The only choice." As he set down the card, I asked, "Do you want it?"

"I've her email, thanks." Stephen rose and shrugged into his jacket. "I'm calling round to Desmond's."

To tell him we were selling, of course. "It's a bit early, isn't it?"

"He's a farmer," said Stephen. "He'll be up."

"Right," I said slowly. "By the way, he'll have some exciting news about the farm." It was a relief to think of more prosaic things, like a new arrival to the community. "He'll want to tell you himself, of course."

Stephen nodded. "After my visit, I'll be off to Hurley's to do email. You're to go straight upstairs and have a sleep."

"I'm not tired." I'd hit that stage of exhaustion where you feel wired and shaky, and the last thing you want is to lie down.

"I. Don't. Care." He looked grim. "Upstairs, or on the couch, it's your choice, but you're going to rest."

"All right," I said meekly. If Stephen wanted me to take it easy because he didn't want me to come with him, I could get that. He'd likely had his fill of his mad, chicken-obsessed wife.

Waving to him from the front stoop, I knew I needed time to myself anyway. To get accustomed to the future I'd put off so long. Unlike when I first arrived here, I would tell Judith and all my friends right away that we'd be leaving. For good.

I headed upstairs, thinking of my phone conversation earlier. "I still have all the paperwork from last spring," Robin said, her voice enthusiastic. "We'll get a sign up and the listing online today—"

"It's too soon for a sign," I interrupted.

"Really, Mrs. McCormack, the sooner we start marketing, the sooner it'll sell."

"I only need another day," I told her. *To say goodbye to the farm.*

"I'll be round tomorrow, for photos," she said. "We can finalize the listing agreement too."

Within a few hours, then, it would be official. Avalon Farm would be for sale.

Fiona

51

$\mathcal{S}$he awakened early, curled up against him.

Fiona resisted the urge to move, for fear of waking him and breaking the spell. The dream she'd been living since he'd found her on the steps of the Galway Cathedral…

"You've been following me!" she accused, jamming her mobile into her bag. "Giving me the fright of my life!"

Davie didn't try to touch her. "You've put me in the horrors too," he said. "Trying to work out how I'd live without you."

Tears sprang to her eyes but she didn't care. After the last few days, living through her heart and not her head, hiding her feelings was beyond her. "Beata isn't enough for you?"

Davie's brows met. "Gil was right, then."

"Right about what?"

"Do we have to get into this here?" He gestured toward the curious passersby trailing up and down the steps.

"I can get into it anywhere." Grasping her bag and sketchbook, Fiona headed for the Salmon Weir Bridge and broke into a rapid stride. For all her brave words, she was *this* close to falling apart.

Davie matched her pace across the river. Once they were on the Corrib Walk, he said, "Gil guessed you thought it was me who fancied Beata. It's him. He's been going to Ballydara to see her."

Fiona nearly tripped. "Gil?"

"It's not the first time people have mixed us up," Davie said gently, a smile in his voice. "In fact, it's a right cliché, how much it's happened."

"But…" She gazed at him, confused. "You were going to buy her pigs!"

"I wanted to help her out, as a favor to my brother—only Beata wouldn't have it. She told me, 'I *hev* been getting helping from everyone in village.'" He did a fair approximation of her Polish accent. "'But cannot take money from you.'" Davie reached for her hand. "But let's don't talk about Beata. You know why I'm here—"

Fiona pulled away. "I don't! What is it with men? They break it off, then after you've learned to live without them, they want you back when it's too late!"

"Is it too late?" Pain flashed in his face. "Okay, I was an arrogant bastard—"

"Yes, you were!" Despite her anger, she was reassured by the almost agonized look on him. "Giving me those narky ultimatums!" She could still recall every word. *The minute you hop into bed with him, we're done.*

"I get it, that was a mistake too—"

"You think? All but telling a woman she'd be damaged goods if she was with another man? It's not the bloody 1960s!"

"I…I was throwing my weight around, because…I knew this other guy was right for you in all the ways I'm not."

His humility took the wind from her sails. "Right for me?"

"You know. An artist. Who could give you all sorts of opportunities, contacts. Give you the moon."

If Colm was going to give anyone the moon, Fiona could have told him, *it would be himself.* "But you didn't even wait for me to be serious about Colm, doing a runner because I went out to dinner with him. With my dad! What did you think could happen?"

"It was all a lot of chest-thumping. But I was desperate."

"You wouldn't even listen to me, let me tell you why I decided to see him."

"I'll listen now."

The rippling sound of the river reached her ears, calming her. "I was torn about seeing Colm again," she said, mollified. "I only wanted to find out if I had any feelings left for him, after you and I…" She couldn't finish.

A flush crept up his lean face. "So if only I'd trusted you, I might never have been reduced to this."

"Stalking me?"

"Following you around Galway like a lovesick eejit."

The pinched feeling Fiona had had in her chest—the one she'd felt for so long she'd thought it was normal—began to ease. "Are you...*love*sick?"

He eased her handbag and sketchbook from her limp grasp, set them on the ground, and took her hand.

She didn't pull away this time. "Are you?" she asked again.

"I don't know what else to call it." Davie laced his fingers through hers. "Gil told me where he'd seen you. And you weren't hard to track—a girl with a faraway look on her face, carrying a sketchbook."

"I've been working on a new project," Fiona said shyly. She'd been so long from her art she'd forgotten what it was to have pride in her creations. "About Irish mythology." She wasn't quite ready to show him her fairies and pookas and banshees, though. "Why did you wait so long to talk to me?"

"It sounds...I don't know, a bit skulky, but I wanted to watch you for a while first. Also, in case you told me to piss off."

"That *is* skulky," said Fiona, hiding a smile.

"I'd finally got up my nerve to approach you, when you went into the church." He nodded toward the Cathedral. "You were sitting under that blue light, face like an angel and something in me just...cracked wide open." He looked so vulnerable that she forgave him everything.

As he drew her slowly toward him, she wrapped her arms round his broad chest. "Davie, I'm no angel."

"I know." His Adam's apple shifted. "You've been living with that bloke."

She knew what he was thinking. "I never slept with Colm. I couldn't." She kissed him. "Not after I was with you."

He took her to dinner, and confessed that in between lurking about to keep tabs on her, he'd been trying to book a hotel or

B&B close by. "In case you did forgive me. But here in the city, with the tourist season on, there's absolutely nothing!"

"What about your flat?"

"It was Gil's place," he confessed. "I didn't want you to know I was still living with my dad, even if I'm doing it to save money."

"A good reason," said Fiona.

"Well yeah, but then you'd *really* think I was a kid. Not that I'd take you to my dad's house tonight or any other, no matter how much I want you."

"How much is that?" she teased. "I've my hostel room."

"Thin walls and a thinner mattress? No way."

"So you've some interesting plans for us?"

"Do I ever," he said, the spark in his dark eyes like a flame. "If you know anywhere…"

Fiona smiled wickedly. "I understand there's lovely place out in Oughterard, where the walls are thick, and the beds, thicker." She had reached across the table to trail her finger up his arm. "Excellent place to get…reacquainted."

Now, lying with Davie in lush bedding of the Harmony Hotel, Fiona watched him awaken, his eyes confused, then his mouth curved in a smile. "If this is a dream, don't wake me up."

Burning with emotion, she couldn't answer. *I want you so much the wanting feels like it could burst through my skin. And it's all of you I want, your heart and your soul…* When he pulled her on top of him, Fiona could only think dimly, *I'll tell you later…*

Afterward, she lay with her head on his shoulder. "Since Ballydara's not far, can we go see Dad? I never told him I left Dublin."

"Sure," said Davie. "I wouldn't mind, though, waiting until tomorrow." He smoothed his hand down her bare back. "I want just one more day with you, before we let the world in."

"I'd like that too," said Fiona. "Although a week or even a month sounds even better."

"I'm all for that," said Davie, his hand lingering on her hip.

They lay quietly for a while, then Fiona said, "I also wanted to let him know about…you and me."

"You're ready to admit we're in a relationship?"

"I don't know how you could doubt it, after the last few hours." She tickled Davie's chest. "He'll be happy to know his matchmaking paid off."

"Since we're official," said Davie, "will you move in with me? We can start looking for a flat—"

"That's terribly fast," said Fiona, delight rising in her at the thought of sharing his life, spending every night in his arms. "We'll have to tell Dad that too."

"He won't be meeting me with his shotgun, will he?" Davie said with mock alarm. "Telling me to get the priest?"

"Hardly," said Fiona, secretly disappointed. *Not that I want to get married! Davie's so young, and I've a career to restart.* But still. "Dad can be modern about a *few* things."

"I'm not," said Davie, and the promise in his eyes was far richer and deeper and altogether lovelier than she'd ever seen in any man's. "Have you forgotten? I'm all for tradition."

Kerry

52

"You'll not believe this," said Robin on my stoop the next day. "We've an offer! Really, it's like a miracle, coming so soon after I posted the listing!"

My heart sank in my chest. "An offer." I stepped back to let her inside and closed the door.

"Well, it's not exactly a *proper* offer, but I think this person is a *very* serious prospect."

"Did they mention a figure?" I couldn't quite associate Avalon Farm with money—it was like working out the price of your child.

"Not...quite. They were definitely interested in farming, though." Robin said. "They'll be looking into farm schemes, and they seemed to know the district well."

Could the prospect be Fiona's brother, I wondered, wanting to expand the Whelan's farm?

Robin added, "I wouldn't be surprised if an offer came in straightaway."

"Stephen's down in the village, doing emails," I said, my voice shaking. "I won't make any decisions without him." *I thought I was ready, but I'm so...not.* "Go ahead and take your photos."

Robin pulled out her phone and headed for the kitchen. It was all I could do not to plant myself in front of the Aga to block her view, then show her the door. Instead, I poured salt on the wound by ambling toward the chicken run. On the way, I rubbed the slight curve of my tummy. "You're worth it, love," I told the baby. "Truly you are. It's only that your mammy is having a hard time with reality." Reaching the pen, I gazed at the chickens. "Girls, I'm so sorry it's come to this, having to leave—"

"So am I," said a voice behind me.

I turned round so fast my head swam. As my vision cleared, I said stupidly, "What are you doing here?"

Fiona looked distressed. "I've just come from Dad's—I wanted to think it was all a big mistake, that you'd never sell your farm, but when Stephen mentioned the estate agent, I knew it was true."

She was wearing her red flats, reminding me of the day we'd fetched the hens. "Stephen's been entirely forbearing." I tried to sound matter-of-fact, while another part of me wondered, what was he doing at the Whelan's? "But I can't put our family through the wringer anymore."

"Oh, Kerry." She gave me a quick hug. "Stephen told me about your poor hen too. I'm so sorry."

"Thanks, love." I felt another surge of regret for letting my girls down. "It was rather the last straw. I'm apparently not meant to be a farmer."

Realizing that dwelling on the chickens would do me no good whatsoever, I touched Fiona's arm, to guide us away from the pen, and noticed her hair was down, tumbling around her shoulders, and she had a glow about her I'd never seen before. "Wait a minute." I squinted at her. The past days had been so mad it took me a moment to remember our last conversation, on the phone. "You and Davie!"

She nodded, her eyes shining. "I think he loves me."

My melancholy receded. "The minute you said your stalker was none other than Davie Killeen, I *knew* I'd been all wrong about him and Beata!"

"You did tell me once you're a hopeless romantic," said Fiona.

"Yeah, though don't I deserve a right bollacking for thinking Davie could ever go for anyone else."

"It took me a bit longer to be convinced," said Fiona, though her face was tender. "It's got to be weird for Dad, though—my leaving Ballydara for one bloke, and coming home with another." She pulled a face. "Feels a bit…well, not exactly *slutty*, but you know what I mean."

"Let's just say you're living the adventurous life." As we strolled toward the front garden, I felt another pinch that my own Galway adventures would soon be over. *Come on, focus on the positive…* "Really, it's fantastic, the pair of you getting together," I said lightly. "Where's Himself, by the way? Not far, I'll bet—I'm sensing a lovey-dovey vibe here."

"He's at our house. For all I know he's telling Dad he'd like to make an honest woman of me, but that I don't want to get married."

"Not yet, anyway?"

"Well…" A faraway look came over her face. "I must say, that hotel in Oughterard is…*something*. Perfect for a honeymoon."

I had a flash of Stephen and me in the hotel's roomy shower. "That'll be one more place around here I'll never see again," I said a little sadly.

"You'll come back for visits, surely?"

I wanted to tell her, *of course I will*. Still, I *had* decided to make friends with reality. "I'll miss you terribly, but I'll have a new baby, and Jamie will be in school. Visits will be few and far between."

"Then I'll visit you," she said stoutly.

I knew she'd try. Yet she had Davie now… "What else have you been up to, besides falling madly in love?"

"Actually, I've one more bit of news," said Fiona. "This morning, I'd finally worked up the nerve to phone up my book contact. But when I got to Dad's, he'd a message waiting for me. My contact—Pauline—actually tried to reach me at home, to let me know the project is mine."

"Fantastic!" I said. "A dream come true."

"I'd give anything if things were different," Fiona said, a catch in her voice. "That you could live your dream too."

"Oh, I am." Giving my tummy an affectionate pat, I pretended that she wasn't talking about the farm. "Now that I'm feeling more myself, I'm really getting excited about the baby."

"I'm sure." Fiona wore a look of understanding. "Dad told me about the bit in the shop, when everyone guessed you were pregnant when you hadn't a clue. 'I could hardly keep a straight face,' he said, 'Kerry was that surprised.'"

"Yeah, I made a right fool of myself." I tried to laugh but couldn't quite manage it. "I guess no one in Ballydara will forget me anytime soon."

"You didn't," Fiona said softly. "And they won't." She seemed to take a deep breath. "Now, about that lunch date we've been planning—shall we try for Hurley's?"

"Hurley's it is," I said, more grateful for her friendship than I could ever express. "And let's make it soon." *I won't be in Ballydara much longer*.

"I've discovered something," Stephen said that evening.

He and I were walking up the steeper stretch of the Ballydara road, past the field where months ago, I'd discovered Fiona lying low after my party. For Stephen's sake, I tried to act like we were simply out for an evening jaunt. Yet in my mind I was saying goodbye to every stone and wall, every cow and sheep we passed.

Ever since the night Laura had been killed, he'd looked utterly wiped out. Tonight, though, his light step was at odds with the weariness in his face. "Let's go to the top—you're up for it?"

"Yes." I couldn't help adding, "but you look so tired."

"Just being outside is helping," said Stephen, "after the long day on the phone."

"Your boss apparently doesn't get the concept of weekends."

"Uh...right. Anyway, people in the village were starting to queue up at the special booth."

"Like who?" I pictured my friends hanging around Hurley's—another memory to take with me when we left.

"Let's see—Bernard was hovering, as usual. Deirdre O'Donnell came in with her aunt Bridie, and so did Beata. Deirdre was there to mind Peter so Bridie could help his mammy shop online for a new mobile."

I managed a chuckle. "Her wages from Desmond seem to be coming in handy. Anyone else?"

Stephen stepped over a pothole. "Maeve O'Donoghue, I think she's called, was in too. And a tall, black-haired girl with a smile like a pirate's."

That would be Grainne, who'd helped me with the ladder. I hadn't known he was acquainted with so many locals. "I imagine no one made a fuss." I swallowed hard. "Everyone here has been such a good neighbor."

"They've been grand." Stephen smiled faintly. "But finally Bridie O'Donnell said, "Mr. McCormack, if you stay in that booth much longer, Pat should charge you rent!""

My laugh was real this time. "I hope you bought a big lunch in return for the long phone session."

"Bought one for Desmond too, when he came in," Stephen said. "With his son soon home to work the farm, he was full of plans, that one."

I followed Stephen as he clambered over a low stone wall into a pasture, thinking how delighted Desmond must be. "What sort of plans?"

"Oh, you know," Stephen said vaguely. "Grants and things."

We were now on the commonage land, sheep grazing close by. I glanced at the inevitable droppings on the ground. Months ago, I would have picked my way through the manure, but now, as I strode right through it, I felt like a proper farmer. *A farmer*, I thought, my blues returning. Just when I'm leaving my farm.

Stephen suddenly took my arm. "Mind the stones."

"Everyone knows to mind them," I said, "since they're everywhere—"

"I mean, *look*!" As he pointed all around us, I suddenly saw all the stones arranged in a square smaller than our front room, nearly hidden by the tussocks of grass. "See? Here's another. And another."

"What...?"

"I learned from Desmond today there was a village here once," he said, his face animated. "I went straight online to get a satellite photo. Forty-some houses. Even a school."

355

No need to ask what had happened. Abandoned during the Famine. "So many people leaving their homes, their villages—their lives." My voice shook. "All those broken hearts." *Like mine.*

Stephen pulled me into his arms. "I didn't bring you here to make you sadder, love."

"But this is one more lovely place I'll be missing."

He was quiet for a long time. Finally he said, "We can hope the folk here went on to something better, though. Can't we?"

I could feel him wanting me to agree. But all I could do was wonder what would happen to Avalon Farm without me to tend it. Would it disappear too, into the mists of time?

Stop, I told myself. You still have Stephen and Jamie, and... I took a deep breath. "I'm still set on selling, but I want you to know something."

"What's that?" He rested his cheek against my hair.

"I've probably romanticized my childhood—you know, playing at Aunt Rose's farm at the weekends—but I'd so hoped to give our baby one just like it."

"It was a good childhood," he said. "Like mine."

I drew away, meeting his eyes. "Stephen—all the chores, the farmwork you did for your granddad, it wasn't so very onerous, was it?" *If I never see another cow again it'll be too soon,* he'd said. As long as I lived, I'd never forget it.

"It seemed that way at the time." He turned away to kneel in the grass, running his hand over a stone. "I've come to realize those days were quite...magical."

Kerry
53

The next morning, Stephen was running late for a meeting. "I'd planned to have the whole day here with you," he said, and I could tell from his expression he was already in Dublin. "But it's…important."

"On Sunday?" If Stephen leaving early wasn't bad enough, while I had a lie-in he'd been on the phone with the boss at dawn. "I hope you'll tell your colleagues that after the baby comes, you're putting your foot down about Sunday meetings."

He managed a weary smile. "I'll do that."

"Before I forget," I said, "we haven't sorted who's to fetch Jamie from Con's. Could you do it after your meeting?"

"I'll…try," Stephen said. "Or your mam could."

Work must be preying on Stephen's mind even more than I thought, if he wasn't eager to see Jamie after his long absence. I bit my lip. "Maybe I should come with you, start house-hunting this afternoon."

"Why don't you give yourself a few more days to take it easy," he said, not looking at me.

I didn't hide my relief very well. "What if that buyer Robin's got on the line does make an offer, and wants us to vacate straightaway?"

"If the buyers are honestly keen on the place, they'll wait until we're ready to leave." He must've seen something in my face because suddenly, he hugged me fiercely. "I'll make this right, I promise—" Before I could answer, he kissed me quickly and was out the door.

I watched him head for the car, then noticed what he'd left by the door. "Wait—your briefcase!" I grabbed it and followed him.

But he was already in the car and backing down the drive. Heading back to the house, I decided to ring him as soon as he was on the motorway. Hopefully he'd get through the week without it.

With Stephen gone, I had to have a little weep. Actually a long one. You'll have this one cry, I told myself, to get losing the farm out of your system. Then it's nothing but happy, positive thoughts. For the baby.

After snuffling my way through a packet of tissues, I sat on the couch, resting my hands on my stomach. "Daddy seemed awfully tired," I told the baby. "But soon we'll have a lovely new place." That thought was enough to get me tearing up again, so when my stomach growled I was happy to focus on something else. "I should probably feed you a proper meal," I said. "Daddy would want you to have more nourishment than tea."

Even after my pep talk, I didn't feel like eating. I was listlessly heading for the fridge when the phone rang. "Kerry, big news." It was Robin. "I told you the market was having an uptick! The prospect we talked about rang this morning and said the programmes they've been looking into are *super* promising."

"Really." I sat on a kitchen chair with a thump.

"They're seriously considering agritourism!" Her voice spiraled upward. "I think they're working up an offer as we speak!"

As Robin chattered on, I couldn't help thinking that if this buyer was Fiona's brother, she would've told me. What if it was a deep-pocketed city person instead, who wanted to turn my little place into a farm-themed amusement park? It didn't bear thinking about. But I was already on the selling train—too late to jump off.

"Who knows, we might have a deal before I get the sign up!"

Robin was saying breathlessly. "But I should tell you…" Her enthusiasm seemed to have taken a dive.

"Tell me what?"

"Well, this prospect may be more like an…*investor*." She paused. "Which could involve more…um, unconventional financing. Is that okay?"

Whatever. Buyer, investor, who cared? Giving up Avalon farm would break my heart whoever bought it or how they paid for it, whether they farmed my place or Disneyfied it. "Okay." My voice cracked.

"Great—actually, it's fantastic!"

"Yeah." I could barely speak around the pain in my chest.

"I got the impression they want to move straightaway on their schemes paperwork, because they're ready to wire us a deposit."

"Let's take it," I mumbled. It came out, *Lez-ta-kut.*

"Sorry?"

"I said, let's take the offer…deposit." For once, I would put Stephen's and our family's wellbeing first. "I'm selling." Ready to let my head sink to the table, I heard someone on my back stoop. Desperate to get off the line, I said, "Robin, I'll ring you right back."

"No need—I'll get everything organized on my end."

"Isn't there some paperwork, listing agreement or something we need to take care of?" I made myself ask.

"Oh, we can do it later," she said breezily. "Cheers."

Replacing the handset, I thought she was being awfully casual about the whole matter, especially with a deposit coming in, but here was Fiona, popping her head in. "It's only me."

Surprised, and completely overwhelmed with the decision I'd just made, I said, "I'm g-glad you're here. I just sold the farm."

She colored. Which was an odd reaction to my news. Instead of consoling me, she said, "I realize it's short notice, but we talked about lunch out at Hurley's."

"Oh." I remembered my tear-stained face. "I thought you meant next week. And aren't you and Davie…"

"I'll see him later."

She seemed very pressurized. I hoped they weren't having a lover's tiff already. "You mean, right now?"

"I've Dad's car. You don't even have to drive."

"Give me ten minutes." Fiona's company meant happy thoughts. For a little while, I could avoid thinking of Robin's buyer, hanging like the sword of Damocles over my head.

Fiona barreled Desmond's small Ford down the hill. "There's a fire somewhere?" I inquired.

"Oh." She let up slightly on the accelerator. Within moments, she pulled to a stop in front of Hurley's.

"I think we're blocking the door," I said.

"Car park's a bit crowded," said Fiona.

I couldn't see the park from this angle, so I'd have to take her word for it. "Must be a big match on? I hope we can find a table."

Inside, though, the bar was deserted. And for the first time ever, the telly was actually *off*. Mystified, I said, "Pat must've closed suddenly. We can do this another day—"

"Upstairs," she said. "Bernard and Gil Killeen fixed up the old banquet room."

"I didn't know Hurley's had a room up there." I heard a creak above my head, and the low rumble of some indeterminate sounds.

"It's where Aislin's been teaching her yoga classes," Fiona said, leading the way. "I thought you would've signed up, but…oh, sorry."

"But I won't be here," I said despondently. "Fiona, maybe I'm not up for lunch after all."

"It's too late." Fiona opened the door.

I froze.

Kerry
54

The room was filled with people.

Front and center was Pat Hurley, standing behind a massive roast. Flanking him was Grainne's friend Justine, sharpening a carving knife the size of a machete. Bernard, near his brother, gave me a courtly bow, and not far away stood Davie and his brother Gil, who was actually *smiling*. Beata waved at me shyly as Desmond, his face creased in a wide grin, held Peter. Judith and her elusive Padraig manned another table groaning with an assortment of steaming dishes and stacks of plates.

Disbelieving, I gazed around to see Aislin, her husband and freckle-faced son, and then Grainne, holding hands with a black-haired bloke who was so startlingly handsome he made me blink.

Mam and Dad were across the room, alongside Mary and Brian, all four wearing broad smiles. Standing between the grandparents was my son, who lifted his hand. My eyes swimming with tears, I took a step toward Jamie to kiss him hello, when a man stepped out of the crowd. A man with a quiet strength I'd sensed from the beginning, who'd *always* been grand in an emergency.

The man I loved.

Still in the doorway with Fiona, I simply couldn't take in what I was seeing. "I don't understand," I muttered. "Stephen's meant to be at a very important meeting in Dublin—"

"In you go." She gave me a tiny push. "When we found out

you were selling, we—Dad and Judith and Aislin and all of us—decided we had to do something about it."

"A goodbye party," I said. "Thank-y-you…"

"Good-bye?" Desmond crinkled his eyes at me. "Wouldn't a celebration be more like it, when your man there is ready to take a chance?" He looked at Stephen.

"A chance on…"

"On us," Stephen finally spoke. "On the farm."

"F-farm?" I felt my knees shake.

"Our Kerry needs a chair," said Bernard. He and Fiona tucked a seat beneath me and I sat down, hard.

Then Stephen, a great one for keeping himself to himself all the years I'd known him, began a *speech*.

He'd been getting more and more weary of waiting in airports and sleeping in strange hotels. Fed up with windowless conference rooms, putting on presentations about sales goals he no longer gave a rip about. He'd been talking with his team all weekend, and had been ready to hand in his resignation. "But when I rang the boss he had a proposal for me—right out of the blue he asked me to stay and telecommute."

"Telecommute?" Now I couldn't believe what I was *hearing*.

"That's it," Stephen confirmed. "But I said, no way, I was done."

Dizzy with disbelief, I said, "You quit your *job*?"

"Resign, they call it," chimed in Bernard.

"Let the man tell his story," Judith chided.

Stephen said, "I tried to resign, only the boss wouldn't have it. 'Take a sabbatical,' he said, 'and we'll talk in six months.' So I have."

"To do what?" I asked tremulously.

"I'm going to invest in the farm," he said. "With myself."

"You mean…we can stay in Ballydara? *Live* here?" Instantly, I was buoyant with happiness. All the plans I'd envisioned burst in my mind like a panorama, apple trees laden with fruit and *young* hens laying eggs and a pasture with animals and me milking Desmond's little cow… Then I glanced at my son and my ebullience whooshed out of me. "But

I—*we* can't do that. Jamie, there's your school, you've had so many disruptions—"

"I didn't tell Dad till this morning," Jamie said, "but I think I've a way around that—" He broke off as the door opened. His cheeks flooded with color.

In walked Deirdre with her Aunt Bridie and Granny Nora. "Sorry we're late," said Deirdre.

"I was told there'd be a proper Sunday lunch," the old lady said, banging her cane on the wooden floor with emphasis.

"Now Mammy, we'll get to that in a minute," Bridie said as Deirdre turned her smiling gaze to my son. "Jamie, you were saying?"

"I've been looking into doing my transition year early," Jamie said confidently, not quite the dumbstruck lad he'd been the last time Deirdre showed up. "It's a long shot, but Con thinks I've a really promising proposal—"

"Brilliant!" In an instant, I was out of the chair. "Oh, love." I hugged Jamie quickly, releasing him before he could squirm away. Then I gazed into Stephen's face. "We're really going to do this?"

He grasped my hands as if we were stepping into a reel. "That's right."

"And you've put your career on hold for *me*?"

"For us," Stephen said, and he nodded toward the crowd. "We're all in this together, don't you see?"

I pulled him close, and dimly heard laughter as I kissed him. Ballydara wouldn't meet the same fate as the poor little village up on the commonage, not if Stephen and I had anything to say about it. When I was finally ready to let go of him, I turned to Fiona. "You were in on this!"

"Not until the last minute," she said smiling, and hugged me. "Stephen made it happen, and all within a few hours. Dad rang Pat who rang Justine, and then everything snowballed."

Amidst the flurry of more hugs and greetings and thank yous, Pat and Justine served up the ginormous lunch of roast beef, mashed potatoes, pureed parsnips and salad, and not a hot pepper in sight. After I asked the grandparents to come up to the farmhouse after the party, I sat down at the big table with a full plate, Judith on one side of me, Bernard on the other.

"The supplier shipped me a second pregnancy test kit by mistake," Judith murmured. "I was going to send it back, then I thought of that pair." She nodded toward Grainne and the black-haired Adonis. "The way things are going, the village will need a primary school soon."

I glanced at Grainne and her man, the pair of them laughing into each other's eyes as if no one else was in the room. She *had* said she was working on a baby...

"I can see Ballydara finally getting on the map," Judith went on, and discreetly pointed her knife at Fiona and Davie. They'd scored a small table in a corner, heads together. "What if Fiona started a gallery or something?"

"Maybe Davie could help her build it," I said, excited.

"The sky's the limit," said Judith. "With Justine's idea for a restaurant, and you not selling your farm—"

"Selling." My eyes widened and I dropped my fork. "Wait!" I croaked. "Wait, everyone! I've a b-b-buy—"

"What's that?" Judith looked puzzled.

Dear God, what had I *done*? "I've a *buyer*!" I said tragically. "For the farm!" I gazed at the merry faces around me, ready to weep with mortification. This was far, far worse than the scene in the shop with my pregnancy. But why was everyone still smiling? "It's only a verbal agreement, but I accepted the offer, investment, whatever, and I can't go back on my word—we've *got* to sell!"

I couldn't look at Stephen across the table, hearing the village gossip already. *Yeah, did you hear about that madzer Kerry McCormack? She got her husband to wreck his career to work their farm, but it was already sold!* "I'm so sorry—you've put on this party for nothing!"

"You'll want to ring the estate agent," Bernard said kindly.

"Robin!" For once in my life, I was too upset to cry. "Her buyer put down pots of money already and applied for an agritourism scheme, and oh, God, what'll I do? I've spoiled everything—"

"You haven't!" Stephen was smiling again, wider than before. "It was me."

"What?"

"I'm the investor!"

I nearly fell off my chair. "Robin's prospect?"

"That's me," he said, and I was suddenly laughing and crying and altogether so gobsmacked I could hardly breathe. I jumped up, rounded the table, and practically ran into his arms.

When I finally let go of Stephen, I saw Brian smiling at me. "Mary and I were the decoy buyers."

"It was my idea," Mary said smugly. "If our Stephen is keen to be a farmer, we wanted to make it happen."

"But Robin...she did a *lot* of work."

"She's grand," Stephen said. "I let her in on my plan early this morning, and she actually thought it was great crack."

Jaysus. Robin was wasted as estate agent. She should be treading the boards at the Abbey Theatre. "What about the deposit?"

"Oh, that's real," Stephen said. "I'm giving Robin a bit of it, but the rest...how about we spend it some on sheep?"

"And a Border collie," said Jamie. "What I didn't get to tell you—I'm to help Dad write up the farm grants for my school proposal."

"You want cows, we'll get those too. I'll even milk them," said Stephen. "You know I'm not mad for cows but for you, anything, and you'll mind the chickens."

"I know where you can get more of 'em," said Pat slyly.

"No chickens from me," said Beata, "but I *gif* you my pigs." Next to her, Gil was bouncing Peter on his knee. "That way I pay you back. And they will *hev* nice pasture to live in."

"I'll invest too," said Davie. "I'll build a pen for 'em."

"I've already started a design for an Avalon Farm sign," Fiona put in. "And I'm up for any chicken wrangling in the future."

"Kerry, you can use my tractor whenever you like," Desmond put in. "Unless Niall needs it."

"I'll give you a reduced rate on some of those garden box

yokes for your root crops," said Bernard. Judith gave him a ferocious frown. "Ah, just having you on. I'll do it for free."

"When the baby comes, we'll all pitch in for the veggie patch," said Judith.

"We'll drive over from Dublin to help," said Mam. When Dad opened his mouth, she elbowed him. "Both of us."

"You need a nanny, I'm your woman," put in Grainne.

"I've got satellite Internet at my place," said her Adonis. He'd an American accent. "You can use it anytime."

"And you'll want to know," Aislin called over, "my Gentle Yoga class is perfect for preggies."

Just then, I felt something...odd. On the side of my stomach. I pressed my hand to the spot.

"You okay, Mam?" said Jamie.

I waited. There it was again. A tiny bubble. "I think it's...the baby," I said wonderingly.

Everyone in the room broke into applause.

After inviting Desmond, Fiona and Davie to join our parents at Avalon Farm, Stephen and I decided we'd walk home as a family. The farm really *was* home now.

Jamie strode ahead, but Stephen and I took a leisurely pace up the hill, holding hands as the birds in the hedgerows filled the air with song. "What changed your mind?" I asked him.

"About leaving?" He stared into the middle distance for what seemed like a long time. "It was more a slow realization of what we could have if we stayed. Then last night, there in the ruins, it hit me, hard."

"What was that, love?"

"That *this* place was what was real—pastures and animals and working the land." His voice vibrated with emotion. "Enjoying your kids, sharing your lives with dear friends. Not cooped up in meetings, away from your family, all for a fat paycheck." His hand tightened on mine. "The night the chickens got attacked..."

I shuddered. "I never want to think of it again."

"I want to. Because that night, I saw what you were made of."

He sounded…proud. "What do you mean?"

"After you found your dead hen, you were so…" he seemed to be searching for words. "Gallant. I can't think of another way to put it. There you were, pregnant and exhausted, but bearing the death and the muck, refusing to go down without a fight. All I could think was, my wife will be entirely wasted in the city."

"It's a safe life, there," I said.

"I don't want safe," he said simply. "I want you."

Jamie suddenly doubled back to walk toward us. "I've been thinking, it'll be easier to avoid Granny McElligott if I live in Galway."

"Now there's an advantage I didn't see before," I said drolly. "I'm sure you'll miss your mates at school, though."

"Well, yeah," said Jamie, "but…" He got a strange look on his face. "I keep forgetting—I'll have a brother or sister to hang with."

"You're ready for that?" I asked.

"Your days as an only child are numbered," Stephen added, smiling.

"I actually can't wait," Jamie said. "Besides, we can have Con out for school holidays."

"Con." An eye roll was almost mandatory here. "God knows what the pair of you will come up with for your next brainwave."

"Ha," said Jamie. "By the way, if our baby's a girl maybe Con will fancy her, and it'll be like in 'Harry Potter' where Harry goes for Ron Weasley's sister. Although Con would be sort of an old dude by the time she was ready to go out with a guy."

"A *real* old dude," Stephen agreed, chuckling. "Good job we don't have to worry about *that* for a while."

I squeezed his hand, my throat catching with the sweetness of this perfect moment, and thought of our baby. We'd raise our child here, in this place of belonging, near the ancient stones of the long-gone village up on the commonage. I raised my eyes to the green hills above us, bathed in mist. Filled with so much joy I couldn't speak, I continued up the Ballydara road with my husband and son, toward Avalon Farm and our future.

Acknowledgments

I'm eternally grateful to the first readers of *The Galway Girls,* Lish Jamtaas, Lori Nelson-Clonts, and Becky Burns, for their critical eyes, insightful suggestions and friendship. Extra appreciation goes to Lori for so generously sharing her process and expertise as a glass artist. And for allowing her dazzling, real-life pieces to be recreated as the artwork in the story!

I so appreciate Twin Brooks Creamery in Washington State for the chance to hang out with their herd of Jersey Cows, and Tomás, our tour guide during our trip to Ireland, who spoke at length about farming in Ireland. A world of thank yous to Glen Keen Farm in County Mayo, Ireland, for the informative and incandescent afternoon; my visit inspired many of my characters' farm experiences. Any errors I've made about Irish farm practices are mine and mine alone!

Great thanks to the wise and big-hearted women of the Northwest Authors 4 Authors for their generous support and cheerleading, especially through the last leg of crafting this book! Big kudos to Courtney Lopes for her beautiful cover design, and to Amy Atwell at Author E.M.S. for her formatting expertise.

Boundless hugs go to my wonderful family—with an extra hug for my mother, whose gift of *Irish Folk and Fairy Tales*, edited by W.B. Yeats, was instrumental in helping me invent Fiona's art in the story! Finally, I dedicate this book to my husband John—and to him goes my deepest appreciation for his ideas, wordsmithing talents and artistic eye, and especially, his love and encouragement.

About the Author

Susan Colleen Browne weaves her love of Ireland and her passion for country living into her Village of Ballydara series, novels and stories of love, friendship and family set in the Irish countryside. She's also the author of an award-winning memoir, *Little Farm in the Foothills,* as well as the Morgan Carey fantasy-adventure series for tweens. A community college creative writing instructor, Susan runs a little homestead with her husband in the Pacific Northwest, USA. Her latest book is the sequel to the first Little Farm memoir, *Little Farm Homegrown: A Memoir of Food-Growing, Midlife, and Self-Reliance on a Small Homestead.*

When Susan isn't in the garden, she's working on her next Village of Ballydara book!

You can sign up for special offers and updates at
www.susancolleenbrowne.com.

You'll also find recipes, book excerpts and
tales from Berryridge Farm at
www.littlefarminthefoothills.blogspot.com

Special Bonus Excerpt:

The 3rd book of the Village of Ballydara Series, and the prequel to
The Galway Girls

The
Hopeful Romantic

County Galway, Ireland

Every fix I've gotten myself into, every eejit thing I've ever done, is because of my fatal flaw—I'm a hopeless romantic. And just look where it's taken me.

I gazed at the snowy pasture from the kitchen window, huddled in Stephen's old work coat, the one item of his I'd taken with me when I'd left Dublin three days ago. Okay, there was the ring too—the new gem-studded wedding band Stephen had surprised me with last month. He'd given it to me over the holiday we'd spent with our friend Will, when everything had changed. Well, more like…imploded. But I couldn't quite go there.

Not today. Not on Christmas Eve.

I rubbed my bare ring finger with my thumb. Why I thought of the ring as Stephen's…I'd never felt such a flashy piece of jewelry belonged to me, even though he'd had *Kerry, Forever*, engraved on the inside—such a sentimental gesture for such a prosaic guy. Out of respect, I'd kept wearing the ring, even after he left. But I'd not worn it since arriving here at the farm. I'd put the ring into a saucer next to the kitchen sink and there it had stayed. I would try not to look at it, but invariably, my eyes would be drawn to the flash of sparkle against the countertop. Whether my ring was mocking me or guilt-tripping me, I wasn't sure.

You may ask, why wear a posh wedding band anyway, after your husband says "we need a break?" *Exactly*. But the bigger question was, what had possessed me to come to the farm at all? On the spur of the moment, I'd decided that staying here for a few days would be like a…well, a mini-retreat. On my own, without distractions, I'd find the answers to all my problems.

371

Instead, I'd done a rash, madzer thing and gotten myself completely stranded. Which is where my fatal flaw comes in.

So I've really done it this time. As the rich, buttery sweetness of the shortbread I'd baked still lingered in the kitchen, I stared bleakly at the mounds of sparkling white surrounding the farmhouse. You'd think I would've been grateful for a white Christmas, such a rare thing in Ireland, but I gave the snow a baleful look. I'd so hoped to hash things out with Stephen on his short Christmas holiday in Dublin. Find a way to get past our troubles...

Well. That *was* optimistic. Now, stuck on the other side of Ireland after it had snowed for two days straight, I was completely isolated. And with no working phone, I'd no way to talk to him at all, even to wish him—and our son Jamie—a Happy Christmas.

I turned toward the front room, my eye caught by the small, bedraggled Christmas tree sitting in the corner. I'd cut it down myself, in the fir grove next to the pasture. I'd tried to make the place festive, but the tree seemed a sad little article, weighed down with fairy lights and cheap glass bulbs. Just hours ago, thinking positive, I'd made the shortbread, hoping for a sudden thaw. Then I could head back to Dublin, see Stephen, Jamie, Mam and all my family. A vain hope, as it turned out—because the snow was just as deep as it had been the last time I looked.

I suddenly strode to the back door, pulled on my wellies and flung the door open. Stepping into the snow, I was desperate to think of something else besides all the wrong turns I'd taken, or how I would be utterly, completely alone for the holiday. After all the solitude since I'd arrived at the farm, you'd think spending another day or two on my own would be no bother. Only I was still reeling after what I'd found in the fir grove two days before. And so here it was, nearly Christmas, and I was in shreds. Along with my marriage.

And I'd no one to blame but myself...

Dublin

1

Two Months Before

*Y*ou'd think I would've been ready for Jamie's question. Or at least wondered why he hadn't asked it sooner.

"Jamie?" I called down as the front door closed with a *thunk*. I certainly didn't expect Stephen this early. "You'd a good time at Con's?"

Hearing my son's subdued "Yeah," I fastened my flowered skirt. Tempted to kick the tailored gray trousers I'd just removed into the closet, I tossed them over a hanger instead. *You are not your job*, I repeated my usual after-work mantra, and headed downstairs. I found Jamie in his usual spot in the kitchen, standing in front of the opened fridge. "And the pair of you finished your schoolwork?" I aimed a kiss at his cheek.

"I did." Jamie didn't duck away from me like he'd been doing the last few months. Which should have been my first clue that something was up. (I'd yet to see him dodge his dad's kisses, a fact that secretly drove me a bit mad.)

Conversations with Jamie felt a bit like pulling teeth these days, so I resisted quizzing him about how his friend was, details about what they'd done after school or any other tidbits he wouldn't want to share anyway. "You'll have a quick bite before we head over to Granny and Granddad's house?"

As he nodded, I gave him a covert look. My mam always said my son was the spit image of me, with my dark eyes, the dimple in my right cheek, and wavy brown hair. Although when I was small, my great-aunt Rose claimed my hair wasn't brown at all, but the color of blackberry honey—*vastly* better, I'd thought, than plain brown. Jamie's hair hadn't changed, but the rest of him had, so quickly that every time I saw him I'd have to stop for a second and think, *right, this is Jamie.* Cheekbones and a squarish chin were emerging from his boyish features, his eyebrows had thickened, and he'd started wearing glasses this past summer.

Tonight he looked even less like the child I'd raised. His face seemed pinched, the new spots on his face more prominent than usual. Maybe he'd gotten over-hungry, growing as fast as he was. Though how that could be I don't know, since he spent most of this free time eating.

"Will Dad be at Granny's?" Jamie asked, still staring into the fridge. Bulky as a Mini, the polished steel appliance was far too large for the three of us (and the way things were going, our family was likely to stay that size). Jamie was studying the sparse contents with the same intensity he applied to his maths equations.

"He's promised to stop by," I said. That wasn't *quite* true. Stephen had texted me as soon as I arrived at work this morning.

> CFO flying in for big meeting 2nite, sorry can't make it to your mam's.

He used to leave me notes on the kitchen table.

In the early years of our marriage: *Last night was...! Love, Stephen.*

After Jamie had learned to read, he'd brought one of the notes to Stephen while we were fixing tea. "What happened last night, Daddy?"

Stephen had met my eyes, his crinkling in a smile. After that, the notes were more...sedate: *Did you sleep well? I'll pick up milk on the way home. Love, Stephen.*

Having taken a stand against texting—call me old-fashioned— I rang Stephen at work for the first time in weeks. I got his voice mail. "You can get away for an hour, can't you? It's our first family do in a long time. And Jamie hasn't seen you in three days." I restrained myself from saying, *Besides, I've had it up to here with the way you've become the invisible man.* Ringing off, I didn't want to think how things you can't see are still entirely...well, *real*. A few minutes later, another text popped up.

OK, will try—but can't stay long.

Mam had invited us to call round this evening, though it wouldn't be for one of her table-groaning dinners, the ones she'd once put on for the whole family at least once a week. "I'm just not into cooking these days," she'd said when she rang yesterday, sounding apologetic. "Of course we'll have a dessert, even if it's from the shop."

Into cooking? Was this Mam's latest attempt to sound hip? She must mean *up for*. "We don't love you for your puddings," I teased her, "though they do help." She laughed gaily, sounding like her old self again. "So...what's up?" I was careful to sound casual. "Did the prodigal ring you and Dad and say he's coming home for Christmas?"

"Liam?" Mam chuckled again. "When has your brother ever made his plans two months before the holiday?"

"We can always hope," I said. "Shall we start thinking about Christmas anyway? You always say it's never too soon to get organized."

Mam *adored* Christmas. In the past, she'd always started her marathon Christmas baking by All Saint's Day, and had the house decorated before the first Sunday of Advent. Besides, focusing on the future would be good for her. And for me. "It's a surprise," she said, sounding mysterious. She ended the call before I could say, *So what's going on then?*

Now, seeing Jamie still staring into the open fridge, I wondered if I should ask him the same question. Instead I said, "Surely you've memorized everything in there by now?" I'd meant to tease him but it came out a bit sharpish.

"Almost," said Jamie.

You're not being sarcastic, young man? I nearly did snap. I stopped myself just in time. Because the last time Jamie had gazed interminably into the opened fridge, Stephen had only said, *Your mam and I might want a go at the fridge ourselves, don't you think?* Jamie had closed the door without comment. I'd looked at Stephen, wondering, how do you do that? And why can't I? But maybe I should stop overthinking this…

"What's the other father called?" Jamie said abruptly.

"The other father?" I echoed, puzzled. An odd question, from a boy who'd never mentioned church or going to Mass except to complain every Sunday morning, "Why do I have to go? Con doesn't have to."

Stephen never said, "Because I'm your dad and I say so!" Or, "You don't want to grow up into a heathen like your friend, do you?" He'd always say mildly, "It won't hurt you to practice being on your knees, before life brings you to them."

Actually, now that I thought of it, he hadn't said that for a while. These days he said, "Because I'd like you to come with us." While I admired Stephen's instinct for the best way to handle Jamie's on-the-cusp-of-teen rebellion, I wish I could do it as effortlessly as he did.

"Mam?" Jamie prompted, an edge in his voice. He finally closed the fridge.

"You mean…the new assistant priest at the parish?" I thought quickly. He's called Father McQua—"

"Not him." Jamie turned around. "The other dad—the dad who made me."

The shock was like a clout on the head. I clutched the edge of the granite countertop for support. "Why…" I began, my mouth so stiff I had trouble forming the words. "Why do you ask?"

"I just want to know," Jamie said, still not meeting my eyes. "I'm old enough. And Con thinks I've a…" His voice cracked.

I could almost see the thought bubble hovering over his head: *I've a right.*

"James McCormack, how could you—" *How could you mention your biological father to your friend before you'd talked to me?* Everything in me wanted to shut this down. Like *immediately.* Still, I knew I'd have to tell Jamie that naturally he'd a right to know the man's name, and more. When he was four years of age, Stephen and I had told Jamie about how he had another daddy. He hadn't seemed that interested. "I guess that other daddy is invisible," he'd only said. I'd breathed a sigh of relief. *It's grand then.*

But suddenly it wasn't. I gazed at Jamie's face, tears behind my eyes. *What'll your dad think, that you asked after this man? And do you realize how hurtful this could be for you? For all I know "your other father" wouldn't care two pins that you exist.*

"Mam," Jamie prompted again. His brown eyes finally met mine, two bright spots of color on his cheeks. "Is his name a secret or something?"

I blinked hard. In a way, it *was* a secret. Stephen didn't know the man's name. He'd never asked. I forced myself to speak normally. "He's called Mike," I said, my face burning. "Mike McElligott." *Stephen will need to know that Jamie asked after his father. Only how will I tell him?*

"Okay," Jamie said.

"Do you…want to write down the name?" I asked. Talking seemed to ease the shock-induced ache at my temple. "So you'll remember it?"

"I'll remember," he said simply. In one of his lightning fast subject changes he added, "We've ham and four kinds of cheese in the fridge—I'm going to make a sandwich. You'll have one too?"

"That's it?" I rubbed my forehead. "Aren't you going to ask me about him?"

"Um…no."

Oh God, he was doing his no-drama Stephen thing. "Why not?"

"I'm after making sandwiches," he said patiently.

"Jamie…" *Never mind,* I wanted to babble, *I'll tell you what I know, he's Irish, he used to work in London, but when I met him he was temping in Dublin, and I don't know his family, or where he lives now…* "A sandwich would be great," I said instead, though I was sure I couldn't eat a thing…